Uptown THIEF

Uptown THIEF

AYA DE LEÓN

KENSINGTON PUBLISHING CORP.
www.kensingtonbooks.com

To the extent that the image or images on the cover of this book depict a person or persons, such person or persons are merely models, and are not intended to portray any character or characters featured in the book.

DAFINA BOOKS are published by

Kensington Publishing Corp.
119 West 40th Street
New York, NY 10018

All Kensington titles, imprints, and distributed lines are available at special quantity discounts for bulk purchases for sales promotion, premiums, fund-raising, and educational or institutional use.

Special book excerpts or customized printings can also be created to fit specific needs. For details, write or phone the office of the Kensington Sales Manager: Kensington Publishing Corp., 119 West 40th Street, New York, NY 10018. Attn. Sales Department. Phone: 1-800-221-2647.

ISBN-13: 978-1-4967-0470-2
ISBN-10: 1-4967-0470-3
First Kensington Trade Paperback Printing: August 2016

eISBN-13: 978-1-4967-0471-9
eISBN-10: 1-4967-0471-1
First Kensington Electronic Edition: August 2016

10 9 8 7 6 5 4 3 2 1

Printed in the United States of America

For Juana, the Jungle Girl

Acknowledgments

I would like to acknowledge the following people for their incredible help in making this book happen: my agent, Jenni Ferrari Adler, and Union Literary; my editors, Mercedes Fernandez and Esi Sogah, and all the folks at Kensington; Lulu Martinez, Sofia Quintero, Dana Kaye, Toni Ann Johnson, Susie Meserve, Galadrielle Allman, Simha Evan Stubblefield, Sara Campos, Shailja Patel, Tracy Sherrod, Jill Dearman, Cara Diaconoff, Tobe Correal, Bishop Yvette Flunder, Pastor Donna Allen, Adrienne Crew, Lisa McCalla, Alicia Raquel, La Bruja, Julia Hutton Randall, Diane Balser, Peechington Marie, Nova Anon, Shannon Williams, *$pread* magazine, the St. James Infirmary, SWOP Bay Area, The Harm Reduction Coalition and Training Institute, Xanthos, Inc., MK Chavez, Sara Kershnar, Alisa Valdes, Cristina Garcia, Tim Hernandez, Brooke Warner, Carolina De Robertis, Pam Harris, BinderCon, HackerMoms, VONA, Sandra Garcia Rivera, Elmaz Abinader, Mat Johnson, Achy Obejas, Aurora Levins Morales, Torrey Maldonado, Gail Burton, Sharan Strange, my Tigress Crew: Kirsten and Jennifer, The Debutante Ball crew: Louise, Abby, Heather, and Jennifer. The crew of women who has helped keep me serene through it all: Carolyn, Peggy, Staci, and Julianna. My family: Stuart, Anna, Larry, Paci, Coco, and Dulari. And Natasha Bedingfield, for my anthem, "Unwritten."

Chapter 1

February
New York City

Marisol Rivera ran down the stairwell of the eighty-story building, trailing the banister with one hand and gripping the stolen brick of $10,000 cash in the other.

The center of the stairwell was open. Three floors above, a door opened and a security guard pointed down and yelled, "There he goes!"

In her ski mask and bulky black jacket, she had been mistaken for a man, but at closer range, they would see her curves and understand their mistake.

Her bare feet thudded down the stairs, pressing off against the concrete steps.

She ran for the fifty-seventh floor.

Tyesha was holding an elevator car on the fifty-seventh. Numbers flashed by Marisol in the stairwell: sixtieth . . . fifty-ninth . . . She heard the boots of security guards thundering down above her head.

Her calf muscles ached, and air burned in and out of her lungs. Her heart beat even faster than the rapid fire of her feet against the steps.

She had just started down the final flight, when another squad of gray-uniformed security guards rushed out of the stairwell on the floor below.

Had they caught Tyesha? Marisol clenched her body to a stop, one hand gripping the banister, and the accumulated forward motion sent her stumbling, almost falling down the stairs. She hurled herself back the way she had come and slammed against the push bar for the fifty-eighth floor.

As she lunged into the hallway, she heard the chime of the elevator and the door began to open, maybe ten yards ahead.

More guards? Would she be cornered?

She ran faster, hoping to . . . to what? Hit the opposite stairwell? Where could she go?

Before she could decide, she saw that the figure stepping from the elevator wasn't a guard, but a brown-skinned woman in a green cocktail dress and platform sandals—Tyesha.

"*Gracias a Diós!*" Marisol breathed, as she peeled off her jacket and ski mask. She balled them up and tossed them into the elevator, as her long hair fell over her shoulders. Some of the strands stuck to her forehead, and a few ends tangled in the lacy neckline of her red blouse.

"Hit some buttons!" she yelled to Tyesha. "Send it up."

Tyesha stabbed the elevator's Door Close button repeatedly.

Marisol pulled her stiletto heels out of her oversize purse and shoved her feet into them. She left the $10,000.

The two women stepped back from the elevator as the security guards stormed through the stairwell doors.

"Please!" Marisol begged, looking into the empty elevator. "Don't hurt us!"

The guards rushed closer as the elevator door began to close. Another few feet and they would see it was empty.

"Step away from the elevator!" the security guard yelled.

"He's got a gun!" Tyesha shrieked.

"Wait!" Marisol wailed. "He might shoot us if you come closer."

The guards slowed their progress, as the metal doors gradually slid closed.

The moment they shut, the two women fell back against the wall, gasping in relief.

"Oh, thank God." Marisol wiped the perspiration from her face with a handkerchief. As she returned the sodden cloth to her purse, she palmed the brick of cash and stuck it in the waistband of her black silk pants.

Five guards approached the pair of women and surrounded them. Marisol shoved her purse back past her hip to hide the cash lump against the base of her spine.

One guard was on the radio. "Suspect boarded the elevator on the fifty-eighth floor, headed up."

"Can you describe the assailant?" another guard asked Marisol and Tyesha.

"Short, stocky build," Tyesha said. "Maybe he was black."

"I'm not sure," Marisol disagreed. "It was hard to tell in the ski mask."

"I'm sorry, ma'am," the guard in charge said. "We'll need to do a search." He called one of the young guards over.

Marisol and Tyesha handed over their purses as a voice crackled over the radio: "Caught the elevator on sixty-three. Nothing but a ski mask and a jacket. A ceiling panel was loose. He must've climbed out. Seal the building for search protocol."

The young guard called to his superior. "Purses are clean."

The older guard stepped forward. "Now we'll do a pat down."

"We'd like a woman to search us, please," Marisol demanded.

The older guard pulled up the radio. "I need a female assist on fifty-eight to frisk two suspects . . ."

Two hours earlier, Marisol and Tyesha had been working in the office when Kim called.

"Marisol, you'll never believe it," Kim said, her voice thick with tears. "We're here at the corporate party but I'm hiding under the CEO's desk. He's a goddamn sex trafficker!"

"He's what?" Outrage swelled in Marisol's chest. It took a few minutes to get the story out. Kim and her girlfriend, Jody, were escorting two clients to the after-party of an awards event where the host had been honored for humanitarian efforts in Mexico. But Kim recognized him as one of several CEOs acquitted—despite extensive evidence—in a Mexican sex trafficking scandal. Kim had followed the CEO and slipped into his office, where he had locked up the award. After he left, she had tried unsuccessfully to crack the safe.

She was sobbing. "I can't breathe. I think I'm having a panic attack. I can't go back to the party and pretend everything's okay. But what was I thinking? I don't know how to open a safe."

But Marisol knew how. An hour later, she and Tyesha snuck into the party and Kim let her into the CEO's office. Marisol had smoothed Kim's glossy hair from her face, and coached her breathing back to normal.

Kim was Korean and in her mid-twenties. Marisol had met her when she was a topless waitress in a seedy club. She worked eight hours, gave the occasional blow job, and didn't have health insurance. Now she worked one night a week and had a 401K.

"I'm sorry," Kim said. "I know these software guys pay a lot of money. I should've just rolled with it."

"No," Marisol said, drying the girl's eyes. "When you're working and anything goes wrong, you call me. Always."

Kim nodded and blew her nose.

"Go back to your date and act like nothing happened," Marisol told Kim. "I'll take care of this."

Marisol had stolen the award and $10,000. She had almost reached the stairwell when someone yelled for her to stop.

On the landing of the seventy-second floor, she'd pulled the ski mask over her face and sprinted down the stairs. She hurled the award down the center of the stairwell. The glass trophy was designed like a map of the world, with continents and the CEO's name in twenty-four-karat gold. As it fell tumbling through the air, the stairwell's fluorescent lights glinted off the crystal planes and smooth surfaces of gold. Seventy stories below, it crashed into the marble floor like a meteor, creating a ragged hole, an explosion of fine glass fragments, and bits of molten gold shrapnel.

On the fifty-eighth floor, the head of security returned with a female guard. A blond bun peeked out beneath the gray uniform cap.

As she patted Tyesha down, the lead guard asked, "What were you two doing on this floor?"

"We were looking for someplace quiet," Tyesha said.

"She's clean," the female guard said of Tyesha.

"We just wanted to be alone," Marisol said, putting her arm around Tyesha. Behind their backs, Marisol slid the cash out and handed it to Tyesha.

The man sneered. "No wonder you wanted a woman guard." He pointed at Marisol. "Step forward."

Marisol let the woman pat her down as Tyesha slid the cash into her own purse.

Marisol felt the woman's gloved hands patting down her body. The guard checked under her hair and ran a hand gently down her back, passing over the spot where the cash had been, barely a moment before.

"Can we go back to the party after this?" Marisol asked. "I need a drink."

"She's clean, too," the female guard said.

"Party's over," the head guard said. "We'll escort you to the ground level, where they'll check your IDs."

The two women stood flanked by both guards, as the elevator descended fifty-seven floors to the lobby.

Marisol watched a uniformed guard do a slipshod job of sweeping shards of glass into a dustpan.

At the security desk, Marisol and Tyesha handed over IDs for Lourdes and Danita, both with Long Island addresses. A guard copied the information, then let them go.

As they approached the street door, the guard yelled, "Wait a minute!"

Marisol turned around, her heart hammering.

"You should use the other exit," the guard said. "There's broken glass on this end."

"Don't worry," Marisol said, steering Tyesha around the crater in the marble floor. "My shoes are invincible."

Chapter 2

Eleven months later

The cargo van sat at the snowy curb like a tropical fish in the middle of a vast white sea. Two inches of powder had accumulated on top of the vehicle. The van had been shrink-wrapped in a colorful vinyl advertisement: "The María de la Vega Health Clinic, serving the ladies of Manhattan since 2001." The clinic's toll-free help line number and location followed. One vinyl patch on the bottom of the door was held down with duct tape.

The van sat in a loading zone in front of the Lower East Side storefront clinic. Three teenage girls hurried into the clinic through the snow, their tight jackets and jeans as bright as the van. A moment later, Marisol Rivera, a caramel-colored woman in her thirties, stepped out of the clinic door into the snow. She carried two plastic shopping bags of homemade sandwiches and a jug of imitation juice. Rush hour traffic sped past, turning the powder to sludge. In contrast to the teenagers' hot girl clothes, she wore a tailored suit sanding down her curves, and high-heeled pumps. Her hair was pulled back into a loose knot. Underneath the suit, she wore a fraying baby carrier with a sleeping infant snuggled against her chest, a son of one of the clients. With her free hand, Marisol tucked the blanket more tightly around him.

She crossed the grimy sidewalk and unlocked the back doors of the van with one of the keys from a ring on her belt. They granted her access to every lock in the clinic building—every door, desk, closet, file drawer, padlock, and supply cabinet.

The two women who trooped out to join her looked like opposites, although both were in their twenties. Jody was a six-foot blonde white woman in athletic gear. Tyesha not only contrasted in size and color—she was African American and much shorter—but also in style. She wore designer jeans and boots, with bling jewelry. The three piled into the clinic's mobile health van. The interior had a plastic corrugated floor, and the walls were stacked with milk crates, which held medical and outreach equipment.

Marisol pulled a clipboard off the wall, and sat cross-legged on the floor. She checked off items the van would provide during their run throughout Lower Manhattan that night.

Tyesha peeked into a wax paper sandwich bag, and her bobbed hair fell forward, obscuring her heart-shaped face.

"Peanut butter again?" she said, tucking her hair behind her ear.

"That's government peanut butter," said Jody, who had to crouch considerably to fit in the van. "No peanuts were harmed in the making of it."

Jody was a fearless street fighter. The muscles in her arms and back rippled as she moved several heavy supply boxes. Tyesha piled the sandwiches into milk crates and poured the juice into a plastic dispenser.

"When I first started working here, we used to get

turkey," Tyesha said. "Real turkeys died for our sins back then."

"These bitches need to be happy they're getting food at all," Jody said, taking a sandwich.

"Hold up, ladies," Marisol said. She brushed the snow from her hair. "Remember, you and our clients are not bitches. You are hoes."

The women laughed.

"Bitches are dogs," Marisol said. "But whores are . . . ?" She looked expectantly at Jody.

"Professionals who get paid." Jody grinned and high-fived Tyesha.

"Thank you," Marisol said. "Show some respect for the trade."

Marisol stood to hand the clipboard to Tyesha, and Jody noticed the infant carrier.

"What the fuck?" Jody asked. "You brought someone's baby into our mobile health van?"

"The son of a client," Marisol said. "She missed her last two counseling appointments and needs help."

"Seriously, Marisol?" Tyesha asked. "You gonna add babysitter to your never-ending job description?"

"If you're gonna start a nanny service in the van, can we at least have heat?" Jody asked. "It's fucking freezing." She tugged her cap further down.

"Waste of gas," Marisol said. She unhooked some of the bungee cords that secured the milk crates. "We'll be out in a few minutes."

Tyesha put on a pair of rimless glasses and flipped to the second page on the clipboard. "Should the outreach team bother to go by Vixela's anymore, after last night?"

"More underage girls?" Marisol asked. Vixela's was a strip club that advertised "private entertainment" in its warren of tiny back rooms.

"Who knows?" Tyesha said. "They wouldn't let us operate there."

"Vixela won't let us park in front," Marisol said.

"We were parked in the back alley," Jody said. "Her security guys kicked us out."

Marisol stopped counting HIV tests. "Out of the alley?"

"I fucking hate her," said Jody. She gripped one of the crates. Inside were stacks of flyers advertising the clinic's gala fund-raiser. "When my ex-girlfriend started working there, Vixela promised she could make good money just dancing. By the end, she was fucking four or five guys a night to make rent."

"Vixela's an old-ass hoe who's jealous of young girls," said Tyesha. "All those pictures of her on the wall showing off her tits. Okay, I get it, Vixela, you were *va-va-voom* back in the seventies. But your moment has passed."

"Like you always tell us, Marisol," Jody said. "Don't build your whole life on being young and hot forever."

"You'll stop making money for yourself and start making it for your plastic surgeon," Marisol said.

Jody nodded. "When my ex worked there, we used to joke that she was fucking the guys just to pay for Vixela's cosmetic retrofitting."

"I don't understand how she could be face-to-face with me and lie," Marisol said.

"Cause that's not really her face," Tyesha said.

They laughed. The baby murmured and shifted in the carrier.

"Marisol," Tyesha whispered. "You should get that baby out of the cold. I can do the setup."

"He's fine," Marisol said, patting him. She checked the expiration date on a box of condoms.

"But won't the snow mess up your shoes?" asked Tyesha.

"Not these," Marisol said. She looked down at her invincibility shoes, classic black platform stiletto pumps, with springy material beneath the balls of her feet that made the five-inch heels tolerable. "They're made outta some indestructible type of patent leather. Wind, rain, sleet, snow. Nothing fucks them up."

"I need a pair like that," Jody said. "What are they, Jimmy Choos?"

"No way," said Tyesha. "Those are Vera Wangs, right, Marisol?"

"I don't know," Marisol said.

"How can you not know?" Tyesha asked. "Take off the damn shoe and check the label."

"That's the thing," Marisol said. "I got them from this lady who sells shoes outta her trunk. She cuts out the designer labels and charges twenty-nine ninety-nine."

"I love deals like that," Tyesha said.

Marisol smiled. "My *mami* always told me that finding a bargain is God telling you He wants you to have nice things." Her mother had described it like a signpost on the way to the good life. And occasionally Marisol saw her mother create the bargain herself by switching the price tags. Or in a big store she would take advantage of a missing inventory tag. This was also God, her mother had explained, because God created the opportunity.

Her mother was always cool and discreet. She never boosted any item unless it was a sure thing. Once she'd left her raggedy sneakers in the box at a department store and walked out wearing snakeskin stilettos under her custodian's uniform. She left the store with her head held high, children in tow. After they got back to their one-bedroom apartment on the Lower East Side, her mother told them never to steal from people. Only stores.

"So, where does your girl sell the kickstunners outta her trunk?" Tyesha asked.

"Sometimes she's at West Twenty-seventh and—"

The van rumbled and tilted.

"What the fuck?" said Jody.

Marisol swung the back door open and sprinted out. The van was being lifted up onto a tow truck by a short, barrel-chested guy.

Jody balled her fists and advanced, but Marisol grabbed Jody by the hood of her jacket and pulled her back. "I'll handle this."

The baby started to cry.

"What the hell are you doing?" Marisol asked the tow guy.

"We're repossessing the van for nonpayment," he said. He pulled a lever, and the chains began to pull the van up onto the back of the truck.

"Bullshit," Marisol said, over the baby's wailing. "Our account is up to date." She bounced up and down, and the movement quieted the baby. Tyesha and Jody stood behind Marisol with their arms crossed. Several girls came out of the clinic and joined them.

"I just tow who they say. Tell your boss we're taking the van."

"I am the boss," Marisol said. "And if you wrongfully remove this vehicle, I'll sue your company in a heartbeat."

"You tell his stupid ass, Marisol," said Nalissa, a young woman with hair dyed bright carrot red. *"Defiende lo tuyo!"*

The guy shut everything off and the van stopped moving. By then it was halfway up onto the truck bed. He stalked around to the cab and pulled out a cell phone.

"Crazy Spanish bitch," he muttered.

"That's crazy Puerto Rican bitch," Marisol yelled back. "Learn your geography."

"Crazy Spanish bitch?" Nalissa said. "I'm a show you a crazy Dominican bitch!" She lunged toward the driver, but Tyesha and Jody grabbed her arms.

"*Cálmate*, Nalissa," Marisol said. "I got this."

With all the noise, the baby began to squirm and fuss. Marisol pulled him out and held him to her chest. He reached up and played with the locket around her neck.

"Yeah, *papi*," she said, opening the locket to reveal a little girl with two puffy blond pigtails and a missing front tooth. "You see that girl? That's Cristina, my baby sister."

Cristina was six years younger and had been more like a daughter in many ways. Now that Marisol was in her thirties, the difference wasn't so pronounced, but when Cristina was a baby, Marisol had cared for her at night, while their mother worked. Holding babies always reminded her of Cristina. Their mother died of breast cancer when Marisol was in middle school, her sister in elementary. After that, Marisol had fallen solidly into the mother role.

As the baby tickled against her neck, Marisol had a bitter ache in her chest. Cristina was her family, the one person who really mattered.

The engine rumbled. Marisol cursed and handed the child to Jody. The baby wailed. Marisol kicked off her heels and handed them to Tyesha, then scrambled onto the back of the tow truck, slush dripping from her stockinged feet.

She opened the van door and yelled down to Jody, "Gimme the baby."

"You want me to—?"

"Now!" Marisol yelled, stretching both hands out.

Jody handed back the screaming baby. Marisol slid into the van's passenger seat and locked the door. The tow guy came around from the cab of the truck with an armful of brake lights.

"What the fuck are you doing?" he yelled over the noise of the engine.

Marisol rolled the window down a crack. "Watch your goddamn language in front of the baby."

"You need to get down from there," he said. "It's not safe."

"I'll tell you what's not safe," Marisol said, jiggling the baby on her knee. "Women working on the street with no health care. The city pays us to drive this van around and provide services for girls who can't come to the clinic."

"I'm calling the police," he said.

"Go ahead," she said. "I'm calling the leasing company." The baby flailed in her arms and knocked some papers off a bulletin board.

She dialed her phone, and asked for the manager on duty. As she waited on hold, she rummaged through the clinic supplies. "Are you teething, *papi*?" She found a tongue depressor and he began to chew on it.

The manager came on the line, as she dried the dripping slush from her freezing feet.

"This is Marisol Rivera, executive director of the Vega Clinic on the Lower East Side. There's been a mistake. They're trying to repossess our van." Marisol only called it the Vega Clinic when she was particularly pissed off. The place was named after her mother, so she enjoyed saying the full name: María de la Vega.

"No mistake," the manager said. "You've been late with every payment since last June."

"I have an arrangement with your bookkeeper," Marisol said. "She gives me until the tenth."

"We have no record of that," he said.

"Put her on the phone," Marisol said.

"She no longer works here."

"She was working there when we made the verbal contract," Marisol said. "I have her cell number and I bet she'd testify in court."

"What's the big deal?" he asked. "You'll get it back once you pay up."

"The big deal is the thousands of dollars of medical equipment we have inside. Besides, your driver can't take the van anyway, since I'm sitting in it."

"The van is already on the tow truck," he said.

"I'm in the passenger seat."

"You're what?"

"With a baby on my lap," Marisol said. He was happily chewing the tongue depressor. "In fact, the van was occupied when the towing process started. Highly illegal."

"You're wasting everyone's time," he said. "We'll send someone to find the van later via GPS."

"Be my guest." Marisol laughed. "Your repo guy can watch urban health care in action all over Manhattan. I told your girl I'd have the money for you tomorrow, and I will—in cash."

"Tomorrow morning," the guy said. "Just this once. You need to start paying on time."

"Great," Marisol said. "Now you and I have a verbal contract. Which I recorded on my phone. Is nine a.m. good for you?"

The tow guy lowered the van off the truck. Marisol put her shoes back on and handed the baby back to his mother.

Nalissa, the young hothead with dyed-red hair, approached Marisol. "You remember how I been looking for business opportunities?" she asked.

"I'm rushing right now," Marisol said. "Talk to my assistant, Serena. Tell her I said you're a priority appointment."

Marisol and Tyesha watched Nalissa switch back into the clinic on high-heeled sneakers. With her extreme curves and long red hair, she was popular with the escort clients.

"What does Nalissa want?" Tyesha asked. "Better bookings?"

"She can smell some more hustles going on besides the escort service," Marisol said. "I think she wants in."

"You considering it?" Tyesha asked, handing Marisol a duffel bag.

Marisol shook her head. "That first award heist was a fluke, but it taught me I could trust you, Kim, and Jody," she murmured. "The last seven or eight jobs taught me to stick with a good thing. After we get these two final 'donations,' we'll be home free."

She said good-bye to Tyesha, and ducked back into the van with the duffel.

Jody took a drag off a cigarette and blew smoke out the driver's side window. Marisol reposted the papers that the baby had pulled off the van's bulletin board. On top were two press clippings. One, dated over a year before, was about the Mexican sex trafficking scandal. It carried the photo of the eleven CEOs on the board of the fraternity Ivy Alpha, who were allegedly involved. The other article, dated eleven months before, reported that one of the Ivy Alpha CEOs had been robbed at an award after-party—details were sketchy as to what had been stolen. However, it did mention that security was able to recover the award, which had been "damaged" in the chase.

"I haven't had time to check my phone," Marisol said. She stripped out of her office clothes, exchanging them for a black turtleneck, yoga pants, and sneakers from the duffel bag. "Is Kim at the 'donation' job already?"

"We just talked," Jody said. "Since it's snowing, she was going to move—"

"Tell your girlfriend to stick to the plan and stay where I put her," Marisol said, holding up a hand. "I'm already fourteen minutes behind schedule. Can you stay with the van until the outreach crew arrives?"

"No problem," Jody said. "I hope some dick does come for the van. I haven't given out a good ass-kicking since I left the dominatrix biz."

Marisol said, "Tell Kim that Tyesha will be there to relieve her momentarily."

Jody pointed to a pudgy, graying man in the newspaper clipping. "Give the tech CEO my love," she said and lit another cigarette.

Chapter 3

Marisol looked out of the sixth-floor window. Snow obscured the visibility across East Seventy-second. She could barely discern the outlines of the windows on the building across the street, and she had no way to see whether anyone was standing on the sidewalk below. She and Tyesha had arrived in separate cabs, while Jody stayed with the van at the clinic.

U in place? Marisol texted to Tyesha.

All clear, Tyesha texted back.

Marisol picked up her worn tool bag and got to work.

Out in front of the opposite building, Tyesha made eye contact with Kim. The young Korean woman wore a hooded parka and high-heeled boots. After their eyes met, Kim walked away, letting Tyesha take over as lookout. The doorman came to shovel the curb, so Tyesha paced back and forth between two piles of snow.

Three tourists exited a nearby restaurant.

"Oh my God, it's snowing," one shrieked.

Tyesha watched the cab pull up in front of the building where Marisol was working. The snow muted the voices of an arguing couple that drifted out of the open cab door. They'd come back home to retrieve their forgotten theater tickets. The woman had her wallet out, platinum credit card in hand, and one rust-colored pump already planted in the snow. Her husband said they should hang on to the cab.

Above, in the couple's apartment, Marisol Rivera tapped twice on the door of their wall safe. She put her stethoscope to the door and slowly turned the dial. The pads of her fingers pressed against the serrated surface of the metal. She turned it carefully to the right, then left, then right again. She breathed to calm her jitters, and listened for the safe's three-click reply. She relied on the ritual of the two-beat/three-beat call and response in clave rhythm to guide her conversation with the safe. When the door swung open with a slight hiss, she mouthed "*gracias*."

Marisol reached in, and pushed aside several disk drives, a stack of CDs, and a jewelry box that contained a diamond necklace set and an Ivy Alpha membership ring.

Marisol's anxiety escalated as she found several stacks of papers, some kind of patent materials, but no sign of cash. Had she really masterminded this job only to find a safe full of stuff they couldn't use?

The back of the safe seemed to move. The surface she had thought was the rear wall of the compartment turned out to be the back of some kind of metal box. The safe was deep, and she had to stand on her tiptoes to pull the box out. She set it on the hardwood floor and lifted the lid. She found stacks of twenty-dollar bills.

The woman paid the cab fare, and her husband climbed out behind her. All at once Tyesha recognized the graying man and his young wife as they hurried into the building. Tyesha had been watching to make sure the housekeeper didn't return, but she hadn't expected the owners. She snatched her phone to warn Marisol. As she dialed, one of the tipsy tourists swayed into her, knocking her phone into the snow.

Tyesha leaped to retrieve it.

"I'm so sorry," the tourist wailed. "Let me help you." She stumbled forward, spraying new powder onto the spot where the phone had fallen.

"Back the fuck off me!" Tyesha elbowed her and dug into the snow.

The tourist wobbled across the street to her friends, complaining about rude New Yorkers as they piled into the available cab.

Tyesha tore off her leather gloves and dug barehanded, the cold biting into her fingers.

Marisol's own gloved hands gripped the bricks of cash as she loaded them into the oversized handbag strapped across her chest. She eased the safe shut and replaced the painting that had concealed it, a headless reclining female nude in shades of yellow-green.

One of Kim's escort clients had brought her to a party here a few weeks before. Kim had bumped the painting and seen the edge of the safe.

The apartment belonged to the CEO of a tech manufacturer. On the wall opposite was a photo of him with the mayor.

The snow floated down past the window, hushing the noise of the city. Down the hallway, an elevator sounded a faint *ding*.

Marisol set the bag down on the living room floor, and knelt in front of the open-air vent through which she'd crawled in. She had just turned to grab the screwdriver to refasten the grate, when she saw something in her peripheral vision. It was a little model building, about eight inches high. As she turned her body for a closer look, she heard a key in the door. She grabbed the bag of cash and shoved it into the vent.

The apartment was secured with three locks, which allowed her time to slide into the vent feet first. The space was narrowest just outside the apartment. Her hips and ass, the widest part of her frame, barely fit. The squeeze of her lower body had been a challenge crawling in, but it was even more difficult in reverse. She wriggled backward, pulling the grate into place. She held a flashlight in her teeth, a press-on/press-off type she could operate by biting down. She scanned the room.

Three of the four screws from the vent lay brazenly exposed on the hardwood floor, just beyond the camouflaging reach of the Oriental rug. The beam of her light illuminated the flat head of one of the screws on the floor. It glinted up at her, taunting.

The couple entered the apartment. Marisol bit down, extinguishing her light.

". . . And did you see her dress?" the woman said. "What was she thinking with all that pink shimmer?"

The husband murmured something, and the woman said, "Honestly, I'm halfway glad we forgot the tickets. Not just because of the snow. I'd hate to walk in with her wearing some prom dress–gone–wrong."

They flipped on the living room lamp.

Marisol's eyes darted from the couple's shadows on the carpet to the loose screws on the floor.

"And her daughter?" The wife's voice got louder as she walked into the living room. "Did you see what she had on? Some of these teenage girls look like roadkill."

Marisol's phone vibrated. The vent lit up with Tyesha's belated warning. It rattled slightly, rumbling against the metal of the vent through the fabric of her pants. She saw the rust-colored tip of the woman's shoe through the metal slats. Marisol held her breath. The woman kicked off her wet high heels and walked out of view.

What the hell had happened with Tyesha? Why was the warning text so late?

"Honey, you forgot to set the alarm again," the wife said.

"I was sure I had," he said. "Your husband is getting senile."

But he had set it. Kim had videotaped the husband entering the code while pretending to take selfies with her date.

Marisol's phone buzzed again. She itched to turn it off, but her bent arms were pinned to her chest like chicken wings, holding the grate in place in front of her. Marisol's fingers gripped the latticed metal on either side of her head, the crown of which was practically pressed against the grate. Strands of her dark hair and her fingertips would surely be visible to anyone looking closely.

"Good thing we came home," the woman said. She padded across the carpet and picked up her shoes. "I had to pee and that restaurant bathroom was disgusting." Her voice trailed away as she moved toward the back of the apartment.

The screwdriver dug into Marisol's right hip. She angled her body to take off the pressure. As she did, she heard a tiny rustle of paper. Folded up in her bra was the same newspaper article from the bulletin board in the van. She carried it as a talisman.

Ivy League Fraternity CEOs Cleared in Sex Trafficking Case

Houston, TX (January 17th)—A federal judge dropped all sex trafficking charges against the organization Ivy Alpha, the national men's organization whose members are all Ivy League alumni and Fortune 500 CEOs. A complaint alleged that the organization brought in young Mexican women as prostitutes at Ivy Alpha's annual conference in Houston last year, under the guise of a "dance performance." The fraternity was charged with several misdemeanors and felonies, including child prostitution, as some of the girls involved were underage. "The hypocrisy is particularly outrageous," said the attorney who filed the complaint. "All the CEOs have factories in the region that offer low-wage jobs to women as part of anti-trafficking efforts to provide 'jobs with dignity' to women who have been 'rescued and rehabilitated.'" One CEO's bookkeeper turned whistleblower when she suspected trafficking: "I requested the lodging invoice for the women since the transportation invoice clearly showed that they came early Saturday evening, but didn't leave until Sunday morning. My boss said, 'Don't worry about it,' but I dug around a little, and it became clear that those girls spent the night in the CEOs' rooms." Criminal charges were dropped despite several firsthand accounts by the women allegedly involved. According to the judge, the evidence

> was insufficient to proceed with a trial against the organization. Defense attorneys insisted that the firsthand accounts were "suspect" because "these women from Mexico would say anything in order to come to the US."
>
> *Pictured above, the eleven New York–based CEOs who are board members of Ivy Alpha.*

"Where did you leave the theater tickets?" the man asked.

"In the breakfast nook," the woman called back. "I used them as a bookmark."

"What time is it?" he asked, over the sound of running water. "You hate to miss the beginning of a show."

Marisol saw the woman's feet as she stepped into a pair of brown boots.

"You look stunning," the husband said. "Maybe we can have our own little show right here at home?"

Two pairs of feet moved closer to each other.

The woman giggled. "Easy there, big fella. I promised my brother I'd come backstage afterward—mmmmm . . ."

"Well . . ." The husband's voice was low, seductive. "We can't really be seated until after intermission, sweetheart. We have at least half an hour."

"Half an hour is not enough time to get into anything naughty," she said.

"Usually it's not," he said. "But I took a little trip to the fountain of youth."

"I thought the Viagra made your vision bluish," she said.

"My doctor got me something else," he said. "I can see you perfectly. Can you see what I've got for you?"

"Wow," she said.

The man's pants dropped around his ankles.

The couple laughed, murmured, and moaned. The woman's bra fell next to her stockinged feet, and then both of their bodies sank into Marisol's view. Their foreplay continued on the carpet.

The husband knelt on the rug, in front of his wife's parted thighs. He slid off the lacy beige panties below her skirt.

As he lowered himself between the wife's legs, she moaned.

"Am I rocking your world, baby?" he asked.

"Oh yes," she called back. "*Yes!*" The young wife had the practiced, breathless affectation that any pro could recognize.

Marisol distracted herself by trying to guess the take from the safe. How many bricks of cash had there been? Seventy-five hundred would cover this month's mortgage payment on the clinic. But $14,750 would make payroll.

Government cutbacks had hit the clinic hard a few years before, and Marisol had opened a discreet escort service to cover the $5,000 gap every month. Then, one of their private foundation supporters came under fire for funding birth control, and didn't renew their operational grant. Previously, it had been one of their most reliable income sources. Marisol kicked the escort service into overdrive, hustling to hang on until later this spring, when a different foundation would disburse a grant award for 1.3 million dollars. Her scheme was working until their biggest corporate sponsor went bankrupt. But that same week the chance to heist the first corrupt CEO practically fell into her lap. Her mother would have called it a sign from God.

A hand swung into Marisol's view, almost touching the screw that lay just beyond the perimeter of the carpet. Marisol jerked and nearly banged her head against the roof of the vent. Holding her breath, she watched the woman dig the back of her fingers into the carpet. With each thrust, her little finger moved closer to the screw.

"Oh God!" the woman moaned.

When her hand touched the screw, she didn't seem to notice. Then they changed positions, with the wife on top.

Marisol felt jagged from the tension between the adrenaline rush and the need to stay still. Her leg twitched, and she breathed to calm her system. She willed herself toward soothing thoughts, recalling the last place she felt she could really relax. She imagined *la playa*, El Escambron Beach, in Puerto Rico, and being with her grandmother when she was eleven. She recalled humid nights sleeping under a mosquito net with Cristina, laughing and admonishing her younger sister not to scratch her bites, even as Marisol secretly scratched her own—not scratched, but pressed the tip of her nail on the bite, making an X across the surface of each one. Scratching broke the skin, made it bleed, invited infection. The nail press brought delicious relief, but left no trace.

The sharp *clack*ing of the woman's boot heels on the hardwood floor brought Marisol back. Back to the screwdriver digging into her hip, her cramping fingers as she held the grate, the pain in her jaw from biting down on the flashlight, and her stiffening muscles.

"I just need to freshen my lipstick," the wife said, slightly breathless. "You have the tickets?"

"Got them," the husband said.

Marisol waited in the dark, at the edge of her endurance. The vent air was starting to taste stale, and her fingers and neck cramped. As she turned her head slightly she saw the little model building, and recognized the logo on it from the CEO's tech factory in Mexico. Suddenly she didn't feel discomfort, just a furious, cold resolve.

Before the scandal broke, this CEO was hailed for providing "decent" jobs for formerly trafficked girls. Yet building a tech assembly factory beside a notorious red-light district simply meant rescue operations could send a never-ending supply of cheap labor. Marisol could have stood the hypocrisy of hiring sex workers for his conference. But she had read the court transcripts. According to the women involved, some corrupt members of the anti-trafficking organization had handpicked the girls they considered most attractive and then groomed them as dancers. They dangled promises of green cards to the United States. Then they just shipped them into the conference to provide sexual services to the CEOs.

The bag of cash pressed against her ankle. As always, she would send some of the funds to a group in Mexico that worked directly with the women.

She kept her eye on the edge of the logo until she heard the alarm code. She waited until all three locks were bolted into place before she unpacked herself from the vent, spilling her body out onto the floor and spitting out the flashlight.

She heard the ding of the elevator. Pulling pliers from her bag, she snipped off the ends of the screws and used epoxy to glue the four screw heads onto the front of the grate.

As she waited for it to dry, she swept her arm along the living room shelf, knocking everything onto the floor. The ceramic and glass framing a picture of the man and two teenage kids shattered on the hardwood floor, but the plastic cover on the little model building only cracked slightly. It wasn't nearly as satisfying as dropping the award seventy stories during her first theft.

It was just past midnight when Marisol's taxi crossed into Alphabet City. She drove by a couple screaming outside one of the bars: "*You were flirting with her! You were totally fucking flirting!*" They drove through traffic backed up from an accident on the Williamsburg Bridge.

With all the gentrification, the Lower East Side felt muted these days. When Marisol was a kid, Loisaida had a different soundscape: Mamas calling, "*Oye, Yunior, get your ass inside!*" Salsa blasting from apartment windows, and summertime outdoor conga jam sessions with the splash of hydrants.

Over time, many of the murals had become discolored. Red paint faded quickly, so the Puerto Rican flags were now pale pink, white, and blue. These days offered plenty of bright red neon for ATM or Under New Ownership signs. Where there used to be glinting mirrored mosaics on somebody's storefront or crazy sculpture installations in a vacant lot, now there were galleries, and graffiti lettering to advertise beauty salons that mostly catered to straight hair.

Even people's fashion colors had dulled. The visual riot of Latin clothes had yielded to subdued hipster hues. Tropical turquoise, magenta, yellow-green, and violet still appeared in women's outfits, but no longer all together.

The cab dropped her on a quiet street between Avenues D and C. She held her purse closer. It wouldn't do to get mugged on the way back from a burglary.

With the exception of that small hitch tonight, her burglary modus operandi was working flawlessly. Kim had a client who was a tech consultant with these Ivy Alpha guys. He and his lovely Asian "girlfriend" got invited to their parties. Kim could take pictures with her date in strategic locations, and Marisol would research the technology in preparation to do the hit. With wealthy Manhattanites, it was easy to pick a night they'd be out.

Half a block from her apartment, Marisol noticed a figure huddled in a doorway. The block was deserted. At first she stepped back, in case it was a setup. But as she got closer, she could see it was a young woman. Her face was hidden, but Marisol could see a bare bruised leg in a scuffed-up pair of eight-inch, silver platform boots.

Chapter 4

"You okay, honey?" Marisol asked the girl in the doorway.

She didn't stir.

"Hello?" Marisol saw the slight rise and fall of breath. She tapped the spot she estimated to be a shoulder.

The girl shrieked and curled into a ball. "I'm sorry! *Descúlpame!*"

Marisol saw the girl's face for a second. So young. Marisol had a flashback of her own bruised teenage face, a late-night trip to the emergency room, lying to a social worker.

"It's okay," Marisol said, placing a hand on the girl's back to calm her. "Nobody's gonna hurt you, *nena*."

The girl released the fist that her body had become.

A hospital ID bracelet peeked from under the sling on the girl's arm. Marisol recalled the times she'd cut hers off before she returned to her uncle's house. She didn't want to get in trouble for involving the authorities.

"*Mamita,* you shouldn't stay out here," Marisol whispered. "I'll take you to the clinic down the street."

"They're closed for the night," the girl muttered into

the sheet that fell back from a heavily bruised face. She was Latina, with honey-blond hair, midnight at the roots.

Marisol reached out her hand. "I work there. I can get you in. Come on, *mija*. Do you need help up?"

"He said he'd kill me if I ever went there," the girl said, tears spilling across the plum and violet of her face. "He dumped me at the ER and said to come home when I could walk. There ain't many places in the city a beat-down whore can go. He said he knew all of them and he'd be watching."

Marisol felt a flash of rage. She remembered her uncle's words, decades ago: *I'm your only family now. Nobody else wants you*. His words stung. He had reached toward her body, but she sidestepped him easily that night since he was falling-down drunk.

"*Mira*," Marisol said to the girl. "Of course you're scared of whoever did this, but he's not here now. There's a place for you a few buildings down."

Marisol took the girl's good arm to help her up, but she stayed put.

"*Corazón*, look around." Marisol knelt down. "There's nobody here but us."

The young woman looked out at the empty street. Every car was perfectly covered in white. "He has guys on his payroll who follow us sometimes."

Marisol knew the risk the girl would be taking to go to the clinic. Still, if she could just get her into the building, she could protect her.

"Jerry was right," the girl said. She was on her feet now, unsteady on the torn platform boots, and still wrapped in a hospital sheet. "I really—" She took two steps, wavered, collapsed against the doorway, and threw up into the snow.

"I'm taking you in," Marisol said. She put her arm around the girl, half-carrying her down the block to the clinic.

The girl stumbled along. Marisol unlocked the door. She turned on the lamp next to one of the couches.

In the dim light, the lobby would have looked like a living room, if not for the large reception desk and the vending machines under the stairwell. The room was filled with comfy couches and reclining chairs. A large flat-screen TV sat against the far wall, and beside it was a shelf filled with books, magazines, and board games.

The clinic was a former storefront that had sold tobacco, and whenever Marisol leaned against the walls, she detected the faint smell of sweet pipe smoke. In the rear of the lobby, a security door opened up to a stairwell. The upper floors had mostly been converted from apartments to clinic offices.

"What's your name?" Marisol asked.

"Dulce."

"Dulce, I'm admitting you to the shelter for the night. You'll have an intake appointment in the morning. Wait here." Marisol gestured toward the couch. Dulce collapsed onto it.

"What if they won't let me in?" Dulce asked.

"I'm the executive director," Marisol said. "I say who comes in."

She scanned her ID card and opened the door to the stairwell. She ran up the stairs, the oversized bag filled with stolen cash bumping against her hip.

On the second floor, Marisol saw a strip of light coming from under one of the doors. She knocked, and Dr. Eva Feldman let her in.

Marisol walked into the office and hugged her codirector. Eva was in her early sixties, her body thick and solid.

"Three more light bulbs blew out today," Eva said, shutting the door behind Marisol.

"I know," Marisol said. "They're defective."

"Defective? They're black market," Eva said. "You got ripped off."

"No, I didn't," Marisol insisted. "The guy made good and sent ten replacement cases. It was still a great deal."

"Not if you factor in staff time replacing bulbs," Eva said. She leaned her cane against the wall and sat down at her desk. Childhood polio had rendered her left leg weak and unstable.

The long, rectangular office had a split personality. On the administrative side, the desk overflowed with papers and books. The therapy side was open and peaceful, with two chairs, a couch, and a Zen sand garden on the table.

"I'm not here to debate supply issues," Marisol said. "I've got a late admit for the shelter."

"Sorry," Eva said. "We're full."

"Put her on the floor if you have to," Marisol said with a shrug. "We have sleeping bags."

"The floor is full, too," Eva said.

"No problem." Marisol began to pull cushions off the couch. "We can make a bed for her in the hallway."

"We can't," Eva said, standing up. "Another citation from the fire marshal would finish us." She picked up her cane and walked over to Marisol.

"A surprise inspection is a chance we have to take," Marisol said. She balanced the pile of pillows against her hip.

"You need to stop," Eva said. She put a hand on Marisol's arm. "I know you're coming in from a job, full of adrenaline. You feel invincible, but the clinic is much too vulnerable."

Marisol snatched the throw blanket off the back of the couch, and slung it over her shoulder. "I did not spend an hour crawling through a fucking air vent just to turn somebody away who needs us. This girl is vulnerable. She's half-dead with some pimp looking for her." Marisol put her free hand on the bulge of cash in her bag.

"We have an agreement, Marisol," Eva said. "You fund the clinic. I run the clinic. It doesn't make sense to save one girl for one night if the clinic gets shut down."

Marisol sucked her teeth. "It doesn't make sense to you because you've never stood in that girl's shoes."

During high school Marisol had felt the urge to vomit every time she entered her uncle's apartment.

"I am not putting that girl back out in the snow," Marisol said.

"Then I'll put her out in the snow," Eva said. "I won't have the whole clinic at risk because you can't see the big picture." She pulled a list of shelters off the crammed bulletin board. "I'll call to see if there's an open bed." Eva picked up the phone receiver.

"Her pimp is looking to finish her off," Marisol said, hitting the Off button on the base of the phone.

"We're not the only clinic in the city, Marisol. We can't save everybody."

"Not without a bigger building," Marisol said.

"You're delusional," Eva said. "Bring the girl in here and I'll break the bad news then call the shelters."

Eva set the shelter list on the desk. Between tall stacks of client files sat a half-eaten container of Indian food.

"Never mind," Marisol said. She put the cushions back onto the couch. "I know where to take her, and it won't break the fire code."

"Not your apartment."

"Don't worry about it," Marisol said. She walked to

the office door. "I just funded the clinic. You run it. I'll see you tomorrow."

"Boundaries," Eva said, as she followed her to the door. "You ever hear of professional boundaries?"

"Is that what they taught you in law school and shrink school?" Marisol asked. She unzipped her bag and held a brick of the stolen cash aloft. "I think I would've flunked ethics."

"Don't even go there," Eva said.

Marisol put the cash back in her purse. "If I wake up in the morning with my TV missing, you can say 'I told you so.' But if I wake up with a girl ready to dump the pimp, let's get her some services, okay?"

"Fine." Eva sighed. "I'll set up an intake."

"I love you," Marisol said, kissing Eva on the cheek.

"Glad you're back safe," Eva said.

Marisol trotted back down the stairs.

"Come on, Dulce," she said when she got down to the lobby. "Change of plans."

It took nearly fifteen minutes to climb the four flights of stairs. Marisol helped Dulce limp up past the upper floors of the clinic and the administrative offices, and then up to her apartment.

Dulce leaned against the wall of the hallway as Marisol unlocked the door. She led the girl into a cozy studio with hardwood floors. The walls were bare except for a few family photos. Above the stove, an aloe vera plant struggled to survive. Marisol only remembered to water it when she emptied the teakettle, every couple of weeks.

"I can't believe you're taking me in like this," Dulce said, slumping into an armchair.

"Make yourself at home, *nena*," Marisol said. She walked into the bathroom, a closet-sized box that only fit a full-sized bath because the sink was above the toilet tank. Marisol turned on the tub's hot water.

"You'll feel better after you soak in this," Marisol said. She poured in some Epsom salts.

Through the open bathroom door, she saw Dulce looking at a photo of ten-year-old Cristina, with sandy brown hair and similar features to Marisol's. "Is that your daughter?" Dulce asked.

"My little sister." Marisol walked back across the main room. "But I basically raised her."

"Is this your mom?" Dulce asked, looking at a heavy-set gray-haired woman on a rural porch in the Caribbean.

"No, my *abuela*," Marisol said. She indicated a photo of a thirty-something woman in a brightly colored dress, smiling on the Staten Island Ferry. "This is my *mami*."

"She's so pretty," Dulce said.

"Forever young," Marisol said. "They both died around the same time. Come on. Get in that tub."

Marisol had longed for this as a teen. An aunt or female cousin to appear out of nowhere and rescue her. Not another worker or counselor she'd have to figure out whether she could trust, but someone who would claim her and take her in—both her and her sister. *Mija, you don't have to live like this anymore . . .*

Marisol carefully closed the apartment's shades. She listened for the gentle splash of the water as she pulled all the books off of a shelf in the bedroom alcove. Behind it, she lifted out the false back and piled in the heist cash from her purse.

The splashing stopped.

"You okay, honey?" Marisol asked.

"Yeah," Dulce answered in a sleepy voice.

Marisol secured the false back into its place and returned the books to the bookshelf. She knocked on the bathroom door and stepped inside.

Dulce lay in the tub with her eyes closed. Her body

looked like a garden with burgundy, violet, and navy blue flowers blooming.

Marisol's jaw was tight as she washed her hands in the sink. So many days she'd gone to high school with bruises under her own clothes.

"I don't know the last time I took a bath," Dulce said. "The guys have hot tubs sometimes, but you never get to soak before they want to fuck."

Marisol laughed. "I remember."

"What?" Dulce opened her eyes. "You used to be a hoe?"

"I prefer the term 'sex worker,' but yeah." Marisol laughed. "Why do you think I run the clinic?"

People thought having sex for money was the worst thing in the world. For Marisol, it had been a step up.

"You're pretty enough," Dulce said. "But you must've not had a pimp if you still look so good."

"I had a pimp at first, a Russian guy named Sergei," Marisol said as she took the rubber band out of her long, wavy hair and began to brush it out. "But he was only a businessman. He would have been just as happy to sell farm animals if he could make as much money."

Dulce laughed.

"He protected us," Marisol said. "Made sure we got to a clinic when it hurt to piss. He even paid for the antibiotics." She ran some warm water and got a facecloth.

"And he was okay with you leaving?" Dulce asked.

Marisol looked up from washing her face. "We were like cows or horses. It wasn't personal."

"Why'd you get out of the business?" Dulce asked.

Marisol shrugged. "I wanted to be the businesswoman. I had ideas about how to make more money. Make things safer. He wouldn't give my brains the time of day. These young Eastern European guys ran his errands, or called my pager with his messages. Maybe he listened to their business ideas. But he just wanted the women on their backs."

"Then why'd you stay and give him your money?" Dulce asked.

"Half my money," Marisol said. "He had one of the safest operations in the city. He provided clean hotel rooms, protection, some alcohol. We were lucky. If he thought you were cheating him, he just told you not to show your face in any of his bars. I remember girls getting stiffed by clients, then servicing an extra client to pay Sergei so they wouldn't get fired. And when girls left, he'd just find someone else. See? Not personal."

"You really were lucky," Dulce said. "Everything with Jerry is personal."

"Did he start out as your boyfriend?" Marisol asked, blotting her face with a towel.

"He was never really my boyfriend," Dulce said. "I was just too young and dumb to know that. I met him when I was fourteen. Cutting school with my best friend, smoking weed in the park. He approached us both, but she wasn't interested. He said he wanted to be my man. My friend found out he was a pimp and begged me not to mess with him. Easy for her to say. Her dad lived with them and had a job. I had four brothers and sisters at home in our small-ass apartment, including my big sister with her two kids."

"Your dad wasn't around?" Marisol asked.

"Left when I was five," Dulce said. "My older brother was the man of the house. Every fucking thing fell apart after he got deported. He had his green card, but he was selling drugs. They sent his ass back to Santo Domingo."

"You two were close?" Marisol slid the mirrored door

of the medicine cabinet to the side and took out a small tube of lotion.

Dulce shrugged. "He looked out for me. The same month he got deported I met Jerry. Hooking up with an older guy with money was like having parents again—at least in the beginning."

Marisol had had a sugar daddy when she was in her twenties. At first it did feel like a fairy-tale rescue. For different reasons, her honeymoon had also been short-lived.

"Sometimes it's okay," Dulce said. "Sometimes me and him and the girls are like a family. His brother Jimmy is kind of a dick. But other times . . ."

"Other times you end up in the emergency room," Marisol said. She capped the lotion and put it away.

"I've tried to leave him before," Dulce said. "I guess I'm not strong enough."

"Here's the thing," Marisol said, sitting on the edge of the tub. "For almost every woman in a bad situation, it takes more than one try to get out. Maybe your number is two. Maybe five. Maybe more. I've seen girls trying to leave some asshole for ten years. And then one day it clicks. I don't know why. I just know you can't be afraid or ashamed to keep trying."

It had clicked like that for Marisol, the day she decided to get away from her uncle.

"I wish I could stay here forever," Dulce said. She trailed the hand of her good arm back and forth in the bathwater.

"Maybe you can," Marisol said, rubbing the excess lotion into her hands. "You can stay in the shelter short-term, and the case managers can help you figure out your next steps. We've got partnerships for housing, job training, and school. Plus entrepreneurship classes if you wanna stay in the business."

"Now I know why Jerry didn't want us coming here," Dulce said and closed her eyes again.

"Come on, *nena*," Marisol said. "We can't have you falling asleep and drowning."

After Dulce came out of the bathroom, Marisol gave her an oversized T-shirt and a clean pair of underwear, and they put her arm back into the sling.

Marisol tied Dulce's dark hair in a loose bun on her head, and the two women climbed into her queen-size bed.

"So, if your pimp didn't pressure you, how'd you get started?" Dulce asked. She shifted around under the beige down comforter.

"Me and my sister were orphaned," Marisol said with a yawn. Her body felt drained. "I was seventeen, a senior in high school, with an eviction notice in my hand. My little sister was not going into foster care."

"You did it for her?" Dulce asked.

"I'd do anything for her," Marisol said. Under the covers, her hand closed on the locket around her neck. "I haven't seen her in over a year. I usually pay for her to fly here for the holidays, but I was too broke this year."

"I wish I'd had a big sister like you to look out for me," Dulce said, reaching with her good hand for Marisol's other hand under the covers.

"Everybody deserves to be protected," Marisol said, squeezing Dulce's hand. She smoothed the girl's hair back from her forehead again and again. It was pressed straight and bleached, but it had grown out dark and tightly curled at the roots. Dulce had a pair of deep cuts beneath her bangs. The bruised skin was held together with Steri-Strips. The shape of the cuts looked like heel marks. Marisol recalled tracing her finger along a similar crescent shape on her own jaw, decades before. She let Dulce's hair fall back in place, as the girl began to snore.

During Marisol's twenties, she spent two years as a mistress to a Fortune 500 VP named Campbell. After their first night together, she had woken up between Egyptian cotton sheets on a Memory Foam mattress. He left for work saying he hoped she'd still be there when he got home. Finally, she had found a man to keep her. She never bothered to get more than a couple of suitcases out of her dank basement apartment.

Other than a little boredom, she had no complaints for the first six months. He wanted her to be on call, in his apartment, for that lunchtime quickie or that casual blow job when he changed for a dinner party with his colleagues. She was a convenience. She slept there, because he might wake up in the middle of the night and want a tumble. She had her own room, as he hadn't wanted to sleep in the same bed with another person. She was more of a workout than a lover, a way to relax and blow off steam.

Early in their relationship, there had been dinners, when he had asked her all about herself. She invented a bootstraps Puerto Rican immigrant story, quaint and spunky. When he asked her to quit her "waitressing" job to move in, he explained that he wanted a passionate woman who would be available to meet his needs. He promised he would give her everything: a lovely place to live, the latest technological toys; she could shop from home, buying all the clothes she wanted—within reason. He had a room in the apartment, which had housed his previous mistress, who hadn't understood the arrangement. He provided the money, and she provided a soothing presence.

Marisol understood. She aimed to please because it was a good gig. Unlike the ex-mistress, she made friends with the domestic staff, also on call, waiting for "his lordship" to get home and declare his desires. She played dominoes with them, ordered them gorgeous dresses off the Internet. The maid's daughter went to her prom in Prada.

Eventually Marisol understood why the ex had gotten stir-crazy. She rarely left the house. She was on call. She needed to be no more than half an hour away from the apartment at all times. You couldn't get anywhere from midtown in half an hour—not uptown to Spanish Harlem, not downtown to the Lower East Side. She almost left him ten months in when she realized he had put a GPS in her cell phone.

Her sister was a premed sophomore at Syracuse then. They hadn't seen each other since Marisol had moved in with Campbell, but they talked a few times a week on the phone. Mostly Marisol listened to Cristina's fragmented rants on why the microbial biology prof was an asshole or how the study group system was hard on female students.

During one call Cristina asked about their plans for Thanksgiving. It turned out that "his lordship" was going to see his family in Delaware. Of course the mistress wasn't invited. At the last minute, Marisol went upstate to see Cristina. They had Chinese food for Thanksgiving, and later slept in Cristina's twin bed.

"I know we don't have money for medical school," Cristina said over the cartons of takeout. "So I'm thinking of going to school in Cuba. They'll pay for it and everything. But I'll only go if we can still see each other."

"Of course," Marisol had agreed. "I don't care if you go to Siberia. Wherever you go, I'll always find a way for us to be together."

After Marisol got back to Manhattan, the boredom and the loneliness were worse. One day, she was at her wits' end. Everything on television was stupid, and the cook wasn't coming in until evening. Marisol wandered into Campbell's library. She had dismissed it as a source of amusement because he didn't have any novels, only books on finance. She picked up one of the books, *Globalization and Microeconomics in the US,* and found herself interested. She devoured the book in the next couple of days. She was glad just to have something in her head other than her own spinning thoughts. She went online and looked at MBA programs. What books were business students reading? His lordship had most of them in his library. Marisol began her MBA training. She supplemented with a few more liberal texts she found online, as well, reading the work of feminist economists, Caribbean economists, socialist economists, liberals, and conservatives.

What had been a prison became a graduate program. She looked forward to seeing Campbell when he came home. She asked him leading questions about his company. He went on at length about profit shares and stockholder pressure, interrupting his own monologues occasionally to ask if he was boring her.

"Oh no," she said. "I don't really understand it, but it's still fascinating to hear you talk about it."

After a year, she had read all the books in the library. She did the MBA informally—never set foot on a college campus. She completed her GED and got an online degree in bookkeeping. Wandering through Campbell's study, searching for something to amuse herself, she came across his wall safe—a Superlative model.

It took her a week to work up the nerve to touch it. It might have had any number of security measures. But touching someone's wall safe wasn't against the law when you lived there.

She slid the picture aside and moved her hand toward the dial. Just one finger. Just a touch. The silver metal was cool. She tapped it twice.

Marisol held her breath. No alarm. No lights. She put the picture back and was on edge for the rest of the day. But when his lordship came home, cranky about a board meeting, he said nothing about a safe, an alarm, or anything.

The next day, Marisol got some of the maid's latex gloves and began to move the dial.

It took her two months and a stethoscope she bought online to learn to listen for the *click* of the tumblers. Four months to crack it.

As the safe door swung open, Marisol gazed at more cash and bonds than she'd ever seen before in one place. She also found his will. Campbell was leaving everything to a boy in Belgium, a son he never talked about.

She closed the safe. She never stole a dime from him in cash. Instead, she would buy designer clothes and then sell them on eBay (never worn—tags still on!). For herself, she started buying business suits and briefcases.

She kept practicing safecracking. Blindfolded—so she couldn't see the combination she already knew. She tried it without the stethoscope. After six months she could do it in three minutes. She felt elated every time the safe clicked open.

Chapter 5

The María de la Vega Health Clinic was one of five adjoining properties on either side of one corner on Avenue C. The clinic faced east, and had been carved out of a brownstone storefront.

Marisol had bought the property just after September 11, 2001, in that brief moment when property values in lower Manhattan dipped. At the time, she and Eva were running a clinic in Chelsea. Marisol's down payment included the cash she had accumulated from her eBay racket with Campbell. As time went on, she rented several properties in the adjacent building, as they became available. After the recession hit hard, she began the escort service to supplement the clinic income.

Behind a bookshelf in the clinic's fourth-floor hallway, Marisol had cut a door. The bookshelf slid to the side, and the door opened into a small loft in the adjoining apartment building. The "gift gallery" was where high-end clients could select escorts. The loft was leased by Loisaida Talent, but there was no sign on any of the doors or windows. Loisaida Talent was owned by a corporation with an offshore account. The corporation also leased the street-level offices, which were subleased to a chiropractor who worked exclusively with health center clients. Government reimbursements for chiropractic work covered only a tiny fraction of the fees. Most clinic clients couldn't afford the co-pays, but sex workers really needed the bodywork. So the chiropractor was paid mostly with stolen cash. She had an appointment log of phony cash-paying clients, which effectively laundered some of the money. The adjoining door between the properties had been built without city permits and without the owner's permission. Marisol was hoping to pay off the mortgage, close out the escort operation, and Sheetrock over the door before anyone found out. Unfortunately she had just received the official letter from the landlord of the modeling agency and the chiropractor that their leases were up later this year. He confirmed that he would be raising all rents significantly, and the building might be converted into condominiums.

By 10 a.m. the morning after she'd met Dulce, she had already walked the girl downstairs to an intake appointment, rushed across town with cash for the van lease payment, and was now sitting in her clinic office waiting for a new client.

She kissed her index finger and touched it to the photo of herself and her sister that sat on the desk. For luck. The photo was taken five years before at the airport, just before Cristina left for medical school in Cuba. The two of them were squeezed close, smiling at the camera but both had cheeks wet with tears. That was the last time Marisol had cried.

The sisters had similar faces, but Marisol was curvy and dark while Cristina was slender and fair. They had the do-they-or-don't-they likeness of sisters with different fathers. Marisol had never met her dad, who—according to her grandmother—had a temper. She vaguely recalled Cristina's father: a fair-haired charmer who gave Marisol candy when she was little. Apparently, he liked to spread his charms around.

Her mother had died over twenty years ago, when she was in middle school. Afterward, Marisol had pestered her grandmother for information about both dads. Her grandmother had given her euphemisms and minor tidbits of information appropriate for an eleven-year-old: Cristina's father was a fantastic cook. Marisol's father was a great *merengue* dancer. *Merengue*? Later, she wondered whether her father was Dominican.

Cristina left for Cuba with a promise to work at the clinic after medical school. Marisol promised there would be a clinic to come back to.

As Marisol's watch signaled the hour, the light bulb above her desk blew out. She cursed and scrambled for the legit bulbs in the cabinet. She had kicked off her heels and was on the desk replacing the light when her assistant buzzed.

"Stall him for a minute, Serena."

When the client came in, Marisol was sitting at her perfectly illuminated desk, brushing a dust smudge from her slacks.

The client was a short white guy with glasses and an upscale suit. He represented Thug Woofer, the notorious gangsta rapper from South Carolina who needed adult entertainment at an engagement party. The idea of matrimony didn't match Woof's bad boy image. He and his entourage had cut a path up to New York, leaving a trail of DUIs and trashed hotel rooms. Thug Woofer had moved into the penthouse of a midtown apartment building to record his next album.

Marisol tilted back and studied her visitor. People like him were the reason she'd had the office done in mahogany and black leather. Marisol could have sat in a folding chair at a card table with piles of paper all around her and an old laptop. But for clients like this one, she'd hustled up designer leather furniture, wood panel walls, and a massive wooden desk. Southern exposure brought warm indirect light into the room and sustained several plants. Marisol loved green things at work—plants and money.

She dressed to match the office. Dark suits and tailored blouses.

She frowned down at her notes from their phone call.

"Thug Woofer is getting engaged?" Marisol asked.

"His brother," the manager said. "This is just a small party. Woof, his brother, and cousin. The bachelor party will be much bigger—at least twenty girls. My friend with the Yankees said you could handle it no problem."

"No problem," Marisol said. "But we have rules. You and I agree ahead of time on the sex acts. I've seen your boy's videos. No one's gonna be putting any of my girls in the trunk of a car. There are a million assholes in this city who cater to any twisted motherfucker. Go find one of them."

"So if my guys want something freaky, your girls are out the door?"

"Anything freaky we don't agree to ahead of time," Marisol said.

"What about spontaneity?"

"When a contractor remodels your bathroom, you don't ask him to cook you lasagna. These girls are professionals. We negotiate up front on price, terms, and services. No surprises."

"This is bullshit. I can get more bang for my buck at Vixela's."

"Vixela's strip club downtown?" Marisol scoffed. "You want your guys to get caught screwing minors?"

"We're buying hookers," the manager said. "Not exactly legal, anyway. I want my guys satisfied. This isn't a charity event."

"No?" Marisol asked, raising an eyebrow. "Then your Yankees guy didn't mention our biggest perk?"

"I don't see any perks," the manager said. "Sounds like three cranky-ass girls give my guys some listless hand jobs."

"No, honey," Marisol said. "Three lingerie-model types. Gorgeous and enthusiastic, who will strip, provide private entertainment for each of the three guys, and act like their dream in life is to perform whatever acts we agree upon in this office. Ten thousand dollars for the package. And—" Marisol paused and leaned back in her chair. "Every penny will be tax-deductible."

"What?" The manager blinked behind his glasses.

"Your credit card statement will include a donation to the María de la Vega Health Clinic. Our workers will be thanking your guys personally for supporting women's health care."

"You're fucking kidding me." The manager's mouth fell into an open grin.

"You want the write-off, you keep your guys in line." She showed him where to sign the donation paperwork.

"And our gala fund-raiser is tomorrow." She handed him an invitation. "In case you or Thug Woofer would like to join us."

Marisol liked potential clients to see what the funds were supporting, so she walked the manager out through the clinic lobby. More than a dozen young women, mostly black and Latina, lounged around on couches. On the walls behind them, images of attractive, confident young women from their demographic encouraged them to:

Use condoms . . . every time.
Watch your drink.
Recognize the signs of an abusive relationship.

In the background, a bass line thumped from the speakers of a wide-screen TV playing rap videos. In an armchair, one young woman nodded her head to the beat while gluing in a weave for a girl who sat between her knees. The game table held four domino players and a second circle of observers talking trash.

"Who's your friend, Marisol?" Nalissa asked, gesturing to Thug Woofer's manager from the domino table.

"Business associate," Marisol said.

"If she ain't your friend, I'm tryna be your friend," Nalissa said.

"I like that suit," another girl said. "You can have more than one friend."

The manager blushed as Marisol walked him past the reception desk and a framed movie poster for *Live Nude Girls, Unite!* featuring three comic book hero–styled women, half-naked, with a "Strippers Union" picket sign and a fist in the air.

Marisol opened the front door and shook the manager's hand.

She tilted her head subtly, indicating the young women in the lobby. "If you ever wanted to become a client yourself, we have packages in a wide range of price points."

"Me?" The manager's blush deepened.

"Think about it." Marisol gave him a warm handshake. "A pleasure doing business with you."

Marisol closed the door as a young woman in a bright pink halter top slammed her final domino down on the table. "*Capicú*, motherfuckers!" she crowed as the watchers erupted in a loud wail that rang throughout the lobby. The other players grudgingly tossed in their leftover tiles and the winner counted the points.

As Marisol walked back across the lobby, Nalissa fell into step next to her. "I'm on your drop-in list next week," she said. "But I can't wait to tell you some of my business ideas—"

"Nalissa, you can't charm me like a client," Marisol said. "By looking sexy and eager. You wanna talk business, but you haven't signed up for a single entrepreneurship class here at the clinic?"

"I'm no good at school."

"This ain't school, *mami*. It's community education."

"I'll sign up right now," Nalissa said, and headed to the reception desk.

The sound of a police siren drew Marisol's eye to the TV screen. A gold-toothed rapper threw money out of a limo as a cop chased him down the streets.

Marisol grabbed the remote. "I'm putting the money management video back on."

The women's voices rose in protest.

"But it's Thug Woofer!" someone said.

"I'd like to be the hoe in the back of his limo," one girl at the domino table said.

"Not if he was throwing out the money," said Nalissa.

"You need to stop trying to be the hoe in the video and be the hoe making the video," Marisol said. "And aren't you all late for entrepreneurship training?"

"Oh shit!" one of the girls said, checking the time on her phone. They all grabbed purses and coats and rushed for the stairs. Nalissa fell in with the group.

"Sorry, Nalissa, this session has already started," Marisol said.

"Please, I'm ready to learn," she said. "And the next session is full."

"Tell her I said to take you in on probation," Marisol said. "If you're not caught up by next week, you're out."

"*Gracias!*" Nalissa said, and disappeared into the stairwell.

Later that afternoon, Marisol was in the community room, teaching her seminar, "The Happy, Healthy Hoe." January sunlight filtered into the room.

"Everybody's in this business for the same reason," Marisol said to the thirty or so young women. "You're broke, you got no real marketable skills, but guys will pay to screw you."

She walked over to a young woman texting and raised an eyebrow. The girl put the phone away. "But this is a burnout profession," Marisol went on. "If you don't plan your future, you'll end up broke, with no marketable skills, and those same guys won't still wanna screw you, or won't wanna pay much."

The young women laughed. Every folding chair in the room was full, and a few of the girls sat on the floor. Against the wall were stacks of foldaway cots and a pile of sleeping bags that came out at night when the room became a temporary shelter.

"So be smart," Marisol went on. "Some countries have government-sponsored retirement plans for their sex workers. Not the U.S."

A wide-eyed Nalissa stuck her head in the door.

"Entrepreneurship's not until tomorrow—"

"He's got a gun!" Nalissa said. Her arm waved wildly toward the street. "Crazy motherfucker outside the clinic with a gun!"

Chapter 6

Marisol jumped up and ran down the stairs to the front door. Her hand reached involuntarily for her locket.

Eva stood frozen in the middle of the lobby. The receptionist and several women stood huddled behind the front desk. They watched the street through the two-way mirrored glass of the street door.

"Dulce, I know you're in there! Bitch, I'm a kill you if you don't come out right now," a thugged-out Latino yelled from the sidewalk. He wore oversized shades and a cap pulled low over his face, a large-caliber gun dangling from his right hand.

Jerry. Marisol had a feeling of déjà vu. As if Dulce had not only described Jerry, but also shown her a picture.

Marisol texted Jody for backup, but she might be anywhere in the city.

The thirty or so girls who had come down behind Marisol stayed hunched in a knot by the stairwell at the back of the room.

Eva rushed to the reception desk. "I'm calling NYPD."

"No cops!" Marisol said. "We got girls in here with warrants or no immigration papers."

"He has a goddamn cannon in his hand, Marisol," Eva said. "I don't like police, either, but it's better than getting shot."

"Only a psychopath would shoot us in broad daylight with witnesses," Marisol said.

"What about that guy doesn't say psychopath to you?" Eva asked.

Jerry hulked back and forth like a caged jungle cat.

At the corner, he had parked his tricked-out Hummer across two lanes of Avenue C traffic. Cars honked, and clusters of passersby rubbernecked.

"Shut the fuck up!" Jerry yelled, turning to the motorists.

Marisol peered down the street and counted five heads in the Hummer: three female, two male.

"He's not gonna kill us," Marisol said. "This is for show. I'm going out."

"Are you nuts?" Eva asked.

"It's just like that dad at the Chelsea clinic," Marisol said.

"That guy only had a hatchet," Eva said.

"Motherfuckers don't just get to intimidate women in our clinic." Marisol put a hand on the door. "I'm going with or without you." She pushed the door open a crack. A gust of wind blew in, and Jerry swiveled in her direction.

She stepped out in the street without a backward glance.

Eva grabbed her cane and stepped out the door, her limp more pronounced than usual. Although she wasn't a brawler like Jody, Eva had a fierceness on which Marisol had come to rely. Not only had Eva survived polio, but her parents had survived the Holocaust as children. Eva wasn't looking for a fight, but she was prepared to survive one.

Marisol felt the adrenaline surging through her. Where her shoulder touched Eva's she could feel the other woman trembling slightly.

She and Eva advanced. Underneath Eva's plus-size suit, she was solid. Still, the pimp's tall, broad-shouldered, and heavy frame dwarfed them both. Marisol was a head shorter than him and probably half his weight.

They walked into the middle of the street. "Can we help you?" Marisol asked.

"You bitches better send Dulce out right now." His scowling expression had etched deep, taut lines into his face. His rugged skin contrasted strangely with the oversized cartoon characters on his designer jeans outfit.

This was how Marisol had always imagined her uncle showing up. If she had ever called the cops or social services and had gotten away from him. Somehow he'd find her. Come after her. All the more outraged for her defiance. She had to bite back the memory.

"Dulce came in several days ago with two black eyes, a dislocated elbow, three broken ribs, and a fractured femur," Marisol said with a steely calm she didn't feel. She bluffed about the ribs—they were only bruised. "She can barely walk."

"So fucking what? Bitch deserved it."

Marisol remembered the garden of bruises on Dulce's body in the tub. She narrowed her eyes. "She was practically unconscious when we brought her in. For medical reasons, we can't send her out. When she's healed up, she can decide for herself whether or not she wants to return to working with you."

"Bullshit. I tell Dulce what she wants." The gun rested at his thigh. He stepped closer to Marisol and looked as if he might hit her with his other hand. Marisol's body clenched.

Eva stepped forward as if to break it up, when they all heard a police siren coming up the block in the opposite direction. The pimp stepped back and slid the gun into the waistband of his jeans, pulling his baggy shirt down over it.

The cruiser pulled up and two cops got out. One stepped up to the Hummer, and the other approached the altercation on the sidewalk.

"What's going on?" the cop asked.

"My friend just came to say hello," Marisol said. "But he didn't park very well."

"If he doesn't leave, we'll tow his oversized vehicle."

"I'll be back," Jerry said, stalking to his car.

As she watched him walk away, there was something familiar in his voice, his walk, but she couldn't place it. He was unforgettably imposing. She would have remembered meeting him.

"You know that's Jerry Rios, right?" the cop asked when Jerry was out of earshot. "Was he looking for a girl in the clinic? Do you want to lodge a complaint? We can get him for disturbing the peace."

"No thanks," Marisol said. "We've got this under control."

The cop rolled his eyes. "Just don't go complaining when he beats the girl to death."

"Let's say I did cooperate," Marisol said. "You couldn't lock him up for long. Where would you be when he comes back even more pissed off at us for getting him arrested?"

He didn't have an answer to that.

She sucked her teeth and went to catch up with Eva in the clinic.

"Has he ever come by before?" Marisol asked after closing the door behind her.

Eva shook her head. "Who could forget a guy like that?" she asked. "I thought I was gonna piss my pants."

"I fucking hate pimps," Marisol said.

"You're shaking," Eva said.

"We need extra security," Marisol said. "For tomorrow while the staff is at the fund-raiser."

"Can we afford it?" Eva asked.

"I'll make the money happen somehow."

That evening, on the subway, Marisol held her dry cleaning in front of her body, like a shield. A pair of women with fashionably torn clothes pressed against her in the uptown train. The seats had been filled since the first Manhattan stop near Wall Street. Two men in expensive suits sat to the right of her. Across from them was a browner cluster of passengers who had been on the train since Queens and Brooklyn.

Throughout midtown, passengers embarked and disembarked, an inhalation and exhalation of humanity. Somewhere around Harlem, the crowd thinned, and Marisol hung her dry cleaning on the upper handrail. She got off at Washington Heights, and walked several blocks to a quiet watering hole.

Marisol didn't have a significant other. She was married to her work. But she couldn't fuck her work. At least, not anymore.

She sat at the end of the bar and ordered a shot of tequila. While she waited for her drink, she slipped the locket with the picture of her sister into the change purse of her wallet. Someone was playing a tortured bolero on the jukebox. The tenor's voice crooned heartbreak, as Marisol savored the taste of lime and salt on her lips and the cool touch of ice on her tongue.

A man walked in and looked her up and down. He was a little shorter than her, but with gorgeous tawny skin, hazel eyes, long, hard limbs, and a devious smile.

She smiled back, but with no teeth, feeling a tingle of excitement. She offered him only the briefest of glances, and a shadow of a shrug.

He nodded to the bartender, and then walked to the other side of the room to watch a large flat-screen TV. The Knicks were down by fifteen, but he turned away just as they scored a three-pointer.

He hitched up his jeans and slid onto the bar stool next to her.

"Quieres otra?" he asked.

"No thanks," she said in Spanish. "But I'll buy you one."

He raised his eyebrows, but then leaned back and smiled. *"Como no?"*

She told the bartender in Spanish, "A rum and Coke."

"How do you know what I want?" he asked.

"I know exactly what you want," she said, leaning back on her own stool, tossing her head, and arching her back. "Does the drink really matter?"

"Maybe not," he said, downing half the drink.

"Boricua?" he asked.

"Sí." She was Puerto Rican. From his accent, she could tell that he was Dominican.

"De aquí o de allá?" he asked.

"Los dos," she said, having grown up both in Puerto Rico and in the United States.

"I don't know about you Puerto Rican girls," he said, swirling the dark liquid in his glass. "My brother married a Puerto Rican. Beautiful but too independent."

Marisol put a hand on his arm. "No need to worry about that with me."

"You're not independent?" he asked, skeptically.

She laughed. "I'm never getting married."

"Don't say that." He took another sip of his drink. "Maybe later you will. Maybe now you just want to have a good time."

He used his index finger to move a stray lock of her hair off her shoulder. He didn't touch her skin, just moved the hair in a slow arc, so that it teased along her collarbone. "Maybe now you want company after a long day at your job." He spoke in a murmur, as the lock of hair slipped off the edge of her arm. "Maybe you just want somebody to make you feel really good." He traced his hand down her arm and onto her knee.

"I like to feel really good," she said. "But there's a problem."

"Really?" he asked. "What's the problem?"

"Los hombres," she said.

He laughed, tracing circles on the tip of her quadriceps. "Men are the problem?"

"Not exactly," Marisol said. "But condoms. Sometimes men have a problem with condoms."

"Condones?" he asked, sliding his hand farther up her thigh.

"Do you have that problem?" she asked.

"No," he said, walking his fingers gently up to the meeting of her thighs. "I think I have one."

She pulled his hand from between her legs and held it. "No need for that," she said. "I bring my own."

"You live nearby?" he asked. "I'm staying with family. I can't really—"

"I know a place," Marisol said, dropping a twenty on the bar and leading him out the door.

At a nearby hotel in Harlem, she paid cash. She grabbed him in the elevator, and they tangled. Her tongue in his mouth, his hands groping her breasts through her blouse, pressing her hand to his hardness.

"Any other *problemas* I might need to know about?" he asked, hot rum breath on her neck.

"Me being on the bottom would be a problem," she said. "I like it like this. I like it standing."

"I bet you like it on top, too," he said, his hips grinding against hers.

"And I like it from behind," she said, twisting quickly so his hips pressed against her ass.

The hotel room was a small but clean mass of pale corners with a blond wooden desk and crisp white linens.

They tossed their dark clothes on the white woven rug. She rolled the condom onto him, and he knelt on the pile of clothes. She had him enter her while she sat, open-thighed, on the blond wooden chair.

She could see that he was well-endowed, but she couldn't really feel him inside her, even with him pounding so hard that the chair thudded against the desk. She thrust her hips forward and toppled him back onto the floor, riding him atop the pile of clothes. She tossed aside a stiletto heel as it dug into her knee.

She swiveled around so that she had her back to him, and he moaned with the deeper angle. She still couldn't quite feel him, so she stepped abruptly off of him.

"Que pasó?" he asked, startled.

"Aquí." She led him to the dresser, grabbing a pillow off the bed. She guided him to enter her from behind, sliding the pillow between her hips and the edge of the dresser.

"Te gusta?" he asked.

He gripped the dresser with one hand and lifted the other one to caress her shoulder.

She brushed his hand off. "Don't touch. Just fuck me."

"Okei," he said, putting the other hand on the dresser to get better leverage.

"Da me más!" she said.

He pumped furiously, and she focused all her attention on the spot between her legs. She blocked out the rest of his body, the room, the sound of his breath in her ear. She tried to inhabit only a center of pleasure, ride him like a horse to the finish line. She was almost there.

Suddenly, she heard him gasp and spasm. *"Coño!"* he said.

She slid her fingers between her lips and masturbated herself to a climax, and the two of them slumped forward onto the dresser.

After the last wave of the orgasm subsided, he was too sweaty, too hot, too much on top of her. She slid out from under him, holding the top of the condom so it wouldn't slip.

"You should go," she said in Spanish.

He nodded, a bit taken aback, and he disentangled his clothes from the pile on the rug.

She stood, naked, just watching him dress.

"Adiós, Boricua," he said.

After she closed the door behind him and put on the safety lock, she climbed into bed and let her body unwind, sex-drunk, into the still-fresh sheets, and relaxed for the first time since she'd laid eyes on the pimp in front of the clinic.

The next morning, she woke up looking at her dress. Weak sunlight filtered around it through the clear plastic bag that hung in the window.

Marisol put on yesterday's outfit and swung the drycleaned dress over her shoulder. She didn't really feel like emerald silk this morning, more like crumpled black lace.

She rode the train home, surrounded by commuters running late. She wouldn't feel right until she showered and put on clothes that didn't smell like a stranger. And tonight, she'd bathe again then put on the dress.

Chapter 7

Manhattan offered hundreds of choices for a gala fund-raising event, but Marisol had always planned on using La Fleur Hotel in midtown. The hotel had loomed in her memory since she was little. That autumn afternoon, she and her mother had just run an errand when Marisol had to pee.

"Wait til we get home," her mother had said. She was pregnant with Cristina, and just starting to show.

"They gotta have a toilet in there." Marisol had pointed to La Fleur. Such a big building, with people going in and out, certainly there would be a *baño* inside.

"It's for rich people," her mother had told her in Spanish.

"I can't hold it," Marisol had said.

"*Coño, mija*," her mother had cursed, but then had taken a deep breath.

Her mother took off her head scarf and shook out her hair. Then she removed her shabby coat and folded it over her arm. She put a hand under Marisol's chin and tilted the child's head back so their eyes met. "Stand up straight. Stay by me, and don't look around."

"I have to go really bad," Marisol said, on the verge of tears.

"I know, *corazón*," her mother said. "So we're going to pretend we live here. And pretend we know where the bathroom is." She ran her fingers through Marisol's unruly hair. "We can't ask anyone, because we don't want to make them mad, okay?"

"Okay," Marisol said. "They'll be mad because they only have one bathroom?"

Marisol's mother laughed. "No, *mi amor*. Because . . . because they're rich. They have more bathrooms than they need, but they don't like to be close to anyone."

Her mother crossed herself. She never went to church, but she genuflected when she was worried. "It'll be okay, *nena*. It's an adventure."

Marisol's first midtown theft. Unauthorized use of a four-star-hotel toilet at age six. She was dying to gaze at the marble floors and chandeliers and velvet couches. In her peripheral vision, she glimpsed flower arrangements taller than she was.

The toilet had felt exactly the same as the one in her apartment. She didn't understand the big deal. Afterward, they giggled all the way to the F train.

Nearly twenty years later, she had stayed at the hotel as the guest of a wealthy media mogul from Barcelona. While he was in his business meeting, she sat in the lobby for over three hours, gazing at the delicious, once-forbidden sights.

The sun was setting when Marisol walked into La Fleur Hotel for the gala. Under her winter coat, she wore the emerald gown that had been altered to fit her perfectly. A fifties-starlet style in raw silk that flattered her hourglass figure, with spaghetti straps, a low neckline, and a narrow skirt that flared below the knee. Her invincibility shoes were hidden beneath the skirt's tulle. Her hair was swept up in a French twist, and the pearls at her wrist and ears flattered her dark hair and light brown skin.

The sign in the lobby read:

Gala Fund-Raiser
María de la Vega Health Clinic
7 PM Grand Ballroom

"We finally made it to the big time," Eva said to Marisol. They looked through the open double doors into the Grand Ballroom, with its high ceiling, chandeliers, velvet walls, and plush carpet.

"Ms. Rivera," the director of special events greeted her with an outstretched hand. "Let's do a quick walk-through to make sure everything is to your specifications."

The two of them surveyed the event from the mezzanine level. White tables made a polka-dot pattern on the ballroom's dark carpeting.

The gala was the first in a series of fund-raisers for a clinic endowment. They aimed for fifty million in ten years. Then, after they paid off the clinic's mortgage, they could use endowment interest for operations—making them independent of grants and donors.

The sign at the front table said: "Give now. Give big. And your money will keep giving for you." All funds donated tonight would go directly into an endowment account and couldn't be used for current expenses.

All of Loisaida Talent Agency's "models" were hostesses for the evening. They padded around prepping the tables and champagne glasses in low-cut surplice neck blouses and snug slacks. When the event began, they slipped on high-heeled pumps and circulated trays with flutes of champagne and canapés, while they collected donations.

* * *

By 8 p.m. the room was filled with enthusiastic patrons, and the sounds of a jazz trio.

"Marisol," her assistant Serena's voice crackled in her earpiece. "The deputy mayor just walked in."

Serena was a petite, fine-boned girl, with brown flyaway hair and intense hazel eyes—a former clinic client. Serena was transgender, and had been thrown out of the house as a teen by her Greek immigrant parents.

There was still a line at the registration table. At $500 per person, they would have at least a quarter million walking in the door. With any luck, they would raise half a million for their endowment.

The coup for the evening was having celebrity Delia Borbón signing exclusive preview copies of her rags-to-riches autobiography. Borbón's memoir promised to include her exploits as a stripper before her movie career and marriage to a New York congressman.

"Marisol," Serena's voice warned through her earpiece. "The blonde has arrived and is headed your way."

Marisol spotted a woman in a pink dress that barely covered her huge breasts. She hung on the arm of a strapping young man.

"Vixela!" Marisol bit back her rage at the strip club owner.

From a distance, Vixela looked like a pinup girl from some bygone era. Even in a room filled with glamorous women, she turned heads as she strutted over to embrace Marisol.

Up close, Vixela's seams showed. The arms embracing Marisol were tense and ropy. The breasts pressing against her were stiff, synthetic. Vixela's face had a taut, pulled look. She air-kissed Marisol with overplumped lips.

Vixela must be about the same age as Eva—early sixties. Yet Eva wore her wrinkles and her love handles with grace. And wasn't that handsome Bronx Alderman always asking Eva out? He had to be fifteen years her junior. Eva had a face that made you want to get closer, get to know her.

"You belong up on a pole," Marisol said. "I bet you could show these young girls how it's done."

"Sometimes I have to hold myself back," Vixela said.

"The customers' loss," Marisol said. "Will you walk with me over to the stage?"

"Of course, darling," Vixela said.

"I need your help," Marisol said. "I thought my staff was lying when they said they had problems parking behind your club. You know how lazy these girls can be. So I followed them in a cab last night. I was surprised that your security guys stopped them from parking in the alley."

"Must be a misunderstanding," Vixela said. "You can park right in front, just don't block the loading zone."

"I knew it," Marisol said. "Of course you would want the girls to get checked out if they needed it."

"I'm all about helping my girls," Vixela said.

Marisol took a glass of champagne from a hostess and handed it to Vixela. "Don't be surprised if I give you a little shout-out during my intro."

She unhooked the velvet rope, and gathered up the hem of her dress as she stepped up onto the platform.

"Good evening, everyone," Marisol said into the microphone. "*Buenas noches.*"

Serena cued the jazz trio to end the song, and the clamor in the room dropped.

"In these tough economic times, it's good to see that New York cares for its own," Marisol began. "That the gorgeous, the fabulous, and the prosperous give a damn about the marginal, the vulnerable, and the so-called expendable. Everybody deserves health care. No matter what it is they choose to do with their bodies. Delia Borbón knows how hard it is out there. That's why she's here tonight. Because she remembers the tightrope young brown women have to walk. And she remembers all the sisters who don't ever write the book, attend the gala event, or even live to tell the tale. And that's where our clinic comes in. We insist on a real chance for the lives of our young women, and the occasional young man. Every cent we collect tonight will go into our endowment, ensuring that our services will be available for generations to come."

The audience erupted in applause.

"This is a magical night," Marisol said. "Just a few minutes ago, I sealed the deal for a new health initiative in the Financial District." Marisol searched the audience, and easily found the bright pink dress. "Our outreach van is going to be parked at Vixela's every night to offer services to her fabulous girls."

Vixela's mouth grimaced, but her forehead and eyes remained immobile.

"Please, everyone," Marisol said, an open hand indicating Vixela's location. "A round of applause for our own sensational Vixela!"

Vixela smiled and waved.

"And thank you all for your incredibly generous donations tonight," Marisol said. "But not everyone is so pleased with how we protect and support women. We need security volunteers over the next few weeks. Male or female. We'll take anyone who's ready to defend the women who come to our clinic."

The DJ spun a quick sample of a current club song:

"Don't worry," a tenor voice sang over thudding bass. "We gonna work it out, girl. Work it! Work it!"

"Haaaaaayyy!" various voices in the audience chorused the next line of the song.

Marisol laughed. "Thanks, DJ. I need to remember this is a party. And I think some of you might have come out to hear our special guest, right? Well, prepare to be inspired, and *dáme un gran aplauso* for Ms. Delia Borbón!"

Borbón swept onto the stage in a flash of gold sequins and a cloud of her own signature perfume.

Later, Marisol counted the people in the book-signing line. With a donation profit margin of seventy-five dollars per book, the evening's financials looked good.

"Marisol!"

She turned and looked closely at a thirty-something Latino man. He wore a well-cut suit and a wide smile on his square-jawed face.

Was he an uptown hookup who'd managed to find her? He was just the type of guy she liked to help her blow off steam. And there was an intimacy with which he'd called her name. She felt a flush of heat.

She never told those guys her name, didn't even bother with a fake name. While she remembered all her former sex work clients, she immediately forgot the faces of the hookups, remembering only the notable physical quirks: a dick that curved left or a pair of bullet scars in a bicep.

She blinked, trying to recall a shot of tequila, some flirtation on the way to the hotel, maybe the outline of his square jaw against the white sheet on a bed beneath her. He seemed so familiar, but the body was somehow wrong. And his expression was open-faced and beaming, instead of sly and smug.

"I can't believe it's really you," he said.

He said it in perfect English. Definitely not an uptown hookup.

"Do I know you?" Marisol asked.

"I'm Raul," he said, grinning. "You were in my sister's class."

"Raulito?" She smiled. "Gladys's baby brother? *Dios mío!* It's been two decades."

She kissed him on the cheek and they embraced. Her body buzzed with the intensity of the hug. She remembered him as a skinny kid, but the chest she pressed against was broad and firmly muscled. He smelled faintly of spice—maybe a soap or lotion—only detectable when he pulled her in close.

She had hugged over a hundred people that night, but in the squeeze of their bodies, she felt the urge to lean in close and drape herself across him but at the same time she felt desperate to recoil. She stepped back. He continued to hold her hands.

"How are you?" she asked. "How's your sister?"

"Good. Married, on Long Island. Two kids."

"Give her my love," Marisol said. "You still here in Manhattan?"

"Yeah, I just moved back to the Lower East Side," he said. His eyelashes were too long. He would have looked feminine, if not for the body.

She gave his hands a squeeze and let them go.

"What have you been up to all this time?" Marisol asked.

"Wondering about you," he said. "I had the biggest crush on you in high school."

"Whatever," Marisol said, embarrassed.

"Yeah," Raul said. "I asked around after you graduated, but you'd disappeared. I even Googled you a while back. Did you know there are hundreds of women named Marisol Rivera? I looked at the pictures, but none of them were you."

"Isn't stalking a crime?" Marisol asked with a laugh.

"It's not like that," Raul said. "You were always so smart. I knew you'd be doing something big, I just wanted to know what."

"That's how you saw me in high school?" Marisol asked.

"Definitely." Raul nodded. "Like that time you spoke up about the girls' dress code. You threatened to sue the New York School System for discrimination."

"Like it did any good." She laughed. "They just changed it so both boys and girls had to 'dress modestly.' But what have you been up to?"

He opened his mouth, and she put a finger to his lips. "Wait," she said. "Don't tell me. You became some kind of activist?"

He shook his head.

"Social services? Corporate America? Internet start-up?"

"Colder." He grinned. "I been—"

"Don't tell me." She put a hand on his wrist. "You're . . . you're a stay-at-home dad with three kids and a Fortune 500 wife!"

Raul busted up laughing. "Not married. No kids. No girlfriend. Worked the same job from the time I was twenty one."

"Bartender?"

Raul laughed and shook his head.

"Let me see your hands." She turned his palm over and ran her fingers across it, looking for calluses.

"You're obviously not in the trades," she said, tracing her index finger along the slight ridges just below his fingers.

"Nope," he said, his hand reaching after hers.

"Okay," Marisol said, pulling her hand out of reach. "I give up."

"I went into the police academy."

"A cop?" Marisol asked, the laughter dying in her mouth.

"Not anymore," he said. "I worked in the Bronx for years until I sued them for racial discrimination."

"I can only imagine," she said. "You win the case?"

He nodded. "I just got the settlement and bought a co-op apartment in the old neighborhood."

"Congratulations," Marisol said.

"For winning the settlement or buying the apartment?"

"Neither," Marisol said. "For escaping from the NYPD."

He laughed. "Well, I'm not crazy about them anymore, either." He looked down at the floor and then back up at her. With a pang, she remembered that look from high school.

"So it looks like you'll make good money tonight," he said. "Marisol Rivera. Still in the hood doing good."

"Using all my smarts to afford the rent."

He nodded. "I got a deal on this co-op, but I could never have bought it without the settlement."

"I know," Marisol said. "We own the clinic brownstone, but we rent offices in the building next door. That lease is up soon, so rents are gonna skyrocket, or the owner might convert to condos."

"Some days I'm sorry I moved back," Raul said. "Nobody we grew up with can afford to live here now, right?"

"I never see anyone from back then," Marisol said. "Except the family who owns the bodega on the corner, and they're getting ready to sell to Starbucks."

"I just joined a couple of organizations fighting gentrification," he said. "But only money talks. Back then this was our little bit of Puerto Rico. Our music. Our food. Our loud-ass *tías* talking ghetto Spanish in the street. Our nephews leaning out of cars saying inappropriate shit to the girls. Our little kids playing on the block at all hours."

"Those were the good times," Marisol said. "When me and my *mami* first moved back here from Puerto Rico, you could be poor and still stay in Manhattan. That's why we're hustling so hard tonight. *Coño*, these economic times wanna turn poverty into a death sentence."

"*Eso*," Raul said.

"Speaking of inappropriate," Marisol said. "You got me all riled up and cursing in Spanish."

"You can curse at me anytime." Raul smiled. "God, it's great to see you." He put his hands in the pockets of his suit trousers. "So . . . now that we're gonna be neighbors, you wanna maybe get a cup of coffee sometime?"

"I—couldn't—I mean, I'm really busy," Marisol said.

"Of course." He waved it off. "Hey, I'll tell my sister you send your regards."

"Please do," she said. "Thanks for coming. We appreciate your support."

"Aren't you going to introduce me?" An older white guy stepped forward and extended his hand.

"Sorry," Raul said. "John Mathias. Friend and former partner."

"Pleased to meet you, Mr. Mathias," Marisol said. They shook hands.

"Call me Matty." He looked her over. Mathias read

like a cop. He had salt-and-pepper hair and a protruding belly beneath his worn charcoal suit.

"So," Marisol said to Mathias. "You work in the Bronx?"

"Not anymore," Raul said. "My boy was promoted to Central Robbery."

"Congratulations," Marisol said with a smile she didn't feel.

"Just means more paperwork," Mathias said.

"I really want to thank you both so much for coming," Marisol said. "But I should check on the book signing. Excuse me."

She got about ten feet away when a stocky, well-manicured man stepped into her path. "Ms. Rivera?"

She knew the face well. Billboards. Magazine covers. Tabloids.

"Please, allow me to introduce myself," he said. "I'm—"

"Jeremy VanDyke," she said, her heart beating fast, as she recognized the billionaire.

Chapter 8

"Are you crashing the party?" Marisol asked Van-Dyke. "I would have noticed your name on the list."

"I used an alias," he said.

"I'm honored you could join us." She shook his hand. He wasn't handsome like Raul, but his touch was magnetic.

He grinned. "The pleasure's mine."

She could see the gray in his blond hair. He had a ski tan, lighter around the eyes.

Marisol touched his sleeve. The fabric was unexpectedly soft. She looked around to see whether he had a date, one of the starlets or models he was linked with in the gossip columns. He had just split with the Italian race car heiress.

Nalissa walked by, on duty as a hostess. Marisol took a flute of champagne from her tray.

"Please forgive me if I gush a little here," Marisol said. She handed him the champagne and pulled an annual report from a nearby table. "I have all your books, and I honestly can't believe you're here at my event—it's like a dream. I'd ask you to pinch me, but that would be inappropriate."

"Yet it might be enjoyable."

"I heard you were naughty," she said.

"Work overtime, play overtime," he said.

"I've only mastered the work part," she said. "But it's paid off. Our big economic reorganization was based on theories from your second book."

"I love a success story," he said, making direct eye contact. "Your pitch for additional donations tonight was impressive. I'll donate tonight—anonymously, but you'll know it's me."

"Thank you so much, Mr. VanDyke," she said, squeezing his free hand.

"Please, call me Jeremy. Every quarter my foundation selects a charity to highlight. We pick nonprofits with entrepreneurs who have been implementing our strategies." He tilted his head. "I'd love to talk to you more about it."

"I'm honored that you would consider us." She reached into her bag. "Here's my card with my direct line." He grasped the card between his thumb and finger. Marisol held on.

He looked up from the card.

"Please do call," she said. "I'd love to set up a meeting."

"You'll be hearing from me," he said.

She smiled and let go. He slipped the card into his inside jacket pocket.

"It's not only a good cause," she said, "but we're operating in the black." She offered him the annual report.

"Thank you," he said and handed it to an assistant who materialized behind him.

He squeezed Marisol's hand again and took his leave.

Eva walked over to Marisol. "Is that who I think it is?"

"Holy fucking shit," Marisol said. "Jeremy VanDyke just took my card and told me he wanted to meet with me. I can't tell if he's trying to adopt the cause or hit on me."

"In that dress?" Eva asked. "Probably both. I've been hoping you would start dating someone. A billionaire will do nicely."

"I wouldn't mind having a fling with the guy," Marisol said. "A few swanky dinners. The occasional yacht ride. A little sex on the high seas. The clinic gets fifteen minutes of fame as one of his pet charities. Everyone wins."

"Oh my God," Eva said, looking over Marisol's shoulder. "I can't believe that fucker has the nerve to show his face here."

"Who?" Marisol asked.

"That cop over there." Eva nodded to where Raul and his ex-partner stood. "He's dirty."

"The Latino cop?" Marisol asked.

"No, the old white one," Eva said. "He used to 'arrest' girls in Times Square. He liked them young. Seventeen? Eighteen, maybe? Him and his partner would drive the girls around for a while, and then offer to let them go for a blow job."

"I fucking hate cops," Marisol said.

"I can't tell you how many girls would cry on my couch about it," Eva said. "He acted like they should be grateful, like he was doing them some big favor."

"He works robbery now."

"Sent one girl over the edge," Eva said. "First sex worker client I had who committed suicide."

Eva's face puckered, and Marisol pulled her into a hug.

Eva let go and wiped at her eyes. "This champagne's making me all sentimental. I gotta focus. We need the clinic to help protect girls from assholes like him."

* * *

At 1:30 a.m., the hostesses and clinic staff lounged around in stocking feet finishing the champagne. The hotel staff cleaned crumbs from the quiches and crab cakes. Serena packed up the registration table. Kim, Jody, and Tyesha counted all the cash donations the hostesses had collected.

"Can I help?" Nalissa asked. "I'm really good at counting cash."

Marisol shook her head. "They got it," she said.

"I got one hundred percent on both quizzes in entrepreneurship training."

"Nice," Marisol said. "When you get through level three, let's talk about your ideas."

"Level three?" Nalissa said. "That'll take a year. Shouldn't I get some credit for life experience? I used to help my cousin when she was selling meth. I was deep in the business."

"So where's your cousin now?" Marisol asked.

"Locked up," Nalissa said. "But only because her boyfriend ratted her out."

"Finish the class, then we can talk."

Nalissa was going to say something else, but Kim interrupted and handed Marisol the cash total. She smiled, then walked over to the podium on the stage. One of the hotel staff was prepared to wheel it away, but she put a hand on his arm.

"*Momentito, papi,* okay?"

He nodded and Marisol stepped up to the mic.

"Overworked clinic staffers and drunken hot girls with aching feet, may I have your attention, please?"

"The mighty one speaks!" Tyesha called out.

"Thank you all for working your asses off," she said. "And we raised over six hundred thousand for our endowment. After expenses!"

The staff cheered.

"Hell, yeah!" Jody shouted. Kim was sitting on her lap, and Jody had a casual, possessive hand on Kim's thigh.

"And thanks to our excellent staff from La Fleur," Marisol said. *"Un aplauso para los trabajadores del hotel!"*

The clinic staff and hostesses stood up and cheered for the hotel staff. The man wheeling a stack of chairs toward the door waved away the applause. The woman on hands and knees scrubbing at a wine stain on the carpet didn't look up, but she did smile.

Six hundred thousand dollars. Marisol had stopped at her office to lock up the donations. Her body still buzzed with the excitement of the gala, but she could feel the exhaustion underneath.

On her way out of the hotel, the director of special events had stopped her. "Fabulous job tonight," she said. "Looks like your clinic's crisis is over."

Marisol had sighed. "Unfortunately, no. Tonight's funds are promised for our endowment. We can't touch a penny of it."

Now, as she looked around her office, she saw the folders on her desk, and the stacks of unpaid bills and invoices. Over half a million, but the daily grind was unaffected.

She peeled off the dress and exchanged it for a T-shirt and yoga pants.

Pulling a phone out of her purse, she dialed a number in Cuba. Since the end of the embargo, it was theoretically easier to get through. But she hadn't yet gotten Cristina the right kind of cell phone and plan.

The landline number she had just rang and rang.

Marisol went to her phone's digital recorder, and played a voice mail from her sister she'd gotten six months ago. At this point, she knew it by heart.

"*Hola, hermana*. Just wanted to let you know I'm thinking of you . . ." Marisol set the file to play on loop. She curled up on the couch and closed her eyes for just a moment. When she woke up in the morning, the battery on her phone was dead.

Marisol remembered the night after her grandmother's funeral. They were still in Puerto Rico, staying with cousins. The house was somewhere in the mountains—there was a breeze and thick insect noises. She and Cristina curled together in a narrow single bed. She was in middle school and her sister was still in elementary. Marisol felt the rise and fall of her sister's sleeping back against her chest.

In the other two beds, her teenage girl cousins snored gently. Even then, surrounded by family, Marisol understood that it was just her and Cristina now. No one else in the world really mattered. They were going back to the States to live with some uncle. Maybe if it had been an aunt she would have had some hope. But men? Men were pretty much useless. Loud and unreliable. They went around promising her mother things in seductive voices. They promised Marisol things—trips to the zoo, sweets, movies. No suitor wanted a sullen little girl to ruin his chances. But after a few broken promises, she didn't even crack a smile when they made the offers. Cristina was easier. At two, she was charmed by a game of peek-a-boo. Marisol, the sentry, guarded both mother and sister. She comforted her *mami* when the men left.

Her grandmother comforted both of them when her mother died of breast cancer. A year later, her grandmother died of a massive stroke. Now it was up to Marisol to do the comforting again, stand sentry again.

"Tú y yo," Marisol murmured into her sister's honey hair in the humid night. "We'll always be together. You can count on me." Marisol clung to her sister's narrow torso in the darkness. "I'll never leave. I'll never let you down. *Tú y yo. Siempre. Tú y yo.*" She said it over and over, her thin arms gripping her sister's warm body, until she had chanted herself to sleep.

Chapter 9

For a week after the benefit, the staff called Marisol "Make-It-Rain Rivera." Then some younger clients said that was dated, and started calling her "Market-Rate Rivera," from Thug Woofer's current song:

Market rate. Market rate. I make money like the market rate.

Marisol waved off the praise, but she found herself singing the catchy hook as she set up the call for Thug Woofer's private party.

She had Tyesha, Kim, and Jody on her heist team, but that didn't necessarily mean they would all fit the clients' tastes. Thug Woofer had mostly African American women in his videos, so the first picture she texted to his manager was of Tyesha. The photo had her work name, "Candi Jones," and she wore a lacy white merry widow with matching thigh-high fishnet stockings. Her feet nestled in six-inch Lucite stiletto platform sandals. She lay on her stomach, her ass bared in a thong, her breasts spilling out of the white demi-bra, and her long hair wound up into a beehive cloud, with a spiral vine of small white flowers cascading down around it. She was a rap star's video vixen dream, with her doe eyes, full lips, and slightly open mouth. Marisol typed: **For the groom-to-be?**

The text had come back that she was a yes for Thug Woofer, but the groom wanted a white girl.

Marisol sent a photo of Jody. "Heidi Honeywell" wore a black patent-leather bustier and matching low-rise booty shorts. Her long legs straddled a chair in thigh-high black leather boots with seven-inch heels. Her muscular limbs and six-pack would have made her look like an athlete, if not for the cleavage pressed up by the bustier, and the long blond fake ponytail. She was the über Amazon fantasy looking up at the camera with a lustful smirk.

Marisol texted: **The ultimate white girl.**

She sent a third photo of Kim. "Luscious Lee" wore a pink bra and ruffled hi-cut panties. Her jet-black hair swept down in two pigtails, and her eyes were heavily outlined in black. She wore pink patent-leather pumps, and held a matching pink lollipop just inches from her glossy mouth.

Marisol had supervised the photo shoot for all three pictures to maximize each woman's strong allure and porn racial stereotype. She wasn't surprised half an hour later when she got a message: **Yes to all three.**

Marisol texted the girls that Thug Woofer was a go. On her way out the door, she checked on Dulce.

"I was just headed to Dr. Feldman's office," Dulce said.

"Smart move," Marisol said. "She was my unofficial shrink when I left the business. I still talk to her sometimes."

Dulce's swelling had gone down, but bruises still covered a lot of her face.

"She keeps asking what's my vision for my life," Dulce said. "I don't fucking know."

"My vision for my life was to run a clinic for girls like me," Marisol said. "And then take over the world. Mua-ha-ha." She smiled and elbowed the girl.

"*Coño*," Dulce said. "Maybe I wanna aim a little higher than not getting my ass beat."

"Maybe you do," Marisol said.

As Marisol walked out of the clinic, she absently nodded to the security guard who opened the door for her.

"You need a taxi, *guapa*?" he asked.

Startled, Marisol looked up from her phone at a familiar face.

"Raul, what are you—?"

"I'm volunteering," he said.

He leaned in for a hello kiss on the cheek, and her purse bumped him. Just as she moved it out of the way, he leaned back and her kiss grazed his shoulder.

"What a surprise," Marisol half-stammered, hitching up her purse.

"In your speech you requested volunteers to protect the clinic," Raul said, shoving his hands in his pockets. "So I'm here on security detail."

"That's—that's great," Marisol said, suddenly wary. "Is your cop friend volunteering, too?"

"The one you met at the gala?" Raul shook his head. "We don't socialize, just former colleagues. Hey, am I crazy or didn't this used to be a cigar store?"

"Yes," Marisol said. "Nobody else remembers."

"I knew it," Raul said. "It's that—"

"Smell," Marisol finished his sentence.

Raul nodded. "My uncle used to come here when I was a kid."

"The lady who worked here was really nice," Marisol said. "A Cuban woman—"

"—with a little yappy dog," Raul said. "*Señora* . . . I forget her name."

"Me too," Marisol said. "It's on the tip of my—"

"Raul." The receptionist at the desk waved him over to help a woman on crutches.

"See you around, *guapa*," he said.

Marisol smiled and they managed to navigate a goodbye kiss on the cheek without incident.

As she sat in the cab to her midtown meeting, she felt a clutch in her solar plexus. She felt it every time they met. Not to mention a tingle between her legs. Raul? In her clinic? How was she going to concentrate on anything with him in the same building day after day? Not to mention his inconvenient status as an ex-cop and hers as an active thief.

Yet part of her was relieved. She felt safer. For the first time since Jerry had shown up, she could go to a meeting without worrying that the pimp would burn the place down while she was gone.

A week after the gala fund-raiser, Tyesha waited for a cab in front of the clinic. Raul wished her a polite good night as he left for the evening.

A moment later, Nalissa came out, looking up and down the street.

"Which way did Raul go?" she asked.

"None of your business," Tyesha said.

"What?" Nalissa laughed. "He's your man or something?"

"Not mine," Tyesha said. "But not available."

"I don't see no ring on his finger," she said. "And I didn't see no other woman's name on the mailbox at his apartment."

"He invited you to his place?" Tyesha asked.

"No, but I know where it is."

"It's not about his status," Tyesha said. "It's about your status. You seem like you wanna advance in the business, so don't mess with the clinic volunteers."

Nalissa tilted her head to the side and surveyed Tyesha. "I know Marisol got two kinds of girls on her roster. There's you, Kim, and Jody, then there's everybody else. You three get all the good shit."

At the curb, a taxi pulled up with Kim and Jody in the back. Both wore full makeup, trench coats, and stiletto heels.

"See?" Nalissa said. "You three got something going tonight."

"Now we're back where we started," Tyesha said, stepping into the cab. "None of your business."

She slid in next to Kim and Jody, and shut the door.

After they drove off, Kim asked, "What's with Nalissa?"

"I don't know, but she's trouble," Tyesha said. "You get my text?"

"Yeah, but I must've misunderstood," Jody said.

Kim laughed. "It sounded like Marisol said to case Thug Woofer's apartment."

"She did," Tyesha said.

"What?"

"His new video was playing in the lobby," Tyesha said. "The hook is 'all these hoes tryna take my money.' He says it like fifty times. I could see Marisol getting more and more pissed. Later, she said to case the place."

"But she always stresses to girls in the industry that there needs to be honor among sex workers," Kim said. "Work smart and charge what you're worth. I thought Rule Number One is never to rob the clients."

"Although their corrupt CEO friends are fair game," Jody said.

Tyesha shrugged. "Apparently Rule Zero is don't go on and on about hoes tryna take your money if you don't want hoes taking your money. You know how she gets when clients are disrespectful."

Jody laughed. "Serves him right."

"But seriously," Kim said. "Do you think she's desperate for cash?"

"I been wondering the same thing," Tyesha said. "She won't let me look at the clinic's books, but I saw some warning notices on the utilities."

The cab pulled up in front of the luxury apartment. Jody went to get their equipment from the trunk and pay the driver.

Jody stuck her head in the cab. "Do you have cash for the fare?" she asked Kim.

As Kim handed over a twenty, she turned to Tyesha. "See?" Kim said. "These hoes really are tryna take my money."

Tyesha laughed. "You hoes is crazy," she said, as they got out of the cab.

Marisol had instructed them to do the "delivery" routine for this call. Accordingly, Tyesha opened the lobby door of the rapper's midtown penthouse apartment in a delivery uniform that hid her curves. She wore leather work gloves, and pushed two hand trucks with several large boxes on each one. Her cap covered heavily made-up eyes, and she wore no lipstick.

A security guard sent her up in the freight elevator. The team had instructions from Marisol to find out whether there was a safe. Tyesha was becoming irritated with Marisol's inconsistency and secrecy. "Relax," Marisol had said. "Let me worry about the financials."

But how could Tyesha relax while she was casing the apartment of a famous rapper?

She rang the bell.

"It's unlocked," someone yelled.

She opened the door and backed into the apartment, taking note of the alarm panel just inside the room and the contact plates on the sides of the door. Turning around, she found herself in a high-ceilinged room with spectacular views. To the east, the apartment looked out on glittering city buildings. The view to the west was much darker, with strands of lights zigzagging across the flat expanse of Central Park.

On the far living room wall were several huge reproductions of Thug Woofer's album covers. The largest one was the twelve-inch single "Backhoe Loader," off his *$kranky $outh* album. The image featured a rural field with rows of plants that had hundred-dollar bills where cotton bolls should be. Thug Woofer wore a straw hat and had a wheat stalk sticking out of his mouth. He sat on a solid gold tractor with loaders on the front and back, each filled with women wearing bikini tops, thongs, and booty shorts, rumps in the air.

In the center of the apartment was a sunken living room, where two black men lounged on couches. A muted 1970s mobster movie played in the background, featuring a man in a pin-striped suit shooting a machine gun into a restaurant.

Tyesha recognized the two men on the couches as the cousin and the groom-to-be from the photos Marisol had shown them.

"Hey, fellas," Tyesha said. "I came to drop off some party drinks."

"Over there," the groom said, pointing to the large kitchen area, which was separated from the living room space by a counter partition.

Tyesha proceeded to wheel in two huge hand trucks, each with six boxes of liquor. "So do you need me to unload?"

"What is all this?" the cousin asked.

"Twelve cases. Six of rum. Six of tequila."

"Twelve cases? We didn't order no twelve cases," the groom drawled in a Southern accent. He was tall and chunky, with his hair in short cornrows.

"Are you Mr. Johnson?" she asked. "I'm supposed to get your signature."

"I ain't signin nothin." The groom turned and looked over his shoulder. "Woof! You need to come on in here."

"What?" Thug Woofer came out to the living room, zipping up his low-slung designer jeans, a bottle of whiskey in his hand. He wore shades and several gold chains over a white undershirt, pulled halfway up to reveal a six-pack and gold-seamed boxer shorts.

"Who ordered twelve cases of liquor? I thought this was just gonna be a private party," the groom said.

Woof was already calling his manager. "What the fuck did you order?" Woof slurred into the phone.

"Congratulations on your engagement," Tyesha said. "We'll give you a free bottle to celebrate."

Tyesha undid latches on both stacks of boxes and the false fronts fell forward, acting as a runway. Marisol had had them made by a theater designer, with tiny lights along the sides. Jody and Kim burst out from behind pink velvet curtains, wearing uniforms that matched Tyesha's. The tops of the boxes flipped up into speakers. Tyesha kicked off her delivery boots and slid into high-heeled pumps.

Delivery, I've got a delivery for you . . .

"What the fuck?" Woof said, but when the women began dancing to the low growl of the music, he hung up the phone.

The women began by tossing their delivery gloves aside.

Tyesha applied red lipstick suggestively, as the other two women ran their hands down along their bodies.

Next, they each unsnapped their blouses and pulled off the sleeves, to make low-cut halter tops. At a climactic point in the music, the singer screamed out a high note, and with practiced choreography, each of the girls shimmied toward their dates.

They pulled off the legs of their tear-away pants to reveal booty shorts. Garter belts peeked out from beneath the shorts, holding up fishnet stockings.

Delivery, I've got a delivery for you . . .

The three women led their dates to the couches and continued to dance for them.

Delivery, I've got a delivery for you. Where do you want it, baby? Oh, how do you want it, baby?

Slowly, the three of them undid the final snaps on their shirts, and revealed demi-bras and belly-button piercings.

Delivery, I've got a delivery for you. Where do you want it, baby? Oh, how do you want it, baby?

The women gyrated to the throbbing bass of the music, rubbing their hips, asses, and crotches until, with an explosion sound effect in the music, they tore off their shorts to reveal thongs. They each gave their dates a lap dance.

Where do you want it, baby? Oh, how do you want it, baby?

After the dance, the women giggled and cooed.

"Oh my God," Kim said. "I can't believe we're really here with Thug Woofer and his hot brother and his *really* hot cousin." She pressed her breasts against the cousin. He had a baby face and seemed the most reserved of the three.

"Before we move into the private party section of the evening, can I please get a photo with you?" Kim asked the cousin.

Jody snapped photos of Kim and the cousin on the couch. Then, under the pretext of sending them, she snapped several zoom shots of the alarm system by the door.

"When does the private party start?" the cousin asked, sliding a hand onto Kim's ass. She and Jody exchanged an amused look.

"Party starts now," Tyesha said, leading Woof toward the bedroom.

"I ain't the groom," Woof said, as Tyesha closed the door behind them. "Just givin a nigga his last fuckin hurrah before getting married." He took another slug of whiskey. "I ain't neva gettin married. Bitches just want half yo shit."

He sat down on a water bed. Tyesha was annoyed by his monologue. Besides, the drunker he got, the longer sex would take. She sat down beside him.

"Half? Oh, I don't want half, Woof, baby. I want it all. Are you ready to give it to me?"

"What? You sayin you want all the damn money?"

"No, baby, I want all of this." She stroked his crotch.

"Oh right. My manager already paid y'all."

"That's just for the madam," Tyesha lied. "When I found out it was you, I would have done it for free. I mean, I been wanting to get with you since your first video."

"S'what I'm talmbout." He took another swig from the bottle. "Females see you on stage or on the video and wanna just throw pussy at you." He fell into the lyrics of one of his signature hits:

I got scantily clad jailbait
Chasin me down

They gotta wait
Get in the pussy line, bitches
If you wanna fuck me
betta show some ID
like I said on TV
No bitch gonna trap me.

"Woof, I've always loved that song," Tyesha cooed. She pressed her breasts against him, but he just brooded. He was a "whiner" type—lots of access to sex, but mostly they just complained.

Tyesha liked sex. She didn't mind fucking to pay graduate school tuition. But with this drama, she felt like she was really earning the money.

"That nigga crazy," Woof said. "He could have all this, but Brandon would rather go back to South Carolina?"

"Brandon's your brother?" Tyesha asked. Maybe if she drew him out to have a nice bitch session, it would settle him down. She wanted to fuck him and get home to study for her exam on maternal and child health outcomes in rural versus urban areas.

"My mama act like this wedding the damn second coming of Jesus," he mumbled. "But Brandon rather be a king in Carolina, than be just the brother of the king in New York. I see how it is."

"You can be my king tonight."

"It's that hater bitch he gon marry." Woof took another pull on the bottle. "She don't want him on the road with me. Know she ain't got the world's only pussy."

"If she met him on the road—" Tyesha began.

"Naw, she ain't met him on the road. They went together in high school. She ain't never give me the time of day. Bitch ain't even halfway cute. But he wanna be with her forever? Live in a small-ass Cackalacky town when he could be livin like this?"

"Everybody can't be a big man like you, Woof."

"S'why I wanted hoes for the party tonight. I'ma be like fuck you. Takin my brother away? You ain't got the world's only pussy."

"Speaking of pussy." Tyesha straddled him. She could feel his penis dragging into action. "I wanna give it all to you." She ground her hips around in a circular motion, and leaned him back. They rocked with the motion of the water bed.

He let out a low moan. She unhooked her bra and let her breasts tumble into his face, grazing his lips.

"Aw yeah, girl, I—I—"

Suddenly, his body clenched. He heaved her off of him, and struggled out of the water bed. He ran to the bathroom and vomited.

Tyesha put her bra back on and followed. This was not the I-fucked-a-superstar story she had been hoping to tell.

"It's gonna be okay, Woof." She set a towel beside the toilet and sat down, rubbing his back.

Five minutes later, she walked him back on unsteady legs and he lay down on the water bed.

"I'm the king, but how come I gotta get a hoe for my brother? I got everything, but he got a woman who really love him, you know? Loved him when he ain't had shit. Wanna have his baby. She pregnant now. And he know the baby his. She don't wanna fuck wit nobody else but him. Me, I got hoes chasing me but they just want the money. Then they gon go fuck wit the next nigga. Like you. You fine as hell, but you jus want money. I bet you ain't givin no pussy to a broke-ass country nigga from Cackalacky . . ." He began to drift off.

"Woof, baby," Tyesha said. "I'm gonna turn you on your side so you don't choke on your own vomit, okay?"

Woof began to snore. Carefully, Tyesha climbed out of bed, but the motion of the water turned him over onto his back.

She climbed back into the bed and planted him firmly on his side, arranging him to stay put. But as she got out of the water bed, it sloshed him onto his back again. She kept wrestling him onto his side, but he rolled back each time she got up.

She called Marisol and explained the situation. "What should I do?"

"You can't leave," Marisol said. "Picture the headline? 'Rapper Thug Woofer found dead—police seeking three escorts.'"

"But I have a midterm tomorrow at ten," Tyesha said. "I need to pull an all-nighter."

"Did you bring your books?"

"I was studying on the train ride over."

"So pull your all-nighter there," Marisol said.

"I want a bonus for this," Tyesha said.

"Time and a half," Marisol agreed, and they hung up.

Tyesha tiptoed out into the darkened living room to get her book bag out of the bottom of the liquor boxes. While she was at it, she raided the fridge. Only beer, orange juice, and energy drinks. Tyesha grabbed four cans of Ramp Up! and crept back into the bedroom.

Chapter 10

After she left, Kim and Jody popped up from the couch.

"Did she see us?" Kim whispered. "Marisol would kill us for getting our freak on here."

"I don't think Tyesha saw," Jody said, "but we'd better get down on the floor, just in case."

Kim chuckled. "Always looking for an excuse to get down on the floor."

Kim lay back and Jody straddled her, sliding her hands up under the black lingerie to caress Kim's breasts.

"Was he any good?" Jody whispered.

"He thought so." Kim stifled a giggle.

"Mine hadn't been with anyone but his fiancée in years," Jody said. "She may be black, but she was keeping it vanilla in bed. I pulled a few prostate tricks. Knocked him right out."

"My guy, too," Kim said. "I left him sleeping like a baby. All that booze they drank didn't hurt, either." She leaned in and gave Jody an openmouthed kiss. "When I was with him, I was definitely wishing it was your hands, your lips, your body."

"My guy had a decent-size dick," Jody said. "I wanted to ask him, hey, can I borrow that for a minute after we're done?"

Kim laughed, and Jody shushed her.

"Sorry. I was just thinking you'd know better than him what to do with it. Did you bring any toys?"

"No room in the boxes with all of Tyesha's books. But I did bring ten fingers and a tongue."

Jody ran her tongue in circles around Kim's nipples and then began to lick them in earnest, as she traced her fingers down into her panties.

"Are you wet for me or for him?" Jody asked.

"I took a shower afterward, so what do you think?"

Jody slid her finger up and down.

"I want you to tell me," she encouraged.

Kim moaned.

"It's okay, baby." Jody smiled. "You can tell me."

Kim pulled a pillow off the couch and bit into it to contain the noise of her moans.

Jody kissed both of Kim's breasts, the crests of her ribs, her belly, working her way down between Kim's thighs.

Jody opened Kim's lips, and after a moment of soft licking alternated with firm fingers, Jody asked again, "Who're you wet for, baby?"

"You," Kim gasped.

"Tell me again," Jody said, thrusting four fingers inside Kim, but keeping her thumb on the clitoris still rubbing insistently.

"All you, baby," Kim whimpered. "Oh—you! All you."

And then Kim proceeded to rip the seam on the couch pillow with her teeth, as she tried to keep quiet amidst the intense bucking of her orgasm.

Afterward, Kim and Jody lay on the couch.

"I love you," Kim said, stroking Jody's face.

"I love you, too." Jody leaned in and kissed her softly.

"Maybe one of these days you'll let me do you after a hard day at work."

"Not a chance." Jody shook her head. "I get off making you get off. You can do me on nights when it's just the two of us, start to finish. Not on work nights."

"Speaking of work," Kim said.

"I know," Jody agreed. "Let's case this place so we can go home."

Tyesha didn't understand why Marisol had her looking for Thug Woofer's safe. Still, it was exciting to snoop around a superstar's apartment.

She tiptoed through the rooms, feeling the walls in the dim light and reaching behind framed posters of him.

Woof had the predictable rugged good looks of a rap star. In one image, he had his shirt off, showing his chiseled chest and abs above his boxers and low-slung belt.

On top of his bureau was a photograph of him hugging a thickset black woman in front of a modest, single-story house with a giant red bow on it. The woman was crying and grinning. Woof grinned, too, and his eyes were closed. He seemed to be sinking into the hug. Tyesha was surprised at how handsome he looked. Not glamorous, just a regular guy with a great smile, and kind of sweet. How had he gone from that cutie in the photo to the drunken dick on the bed next door?

As she met up with Kim and Jody in the living room, she chuckled to see Kim adjusting her bra.

"I searched the whole master bedroom suite," Tyesha said.

Kim and Jody reported finding nothing in both guys' bedrooms, as the three of them pulled out pen flashlights. They found nothing behind any of the framed albums in the living room. They crept down the central hallway of the apartment, peeking behind pictures.

There was a total of five doors in the hallway. They could account for all of them, except a door to the right of the bathroom, recessed slightly into the hallway. Kim tried the doorknob, but it didn't open.

"Okay, Lock Whisperer," Tyesha said. "Do your stuff."

Tyesha had given Kim the nickname. Even before she'd started to work with Marisol, Kim had been able to open locks and hot-wire cars. Kim knelt at the door and pulled out her lockpicks.

Jody shone the flashlight beam on the doorknob.

Kim was inserting the pick when they heard a noise from farther up the hallway. Jody snapped off the light and they all froze.

One of the bedroom doors opened, and Brandon shuffled groggily down the hallway toward them. Barely breathing, the three women stood in the slightly recessed alcove only a foot deep. As he approached, they tensed.

Brandon went into the bathroom. When the door closed, the women caught their breath. They heard the seat *clack* up and the sound of the stream into the toilet bowl.

Jody pulled forward as if to move back into the living room, but Tyesha caught her arm.

"Boys are quick," she whispered. "Stay put."

The three of them stood flattened against the wall.

Brandon opened the door and went back to bed.

"He didn't even flush or put the seat back down," Jody said.

"I pity the fiancée," Tyesha said, as Kim got back to work.

"Ooh, that close call got my adrenaline pumping," Jody said. "Hurry up so I can get you home." She tangled her fingers in Kim's hair.

Kim gave Jody a quick kiss on her pelvic bone. "Later, babe, I'm working."

"Calm the fuck down and focus," Tyesha said as Jody ran her finger along Kim's ear.

"Don't distract me," Kim hissed, and then the lock clicked.

The three of them entered what was apparently Thug Woofer's study, a wood-paneled room, where the recessed door had made space for a bookcase. The safe's dial was clearly visible on the wall behind the desk.

"A Muscle Man safe," Kim said. "My favorite."

"Wait," Tyesha said, sliding a fingernail underneath the edge of the door. "It's not locked." She swung the safe's door open with her nail.

The only thing inside was a half-empty bottle of expensive Scotch.

In the morning Woof blinked a few times, looking disoriented. "Who the fuck are you?" he asked Tyesha.

Clients never recognized her with her ponytail and glasses, especially not reading a book.

"From last night." Tyesha shook her chest facetiously, and recognition dawned in his face. "You okay?" she asked.

Woof lifted his head and groaned. He winced as he rolled out of bed and stumbled to the bathroom.

Tyesha packed up her books. She'd gotten a lot done, but now it was time to go home, take a shower, and do a final review of her flash cards before the exam.

Woof stepped out of the bathroom with a condom packet in his hand.

"Where'd we leave off last night?" he asked, biting the end of the package and tearing it open. "I know you stayed to get some of this." He began to unbuckle his belt.

"Woof," Tyesha said. "I stayed because I didn't want you to choke on your own vomit. You passed out. Now you're awake and safe and I'm leaving."

"Wait a minute," he said. "I paid my money."

"You paid for three strippers and a private party last night. The party's over."

"But I paid for some pussy," he said.

"You paid for some time," she said. "And the time is over."

"Fine," he said and began to look around for his wallet. "How much more do you want?"

"I'm an escort, Woof. That means you call the agency. I don't work for cash. I shouldn't even be here. I just wanted to make sure you woke up breathing."

"You worried about me?" He smiled.

"Woof, this is business."

"Fine," Woof said, pulling out a credit card. "If you an escort, who do I call to get you to suck my dick right now?"

"Nobody," Tyesha said. "I'm not available today."

"You don't even know how much I'm willing to pay," Woof said.

"If you wanna set up another date with me, have your guy call the agency and ask for me—Candi Jones."

"Girl, what's your real name?"

"Candi Jones is all you need to know." Tyesha smiled. "Have your guy call if you've got a jones for more candy." She pulled her bag onto her shoulder and walked to the door.

"Probably gonna see some rich guy who like early morning pussy," Woof said. "Can't keep yo sugar daddy waiting for a nigga like me, huh? I bet he's white."

"I have a midterm, and I been here all night, watching over your drunk ass." She cocked her bag up higher on her shoulder and put a hand on her hip. "You wake up demanding pussy because you passed out last night? This is bullshit. You know what? Don't call the agency. I wouldn't fuck your no-home-training ass for a truck-load of money."

Chapter 11

The Monday after the three girls did the call, Thug Woofer's manager began calling Marisol. "My guy wants to hire Candi Jones again," his voice-mail message said.

Marisol called back from a cab en route to a breakfast meeting. "Your guys were satisfied with the service?"

"Sure. Woof wants to see Candi Jones again."

"She's not available, but I've got other black girls, equally charming. How about Janice Jackson? She's nasty."

"Not available?" he asked. "I didn't even say when."

"She doesn't want to work with Woof," Marisol said, stepping out of the taxi, paying the driver, and getting a receipt.

"Why not?"

"You're Thug Woofer's manager. You know why." Marisol stepped into a café. She grabbed a cheese croissant and stood in line. "He acted like a dick. That bridge is burned."

"But can't you—"

"Look," Marisol said. "It's the moment on *Love Connection* when the girl says no, she doesn't want another date. Suck it up and move on. Doesn't Woof have a 'pussy line around the block'? Hang on—" She turned to the woman behind the counter. "Mocha, please. Sorry, I'm back."

"What if I double the price?" the manager asked.

"I told you at the beginning, the girls have the final say. I got Janice Jackson. I got Sugar Golden. He'd like these other girls, and they might even like him."

"He's not gonna like this," he said.

"I'm glad our service was otherwise satisfactory," Marisol said. "Your office will get the donation receipt for tax season. Pleasure doing business with you."

That night, she met with her team in the office. "Sorry this is so late," she said. "Things have been crazy since the fund-raiser."

She slung the purse onto the desk and unloaded the bricks of cash. "From the tech guy heist two weeks ago," Marisol said. "I haven't counted it."

"Did he really do the wife with you right there in the vent?" Jody asked.

Marisol grimaced. "Don't remind me." She distributed the bills to the team to count and recount.

Someone knocked loudly on the door. Marisol leaped up, startled. Tyesha jolted and knocked a tall stack of cash off the desk. The loose bills fluttered down.

"Pick those up!" Marisol hissed, striding across the office.

"Sorry," Tyesha whispered.

"Yes?" Marisol asked through the door.

"Marisol? . . . Hey, it's Raul."

"What's up?"

"Front desk sent me. You have a package."

Marisol glanced at her team picking up bills strewn across the carpet.

"Of course," Marisol said. "Thanks for bringing it." She unlocked the bolt and slid out of the barely open door.

Raul held a huge box in both arms. "Lemme drop it in your office."

"I can get it," Marisol said.

"It's really heavy," he said. "I know you're strong, but I had to rest halfway up the stairs with this."

"Sorry, you can't come in right now," Marisol said, peeking back into the office to see Kim squeezing under the desk to get several hundred-dollar bills. "I'm meeting with my outreach team, and we have open client files. Patient confidentiality. It would be—" She glanced back to see Tyesha stuffing bills into a drawer. "It would be illegal."

"Can I just leave it here?" he asked.

Marisol looked at the sender. "No," she said. "It's got syringes and bottles of narcan. That's why security sent it up. It's locked in my office by special protocol."

"Okay," Raul said. "I hope you've been working out."

She heaved the package into her arms. Although she clenched every muscle, it knocked her backward.

Raul caught her. "*Cuidado*," he said and stood behind her to steady her grip.

She felt his warm shoulder against the back of her neck and his pectoral muscle against her shoulder blade. Her pulse picked up. She wanted to tell him to back up, that she had the package, but she was unsteady.

"Nice upper body strength," he said in her ear. His breath tickled the hairs at the nape of her neck. "Lemme help you balance." He pressed up against her, his crotch at the base of her spine. Her body fit so easily with his, and it was an identical temperature to her own. She was simultaneously unaware of it and intensely, chemically aware.

Jody stepped out of the office. "Need a hand?"

"Yes," Marisol gasped.

Jody lifted the box from Raul's arm and swung the office door open with her foot.

Tyesha and Kim sat at the desk covered with nothing but files. Marisol sighed with relief.

"I'll let you get back to your meeting," Raul murmured in her ear.

Marisol nearly jumped. She hadn't realized that he was still behind her. "Yes—I—" she stammered. "Thanks again."

He turned and walked down the stairs, and the women watched his wide shoulders, narrow hips, and firm ass.

"He can deliver his package to me anytime," Tyesha said. "If it wasn't against the rules to date other staff, I would definitely tap that."

"Uh-uh," Jody said. "He's Marisol's."

"No, he isn't," Marisol said.

"Jody came out of the office and you were all squeezed up with him," Kim said.

"I was not squeezed up with him," Marisol said. "I just overbalanced."

"Overbalancing," Tyesha said. "Is that what the kids are calling it these days?"

"Don't talk shit to me right now," Marisol said. "If you hadn't practically made it rain in front of an ex-cop, I wouldn't have been in that position."

"What position is that?" Kim asked.

"Shut up and count this damn money," Marisol said.

Soon there were no sounds but the shuffle and flip of treasury bills and the murmured love songs of women counting.

The next morning, Thug Woofer came to see Marisol. Before inviting him in, she put on her glasses, pulled her long hair back into a bun, and buttoned an additional button on her blouse.

"I want Candi," he said. "Candi Jones."

For a moment, she wanted to laugh. He was such a kid in those oversized, glittering designer clothes, demanding sweets.

"I'm sorry," Marisol said. "She's not available."

"This some bullshit. How you gonna run a business, but won't let me choose my merchandise?"

"The girls aren't merchandise. They're service workers."

"How much I gotta pay to change her mind?"

"You're not gonna change her mind."

"You tell her to name her price," he said. "And then call me."

He dropped a card on her desk. It read *TW* in raised silver letters and had a cell phone number. He hiked up his jeans and strode out the door.

She recycled the card.

At the end of the day, Marisol and Serena had just finished a site visit from the NYC Board of Elections. Marisol had been trying for years to set the clinic up as a polling place. The visit had gone well, and she and Serena were walking back through the lobby toward the stairwell.

Marisol saw Raul in her peripheral vision. Nalissa had a hand on his arm and her head tossed back. Her unnaturally red curls bounced with her laughter.

Marisol willed herself to focus on what Serena was saying about their latest grant, as the clinic's front door opened and a young transgender woman entered.

"Clara!" Serena ran to her. Clara wore a pair of flip-flops and a Dora the Explorer blanket around her full breasts and narrow-hipped body. She wore blond hair extensions down to her butt. Her long, bare legs were smooth and hairless, and her toes were polished pink. Her face was in full makeup, and there were tear streaks down her cheeks.

"You okay, miss?" Raul asked, extracting himself from Nalissa.

"My *tía* put me out for bringing dates to the apartment," Clara said to Serena. "Bitch threw me out in the snow."

"Oh honey—" Serena began.

"She came home early," Clara said, shivering. "And we was going at it on the couch. I'm naked under this shit."

Marisol put her blazer on Clara, pulling her close to warm her.

"Such a fucking hypocrite," Clara said. "How'd she think we was paying the *renta*?"

"That jacket isn't thick enough," Raul said, stepping closer. He pulled off his hoodie. As he lifted up the sweatshirt, it tugged up his undershirt, showing off the muscles in his abdomen.

Marisol could hear Nalissa's audible intake of breath.

"Here you go, miss," Raul said to Clara.

"Ooh, chivalry is alive," Clara said. "Thanks for the flash, *papi*. That warmed me up even more." She ran her hand along Raul's six-pack.

Raul blushed and yanked down the bottom of his white, ribbed undershirt.

Marisol felt light-headed. "Let me get you some hot tea, *nena*," she said. "We also have emergency blankets."

In the back room, Marisol put the kettle on and crossed to the supply closet. She flipped on the light.

Raul appeared in the hallway. "I had to get outta there," he said. "I'm not used to—am I blushing?"

"It was sweet to give her your sweatshirt," Marisol said.

Raul crossed the hallway. The lights were dim, a cost-saving measure, as the hall was illuminated by windows during the day.

"That girl . . . ?" Raul fumbled.

". . . that young woman is transgender," Marisol said.

Raul nodded. "It's good for me working here. Learning new things."

Marisol walked into the alcove where they kept emergency equipment, and Raul followed.

The overhead bulb flashed, then burned out.

"You've got to be kidding me," Marisol mumbled.

"I'll use my phone," Raul said.

"Good idea." Marisol pulled out hers, too, and they searched for the blankets by the glow of the screens.

The emergency corner of the supply closet was small, and she could feel his bicep touching her shoulder, exposed by the sleeveless silk blouse.

"Here it is," Raul said.

Marisol turned as he leaned over to hand her something. Their noses collided, and her cheek brushed the light stubble on his jaw.

She jerked back, dropping her phone. It fell facedown, obscuring the light.

"Sorry," Raul said.

"Not your fault," she said as they looked for the phone. They crawled around, bumping into each other. The moving on all fours, the darkness, the exposed skin. She wanted to jump on him and rip off their clothes so she could press against that smooth chest and those hard abs. She wanted to top him, take him, on a pile of torn silk and white cotton.

"Is that it over there?" Raul asked.

Marisol blinked. The phone had fallen onto some paper napkins on a bottom shelf.

"Got it." She scooped it up.

"Why don't you take the blanket back to Clara?" she said. "I just found a replacement light bulb."

"I can help screw it in," Raul said. "Isn't it a little high for you?"

"Then I'll go." She handed him the bulb and took the blanket. "*Gracias.*"

She hurried down the hallway to the loud whistling of the teakettle.

Marisol locked her office door. How was she supposed to function with Raul under the same roof all day?

She had no idea what to do with these feelings. She couldn't get away from him. She couldn't fuck him. She couldn't concentrate.

She flipped through the mail on her desk. Several tax information statements sobered her. Nothing sexy about the IRS.

She opened the statements and checked them against her records. When she plugged the figures into the tax software, the clinic came out owing $23,000.

What? She rechecked her math. April would bring a $23,000 tax bill on top of the mortgage and other monthly expenses? How could she pay that?

When Marisol had opened the escort service, she swore to Eva, on her mother's grave, that she would find a way to launder the money and pay taxes.

It was simple to declare escort payments as donations. The clients got the services, plus a tax write-off. She paid the escorts as consultants. And there was a clear money trail from the "donor" to the clinic. She kept a small client list of wealthy men who were very discreet—Thug Woofer was the exception. According to the contract, the girls were entertainers, and the sex was off the books. No client was gonna blow the scheme by telling his accountant: "Don't deduct that, it was for hookers." They took the write-off, and they kept their mouths shut.

The tough part was accounting for the heist money, because the funds had no legitimate origin. She disguised some of it as cash payments for clinic services, but since they served mostly low-income clients, a sudden, massive amount of cash income would be a red flag. She deposited a few hundred dollars of stolen cash every week along with the crumpled one- and five-dollar bills they got in the donation buckets. But she needed to launder tens of thousands to keep up with expenses—and now there was this tax bill.

What she needed was a big heist. A multimillion-dollar payoff that she could keep in an offshore account. So instead of scrambling all day for cash to keep the clinic doors open, she could turn over daily management to Tyesha. Then she could focus on setting up the laundering operation that would make it all legit.

Marisol was double-checking her figures when her intercom buzzed.

"Yes, Serena?"

"Jeremy VanDyke on line one."

Marisol's heart began to pound as she picked up. "Mr. VanDyke," Marisol said. "So glad—"

"This is his assistant," a woman's voice said. "Hold please."

Five minutes later, the billionaire came on the line.

"Marisol," he said. "Sorry to keep you waiting."

"Jeremy. So lovely to hear from you. Thank you again for your generous donation."

"My pleasure," he said. "Your innovation is amazing. You applied some of my strategies in ways no one else could have dreamed up. So impressive."

"Okay, Jeremy," she said. "You know it's rocking my

world that the most successful man in the country finds my financial innovations impressive."

"I understand you have some brilliant strategies that involve offering private services as thank-you gifts," he said.

"Our donors are incredibly generous," she said. "We like to offer generous tokens of our appreciation."

"I want in," he said.

"You're selecting our agency for your foundation?" she asked.

"Unfortunately not," he said. "The foundation had already made this round of selections."

"I understand," Marisol said, although she felt let down. "Thank you so much for taking the time to tell me personally."

"I'd like to personally experience your financial strategy," he said. "To see it in action."

"You mean, a site visit?" Marisol asked.

VanDyke chuckled. "Not exactly. Rather that I'd like to make a donation and get my personal thank-you gift."

In a measured voice she said, "I'm not sure what you're referring to, Mr. VanDyke."

"I understand from a colleague that he got a lovely thank-you gift from one of the young women in your employ."

So VanDyke had heard about their tax break/escort hustle and wanted in on it. No date for Marisol and no pet charity project. She swallowed her disappointment, and shifted into her madam role.

"As a businessman," Marisol said, "I'm sure you can understand that I'm not in a position to give out any *information* about young women who work for me. Especially if I have no idea who is authorizing the *information* request."

"Of course," VanDyke said. He named a state senator, one of their best clients. "He's a close friend and suggested that I contact you."

Marisol exhaled. "Well, that's different," she said. "We always like to help friends of friends."

She set up an appointment for him to meet the girls in a few days—Thursday evening—then signed off.

Eva stuck her head in the office. "Is it true that VanDyke called?"

Marisol motioned for her to shut the door. "The asshole wants an escort."

"What a letdown," Eva said.

It was. With VanDyke, she had imagined red carpets, meeting major world movers, and stepping into powerful circles on the arm of a man who could open any door. But then Marisol contrasted that thought with her morning in the supply room with Raul. She'd never been so overwhelmed with sexual yearning—VanDyke certainly didn't have that effect on her.

"I don't know," Marisol said. "Maybe VanDyke himself wasn't sexy, but his power was."

As she spoke, the light bulb overhead blew out. Marisol looked up at Eva. "Not a word," she said and went to get a replacement bulb.

Later that night, in Washington Heights, Marisol met a Colombian guy. He loved to dance. At the hotel, he turned the clock radio to a salsa station and moved his hips in the rhythm of the song. It infuriated Marisol. He had a faraway smile on his face, and his shoulders swayed as if he'd rather be on a dance floor.

"I need to be on top," she said in Spanish.

"*Bueno*," he said.

She towered over him, thrusting her hips so hard he

had to fold his elbows above him to protect his head from banging into the headboard.

Her aggression didn't bother him. He smiled up at her and murmured along with the salsa romántica lyrics:

Nuestro amor, el amor unico, unico, tú eres mi mundo . . .

She rolled off him. "Turn off that damn music," she said.

He shrugged his broad, brown shoulders and complied, but she still couldn't get the feeling she needed. He moved in the same rhythm—the beat clearly still playing in his head. She tried having him move behind her, as well as sitting in the chair.

He went along with everything, stayed hard, didn't complain.

She wanted him to argue, lose his temper, insist. She wanted some kind of resistance. Finally, she climbed on top and rode him fast.

"Slow down," he told her in Spanish. "I'm getting too close. What about your pleasure?"

Marisol couldn't articulate her frustration. She couldn't tell him he had been too agreeable, too deep in the music. She couldn't find the feeling that she was taking him—

"Controlling him." Eva's voice leaped into her mind.

She rode him harder, thrusting her hips to push away the thought, the tears that threatened the back of her eyes.

He gasped beneath her, and in the moment when he lay back, eyes closed, neck exposed, she caught the thread of her own orgasm, and rode him past the moment when he began to soften, to a climax of her own.

He pulled out and disposed of the condom in the bathroom. By the time he came back, she was halfway dressed.

He looked surprised, but caught the hint. He dressed and headed out the door with a formal, "*Buenas noches.*"

She stripped her clothes off again and lay in bed. Marisol didn't feel her usual sense of relief, but slowly she fell asleep.

An hour later, she awoke from a suffocating nightmare.

"Just a dream . . ." she told herself.

She pulled the covers tight around her. She turned on the television, paced around the room for a while, and decided to go find a drink.

Walking up and down the dark and quiet streets, she was spoiling for a fight. But no one spoke to her except the convenience store clerk when she bought the bottle of wine.

Back in the hotel, she drank it all and watched an old episode of *The Bionic Woman*.

The dream she passed out into was a version of her recurring nightmare. Her uncle's cramped Lower East Side apartment, her sister across the room. Marisol not asleep anymore. Never asleep after she heard her uncle come home. The beige wallpaper and suffocating brown marble carpet. Dank. In spite of her scrubbing, the smell of mildew and bad plumbing hovered just beneath a chemical rose scent from the 99 Cent Store's all-purpose cleaner.

Eventually at night, her exhaustion would eclipse her will to stay awake. Then the terror at the sound of the front door opening. She felt overwhelming desperation to run, to hide under the bed, to climb out onto the fire escape before he came into the room. But then he'd find Cristina and she was too little. She couldn't handle it. In the dream there was always the smell and the feeling of her body crushed under a familiar hated heaviness. But in this particular version of the nightmare, her fifteen-year-old legs moved in slow motion, the *Bionic Woman* soundtrack making all the right noises of superstrength, but not able to push him off. Usually she would have woken up at this point in the dream, but the booze did its own part to hold her down, and the dream eventually morphed into a forest scene where she had to save Cristina from a huge, ferocious bear. Just as she had locked her sister safely in a cabin, she found herself standing in a green botanical garden with the hulking figure of Jerry the pimp.

Marisol woke up feeling slightly sick to her stomach. Not just from the hangover, but it was an anxious nausea, like she was forgetting something important. The tangle of the dream came back to her. The forest. Jerry. Worrying about her sister. She hadn't been to the botanical garden in twenty years. Since high school.

In the quiet Harlem hotel room, Marisol felt a jolt of recognition as she recalled—over twenty years earlier—meeting Jerry for the first time.

Chapter 12

The memory took her back to high school. The knot in her stomach had started around 2 p.m., when their biology teacher led them out of the botanical garden toward the subway.

The school day was when she could relax and laugh with her friend Gladys. On bad days—like if she'd been to the hospital the night before—the school nurse would usually let her doze on a cot. Field trips were the best. She could lose herself in the change of routine.

After ten minutes of walking through the Bronx, they were on a wide street, passing a corner bodega and a check-cashing place. Gladys had worn a short dress with platform shoes, and she complained that her feet hurt.

"Trade shoes with me?" She begged for a chance to wear Marisol's sneakers. "Please. Just back to the train?"

"No way, *tonta*," Marisol said. "You're the one tryna look cute for these stupid boys, not me."

"Don't be such a bitch," Gladys said, gesturing to Marisol's oversized button-down shirt and jeans. "With your *tetas* and *nalgas* you can wear a fucking tent and these boys are all over you. Some of us gotta try a little harder."

"I wouldn't mind if Marisol tried a little harder," one boy said. "I wouldn't mind if she made it a little harder." He rubbed his crotch.

"*Por qué?*" Marisol asked. "So I could be like, 'I don't feel nothing. Oh wait. It's kinda like being poked with a toothpick.' "

"Fuck you, *puta*. I got something for you." He raised a middle finger at her.

Marisol flipped him the bird right back. "Fuck you?" she said, then retracted her middle finger and extended her pinkie. "Isn't this more scientifically accurate?"

A few of the kids cracked up.

"Mr. De Guzman," the teacher said sternly. "Please join me at the front of the line or get detention." He turned to Marisol. "And Miss Rivera, you might focus more on scientific accuracy on your next test."

Gladys laughed and threw an arm around Marisol. "You told De Guzman's skinny ass."

As they arrived at the subway station, however, the laugh evaporated in Marisol's throat. There was some problem with the train.

"Hey, guys," the teacher called. "We'll have to walk to another station. I'll have the secretary call to tell your parents we'll be late."

No.

Not with Cristina at home, letting herself in with her key around three thirty, and her uncle getting off work at five thirty. The field trip was already a risk getting her home around five. He sometimes came home early.

Marisol hustled up to the front of the line. "I can't be late," she told the teacher. "I gotta take care of my little sister."

De Guzman grabbed her ass, and she elbowed him hard in the ribs, but didn't turn around.

"I don't know what to tell you," the teacher said. "It's not like I have a car."

"Can you loan me cab fare?"

"To the Lower East Side?" he asked. "At rush hour? Do you know what that costs?"

"I don't care," she said. "I'll pay you back."

"I don't have that kind of cash, Miss Rivera. Please get back in line."

An SUV went by, blasting hip-hop, and a guy leaned out of the passenger side, making a kissing sound in their direction.

Marisol went back to Gladys. "Gimme those platforms," she said.

As the two girls traded shoes, they fell to the end of the line. Then Marisol pulled out her ponytail holder, and shook out her hair. She tied the oversized shirt around her narrow waist and undid several buttons.

"*Eso!*" said one of the boys. "Finally, Marisol showing what she got. Ass for days!"

"Can you please get your fat *nalgas* outta my boyfriend's face?" the girl on his arm asked.

Marisol ignored them. She turned to the cars coming toward them on the broad street, and stuck out her thumb, pointing downtown.

"What the hell are you doing?" Gladys asked.

"Getting home on time."

She turned back to the street with a wide smile. They walked a block with cars speeding past. Finally, a beat-up black Datsun pulled up with a Puerto Rican flag hanging from the rearview mirror.

"Looking good, *mami*." The curly-haired young man smiled at her appreciatively. He might have been in high school, as well. She advanced toward the car.

Horns honked behind them. Gladys stood on the curb in Marisol's sneakers just out of earshot, her arms folded across her chest.

Behind the passenger, the driver leaned toward her. His face was partially obscured. He had paler skin, and was maybe a bit older, with a scraggly goatee.

"Need a ride, lil' girl?" he asked. She drew back from his creepy come-on and squinted into the car. She could barely see hard dark eyes under the brim of a baseball cap, pulled low.

She hesitated at that face, but then looked at her watch. "Yeah," she said. "To the Lower East Side. You going that way?"

"I could be," the driver said. "How about a ride for a ride?" he asked, jutting his chin toward her hips and pressing the tip of his tongue to his upper lip.

The passenger turned to the driver and said in Spanish, "Come on, Jay, be a gentleman."

Jay shook his head. "Nobody rides free."

"Fine," she said. "I'll give you a blow job."

"Only if you get your friend to do my cousin," he said, indicating Gladys.

The cousin looked stricken. "I'm not in this," he said.

"She's not in this, either," Marisol said. "If that's your price, I'll do both of you."

The driver agreed, but the cousin shook his head.

"First the ride," she insisted, and reached for the door handle.

"Have you lost your fucking mind?" Gladys yelled from the curb, as Marisol climbed into the backseat of the car.

"Tell the teacher I saw someone I knew," she called back, just before the Datsun took off down the street.

"What are you?" the driver asked his cousin. "A faggot?"

Jay drove fast and recklessly, baiting the cousin the whole time.

"Maybe you'd let a boy suck your dick, huh?"

Marisol kept her hand gripped on the door handle, ready to bail out.

The cousin stayed silent.

Once they hit her neighborhood, she directed them to drive into an alley.

Without ceremony, she went down on Jay beside a dumpster, kneeling on the concrete in her jeans. Afterward, she started on the cousin, but he couldn't seem to get an erection. She glanced down at her watch: 5:26. Startled by the time, she bit down anxiously and the cousin gave a brief howl of pain.

Marisol wasn't sure how to apologize. She didn't want to piss him off.

Unexpectedly, Jay said, "Feels good, huh?"

"Yeah." The cousin gave a moan of feigned pleasure.

He and Marisol made a split second of eye contact, then the two of them began to work together. He moaned more and moved faster. She made gagging sounds, although his penis was soft in her mouth.

"*Eso!*" Jay said, as if cheering an athletic event. "Bang it right in her face!"

After a few moments, the cousin faked ejaculation, then quickly zipped his fly over his flaccid penis.

Marisol shook his hand off the back of her head, and made a big show of spitting, as she turned to run the six blocks home.

After a quarter mile, she stopped at a red light. Her chest burned and she could feel raw blisters on her feet in the cheap, pinching shoes, a size too small. She looked at her watch. 5:37. When the light changed, she began to sprint. At home, she shoved the shoes under her bed so her uncle wouldn't call her a slut.

By the time he walked in the door at 6:03, Cristina was no longer hysterical, and Marisol was gargling with Scope for the fifth time, feeling the alcohol and camphor mint burn in the back of her throat.

Chapter 13

The fourth floor of the María de la Vega building held the clinic's administrative operations center. It consisted of Marisol's office, a file room, and an outer reception area. Marisol's assistant, Serena, had her desk there, and was always managing several crises at once.

It was Thursday afternoon, and Marisol and Serena had just met with several funders.

"You didn't just impress those women," Serena said. "You freaking dazzled them."

"I hope we get the grant," Marisol said. They stood among the bustle of the outer office.

"How could they turn us down?" Serena asked. "You're wearing your invincibility shoes."

"Marisol has invincibility shoes?" Raul Barrios asked, suddenly next to her. He wore the clinic T-shirt in turquoise, and it fit him nicely. He smelled like coconut oil and wood spice.

"I knew Marisol was some sort of superhero," he said. "But I didn't realize she actually had a costume."

Marisol blushed. How could you explain something like perfect shoes to a guy—a straight guy?

"It's nothing," Marisol said.

"Just so long as you keep them on," Serena said. "Jeremy VanDyke should be here soon."

"VanDyke?" Raul asked.

Marisol shrugged. "Exciting, huh? He could really set us up."

Raul nodded. "I'll leave you to it." He walked toward the stairwell.

Why did she feel the need to explain herself to him? It wasn't any of his business what she did with VanDyke or anyone else.

Marisol headed for the hallway behind her office, and slipped through the hidden door. In what she called the "gift room," she prepared the girls for display. Thug Woofer got photos via text, but a billionaire got VIP service.

"No, Kim," Marisol said. "That fringe thing is too busy. I want you girls in solid colors."

The gift gallery's windows were blacked out, and the illumination came from track lighting and colored spotlights. Marisol planned to put Jody on the top platform, Tyesha on the second one, and Kim on the lower one, with the least flattering lighting and lingerie.

"Jody, try the dark wig," Marisol said. "In the tabloids he's always with brunettes."

Kim's brick-red halter and booty shorts looked dull compared to Jody's black patent-leather demi-bra and thong, and Tyesha's royal blue bustier and garter belt.

"Climb up, girls. He's due any minute."

"He'll be late," Jody said.

"How do you know?" Marisol asked.

"I used to whip a billionaire at the dominatrix dungeon," Jody said. "He'd come an hour late, pay a fee, and have me whip him extra for tardiness. It's part of the game."

Next to Tyesha, a phone began to buzz. "Kim, your cell's ringing."

"No calls right now," Marisol snapped.

"Okay." Tyesha silenced the phone. "It said MPH. Are you considering a master's degree in public health?"

"MPH?" Jody asked.

"I wasn't gonna pick up," Kim said.

"He has your new number?" Jody demanded.

"Apparently not a master's in public health," Marisol said.

"Mr. Potato Head," Kim said. "This old guy client."

"Clients pay," Jody said. "This guy is always looking to get some free time."

"He says he's in love with me," Kim said.

"They always say that shit when they want free time," Tyesha said.

"He once gave me a five-hundred-dollar tip," Kim said.

"Years ago," Jody said. "Since then, he acts like he prepaid."

"Are you jealous?" Kim asked, pressing close to Jody.

"No," Jody said. "I'm pissed."

"Don't be mad," Kim said, running a finger down Jody's chest.

"I'm pretty cute while I'm angry, right?" Jody said, pulling Kim into a kiss.

"Speaking of cute," Tyesha said, changing the subject. "Marisol, when are you gonna get a piece of Raul?"

"And you need to hurry," Kim said. "Because Nalissa is trying to take your man."

"He's not my man," Marisol said.

"What's wrong with you, Marisol?" Tyesha asked. "He's a walking advertisement for fucking."

"I gotta say." Jody was pulling the brunette wig on. "I'm one hundred percent gay, but I would totally fuck him."

"Excuse me?" Kim said.

"If I was single," Jody said.

"He's just an old friend," Marisol said.

"Bullshit," Kim said. "You gave him the real smile."

"I saw that, too," Jody said. "At the gala."

"Every pro knows the difference," Kim said.

"Psychobiological research shows that you can fake the mouth-smile part," Tyesha said. "But when you're really feeling it, there's an involuntary muscle movement around the eyes."

"Moving right along," Marisol said. "Tyesha, Thug Woofer told you to name your price. What's it gonna be?"

"Don't sell yourself short," Kim said to Tyesha. "Tell Thug Woofer you'll fuck him for a quarter million dollars."

Marisol shook her head. "Thug Woofer won't get you into the 'Platinum Pussy' club. I checked his financials. Ten grand, max."

"You don't want money," Jody said, adjusting her breasts in the bra for maximum cleavage. "You want something better than money. Something personal. Like his signature Woof chain."

"I don't want any of that shit," Tyesha said as she pulled up the fishnet stockings. "What am I gonna tell my grandkids? I once fucked a rapper for a gold chain that says 'Woof'?"

"If it's not about the money, make him take you to something special," Kim said. "Like his album release party. And get your picture in the paper."

"Yes!" She high-fived Kim, and turned to Marisol.

"No, Tyesha," Marisol said, pulling a piece of lint from Jody's waistband. "This is a cash business. I can't take a percentage off a picture in the paper."

Tyesha looked up from adjusting her garter belt. "Then gimme his number, and I'll negotiate."

Marisol stood up and turned to Tyesha. "I said no. He's off the list."

"What if he pays your fee?" Tyesha asked.

Marisol put her hands on her hips. "Why have I told him no if you wanted me to book him?"

"Because," Tyesha said, "I want the dynamic to be more like a real date."

"Which is precisely the point," Marisol said. "We don't date the clients."

"But it's Thug Woofer," Tyesha said. "The number-one rapper in America. Can you make an exception?"

"And he's public enemy number one on our client list this week," Marisol said. "No exception."

"But, Marisol—"

"Look, Tyesha," Marisol said. "New York has eight million people. Forty-seven percent men. Twenty-six percent of those are in your age bracket. Seventy-five percent of them are unmarried. Three quarters of a million men. And you want the one who was already an asshole to you?"

"Is she doing the math in her head?" Kim asked Jody.

"I only date black men," Tyesha said.

"Fine," Marisol said. "New York is twenty-five percent black. A hundred and eighty-five thousand men."

"Ten percent are gay," Jody put in.

"Eleven percent," Kim said. "We've been recruiting."

"No," Jody said, laughing. "We've just been setting a sterling example."

"Okay, ten percent are gay," Marisol said. "A hundred and sixty-six thousand. Date one who's not a client."

"She's definitely doing the math in her head," Kim said. "Damn."

"Most of those guys are struggling," Tyesha said. "And the successful ones don't want a ghetto girl. I cussed Woof out and expected he'd move on to the next chick.

But if he keeps calling it's because he saw the real me and he's still interested."

Marisol shook her head. "If you wanna try the 'do you love me even though I've been a hoe?' experiment, it's not gonna be with a client."

"Wow," Kim said to Tyesha. "Marisol is officially cockblocking you."

"Call it whatever you want," Marisol said.

"Marisol's right," Jody said. "He's a dick. Forget him."

Before Tyesha could speak, her phone sounded an e-mail alert.

"Phones off," Marisol said.

Tyesha muted the phone. "What the fuck," she said.

"A client?" Kim asked.

"The public health department," Tyesha said, laughing. "I put a résumé on file with them when I was job hunting last year."

"A year later?" Kim asked.

"Dear public health department." Tyesha fake-typed. "Please kiss my black ass. I am now an escort fucking one client a week, and making better money than any of your sorry-ass jobs."

Kim laughed. "You should sign it, 'One of the smartest bitches on the block.'"

"Ladies—" Marisol began.

"That's right," Jody said. "We're not bitches, we're hoes." All three girls high-fived.

Marisol was glad her escorts felt good about their choices, but her own years as a sex worker weren't high-five material.

The intercom buzzed.

Marisol rushed over to answer. "Hurry up and get into place."

"Elvis is in the building." Serena's crackly voice came through the intercom.

* * *

When he knocked, it was forty-five minutes after the appointed time.

"Mr. VanDyke." Marisol opened the door. "Welcome to the gift gallery." She ushered him in with a smile that didn't quite extend to her eyes.

VanDyke barely stepped into the room. "Lovely," he said, glancing at the women. "Can we go to your office?"

Marisol supposed that the man who could make billion-dollar corporate takeover decisions in two minutes could decide between three women in two seconds.

"Certainly," Marisol said. "Serena will get you the donation paperwork, and I'll be right with you."

When the door had closed behind him, Marisol turned off the spotlights and opened the mirrored sliding doors of a walk-in closet. It held a selection of wig heads that ranged from green bobs to honey-blond Afros.

Kim unhooked the long straight ponytail to reveal her own hair, dark and shoulder-length. Tyesha pulled off her wig to reveal cornrows.

As Marisol walked back to her office, Nalissa, the eager young redhead, approached her. "Serena had to go run an errand, but she said this grant proposal needs your signature ASAP."

She handed Marisol a pen and murmured, "Look, I know you got a lot of different kind of projects happening. Whatever you got going, if you need more hands on deck, I'm your girl."

Marisol met her eyes. "Good to know," she said. "Now, run that down to the front desk, please."

Marisol hustled to greet her VIP guest in the inner office. Once inside, she went to the liquor cabinet behind her desk.

"A drink, Mr. VanDyke?"

"Scotch straight-up," he said.

She poured her best Scotch into a wide-mouth glass and handed it to him on a coaster. He drank.

She poured herself a glass of rum and sat down.

"So, which young lady appeals to you?" she asked.

"You," he said.

"Excuse me?" Marisol blinked several times.

"Ten times hotter, even fully clothed, in glasses, and with no makeup." He sipped his drink. "Revise that. Mascara and a light lip gloss."

"I know what you're doing," Marisol said. "Your chapter on negotiation. 'Throw in a curveball. Put your competitor off-balance.' "

"I want the woman who reads my books and devises brilliant, unethical, scandalous applications for my theories. The woman who has New York eating out of her hand," he said. "You netted a quarter million at that benefit, didn't you?"

"Six hundred thousand," she said.

"Money talk is foreplay to me," he said. "Name your price."

"I don't have a price, Mr. VanDyke." She smiled her standard donor smile.

"I do my homework, Ms. Rivera. You've provided this service in the past."

"And you started in the mailroom. We've both moved up."

"Fifty thousand?"

Marisol raised her eyebrows. "A tempting offer. But do you have a second choice?"

"I don't do second choices, Ms. Rivera. First choice or no deal. You can make it seventy-five. Call my assistant. It's been a pleasure." He walked out of the office, leaving the quarter-full glass with a complete set of fingerprints on it.

After VanDyke left, Marisol went to the downstairs kitchenette for coffee.

"Hey, boss lady," Raul said, stepping in. "How's your evening?"

Her pulse quickened. "Busy," she said.

"Tonight's my last shift," he said. "I got a consulting job."

"Thanks so much for your help," she said, as Serena came running down the hallway.

"Marisol," the young woman screamed, waving her cell phone. "We got a huge plug from Delia Borbón on *New York Entertainment Roundup*."

"That's fantastic," Raul said.

Serena grabbed Marisol in a tight hug, while their phones kept beeping.

"We're trending on 'Give Mo Money dot com,'" Serena said, jumping up and down. "The story's been up twenty minutes, but already our online endowment donations are nearly fifty thousand dollars!"

As Serena ran from the room, Marisol screamed and threw her arms around Raul.

He seemed startled, then relaxed into the embrace. As he looked down at her, she noticed the softness of his lips. She inhaled the cool, mint, and coffee smell of his breath. He leaned in close—their faces were inches apart.

She tensed.

Raul stepped back. "Sorry," he said. "I was just so happy. For the clinic."

He dug his hands into his pockets. "I don't want you to get the wrong impression about me. I didn't volunteer just to hit on you." He shook his head. "I mean—

you know how I feel about you. But that's not what I'm here for."

"What are you here for, Raul?" Marisol asked, exasperated.

"Since I left the NYPD, I just felt bitter," Raul said. "And lost. Then Matty invited me to the gala, and I saw you and I saw what you were doing for the community. I just wanna be a part of it."

"We appreciate your help," Marisol said again.

"I respect you," Raul said. "You were happy and you hugged me. I read the moment wrong."

Marisol shrugged.

"So that's about all the awkwardness I can take." He chuckled. "I'm gonna go finish out my shift. Congratulations. Again."

She ached as he walked away, but men were not part of the plan.

As a kid, she had observed her mother with boyfriend after boyfriend. They had all behaved like Raul at first. But once her mother let them move in—things got foul. They started cheating or treated her *mami* like a maid. Some were the yelling type, but just about all were controlling and jealous.

At the clinic in Chelsea, Marisol had had a fling with a Honduran food delivery guy from the German deli. It was sexy for a week. Drama for three months. She hadn't been able to eat sauerkraut since.

Marisol knew how Latino men were. That was why she kept things strictly uptown. Plenty of guys had thick arms and long eyelashes uptown. Guys with no complications, who didn't volunteer in her clinic, and who certainly weren't ex-cops. If only she'd met Raul uptown. She'd sink her teeth into one of those shoulders, tasting him down to the bone.

* * *

As he left the clinic, Raul heard someone calling him. He turned around to see Nalissa waving.

She ran and caught up to him. "A shame it's your last day," she said.

"It's been great helping out," Raul said, and the two of them crossed the street.

"You know what's an even bigger shame," she said. "The way Marisol takes you for granted, *papi*. Like you wouldn't be the best thing to happen to her."

"Nah," he said. "We're just friends."

"You light up when she walks in the room," Nalissa said.

"I just have so much respect for her," he said. "For everything she's accomplished."

Nalissa put her hand on his shoulder as they crossed another street. "Accomplishment won't keep you warm at night."

Raul shook his head. "This is my building. You be safe getting home, okay?"

He unlocked his front door.

"Let me come in," Nalissa said, pressing up against him. "If you was with me, I would treat you so good, *papi*. I would make you forget all about Marisol Rivera."

She leaned forward and kissed him. Raul felt the warmth of her body—the eager openness of the invitation—and kissed her back. He opened the door with one arm and pulled Nalissa inside with the other, his tongue still in her mouth.

Chapter 14

The moment after his orgasm, it felt wrong. All wrong. How old was this girl? Twenty-five? Thank God he'd used protection.

They lay on the living room rug. His shoes were off, and his pants were down around his ankles. Her bra was off, and her skirt was hiked around her waist.

He didn't know what to say.

"Looks like I only made you forget her for a few minutes," she said with a laugh. But then she rolled over, halfway onto him, her full breasts warm against his chest. "It might take a little more time than I thought. Wanna try again sometime soon?"

"Nalissa . . ." he began. He slid out from under her and sat up, the carpet scratching against his bare ass. "You are a beautiful, sexy—"

She cut him off. "Save the awkward speech." She stood and pulled on her clothes. "My ego's bruised, but I'll recover."

Yet as she dressed, he could see a bitterness in the line of her mouth. When his front door shut behind her, he sank back down on the carpet. What the fuck had he been thinking?

* * *

"I've been picking up guys in bars again," Marisol confessed to Eva the following night. They were in a Village sushi restaurant.

Eva stopped mid bite of her tempura appetizer. "And using condoms, right?"

Marisol nodded. "I didn't escape my twenties HIV-negative just to get infected from some recreational fucking." She didn't mention that he looked like Raul. It would just get Eva started on the open-your-heart bullshit.

"Recreational fucking?"

"I just need to blow off steam," Marisol said, drinking sake.

"Marisol, I've been noticing something about your sex life," Eva began.

"Uh-oh," Marisol said. "Here comes the talk."

"You've only chosen to have two kinds of sex in your adult life—the kind where you're in total control with a stranger or the kind where you're getting paid with a stranger."

"Strangers can be sexy," Marisol said. "Sometimes I just want an uncomplicated fuck, Eva. You wanna send me to a convent?"

"Jews don't do convents," Eva said. "And why always uptown? Why always immigrants?"

"What's wrong with immigrants?" Marisol asked. "My mother was an immigrant."

"Mine, too," Eva said. "I just wonder if it makes you feel more in control because you're a citizen and they're not."

"Look," Marisol said. "Puerto Rico is a third world colony. We've all got American citizenship whether we like it or not."

"Fine," Eva said. "You fuck any Puerto Ricans?"

Marisol laughed. "It's not like I ask to see their passports. You have no idea what you're talking about."

"Fine," Eva said. "I counsel sex workers all day, plenty of them Puerto Rican, but I don't know shit about Latina women who have control issues in bed."

"You make me sound like a cliché," Marisol said. "I was abused and chose to be a sex worker, and now I have issues."

"No, Marisol. Other sex workers can have sex with people they trust," Eva said. "Look at Kim and Jody. They have sex with guys for money, and then they have sex with each other for love. You don't trust anybody in bed."

"Well, I might be fucking somebody else I don't trust," Marisol said. "VanDyke says he wants me to do the call, personally."

"Out of the question," Eva said. "Tell him to kiss your Puerto Rican ass."

"He offered seventy-five thousand dollars."

"No shit?" Eva asked. "Are you still attracted to him?"

"I don't know," Marisol said. "Half the attraction was the glamour of being with somebody that rich. Being seen with him or having our names linked in the press. This way he's just a client, and it's confidential."

"Have you talked to Tyesha about it?" Eva asked. "Or Jody or Kim?"

Marisol shook her head.

Eva set down her chopsticks. "Here's what I think," she said. "If you wanted to do this, you'd have told Tyesha. Then she would have high-fived you and said, 'Yeah, my girl got a seventy-five-thousand-dollar solid-gold pussy!'"

Marisol laughed, nearly choking on her sake. "That's exactly what she would say. But solid gold is a hundred thousand. Two hundred fifty thousand is platinum."

"Tyesha would cosign you having sex with him. But I cosign setting your own limits. And you didn't go to Tyesha, you came to me."

Marisol shrugged. "I just haven't had time to talk to them."

"Bullshit me all you want," Eva said. "But don't bullshit yourself."

"It's not that deep," Marisol said.

"So I'm giving you permission," Eva said. "You can say no to seventy-five thousand if you don't want to have sex with him."

"I did wanna have sex with him," Marisol said. "Until he wanted to pay me. Even though I need the money."

"Your choice," Eva said.

"I know," Marisol said. "I'm only going to do it if we can figure out how to solicit an *additional donation*."

"What?" Eva asked. She lowered her voice. "You would try to heist VanDyke? That's a suicide mission. How is it gonna save the clinic for you to be in prison?"

"I think I could pull it off," Marisol said.

"One of the world's biggest stereotypes is that all sex workers are thieves," Eva said. "You think you won't be the first one he suspects?"

"I have a plan for that—" Marisol said.

"Which I don't want to hear about." Eva gulped some sake. "VanDyke is a notorious security fanatic. A heist is way too dangerous."

"He's also obsessed with his privacy, so he'll turn off the cameras if a sex worker is coming over."

"Cameras are the least of it," Eva said. "He has so much money, he could record the DNA of everyone who walks through his door. You're never gonna heist him and get away with it. Just take the seventy-five thousand."

"If we play it right, he could be our biggest donor

ever," Marisol said. "We could pay off all the real estate debt. I can get it up for that."

"Marisol, this is going way too far," Eva said. "When you started the escort service, I agreed, because I know as an attorney that it's a legal gray area. But I never approved of the heists. You've hit nearly all the Ivy Alpha guys. Let's quit while we're ahead."

"But we're not ahead," Marisol said. "And we keep getting away with it."

"We haven't gotten away with it yet," Eva said. "Let's see how the IRS likes all this unexplained cash next tax season."

"I have a plan for that, too," Marisol said.

"Listen to yourself," Eva said. "*I* have a plan. *I* have a plan. *We* are supposed to be partners. *We* had a plan. To rob a couple of the assholes from the Ivy Alpha scandal because Kim's guy took her to parties there. You said you could use the same safe MO until that big grant comes through in the spring."

"And what about next year?" Marisol asked. "If *we* can see a chance to set the clinic up for life, *we* should take it. So I am. *Punto*."

Marisol's phone rang. She motioned for Eva to wait and picked it up.

She listened to Thug Woofer's manager for a minute, then told him to put the rapper on the phone.

Woof came on the line and asked, "What's her price?"

"She doesn't want to see you again," Marisol said.

"Tell her I apologize for being rude," he said. "Ask if that changes anything."

"Mr. Johnson," Marisol said. "This is an escort service, not a game of telephone. You had your shot. You blew it, so move on. Candi will be moving on, as well. She's not a sex worker full-time. In fact, she's getting her master's degree."

"For real?" he asked.

"See?" Marisol said. "Unlike your lyrics, not all women are hoes, and even hoes aren't hoes all the time. So if you'll excuse me—"

"Wait," Woof said. "Ask if she wanna come to the Oscars as my date."

Marisol paused. "I'll get back to you if the answer is yes. Otherwise, please don't call again."

She hung up and turned to Eva. "Thug Woofer said to tell Tyesha he wants to take her to the Oscars? I'm no answering service. I should have told Tyesha no from the start. 'No, I don't know any good escort gigs. Keep waitressing and I'll hire you at the clinic after you graduate.'"

"Bullshit," Eva said. "Tyesha was determined to make some fast cash from sex work. If you had let her go work for somebody else, you'd be putting in just as much time backseat driving."

"No, I wouldn't," Marisol said.

"I can see you now," Eva said. "'Tyesha! Tyesha! Did they show you the guy's picture for approval? Did they check the bad trick list? Did they give you a panic alarm?'"

Marisol laughed.

"You'd be doing all the work and someone else would be getting the commission," Eva said. "No one is gonna guarantee that girl's safety like you."

"But now she's interested in dating a client," Marisol said. "At worst it's unsafe. At best it's a big pain in my ass."

"Dating a client is always a bad idea," Eva said. "But you're considering servicing a client, even after you quit. Tyesha's smart and stubborn, just like you. Frankly, I think this VanDyke job is gonna be the ruin of us."

* * *

VanDyke's offer looped in Marisol's mind. Seventy-five thousand could cover several mortgage payments and months of payroll. She just needed to eat a nice dinner and fuck a guy. Couldn't she spare a fuck for Jeremy VanDyke? Best of all, he would write a check she could declare on her taxes, not add to the pile of cash to be laundered.

She used "PCD" as a code for "private cash donation" on her internal spreadsheets to track the heist money. She had to establish a paper trail for the IRS that could explain all the stolen cash she'd been using to pay the mortgage for the past several months.

Late Sunday night, Marisol met with the team in her office.

"We need to plan the VanDyke job," Marisol said. "I haven't set up the escort call yet, because it might not be feasible."

"So which one of us is fucking the billionaire?" Jody asked.

"Unfortunately," Marisol said. "I'll be fucking the billionaire."

"He didn't like any of us?" Kim asked.

"He's a billionaire," Jody said. "They get off on buying things that aren't for sale."

"And hopefully he's predictable in other ways," Marisol said. "I've researched his business model. Rumor has it that when he's trying to gain control over a company, he offers a million in cash to avoid a hostile takeover. And VanDyke doesn't report it to the IRS, so the competitor can keep it free and clear of taxes. But where does he store the cash? Apparently, he doesn't trust his employees enough to have an office safe."

"Isn't his apartment connected to his corporate headquarters?" Kim asked.

"With a skywalk," Marisol said. "And he covers both with a private security army."

"You think the cash is in the home office?" Tyesha asked.

"How else could he manage it?" Marisol asked. "And I confirmed that his offices overseas used Superlative safes."

"So that's probably what he uses at home," Jody said.

"Here's the setup," Marisol said. "VanDyke is notoriously reclusive in his love life. The press never knows who he's dating until she sells her story to the tabloids."

"You'll probably go to his place?" Kim said.

"Yeah, but it's like a fortress," Marisol said. "VanDyke has higher security than anything we've seen."

She turned her laptop around so the other three could see the Superlative safe specs. "We're only gonna get one shot at this," she said. "We can't use our usual two-visit MO."

"You'll do the job while you're doing VanDyke?" Tyesha asked.

"No," Marisol said. "I'll do VanDyke and still be there when you three hold us up at gunpoint."

"Gunpoint sounds good," Jody said.

"So he won't put you together with us," Kim said.

"I'll do the scared damsel act," Marisol said. "And you'll wear bodysuits to look like men."

"Bodysuits?" Kim asked.

"Muscle suits that zip up," Marisol said. "Broad shoulders. Thick arms. You'll have to bind your breasts down."

"I suppose we can't tell VanDyke that he's fucking a brilliant criminal mastermind?" Tyesha said.

"Probably not," Marisol said, and they bumped fists.

"But this plan graduates us from grand larceny to armed robbery," Marisol said.

"I like guns," Jody said.

"Guns change everything," Marisol said. "Getting caught means mandatory minimum sentences and maximum-security consequences."

"I hate jail," Kim said. "Can't we just use a little of that fund-raiser money?"

"Not from the endowment," Tyesha said. "If Marisol embezzled those funds, alarms would go off."

"We're just scraping by," Marisol said. "I've maxed out my own credit cards, and borrowed from donors. The debt is racking up, and the escort income isn't consistent. Even the burglary cash just barely makes ends meet. I've done payroll late a couple of times to make sure we wouldn't miss a mortgage payment. If we trigger foreclosure proceedings, we're fucked. We'd have to close our doors."

"I won't let that happen," Tyesha said.

"Me, neither," Kim said. "Not if the clinic is on the line."

"But the risk might be for nothing," Marisol said. "We'll be going in blind. Which is why I'm prepping Kim for several possibilities."

"I've been practicing my ass off since last week," Kim said. "I can crack the Superlative safe in four minutes."

"And the other three brands?" Marisol asked.

"Two minutes or less," Kim said.

"Good," Marisol said. "Apparently, if you can crack these top four brands, all the other manufacturers follow the same basic design."

"For the record," Jody said, "Kim hasn't been practicing her ass all the way off, because I got some ass today."

"Focus," Tyesha said, and the four women huddled around Marisol's laptop.

* * *

The next day, Marisol was writing thank-you notes to gala donors when Nalissa walked into her office with a package.

"Front desk sent this up," Nalissa said. "And I wanna let you know I'm in level two of entrepreneurship."

A glance told Marisol the package wasn't urgent.

"And I started driving for my uncle's car service," Nalissa went on. "So keep me in mind if you ever need a ride, okay?"

Serena buzzed the intercom, and Marisol picked up the phone. "Call for you," Serena said. "Raul Barrios."

Marisol felt a little catch in her stomach. "Tell him to hold."

She turned to Nalissa. "I should take this."

Marisol closed the office door and took a breath. The thought of Raul brought back the almost kiss, and the ache she carried around. But things had improved since he'd stopped volunteering at the clinic. She could handle this. She picked up. "Great to hear from you. How are you settling into the new apartment?" she asked.

"The place is great," Raul said. "But I step out my door and everything's different. Nobody in my building speaks Spanish."

"It's the little things," Marisol said.

"Like the park down the street," Raul said. "They took out the domino tables where my dad played on Sundays. Now it's a dog park."

Marisol sucked her teeth. "I remember when dogs didn't get their own park."

Raul laughed. "Listen," he said. "I know you're busy, but I have something work-related."

"What's up?" Marisol asked.

"The mayor and the cops are developing a community liaison committee," he said. "Every time there's a problem, they develop a committee of community lead-ers to advise the police. Not that they take the advice, but it's good to get your two cents in, you know?"

"Absolutely," Marisol agreed. "What's the next step?"

"There's a meeting Thursday on how to apply," Raul said. "I can get you an invitation."

Marisol pulled out her calendar.

"Brown bag lunch at City Hall," Raul said. "Noon."

"I'd love to," Marisol said. "See you Thursday."

Chapter 15

Marisol came in late the next morning, having been up until 2 a.m. working on grant reports. She found messages from Serena that 1) she had missed a funder meeting, 2) she needed to produce financials for a youth/health grant, 3) the heater was acting up, and 4) Tyesha was waiting in her office.

"I been calling you," Tyesha said when Marisol opened the office door. "How can I get you to reconsider about Thug Woofer? They just announced his next album release party."

Marisol blinked at her through a haze. It was like senior year in high school when she was secretly doing sex work and her best friend, Gladys, would ask what dress she was going to wear to the prom.

"You agreed to this policy when you started working here," Marisol said as she turned on her laptop, then put a hand in front of the heating vent to see whether warm air was coming out.

"You said there were exceptions to the rules," Tyesha argued.

"Not this one," Marisol said. "I'm a madam, not a matchmaker."

"It's not even about Thug Woofer," Tyesha said. "It's the principle of the thing."

"Fine," Marisol said, closing her office door. "You want to talk principles, let's go."

"How come I can't decide to date a client?" Tyesha asked. "But you can decide to rob a client? You always said their corrupt CEO friends were fair game, but not clients. Yet now you're robbing VanDyke? I'm all-in for this operation, but I need to know that it's not just gonna change on your whim. What's the bottom line?"

"The bottom line is"—Marisol searched for the words—"is that I'm sick of playing nice when these motherfuckers are ruthless. I've studied VanDyke. He had massive sweatshop operations in Asia. But after some bad publicity, he now owns them through a shell corporation. He became a billionaire by screwing people over in other countries. Like he couldn't just pick a girl in the escort service. He knows I need money, and he's using that as leverage to pry my legs open. So many of these assholes don't play fair, not in business, not in bed. So I'm gonna stop playing by the rules."

"Like your rule that no girl has to have sex if she doesn't want to?" Tyesha asked. "You quit the business. You obviously don't want to do the VanDyke date."

"That's the cost of being the boss," Marisol said. "But the no-dating-clients rule is firm. We got enough girls coming in to the clinic beat up. Dulce's on the mend. And Jerry finally stopped coming around. I don't want you to be the girlfriend that Thug Woofer beats into the hospital."

Tyesha's mouth contracted. "You act like I can't handle myself."

Marisol sighed. "I obviously don't say this enough," she said. "I care about you." She put an arm around

Tyesha. "I saw something in you from that first time when I spoke at Columbia. Of course I know you can handle yourself. That's why I picked you to take over the clinic. Because I trust you with my mother's good name, and the well-being of all the sex workers in Manhattan. And when you're in charge, date all the rappers or fuck all the clients or rob them or both if that's what's needed to keep the place going. Okay?" Marisol squeezed Tyesha's shoulder.

Tyesha laughed and rolled her eyes. "Okay."

On Thursday, Marisol slipped into the City Hall meeting room with a takeout salad. She sat in an aisle seat halfway back, and peeled off her suit jacket to reveal her short-sleeved green silk blouse. Ten minutes into the presentation, Raul walked in.

He nodded to a few people and walked across the room to sit beside her.

They were built like reverse triangles. He had broad shoulders and she had full hips. Their bodies made contact at the widest points of both.

As she ate, their arms brushed against each other. She could barely pay attention to the speaker. Raul opened a takeout container of *maduros*—sweet fried plantains. A fragrant cloud of fried sugar and garlic escaped.

"Want some?" he asked.

She speared one with her fork, enjoying the tang of the fruit and the savory spices.

"Where'd you get this?" she whispered.

"My kitchen, *mujer*," he said.

"You cook?"

"Don't stereotype Latino men," he said. "You need to come over for dinner."

"You need to give me another *maduro*," she said.

Just as she went to spear the *platano*, he yanked the container away without taking his eyes off the speaker.

Marisol let out a giggle, and a nearby woman looked irritated.

Marisol gripped Raul's arm and went for another plantain.

Again, he moved the container out of her reach.

"Don't play with me, *chico,*" she said. "I will stab you with this fork."

Now he suppressed a laugh. "Assault on an ex-cop," he whispered. "Calling all cars."

"Shhhhh!" the woman near Marisol hissed.

"You're gonna get us in trouble," Marisol said.

"I'm just eating my lunch," Raul said. "What's wrong? Your gentrified salad isn't doing it for you?"

"Hand over the *platano* and nobody gets hurt," Marisol murmured.

As the woman shushed them again, the room filled with polite applause. Marisol grabbed the container and wolfed down three *maduros* before Raul could grab it back.

"That was very unprofessional," the woman said as she squeezed past them out to the aisle.

The two of them cracked up.

"I'll go pick us up a couple of applications," Raul said. "Guard those plantains, okay?"

When he came back, Raul looked down at the empty container and then at Marisol. "What happened?"

"I moved them to a more secure location," she said.

"Your stomach?"

"What could be more secure?"

He shook his head and handed her the application.

"On a serious note," she said. "Thanks so much for

inviting me. A committee like this would be a good move for the clinic."

"You'd be great on something like this," he said.

"Eva Feldman would be the one," Marisol said as they walked into the hallway.

"Why not you?" he asked as they put their jackets back on. "You've got the charisma and charm to really make a difference."

She shook her head. "You know this committee isn't about making real change. It would just piss me off. Eva's the patient one."

"You're probably right," he said. "But after that gala event, I think you could do anything. You got wealthy Manhattan to come out and give money to Lower East Side sex workers? You got Delia Borbón and Jeremy VanDyke to make an appearance?"

Marisol laughed. "Not all by myself. I got the best team in the world." She didn't mention some of her escort clients from whom she'd called in favors.

"And she's modest," Raul said.

They walked down the steps to the street.

"Where you headed?" he asked. "I'm catching the train home."

Marisol looked at the slow traffic and decided to take the subway.

"You going home or back to the clinic?" he asked, as they descended the stairs.

"Same thing," she said. "My apartment is above the clinic."

"Like a bodega," Raul said. "Living above the shop. I love it."

"Can't beat the commute," she said. They swiped their MetroCards.

"Marisol, you got that local style, immigrant hustle,

but you run a multimillion-dollar clinic. I read your report. Plus you got billionaires sweating you."

"I wouldn't say sweating me," she said. They came out of the tunnel to the platform.

"Come on, Marisol," he said. "You're having meetings with VanDyke, when you wouldn't even have coffee with me. You still think of me as your friend's little brother."

"It's not like that," Marisol said. "He could be a major funder."

"I get it," Raul agreed. "If I was running a clinic and VanDyke came through, I'd smile like a toothpaste model and give him my card, too."

"So you understand," Marisol said.

"No. I'm jealous," he said. "Even though intellectually I understand that you put the clinic first. He can offer a lot to an executive director. But I'm trying to offer something to you, as a woman."

Marisol didn't know what to say. The train pulled up and they boarded.

"*Oye*," he said, "I'm not hanging around because you're the cause of the day or because I need a little Latin dish on my menu. I'm hoping you'll carve out a little space in your life for real."

"I'm flattered, Raul," she said. "But I don't carve out space for anything but work."

"Has it ever occurred to you that a supportive guy could be an asset?" he asked. "That he might share your vision and help make it happen?"

"It never worked like that in my family," Marisol said. "The men cut out and left the women to hold everything together."

"But that was our parents' generation," Raul said. "Your *abuelo*? Did your grandfather cut out, too?"

"No," Marisol said. "He just died."

"But was he down for the fam when he was alive?"

"He died before I was born," Marisol said. "But yeah, I heard he was a family man."

"I'm like that," Raul said. "Your clinic is one of the best things I see around here. Score one for the old hood."

"If you're so down for the hood, why become a cop?" Marisol asked. "Back in the day we hated cops."

"I was naïve," he said. "Every time cops hassled us, I wished I was looking at somebody brown. I thought I could be that guy. Turns out, it's still a white-boy network."

"How can you say that?" Marisol asked. "You still hang with your white ex-partner."

"We don't hang," Raul said. "He came to the gala to get me to consult on a case. I told him I'm through with cop shit."

Marisol glanced up to see that theirs was the next stop. "That guy fucking smells like a cop," she said.

"I know," Raul agreed. "But he had my back when shit went down at NYPD."

"What the hell happened?" Marisol asked.

"I saw some white cops assault this black kid," Raul said. "He was no Boy Scout, but they beat him into a coma. I knew my cop days were numbered. I wasn't gonna fall in line with that. At first they didn't know I'd seen. But then they tried to play it like, '*oh, ha-ha, those crazy black guys*.' Like my grandfather wasn't the same color as the kid."

"So you snitched?" Marisol said.

"I filed a report and they retaliated," Raul said. "First they would leave me without backup. I almost got killed, but Matty had my back—almost got himself killed, too. Then they framed me for stealing drugs from the evidence room and I got fired."

"How'd you win the case?" Marisol asked.

"Kid in the coma died," Raul said. "When it became murder, one of the cops turned. The department cut a deal. They all got fired but no criminal charges. I got a settlement and so did the kid's family. They offered my job back to me, or offered for me to consult on cases, but I turned them down. I never shoulda become a cop in the first place."

The train slowly squealed to a stop and the two of them exited.

As they walked up to the street, Marisol asked, "What do you wish you'd been?" She pushed through the fare gates. "Instead of a cop."

"Honestly?" Raul said. "I shoulda been a criminal."

Marisol laughed. "Really?"

They walked out into the weak winter sunlight.

"A stickup kid in the nineties," he said. "My crew woulda pulled a gun on every yuppie and hipster who tried to move in. I woulda sprayed graffiti on every 'our neighborhood is great' public campaign. I woulda convinced all the gentrifiers that this area was a dangerous, crack-infested, crazy junkie–filled death trap, and to buy elsewhere."

"You got a time machine?" Marisol asked. "It's not a bad plan." She walked by what had been her favorite bakery as a kid. Now it sold upscale maternity clothes.

"Like speaking Spanish to your folks in front of white people," Raul said. "I woulda kept our hood a beautiful secret among ourselves." He nodded toward the apartments they were approaching. "This is my building."

Marisol looked at the immaculate façade. "Not bad," she said. "Listen, Raul, it's been great—"

"Go out to dinner with me," he said, grabbing her hand. "I know a mom-and-pop *cafeteria* in the Bronx that makes a pork *mofongo* like we used to get down here. And the place isn't located between a poodle grooming salon and a vegan fondue restaurant with wild Alaskan organic pine needles. *Mami*, I'm telling you, nobody speaks English and the food will clog your arteries on the spot."

Although Marisol shook her head, she couldn't help smiling.

But the rules, an inner voice said. *Stick to the rules.*

The rules were in trouble. It was so easy to be with him. Not just the sexual chemistry, but the conversation. The fact that he could play with her, get her laughing. She had been able to use the ex-cop thing as a barricade, but something about him wishing he'd been the robber instead was threatening to melt her.

"I see how it is," Raul said. "You try to steal my *maduros,* but won't go out to dinner with me."

Marisol laughed. "Okay, fine. It's hard to get your arteries clogged with good *comida criolla* these days. But it's gotta be after I finish a big grant proposal on the fifteenth."

"Yes!" he said. "The hottest woman in Manhattan agrees to go out with me." He sang a salsa riff and twirled her by the hand.

"Gee." Marisol laughed. "I might have to go get the book *He's Just Not That Into You.*"

"You wanna say Friday after next?" Raul asked.

"Sure." She hadn't felt this light and playful since she was a kid. Since her mother was alive. "But don't get arrested as a stickup kid before then."

"It's too late for that," he said. "A crime wave can prevent gentrification, not cure it. Like that uptown crime wave going on now. You don't see anyone moving out."

"What uptown crime wave?" Marisol asked.

"The one Matty wanted me to consult on," Raul said.

"A string of robberies uptown they can't figure out. These guys slip in, crack the safe, walk out with the cash. Nobody sees a damn thing. The MO is the same, but they can't find a link. They want me because they know I'm good at making those connections. But like I said, I turned him down."

Marisol froze.

"Listen," he said. "I know you gotta get back to work. But you made my day by saying yes."

Marisol nodded and hugged him good-bye. As she walked toward the clinic, she began rehearsing *sorry-I-can't-make-it* lines in her head.

What had she been thinking? The rules were there for a reason.

Later that night, Marisol had another planning meeting in her office with Tyesha, Kim, and Jody.

"So what's the money on this hit?" Jody asked. "The usual?" She and Kim were on the black leather couch with their feet up on the coffee table.

"VanDyke is different," Marisol said. "Hopefully a game changer. So I'm proposing fifty percent off the top for the clinic, and we split the rest four ways."

"What's the math on that?" Kim asked.

"If we get a million, that's a hundred twenty-five thousand each."

"Sounds good," Tyesha said. She sat in the matching black leather recliner, tipped all the way back. "I'll be able to do public health full-time."

"I'll get my physical education degree and coach soccer," Jody said.

"Jody might've been a world-class athlete," Kim said, "if she hadn't got kicked outta the house in high school."

"You'll be the soccer mom?" Tyesha asked Kim.

"Maybe," Kim said. "But first I'll visit my family in Korea."

"For how long?" Jody asked.

"A year at least," Kim said.

"Then maybe I'll coach Korean girls' soccer," Jody said.

"You'd come with me?" Kim asked.

"I'm not gonna be without you for a whole year," Jody said. "But I don't speak Korean."

"Me neither," said Kim.

"We have to make sure you're not coaching soccer in prison," Marisol said. "So we'll sit on the cash a couple of months to see what the cops suspect."

"We can be pretty patient if we have a quarter million waiting for us." Jody turned to Kim. "Can't we, baby?"

"Yup," said Kim. "We have the patience of Job, like if Job was a sexy young hoe."

Tyesha laughed. "I think I missed that Bible verse."

Marisol hadn't officially agreed to go out with Jeremy VanDyke, but she was reading everything she could about his dating habits. It was frightening how much information she found online. There was a whole website dedicated to "bagging the billionaire bachelor," that gave women advice about how to make themselves over to attract rich guys. One of the billionaire bachelor profiles was VanDyke. He liked brunettes and the color turquoise. He preferred pearls to diamonds.

Another website boasted "virtual cribs," and showed floor plans and 3-D projections of celebrity houses. It was unclear how accurate they were, but Marisol printed out VanDyke's posted floor plans.

No wonder he was tight with his security, given the invasion of privacy and fascination with the mundane details of his life. VanDyke wasn't paranoid. People actually went through his garbage for story ideas.

The following Monday morning, she woke up in her usual Harlem hotel, hung over. She hailed a cab downtown. When she went to pay, she was shocked to find her wallet empty.

All her cards were there, except the MetroCard. Had the handsome, sandy-haired Colombian taken her cash? She dumped the change purse out in her lap and sorted through it. Where was the locket? She couldn't find the gold chain anywhere, but she found the round locket, hidden among the coins. She kissed the photo of Cristina and put it back in the wallet.

That motherfucker. What a hustler with his fresh-off-the-boat-naïveté act. She handed a credit card to the cab driver.

When she reached for her briefcase, it hit her. He could have taken her account books. Her ledger for the escort service and the heists.

She shuddered. It was one thing putting her own life at risk, but the whole team? The clients who trusted them? She'd risked the clinic for some lousy uptown dick.

"Miss," the cab driver said, "are you getting out here or what?"

Marisol blinked at the receipt in her hand. "Yes," she said. "Sorry."

She hustled up to her office and sat down at her desk. She was supposed to be the thief, not the mark. Plus Central Robbery was hiring consultants to investigate her heists? This Jeremy VanDyke thing was a bad idea.

That night, Marisol called a meeting of the team.

"We had a good week financially, thanks to Kim and Tyesha, who did a double for a new client who tips big."

"What about the VanDyke job?" Jody asked.

"About that," Marisol said. "The VanDyke job's off. We've got this other—"

"What do you mean 'off'?" Jody asked.

"As in not happening," Marisol said, her voice sharper than she had intended. "We're out of our league."

"But this job could set us up," Jody said.

"I been looking at co-op apartments in Brooklyn," Tyesha said.

"The job is dead," Marisol said. "End of story."

Jody's jaw was set. Tyesha had a strong frown line between her eyebrows, and she tapped one stiletto heel on the floor with a high clicking sound. Kim's eyes were wide, like a kid afraid she was in trouble.

"Look," Marisol said. "It's been stressful in the past few months with the heists—"

"It's not the heists, Marisol," Tyesha said. "It's your attitude."

Kim and Jody murmured agreement.

"My attitude?" Marisol asked. "Well, Tyesha, my attitude wasn't the problem when you were getting your jaw broken by a bad trick because you didn't have anyone to look out for you. And, Jody, my attitude wasn't the problem when I got you under-the-table chiropractic care because your dominatrix madam didn't give a fuck about your health and practically wrecked your shoulder. And, Kim, my attitude wasn't the issue when I got your juvenile records sealed so you could get off with probation on that arrest last year."

She stood and paced.

"There's a reason I'm the boss," she said. "I know when to push and when to back off. And I'm saying we back off on this."

"Fine," Tyesha said, her voice tight.

"I do realize . . ." Marisol said. "I've been stressed

lately. I'm trying not to let it affect me. But I'm calling the job off because if I'm not at the top of my game, we're fucked. I don't want us to go down like that."

She saw their faces settle into lines of resignation. "Let's focus on the jobs we have coming up, okay? Some high-end escort dates and the last Ivy Alpha heist."

"But how close are we to the edge, financially?" Tyesha asked.

"That's for me to worry about," Marisol said.

"No," Tyesha said. "You acted like the clinic wouldn't survive without the big score. So if we let VanDyke go, I wanna know where the clinic stands."

Marisol sighed. "The government cutbacks threw off our cash flow," she said. "We made a late mortgage payment last August."

"I remember," Jody said. "But you told us not to worry. We'd have to miss four in a year to be in any kind of trouble."

"Right," Marisol said. "But it's a fiscal year—July to June. Last October the big foundation check was late. And in November we got fined by the fire marshal for having too many women in the temporary shelter."

"Three late payments?" Kim asked.

"One more before June thirtieth and the credit union starts foreclosure proceedings?" Tyesha asked.

"Exactly," Marisol said. "If that happened, the entire mortgage would be due within ninety days. But it's almost March when we get the big foundation check. If we stick to the plan, we'll be fine, okay?" Marisol looked around. "Are we good?"

The women mumbled grudging assent.

"People get caught when they get greedy," Marisol said. "Remember, we're in this to save the clinic."

Tyesha sucked her teeth.

"You think I don't want the big payoff?" Marisol

asked. "Believe me. I do. I'm trying to run a multimillion-dollar organization off a five-year-old laptop where the spreadsheet program keeps crashing. I couldn't fucking work for most of the day, because Serena's trying to fix it. We all got a hundred goddamn problems money could cure. But stealing money won't help if we can't get away with it. We stick with simple jobs. And we've got one set up. Kim's favorite client took her to another party over the weekend."

"And she was gone all night," Jody said. "I hate sleeping alone."

"At first I couldn't find the safe," Kim said. "But the host was loaded, so he had to have one. Then I got the client so drunk he had to spend the night. The safe was in the study, and I cracked it with everyone sleeping. I didn't take anything, but I got the combination."

Marisol high-fived Kim and said, "I learned from the wife's Facebook page that the couple will be seeing an avant-garde concert at the Royal Flush Theater. We'll heist them Saturday. I'll be at the Valentine's Day ball for sexual health. Tyesha, you'll keep an eye on the couple. Jody, you'll hit the safe."

"Are you sure I'm the best person?" Jody asked.

"It's an easy hit," Marisol said. "I'd do it myself, but at the ball I'll be accepting an award for the clinic's HIV prevention work."

"Can Kim do the hit and I'll be lookout?" Jody asked.

"I spent the night at their house," Kim said. "Someone might recognize me."

"What about Tyesha?" Jody asked.

"Robbing while black?" Tyesha asked. "Anyone sees me in the building and they'll call the police on general principle."

Chapter 16

New York City had its own army of soldiers—the service professionals who bussed tables of half-eaten steaks, ironed and starched shirts, mixed the perfect martini, or offered an expert lap dance.

One branch of this army simply answered the phone. Some sat in bright lobbies with inviting décor and flirted with delivery guys. Others were the invisible army—answering service operators—many in Delhi, Singapore, and women's correctional facilities.

Marisol refused to outsource her answering service. She paid a monthly rate for the local number, plus a per-call fee, which had been zero since she'd started the service several years before.

On Saturday night, the answering service for the María de la Vega Health Clinic got their first call.

"Doctor's office, how can I help you?" They had been coached not to give the clinic's name.

"There's a girl here named Tammy who's lost," a male voice said.

"One moment," the operator said. "I'll page the nurse."

Marisol was sitting in her office, putting the final touches on her award acceptance speech, when her private cell phone rang.

Marisol answered it and scrambled for her purse. "I'll be right there to pick her up. I just need to get a cab."

Marisol hung up and pulled a nurse's uniform out of her cabinet and put it on. She grabbed a big pair of coke-bottle glasses and a fake hospital ID and ran out the door. Halfway down the stairs she did a 180-degree turn and ran back. She kicked off her invincibility heels and put on flat, rubber-soled shoes.

Twenty minutes later, she was at a luxury building on the Upper East Side where Kim had gone to a party with her client the weekend before.

Marisol was on the ground floor, shaking the hand of the security guard.

"Thank you," she said. "We looked everywhere."

"My pleasure," he said, and showed Marisol into a small office.

Jody sat on a couch wearing pigtails and a dazed expression.

"Tammy," Marisol said. "How did you get here?"

Jody shrugged and picked at her fingernails.

"Good thing she had that bracelet," the guard said. "Or I woulda called the cops." He turned the bracelet on Jody's wrist with the in-case-of-emergency call number.

Marisol pulled Jody up off the couch and guided her out of the office.

"Glad to help," he said, following them into the hallway, as Marisol walked Jody out the front door.

The two women walked down the block. The traffic crawled along beside them. As they turned the corner, Jody straightened up out of her slouch and met Marisol's eye.

"Dammit!" Jody said. "I was too fucking slow with the lockpicks and this guy saw me." Her jaw was set, and she wiped a tear away with the back of her hand.

Marisol raised her arm to hail a taxi.

"It's okay," Marisol said, putting her free arm around Jody. "We'll work it out."

"I made you miss getting the award," Jody said.

"No worries," Marisol said. "Kim's going."

"It's good we cancelled VanDyke," Jody said. "I can't even handle a basic heist."

"Don't waste your time hailing a taxi," a woman walking by said. "Subway's closed for repairs after seven. Trains don't stop on the Upper East Side. Cabs are impossible."

Marisol nodded, and looked down the street. The buses were full and barely moving. She began walking toward Fifth Avenue, where they could cross Central Park at East Eighty-sixth Street to get a West Side train.

Meanwhile, her inner hard drive had begun running calendar and bookkeeping programs. This month's mortgage payment was overdue, and the late deadline was in three days, on the fifteenth. She had already written payroll checks, so she couldn't fudge there. She and Eva hadn't taken a salary for a few months. They were $7,500 short, and this was the job that was supposed to cover it. Her credit cards were maxed out. She had already gotten emergency loans from a dozen donors. Where was she going to get $7,500 in two days?

Jody pulled a cigarette and a lighter out of a pocket in her skirt. She lit up with a shaking hand. "First I fuck up the job. Now I'm here crying like a little bitch."

"The only failure is getting arrested," Marisol said. "You did great for your first time. I'm proud of you. Now we just try again."

"Cristina, stop crying," Marisol said. "Or I swear to God I'll hit you myself."

Marisol had woken up from an afternoon nap in her

uncle's apartment. She and Cristina slept after school while he was still at work. In his house, night was not for sleeping.

Marisol's head was killing her, and she felt muddled. She'd padded into the living room to find her sister hunched over beside the radiator.

"I'm sorry, Marisol," Cristina wailed. "I'm so sorry." On the floor in front of her were the feather duster, a bottle of white glue, and their uncle's old baseball trophy. The aged plastic was brittle, and the little man and the top of the bat had both broken off.

"What the hell were you thinking?" Marisol asked.

"He beat you up yesterday because he found some dust!" Cristina shrieked. "I had to clean the dust!"

It all came back to Marisol.

He had rammed her head into the refrigerator three times. She couldn't remember the feeling of impact, just the burning in her scalp where he'd gripped the fistfuls of her hair. And the terror that he might actually kill her this time.

She woke up in the hospital. Concussion. Today was the twenty-ninth day she'd missed from eighth grade.

"The glue's not working," Cristina wailed. "He's gonna kill me for breaking the little baseball man."

Marisol looked at the broken edges of the figure. White glue didn't stick well to plastic. Marisol peeled it off.

"See?" Cristina said, her voice increasingly hysterical. "He's gonna know. He's gonna kill us."

Marisol's heart began to race, but she willed herself to stay calm and looked at the clock. 5:23. He was almost never home before 5:45, but they might not get to the dollar store and back in time.

"No, he's not. I can fix it," Marisol said. She turned

Cristina's head so their eyes met. "Always come to me. I can always fix it."

Cristina turned and reached out her arms to Marisol, her face puckering. Marisol gathered her little sister into her arms and let Cristina sob.

"It'll all be oooohhhh-kaaay," Marisol crooned. "We'll get some Krazy Glue and stick it together. We'll trick him. He'll never know. But always tell me when something happens. Don't try to fix it yourself because you're too little."

Cristina choked out words between sobs. "I—tried—to—wake—you—up—but—you—didn't—wake—up."

"I'll always wake up," Marisol said. "Even if it takes a little while. Now lemme fix this."

Marisol got a piece of chewing gum. She chewed it up and used two tiny pieces as temporary adhesive. It held. She put the trophy back.

Marisol looked at the clock. 5:47.

"Stop crying," Marisol said. "He'll be home any minute."

Cristina sat in Marisol's lap, shaking. "You—can—still—see—where—it—broke!" she hiccuped. "He's—gonna—know!" At seven, Cristina still perceived her uncle as omniscient and omnipotent.

"No, he's not," Marisol snapped. "Only if he looks closely, which he won't." Marisol took a deep breath. Her head was pounding. "He's only gonna know if we tip him off by doing something stupid like crying. Don't be fucking stupid. Fucking stop it right now. Stop it or it'll be your fault when he beats us."

Marisol could see Cristina clench her body to push down the spasms.

"Good girl," Marisol said.

Carefully, she set up the table with the appearance of

homework. But the two girls sat holding hands, peering out the window at the front stoop below. Marisol's head throbbed.

"It'll be your fault when he beats us." The words rang in Marisol's pounding head. But what had the social worker said?

"It's not anything you do. He beats you because he's a violent man who takes out his rage on the girls he's supposed to be caring for."

Marisol hadn't said shit to that lady. Had insisted she'd been jumped by some girls in the neighborhood.

"No, sweetie," the black woman with the salt-and-pepper dreadlocks had said. "Then you'd have abrasions from the sidewalk. Says here you live with your uncle."

Marisol sat silent.

"I get it," the social worker said. She managed to look concerned and cool at the same time. "You have to live there and he's probably threatened your life." She looked down at the file. "Or your sister's life. He probably blames you for whatever he does. But it's not your fault. It's never your fault."

The social worker had given her a number to call. "I know how it is, so I won't bother trying to give you my card. But here's a number you can remember. Ask for Rochelle." It was a toll-free prefix and the acronym GET FREE. Marisol had never forgotten it.

"He's coming!" Cristina said. The two girls watched through the blinds as he entered the building.

After the front door closed, Marisol was overcome with nausea. She stumbled to the bathroom. Her stomach convulsed, and she threw up into the toilet.

"Cristina!" she croaked between waves. "Get in here."

Her whole body shook, but she tucked her little sister behind her, in the space between the toilet and the shower.

Hot tears burned her eyes as wave after wave of vomit spilled out of her.

"What the fuck is going on?" her uncle demanded, filling the bathroom doorway, towering over the two girls.

"She's . . . sick," Cristina said, barely above a whisper.

"*Asquerosa*," he growled. "I better not find a fucking mess in here when I get back." He stalked into his bedroom to change out of his work clothes.

In her mind, Marisol begged her body to stop heaving but it wouldn't. Her head felt like it was on fire. She continued to dry-heave, and gripped the sides of the bowl with shaking hands.

Finally, he left the apartment. Cristina ran to the window and back to report he was really gone.

Slowly, the vomiting subsided. Cristina handed her a wad of toilet paper. Marisol wiped her mouth, then collapsed back on the floor, sobbing and shaking. Cristina squeezed next to her, pressing her forehead against Marisol's. "You did it," she said. "You fooled him and we get to cry now."

Chapter 17

Monday was Valentine's Day. At 5:30 p.m., Marisol hustled down an icy street in midtown. The snow had melted a bit then frozen as the sun set. In front of her, a trendy young woman in high-heeled ankle boots nearly slipped.

Marisol walked carefully in her soft-soled shoes. Shoes that made no noise on carpet, didn't squeak on hardwood floors, and had shallow treads that didn't leave prints.

On her way to the building where "Tammy" had been lost two days before, she needed to run an errand. Serena was supposed to drop off the advisory committee application, but she had the flu. Marisol hated mixing clinic business with heists, but the rest of the team was booked.

Inside the municipal building's heavy double doors, a security guard had three banker's boxes for proposals. Marisol reached into her messenger bag and pushed aside a hard hat, wig, and ConEd vest. She pulled out the application and set it in the third box.

On her way out, she ran into Raul.

"I'm so glad you decided to apply," he said with a bright smile. "And I like the braids."

Tyesha had cornrowed Marisol's hair into a coil to fit under a wig.

"Maybc you'll wear your hair like that to our date," he suggested.

Marisol laughed out loud. A release of tension. After this final heist solved the financial crisis, she deserved a reward.

"Maybe I will."

As she turned to leave, he grabbed her hand. "I'm glad I ran into you. Happy Valentine's Day." He kissed her cheek.

"Same to you," she said. She felt the imprint of his lips all the way to the train.

As Marisol was dropping off the proposal, Tyesha was walking into the lobby of the "Tammy" apartment building uptown.

Marisol had sent her with a burglary prep plan that had Tyesha wearing a tight red-and-white-striped dress. In white-gloved hands she held a heart-shaped box of candy. No prints.

"Happy Valentine's Day." She smiled at the fifty-something West Indian doorman. "I'm from the Midtown Candy Factory." She held out two wrapped chocolates. "Do you like milk or dark chocolate?"

"Either one suits me fine, young lady," he said with a grin, and she handed him a candy wrapped in red foil with silver stars.

"How about you?" she asked, as she strode across the lobby to the security guard. "You like chocolate?"

"Definitely," he said. He was in his thirties, black American.

She pulled out two candies in pink foil. One with hearts, the other with cupids. Tyesha chose carefully, because Marisol had dosed some with sedatives. The ones for the doorman had just enough to make him drowsy and disoriented. The ones for the guard would put him to sleep.

"Milk or dark chocolate?" she asked the guard.

He grabbed the two chocolates out of her hand. "I'll take both."

"Wait!" Tyesha said as the guard unwrapped the milk chocolate and popped it into his mouth. A double dose could be dangerous.

"Hold up now," she said. "They're supposed to be only one per customer."

"How you gonna tell me I can't have two?" he asked.

"I'll get in trouble on my job," Tyesha said.

"Your boss ain't here," the guard said, toying with the other candy.

"I'm running low on dark chocolate," she said, pulling a silver-wrapped candy out of the box. "Can we trade?"

"It's not for me," he said. "It's for my girlfriend. She likes her chocolate dark."

"It's a gift?" Tyesha asked, her eyes following the chocolate as he rolled it from hand to hand.

"For Valentine's Day," he said.

"That's sweet," she said. "I'm not supposed to do this, but if it's a gift, let me put it in a box." She pulled out a tiny red heart box.

"What's your name?" he asked, still holding on to the candy.

"Tara. What's yours?"

"Dante," he said, rolling the candy between the thumb and fingers of his left hand, making a crinkle sound with the foil.

"Dante, are you gonna let me wrap the candy for your girl?"

"She's not my full-time girl," he said. "I can have friends."

Tyesha set her jaw, and looked him in the eye with her seductive face. "Dante, I want to wrap your candy. Can you? Let me? Wrap your? Candy?"

She reached over the desk and took it from him, brushing against the back of his hand.

He let the candy go with a grin, and she switched it. "It's been a pleasure," she said, handing him the box.

"Be more pleasurable if you gave me your number," he said, holding on to her hand.

"Save your pleasure for your girlfriend," she said, and pulled her hand away with a wink.

Tyesha strode three blocks west to a trendy Asian restaurant. Through the plate-glass window, she saw the hostess seating two middle-aged couples. One of the men matched the photo on her phone—the tall, balding man who had hosted the party where Kim cracked the safe. His wife was a willowy brunette with a highball glass of liquor.

Tyesha called Marisol. "All clear."

"Almost there," Marisol said. "I caught one of the last trains before the subway closes for repair."

"Dante, the security guard, might hit on you," Tyesha said.

"Anything else?" Marisol asked.

"No," Tyesha said. "I'm headed into a midterm."

She was about to enter Central Park, where she'd cross over to Columbia on the West Side. "Who's the lookout?" she asked Marisol.

"Nobody," Marisol said. "Kim and Jody have client dates. Eva's at some fund-raiser."

"I'll skip the test," Tyesha said. She headed back to the restaurant. "You need backup."

"Absolutely not," Marisol said. She passed a row of street vendors. "We need you to get that fellowship for next year. This can't affect your grades."

"But, Marisol," Tyesha said. "You don't even let us do sex calls without backup—"

"Don't argue," Marisol said. "Kim already cracked the safe. I'll be in and out in five minutes. Go take your test."

"Fine," Tyesha said, turning back into the park. "What about Serena? She wouldn't have to know. Just put her in a cab to watch these folks. She could text you if they leave or something."

"She's not part of this," Marisol said. "It's just the four of us plus Eva."

"Except you asked Nalissa to drive you home tonight," Tyesha said.

"That couldn't be helped," Marisol said. "The East Side trains are running express between Fifty-ninth and One-twenty-fifth, and I can't get a cab. I'm not gonna carry a big donation for thirty blocks. Don't worry. She'll be picking me up at the building around the corner to keep the donor anonymous."

"I don't trust her," Tyesha said.

"Me, neither," Marisol said. "But it's just a ride. Stop worrying and go take your exam."

In a restaurant bathroom, Marisol put on tinted safety glasses and the short auburn wig. Her thick gray jumpsuit was perfectly nondescript.

At the mark's apartment, the doorman let her in. She strode straight to the elevator, ignoring the security guard who was beginning to nod. Once the doors closed, she put on latex gloves.

On the seventeenth floor, she looked up and down

the empty hall. The couple who lived there would just be ordering dinner. Her heart beat hard as she fumbled with the lockpicks. The tumbler clicked and she was in. Closing the door behind her, she could feel the razor edge of anxiety subside, but adrenaline continued to pump.

The large living room was decorated in a Middle Eastern theme, with marble floors and Persian carpets. Marisol saw a framed enlargement of an article she had read in *Forbes* about "human interest innovation." She recognized a picture of a tall man shaking hands with the governor, the Ivy Alpha board president whose company was recognized for work on behalf of "the Mexican victims."

Marisol crossed the living room into a hallway, and flipped on her flashlight. She had memorized Kim's floor plan, and she went straight to the study.

Marisol stepped into a dark room dominated by a wide, cluttered desk. Above it was a large wood carving of the Ivy Alpha fraternity crest. The guy was the CEO of a high-end sportswear chain that had several factories in Asia, and one in Juárez.

Marisol slid her hands behind the crest and found the safe. She opened it quickly with the combination Kim had given her. Marisol opened her bag to load the cash, but the safe only had a few jewelry boxes and a stack of five-dollar bills.

She pocketed the cash, and pulled out her flashlight to inspect the jewelry. High-end fakes, not that she would have taken them anyway.

Why would people lock up fake jewelry?

Marisol looked again at the safe. It was built-in. Part of the original building from the 1920s. A decoy?

The phone rang and Marisol jumped. The machine picked up after three rings: "Sorry we can't get to the phone right now," a woman's voice drawled. Marisol felt behind what looked like some sort of diploma in an oversized frame.

Marisol got down on her knees and shone the light on the desk. Could they have a freestanding safe?

"Meredith? Meredith, it's me. Pick up if you're there."

Marisol crawled across the study floor and let out a cry as she stuck her palm on a tack.

Fuck! She peeled off her glove and sucked on the heel of her hand. As the woman's voice ranted about some mutual friend, Marisol dug out a spare glove and put it on. She flashed the light onto the floor to make sure she hadn't bled onto anything. Standing, she pocketed the tack. She walked carefully around the desk and swung her flashlight beam around the study. No safe.

"I'd be pissed if I wasn't worried about her," the woman's voice said.

Marisol crossed the hallway. It had to be in the bedroom, unless it was a floor safe. Given all the Persian carpets, she prayed not.

"I hate to put you in the middle," the woman said. "But do you think I can trust her?"

Marisol stepped through the half-open bedroom door. She felt behind the various wall hangings with no luck. In the center of the room was a king-size canopy bed, and above it, a large painting of a desert landscape. Marisol kicked off her shoes and climbed onto the bed. She slid her hand behind the painting and felt the seams in the wall that outlined a small door.

Standing on the bed, she removed the painting to reveal the safe. In the dim room, she fumbled for her stethoscope.

"So call me when you get this . . ." the voice on the answering machine went on. "And Happy Valentine's Day."

At last, the machine beeped again, and went quiet.

Marisol took a deep breath to hush the jackhammer of her heart and tapped twice on the door of the wall safe. She put her stethoscope to the door and slowly turned the dial. The pads of her fingers pressed against the slightly serrated surface of the metal dial, as she turned it carefully to the right, waiting for the first sound of the safe's three-click reply.

The safe whispered the first *click* in her ear. As she turned the dial to the left, she could feel the pull of the latex where the blood was sticking her palm to the glove.

She had just heard the third *click*, and swung the safe door open, when another sound sent a spasm through her body. She froze, one hand gripping the safe's dial, the other clenched on the stethoscope.

Through the open bedroom door, she heard keys and then footsteps.

"You're drunk, Meredith," a man's voice boomed. "Not tipsy. Drunk."

Marisol couldn't make out the words of the woman's voice, only the whine of protest.

She looked into the safe and saw several bricks of cash. She lifted them out silently and shoved them into her pockets.

A light snapped on in the front hall, bathing the bedroom in an ambient glow. Marisol was clearly exposed.

She tore off the stethoscope and crammed it into her pocket. She grabbed the painting and hung it up. Sitting on the edge of the bed, she shoved her feet back into her shoes and snatched up her bag.

"I don't care about the Colemans," the man said. "You're not fit to be out in public. Now, go sleep it off."

Marisol had left the bedroom door ajar. She crept over to it and peeked out, blinking at the bright light in the living room.

The man had his back to her, but she recognized his

tall frame from the photo. The CEO. The sex trafficker. The pillar of the community. He pulled off a thick coat, and slid a cap off his bald head. He tossed them onto the back of a chair without taking his eyes off his wife. She faced Marisol's direction, unsteady on her high-heeled boots, a scarecrow in her tasseled dress, waving slightly.

Marisol saw the insolent look in the wife's eyes. The two of them weren't moving, just scowling at each other.

The woman spun on her heel, heading for the front door.

"Where the hell do you think you're going?" the man asked, stepping after her.

"To order takeout," the woman said. "I never got any fucking dinner."

Marisol watched the woman rummage through a basket of menus. The man stood over her, glowering, as she dialed the phone.

Marisol transferred the bulky cash and the stethoscope from her pockets into her shoulder bag, and exchanged them for the ConEd hard hat, which she put on. The woman put her finger in her ear and said hello. When she turned away from him to order, Marisol stepped out into the hallway and opened the kitchen door wide, snapping on her flashlight.

"Hello?" Marisol called, pointing the flashlight into the hallway.

"What the hell?" The man wheeled toward her.

"I'm calling nine-one-one." The woman blinked several times and pressed buttons on the phone.

"Sorry to startle you folks," Marisol said. "Feel free to call, but we already alerted them about the gas leak." She shut off the flashlight. "We checked out the units above and below, but I don't know why your upstairs neighbor smelled gas. I'll have the boys check the line, but I couldn't find a thing." She strode right up to them and stood close enough to smell the liquor on the woman's breath. The woman hung up the phone. The man seethed.

"What the hell are you doing in our apartment?" he demanded.

"The security guard let me in," Marisol said, shrugging and putting the flashlight away. "Dante."

"That idiot was falling asleep at the desk," the man said.

"Well, I'm done here, unless either of you has been smelling gas. Have you smelled gas?" she asked as she eased past them toward the door.

"Wait just a minute," the man said, taking her arm.

"Don't put your fucking hands on me," Marisol said. "I'm just trying to do my fucking job. And if your gas lines are as bad as your security, it would serve you right if your damn apartment blew up. You should be fucking thanking me."

She strode past him. In the bag, she kept the flashlight gripped tight in her fist.

Her other hand was on the door and she was turning the knob when the wife spoke. "But our range is electric."

Over her shoulder, Marisol saw the split second when the man's face transformed, his eyes widening with comprehension and fury. He pushed the wife aside and lunged toward Marisol.

She swung the door at him and it knocked him back. She was two steps ahead of him, running out the door, but he leaped after her and tackled her in the hallway, grabbing her at the knees. She pulled out the flashlight, and as the two of them fell, she twisted her body so she wouldn't be facedown. He fell on top of her, and attempted to hit her in the face, but the blow glided off the ConEd hat.

The pressure of his body on her chest brought a spasm of memory. She let out a howl and swung the flashlight with all her strength. She connected with the side of his head. He grunted and slumped down across her body, his chest on her abdomen. Blood gushed out onto the carpet. Marisol wriggled out from under the unconscious man, her stomach threatening to heave.

"See, Steve?" the woman yelled. "I'm not that drunk. I knew we had an electric stove and you didn't, you arrogant bastard."

Marisol ran down the hall. The last thing she heard as she tore open the door to the stairwell was the woman calling, "Steve? Steve?"

Marisol could barely feel the ground under her as she passed the dozing guard and the doorman, blinking against sleep.

In the stairwell, she had removed the hard hat and the ConEd vest, and shoved them into the bag, along with the bricks of cash.

She felt the jagged rattle of adrenaline in her limbs. She breathed in the night air, and the urge to vomit subsided.

Tyesha was right. She should never have done the job without backup. Someone to watch the mark, make sure they didn't come home early. Anyone who could see a drunk woman being escorted from a midtown restaurant and text her a warning.

She moved through the clotted foot traffic in the thick slate-gray outfit and auburn wig. She held the shoulder bag balled up in front of her chest.

Just around the corner, she could see the dark town car, and Nalissa's bright red hair through the front windshield. The image of the man flashed into her mind again. His dark green suit, blood on his bald head.

She opened the door of the car to get in.

"Just a moment, miss." She felt a heavy hand on her shoulder. Instinctively, she dropped her shoulder bag onto the floor of the car. She felt her heart in her throat.

"Can I help you?" she asked, turning around. It was the older security guard and a younger female guard.

"Miss, there was a robbery around the corner," the young woman guard said. "A man was injured. My colleague here said you just exited the building. Do you mind coming back to answer a few questions?"

"Not at all," Marisol said. She closed the door on the bag and gestured for Nalissa to go. The sedan slowly pulled away from the curb.

She walked back toward the building, while the older guard nearly stumbled with drowsiness.

Marisol made to enter the building next door to the one she had robbed. The doped-up security guard followed her.

"Where are you going?" the young woman guard asked.

"He said this building was robbed," Marisol said.

"No, it was the next building," the woman said.

Marisol frowned. "But this is the building I walked out of," she said.

The young woman looked at the drowsy guard and rolled her eyes.

She turned back to Marisol. "I'm sorry. Do you mind if I search you? Just a formality."

"I understand." Marisol shrugged. She stood, feet apart, and put out her arms.

The guard patted her down. She removed a billfold with a twenty-dollar bill, a fake ID, and a MetroCard from one pocket, and her phone from the other.

"Sorry, Lourdes," she said, looking at the name on the ID.

As Marisol walked away, the relief flooded on top of the second surge of adrenaline, nearly wilting her entire body.

As she pressed against the wave of exhaustion, she called Nalissa. No answer. She accelerated her pace away from the building, calling three more times before crossing the park to arrive at the subway. She texted for Nalissa to meet her at the clinic and caught the train.

When she came back aboveground on the Lower East Side, she felt a dull echo of anxiety where her panic should be. She was too emotionally spent, her body unable to manufacture a sufficient response.

By the time she got to the clinic and saw no sign of the town car, she could feel the anxiety turn to dread. She made a couple of calls, then lay on the clinic lobby couch in a stupor. Beside her, a display held condoms and a bright red and pink sign: "Stay Safe for Valentine's Day!" The auburn wig lay in her lap like a forlorn pet.

Two hours later, Tyesha called with a secondhand report. Earlier that evening, Nalissa had left her shared apartment with a suitcase, talking about an unexpected trip to see a sick relative.

After Marisol hung up the phone, it really hit her. Nalissa and the money were gone—maybe twenty thousand. No way to pay the mortgage by tomorrow. The whole thing would come due in ninety days. Ninety days to raise $247,953 plus interest.

She called the number she had for Jeremy VanDyke.

"One moment, Miss Rivera," his assistant said.

The decision had slid into place like a dead bolt, with a sharp *click*, locking her in. Like when she was seventeen and standing in a grimy hallway with an eviction notice in her hand. *I don't care who I have to fuck, we're not gonna end up out on the street.*

She clenched her fist around the locket on her neck. Back then it had been Cristina she'd been determined to protect. Now it was all the girls at the clinic. Marisol needed to ensure that it would always be there for girls like Dulce, girls like herself.

VanDyke came on the line. "Miss Rivera," he said. "What a pleasure."

"Call me Marisol," she said. "I've got a counteroffer for you."

"By all means," he said.

"Two hundred and fifty thousand," she said. "I assume you'd like the donation to be anonymous, but you'll want the tax paperwork for your records."

"Two hundred and fifty thousand?" he said. "You drive a hard bargain."

"I'm bargaining for a hard driver."

He chuckled. "Miss—Marisol, that's considerably more than I was hoping to spend. Far above market rates."

"Supply and demand," Marisol said. "The negotiation cost is admittedly high, but that's because you want a service that isn't presently on the market."

"I could see myself spending maybe a hundred thousand," VanDyke said.

Marisol slumped against the back of the lobby couch. The rush from the job and the fight and the search for Nalissa had rattled her adrenals, leaving her slightly dizzy.

"Jeremy," she said. "You said you don't do second choices. Neither do I. It's a quarter million. Take it or leave it." She wasn't selling it right. She was too used to being a hard-assed madam, and she had lost her touch as a sex worker: the lure, the promise, the fantasy. That was what they paid for.

With her last bit of energy, she mustered the will to flirt. "And frankly, I hope you'll say yes, because I think we could have a very good time together."

"You are quite a businesswoman, Miss Rivera," he said. "I'll let you know."

She awoke the next morning on top of her covers in the gray jumpsuit. She had a text from Jeremy VanDyke that simply said: **yes.**

Chapter 18

"I can't believe that motherfucker stole our money!" Tyesha raged.

It was late the next night, and Marisol's team was assembled in the office.

"I'll break Nalissa's fucking neck if I see her," Kim said.

"I told you not to trust that bitch," Tyesha said.

"I know," Marisol said. "But if 'that bitch' hadn't driven off with our money, I'd be in jail, and NYPD would have the cash."

"It's my fault," Jody said. "For fucking up that first burglary."

"No," Marisol said. "We can't think that way. We took risks here, and out of twelve robberies, we got away clean with eleven."

"But what about the clinic?" Tyesha asked.

"I've agreed to do the call with VanDyke," Marisol said. "That'll solve our mortgage crisis. And while I'm at it, let's do the hit."

"Hell, yeah!" Kim said.

"As long as I'm just the muscle and not fucking with locks," Jody said.

"So what's the plan?" Tyesha asked.

"VanDyke's safe is probably a Superlative," Marisol said. "The top model has a fingerprint ID."

"How do we get past something like that?" Kim asked.

"We need someone to make us a pair of latex fingerprint gloves with VanDyke's prints."

"I know this genius scientist," Tyesha said. "She did this safer sex art installation with latex. I know she could do gloves."

Marisol shook her head. "I need someone I know and trust."

"Trust?" Tyesha said, cocking her head to one side. "This woman's bread and butter is custom kinky sex toys for rich people. She's all about discretion."

"Not good enough," Marisol said. "I'm the boss, and there's only one guy I feel comfortable bringing in. Someone I knew a long time ago."

When Marisol first met Sergei, she was seventeen and desperate for money. Her uncle had recently been killed downstairs in their building—the police said he was robbed. His death was a relief, and Marisol planned to keep paying rent and stay there with Cristina. She'd skipped school for a week traipsing around the city looking for work. No one wanted a minor with no work experience, although an ice cream store owner offered twenty dollars for oral sex. She turned him down, deciding she wouldn't do it for less than fifty.

The next day she put on her mom's polyester print minidress that was so old, it had come back into style. Her chest was nearly spilling out of the damn thing, but that was okay.

She flirted with the token agent to get into the subway, and rode to Times Square. If she could meet a few different guys this week, she'd be able to pay the bills and could stay in school.

She'd flipped through a New York tourist guidebook, and picked a three-star hotel with a restaurant and a large bar.

She held her head high and acted like she belonged there, just like her mother had taught her. She found an empty bar stool, and sat down. She had barely ordered a soda, when two women in tight dresses—one blond, the other brunette—came and looked her up and down.

"Who the hell are you?" the brunette asked, reminding Marisol of girls who'd tried to fight her in junior high.

"Mercedes Lopez," Marisol said, acting bored.

"Like we give a fuck," the blonde said. "This is Sergei's territory. You can't sell your underage ass here without permission."

"I don't see how it's his or your concern," Marisol said.

"I could cut that pretty face of yours, and then we'd see what's your concern," the brunette said.

"Security," the blonde hissed to her friend, and glanced at a man in a suit looking at them.

"We'll be back, jailbait," the brunette said, and they sauntered away.

Marisol's heart pounded. Maybe this was a bad idea. The bar was filled with attractive women in their twenties. Why would anyone pick her?

The bartender brought the soda and took her moist, crumpled dollar bills.

Marisol felt a creeping sense of panic. If she didn't get rent money by the first, they'd get evicted. Cristina might end up in foster care.

Half an hour later, a guy came over. "Good evening,"

he said in an Eastern European accent. "I'm Sergei. You are new around here, yes?"

Marisol nodded as the bartender handed him a clear drink in a short glass.

"All the girls here work for me," Sergei said. "No freelancers."

Marisol nodded, reaching for her purse. "It's nice to have met you."

"Here's some advice," he said, taking her arm. His grip was firm, but not painful. "All the hotels on this block are mine. You can try farther away, but some of those guys are less of a gentleman than me, yes?"

"Can I work for you?" Marisol asked.

"Trial basis," he said. "You don't work for anyone else or on your own. I say which hotel. I send clients. You please them. You collect three hundred each and I get fifty percent."

"Fifty percent?"

"I provide a lot, sweetheart," Sergei said. "Bartender looking out for you. Security won't hassle. I provide clean room. You want to turn fifty-dollar tricks out of car in the Bronx, feel free." He finished his drink. "I don't usually have Spanish girls, but I got a request. Can you do Spanish accent? Your New York accent sounds cheap. Hurry and decide. I've got to go."

"Can I try it out?" she asked.

"Here's my phone number," he said, and gave her a scrap of paper. No name. "I'll be back when the bar closes. Be here."

Marisol cringed with the recollection. Everyone must've known she was a total amateur.

She'd said yes, and Sergei ordered her a strong drink. The alcohol helped her loosen up. All she could remember about the first guy was the anxious, excited feeling in her stomach, the semi-drunk lightness in her head, and the sense that she was the heroine in a movie. She imitated looks she'd seen in music videos and dialogue she'd heard on television, visualizing her actions and expressions from the outside, watching herself as if through a camera. When it came to sex, living with her uncle had taught her how to check out—to exhale her consciousness from the confines of her skin. She would be wandering among the blades of the ceiling fan, tightrope-walking along the edge of the windowsill, numb from the neck down.

The three hundred dollars afterward almost made her laugh. Five minutes of fucking? Although most clients didn't turn out to be as easy as the first one. Some took longer or creeped her out.

She began to cut school. She never graduated, but she managed to support herself and Cristina.

She got to know the girls. Many had started out with awful pimps. Marisol saw it at the clinic, too. Young women beaten, raped, strung out.

Sergei offered protection and kept his word. On the other hand, he made big money, while they did all the hard work.

When Marisol walked into the same Times Square hotel bar looking for Sergei, it was like a time warp. The streets outside had been sanitized of the sex trade, but the bar was the same. It was Tuesday, but it could have been any night of the week. From the bartender's uniform, to the brands of alcohol in front of the mirror, to the red vinyl upholstery on the bar stools, nothing had changed in twenty years.

She had tried Sergei's old cell phone number, but it

now belonged to a man with a Boston accent. Maybe Sergei was in jail, or dead, or had retired on the money she and the other girls had made for him.

She came into the bar when they opened at 5 p.m., and planned to stay until closing time at 4 a.m. if needed. She called to check in on Dulce, and got an earful about the girl's newly established goals in life. After that, she pulled out a grant application. At 7 p.m., she got hungry, and ordered a miserable plate of buffalo wings.

After finishing the grant application, she itched to work on the clinic's financials. But she needed privacy for that, so instead she proofread the clinic's newsletter copy. Each article reinforced her carefully crafted picture of success and stability. Some of it was true. Overall, their assets had increased considerably with the $600K they'd gotten from the gala, and they were pushing two million with the bump from online donations. But, as promised, she had put those funds in a high-yield account where she couldn't touch it.

By 9 p.m., she was stir-crazy, sick of looking from the newsletter to the door, but afraid she would miss Sergei.

He finally strolled in. Gray at the temples. His face heavily lined, and his pores showing the effects of alcohol and cigarettes.

He walked past her table to the bar and spoke to two women in clingy dresses. The bartender brought Sergei's usual drink.

After he emptied the low tumbler, he escorted the women to the door. Marisol walked toward him. "Sergei," Marisol said. "It's been a long time."

The women glared at Marisol as they left.

"Nearly twenty years," he said. "You look well, Mercedes."

The alias took her back. Margarita, Mónica, Magdalena—she had used several.

"It's Marisol," she said. "Marisol Rivera."

The way he looked at her when he greeted her was more like an appraisal than a leer. She felt an odd combination of irritation and nostalgia. Some part of her wanted to tell him she was getting $250,000 for an upcoming client. Platinum-level pussy, as her girls would have called it.

"Can we talk business?" she asked.

Sergei sat down across from her. "Only for a short time," he said, looking at his Rolex.

"I need a particular service," she said. "Someone who can duplicate something for me. Someone good and discreet. Of course, you'd get a finder's fee."

"I know a lot of people," Sergei said. "What needs duplicating?"

"I have a set of fingerprints on a glass, and I need to be able to reproduce them."

Sergei shrugged. "I might know a guy who knows a guy who can make a pair of gloves."

"Gloves would be good," Marisol said.

"Finder's fee is five thousand," he said.

Marisol blinked. "Five thousand?"

"Supply and demand," Sergei said. "If you come to me after twenty years, you don't know anyone else."

"I don't trust anyone else," Marisol said. "When we worked together, you were always straight-up."

"Look at you. Your table full of papers. Whatever you do now, you got no network," Sergei said. "I'm supply and I have monopoly. Five thousand. Take it or leave it."

"I'll take it."

"Let me make a call," Sergei said. He stood and turned his back to her, speaking briefly on the phone in a Slavic language. He turned back to Marisol. "You have the prints?"

She nodded.

"I'll be back in half an hour," he said.

"I thought you said you might know a guy who might know a guy," Marisol said.

"For five thousand I know a guy," he said and walked out.

As Marisol collected her papers, she marveled at how well he read people.

Thirty-five minutes later, Sergei walked in beside a young man with broad cheekbones and slightly Eurasian eyes. He had bleached hair, trendy clothes, and bling jewelry. Sergei introduced him as Gavril.

"Did you bring the prints?" the older man asked.

She dug into her handbag and pulled out a box. Carefully she took out the glass and handed it to Gavril. He held it up to the light to see the prints, but the bar was dim. He pulled out a flashlight from his pocket and examined the glass. Sergei asked him a question, and Gavril gave a curt answer.

"He can do it by Saturday," Sergei translated. "Ten thousand."

"The work is guaranteed?" Marisol asked.

"Gavril is the best," Sergei said.

Marisol looked Sergei straight in the face. "I want the glass back, and no extra copies," she said.

"You have my word," Sergei said. "The money?"

Marisol pulled out an envelope. "Half up-front?" she asked.

"Fine," he said, and pocketed the cash.

"Five for you, five for Gavril," she said. "You're not gonna count it?"

"I have complete confidence," he said.

Marisol dreamed of the beach. *La playa* in Puerto Rico. Not her grandmother's house, but familiar. Waves crashed nearby, and she dozed in the afternoon sun. She could feel the gentle press of another body beside her. A welcome hand reached for hers in the sand. A soft kiss on her forehead. Raul.

"*Voy en el agua, guapa,*" he whispered.

She squinted into the sunlight. "Don't go without me," she said.

Raul stood over her, smiling, his broad shoulders silhouetted against the sky. "*Pues, ven.*"

He reached a hand out and she took it. He helped her up, practically lifting her. As she rose, sand stuck to the back of her body.

They held hands. Raul's palm was cool and smooth as they walked to the ocean's edge.

A wave lapped their feet. The water was warm, and they waded in. They were simultaneously looking out to sea and looking into each other's eyes. They waded deeper, and with each wave, more of the sand on Marisol's body fell away.

When she was up to her chest, a tall wave came, and Raul lifted her up. It crashed over them, washing the remaining sand from her back. She wrapped her arms and legs around him, and they kissed. She tangled her fingers in his hair, pressed her tongue into his mouth, slid a hand down the back of his swim trunks.

"Slow down," he said gently in Spanish. "I love you. There's no rush. We have all the time in the world."

A massive wave crashed over them, and Marisol startled awake.

She blinked against the weak New York morning sun. Everything was unfamiliar. The feel of the sheets under her face. Equally unfamiliar was the amount and direction of the morning light. She had fallen asleep on her office couch.

The dream came back to her. Had she really dreamed

of Raul? That he said he loved her? She could still feel the imaginary press of his palm in hers, the salty taste of his tongue in her mouth.

A romantic moment on the beach? What the hell was wrong with her?

Eva would say her subconscious was longing for him. That she was trying to sexualize it away, but it was deeper than that. *Love. All the time in the world.*

"There must be another explanation." Marisol murmured the thought aloud and stood up. The dream spooked her. She'd never had that kind of dream before.

The date.

She had started to dial his number a few times to cancel, but with all the preparations for VanDyke, she was never in the right frame of mind to talk to Raul. Of course not. She put away her pillow and blanket into the cabinet above the couch.

She was about to service and rob a billionaire. She didn't have time for an uptown hookup, let alone a real date. Today was Wednesday. The date was for Friday.

The dream was a warning, she decided as she headed upstairs. Every day she delayed, he was getting ideas, building up some kind of romance in his head. It was all there in the last part of the dream. She just wanted to fuck him, but he was talking about love. She recalled the salsa riff he sang on the street, the ridiculous smile on his face. She had to shut this down.

Once inside her apartment, she scrolled through her phone contacts for Raul's number. She called and was grateful to get his voice mail.

"It's Raul," his voice said. *"Déjame un mensaje."* Hearing him speak Spanish caught her off guard and brought back the dream. The voice mail beeped, and it took her a second to recall herself.

"Hello? Raul?" she said. "I—well, thanks so much

for the invite, but I won't be able to make it Friday. It's me. Marisol? And I'm calling about our—the *mofongo*. Anyway, work's just piling up, and—I apologize. Take it easy, okay?"

She hung up the phone, flooded with relief.

Friday night, Marisol and her team went over intel on VanDyke, and possible timelines for the robbery.

Tyesha walked in late and slammed her bag down on the coffee table.

"Do you know what I fucking heard downstairs?" she asked. "One of the girls told me Nalissa's in the Bronx spending our money."

"Leave it alone," Marisol said. "We need to focus on VanDyke."

Kim agreed. "That backstabber is so small in our world right now."

Tyesha sat down, and Marisol continued with the security specs.

"If VanDyke's got the safe with the retina technology, we're fucked," Marisol said. "Just go to Plan B: Get the hell out."

"Or just whack him on the head," Jody said. "And hold his eye to the safe."

"Absolutely not." Marisol shook her head. "If we get caught, I want nonviolent robbery charges. And let's limit the physical contact. The bodysuits are awkward and you have women's hands. We want him to think you're all guys. Keep your distance. Tie us up, then get to work on the safe."

"Got it," Jody said.

"If we're lucky," Marisol said, "we'll get the fingerprint safe. You get three chances, then it locks down for twenty-four hours. Some trip an additional alarm."

The phone on her desk buzzed.

"You have a visitor," Serena said over the intercom.

Marisol looked at the clock. Seven thirty p.m. She wasn't expecting anyone.

"Raul Barrios," Serena said.

"What does he want?" Jody asked.

"Isn't it obvious?" Tyesha asked.

"Cut the shit," Marisol told them. She pressed the Talk button on the intercom. "I'll be right out."

She put on her blazer and went into the reception area.

"Raul, I'm sorry about tonight—"

"You're not ready," Raul said. "You told me at the gala, and I shouldn't have pushed." He handed her a bag. "*Mofongo,*" he said. "I promised you dinner tonight. I want you to remember how I keep my promises."

"That's so sweet," she said. "I just—"

"Really, it's okay," he said. "You like me but you're scared. You got a million reasons why this thing between us can't work. But don't forget to think of me when you feel your arteries clogging." He gestured to the greasy bag in her hand.

She laughed. "I will."

"Good night, *guapa*," he said, and closed the outer office door behind him.

Serena pretended to look busy at her desk.

Marisol pulled out a chunk of *mofongo* and nibbled it, letting her tongue linger on the rich mashed plantains and savory pork. It was the best she'd had in years. She walked back into the office wearing her best *don't-fuck-with-me* expression.

"What the hell is that?" Jody asked.

"And why does it smell so good?" Kim asked.

"None of your damn business," Marisol said.

"Sure, it is," Tyesha said. "I need to know how to get

some man I'm not fucking to come drop off dinner for me after I turn him down for a date."

The following night, Marisol watched as Sergei walked up to the bar and the bartender poured him a drink.

It was eleven fifteen on Saturday night, and she'd been waiting several hours, her anxiety increasing. She still had a knot in her chest when he sat down across from her.

"I asked around," he said. "Looks like you're management now. You always wanted my job." He gave the slightest hint of a smile. "But you need to control your people."

"What people?" Marisol asked.

"Some girl in the Bronx," he said. "Alyssa or something. Says she worked for you and now has her own operation. Maybe five girls out of a house. She's pissing people off up there."

"She's what?"

"I have more bad news," he said, interrupting her. He slid a large padded manila envelope across the table to her. It had a lump in the middle, like a stubby snake that had swallowed a cube. "Gavril got deported this week. I'm sorry. Here's your money and your cup."

"And the gloves?"

"They picked him up before he could do the job," Sergei said with a shrug. "I was lucky to get your cup back."

"Do you know anyone else?" Marisol asked.

"Not anyone I can vouch for," Sergei said. "Maybe this is best. Most girls from this business don't look so good at your age. Nobody pays me to give a fuck, but I'm glad."

Marisol opened the package. It had the box with the cup and a much thinner cash envelope.

"Sergei." Marisol put a hand on his arm. "Where's the rest of the cash?"

"You paid for work that didn't happen," he said. "I give money back. You paid for introduction, I introduced you. No refund."

"You've got to be kidding me," Marisol said.

"Go back to your paperwork job," he said and took a last swallow of his drink. "You do charity work, not me. Nothing is free." He stood up. "Take care of yourself, Marisol Rivera."

He turned abruptly and left.

She stuffed her things into the briefcase, tossed a twenty on the table, and rushed after Sergei.

But by the time she'd gathered her stuff and gotten out onto the street, he was gone.

She tried calling Eva, but got no answer. She caught a cab to Eva's house and pressed the buzzer several times.

"Do you know what time it is?" Eva asked after Marisol had come up the three flights of stairs. She stood there in a raggedy bathrobe and motioned for Marisol to come in.

"The pimp's contact couldn't make the gloves," Marisol said as she followed Eva through the dim living room into the kitchen. "But he kept the finder's fee."

"You can't trust a pimp," Eva said. She put two mugs of water into the microwave.

"I figured if he didn't take advantage of me at seventeen, he wouldn't now," Marisol said.

Eva prepared cups of chamomile tea for both of them, and put milk into hers. Marisol took hers plain. The kitchen, like the rest of the house, was cluttered with papers, laundry, and knickknacks.

"Now what?" Eva asked.

"We'll do the heist," Marisol said. "Maybe he'll have a regular safe."

"Marisol," Eva said. "You've done everything in your power to save the clinic. Some things are beyond your control. You're not God."

"Of course not," Marisol said. "If I was God, women would get paid to sit on our asses and think profound thoughts. We'd only fuck people who turned us on. But as long as the female ass outearns the female brain, there are gonna be sex workers who need our clinic."

"I know," Eva said. "But we started this clinic in better times. We can start another one when the economy picks back up."

"Not after all the years we've put in," Marisol said. "We're one fuck away from owning the clinic free and clear. Stop trying to talk me out of it." She took a sip of her tea and scalded the roof of her mouth.

"Then do the date with him and skip the heist," Eva said.

"I can't!" Marisol said, slamming down her teacup. "I can't live with myself if I go over there and fuck him and don't even try for a bigger score. I'm not like Tyesha and Kim. Fucking him won't be fun or funny or sexy for me."

"I know," Eva said.

"And I'm not like Jody, either," Marisol said. "She's the tall ice queen. People expect her to be in charge. They pay her to push them around. I'm the Latina. I'm supposed to be fiery but submissive. I'm done playing that role. Especially with some rich white guy who is only willing to fuck me if he's paying."

"Then don't do any of it," Eva said. "Don't fuck him, and don't rob him, either."

Marisol leaned back in her chair. "But if we're robbing him, then that makes it sexy," she said. "At least sexy enough to go through with it."

"Because secrets are sexy?" Eva asked.

"Because power is sexy," Marisol said. "Heisting

Jeremy VanDyke is totally fucking sexy." She ran her tongue across the tender spot where the tea had burned her mouth.

"You're determined to do this?" Eva asked.

"We've got a shot at a billionaire," Marisol said. "I'm determined to try. This could be the game changer."

Eva sighed and sipped her tea. "Then go to your team," she said. "Doesn't Tyesha know someone who works with latex?"

"The last thing I need," Marisol said, "is some friend of Tyesha's shooting off their mouth."

"How can you trust a pimp you haven't seen in decades, but not your own team?" Eva asked. "Tyesha's smart. She's gonna run this clinic soon. Have some confidence in her."

"That's too much of a risk," Marisol said.

"You don't have a choice," Eva said. "That is, if you really wanna heist this guy."

Marisol gritted her teeth and dialed Tyesha's number.

Chapter 19

That Wednesday—three nights later—Marisol stood in front of an upscale building on Central Park East. Her turquoise Dilani Mara dress peeked out from beneath the full-length fur coat, and made her look like she belonged there.

The evening was chilly. At the opening of the coat, Marisol felt a crisp breeze through the silk against her skin.

A dark limousine pulled up to the curb.

"Good evening, miss," VanDyke's driver said as he opened the door for her.

"Good evening," she said, lifting the hems of the rented gown and coat, and sliding into the backseat.

He was Latino, gray beneath his chauffeur cap. Under other circumstances she would have made conversation. Not tonight. Tonight, she wore big shades and was picked up at a random apartment. Gloves would yield no fingerprints. Nothing but VanDyke's word would link her to the evening.

VanDyke had an unassuming three-story town house right next door to the thirty-floor high-rise that was his corporate headquarters downtown. In the dark, Marisol couldn't see the connecting skywalk.

As they got close to the building, Marisol texted Kim to call her. The phone rang and Marisol picked up. "If my boyfriend asks," she murmured, "I was with you tonight."

Kim laughed, and hung up.

Marisol continued to hold a one-sided conversation, but used the phone in camera mode. The driver pressed a code into the building door, while Marisol looked away, but videotaped his fingers on the keypad. The code changed every day.

She prayed VanDyke wouldn't meet her at the door. A moment alone in the entryway would be her one, brief chance to case the place.

"What was she thinking?" Marisol said into the silent phone as she stepped into the doorway. No one came to meet her. She climbed the stairs, whispering into her phone. "Some people just don't want to hear the truth."

Slowly, as if she was looking around with her own eyes, she pointed the phone at all of the security equipment, and lingered for close-ups.

"Mark my words," she said. "That girl is headed for trouble."

The stairway was hardwood, the walls were white with paintings hung on both sides. At the top of the stairs, Marisol took a slow sweep of the wide hallway with the gleaming hardwood floor, the high ceilings, wide archways, and a Ming vase in a glass case, perfectly lighted and undoubtedly alarmed. How much had it sold for at Christie's? Three quarters of a billion?

"I've gotta go," Marisol said into the phone, and pressed Send, forwarding all the video to the team.

Marisol got a little tingle as she stood at the door. She hadn't serviced a client in over a decade. She waited. She took off the shades. She got warm and took off her coat. Five minutes passed. Ten minutes.

Damn! She could have done the safe herself. Fourteen minutes. Fifteen. Sixteen minutes of standing at the top of a landing, looking at two closed doors and a Ming vase. Sixteen minutes in five-inch heels.

Even in her invincibility shoes, her feet began to hurt. She had to pee. Twenty minutes. What the fuck? Her irritation rose, in spite of all that he would pay and all that they might heist him for. Maybe he was twenty minutes late for everything. Maybe that was just how billionaires got down. Everybody else could just fucking wait. Maybe everyone in the world was a sex worker to a billionaire. Marisol was just about ready to break the glass in order to piss into the Ming vase, when VanDyke opened one of the doors.

Tyesha, Kim, and Jody had watched the video Marisol sent, and had just finished researching the alarm system. Kim had packed all their tools in a backpack, and they were pulling their cell phones off the chargers.

The three of them stepped out of the clinic in jeans and sweatshirts. Kim carried the bag with male bodysuits and men's clothes for her and Tyesha. Jody was tall enough to pass for male, and had just needed to bind her breasts. Tyesha had a gym bag that contained three ski masks, three sets of shades, and several big duffels, in case the haul was large. They had also bought some fake stubble to put on their upper lips under the ski masks. Kim had the latex fingerprint gloves in her purse. Tyesha's contact had made them for three grand.

They would take a cab to a midtown restaurant. A

few blocks farther uptown, they had parked a van around the corner from VanDyke's place.

"Candi Jones!" someone called from across the street.

Thug Woofer stood alone beside his SUV, waving for her to come over.

"Get rid of him," Jody said as she raised her hand to hail a cab.

Woof trotted across the busy street with a bouquet in his hand, dodging traffic.

"I'm sorry to roll up unannounced," he said.

"Woof, what are you doing here?"

"Look," he said. "I don't mean to bother you on your job, but I just wanted to apologize." He looked at Kim and Jody. "Nice to see you ladies again. Candi, can we have a minute?"

"I'll be right back," Tyesha said. She stepped out of earshot with Woof.

He handed her the fifteen red roses. "I'm sorry I acted like such a stupid motherfucker when I met you. I came to ask for another chance. If not, I understand, but I wanted to let you know that I'm sorry and you deserve better."

"You got that right," she said. Over his shoulder, she saw several cabs pass Kim and Jody.

"I'm hoping you'll reconsider being my date to the Oscars on Sunday," he said.

Tyesha's mouth fell open. "Are you serious?"

"Your madam didn't tell you?" he asked.

"I would've remembered," Tyesha said. "The Oscars?"

"In less than a week."

"Hell, yeah," she said.

His face lit up, although his smile was almost shy. "I appreciate the second chance. Do you know how many times I've driven by here hoping to run into you?"

"Why didn't you just come in?"

"And ask for who? Candi Jones? What's your real name, girl?"

"What's your real name, boy? Thug Woofer?"

"Everybody calls me Woof," he said.

"What does your mama call you?" Tyesha asked.

"I'll tell you mine if you'll tell me yours," he said with a sly grin.

"Tyesha," she said.

"Now, there's a black girl name." He laughed.

"Quit stalling," she said. "What's your real name?"

"Melvyn," he said. "Don't tell nobody."

"Can I call you Mel?"

"You can call me Woof," he said, an edge of irritation creeping into his voice.

"Okay, Woof," Tyesha said.

He nodded. She looked out at the midtown traffic, watching a car nearly run into the side of a pickup truck.

"So, what's up with your friends?" he asked. "They graduate students, too?"

"No," Tyesha said, the lie slipping out easily. "Just working on their taxes."

"Y'all pay taxes?" Woof asked.

"Of course," Tyesha said. "They came with me because at home they'd procrastinate."

"They roommates?" Woof asked. "Aw, hell naw!" he said, and Tyesha could see realization dawning. He laughed uproariously. "Brandon and Mike was fucking some dykes."

"Please don't tell them—" Tyesha said.

"Plenty dudes would pay for two girls," Woof said. "Or just watch."

"It's not like that," Tyesha said. "There's work and pleasure. They don't mix it."

"You gay, too?" Woof asked. "That why you turned me down?"

"It's not that," Tyesha said. "I'm just turned off by men who act like the world is just one big pussy waiting to fuck them."

Woof laughed, and a taxi beeped behind him.

"Gotta go," Tyesha said.

Woof handed her his card. "Text me your info for the plane ticket to LA."

Tyesha nodded and waved good-bye as he crossed the street to his SUV.

She got into the cab.

"What the hell?" Jody asked as the taxi pulled away from the curb.

"He invited me to the Oscars and I said yes!" Tyesha blurted.

"Fuck, yeah!" Kim said.

"Marisol's gonna kill you for dating a client," Jody said, her jaw tight.

"Aww, he gave you roses." Kim gestured to the bouquet in Tyesha's lap.

"Are you two fucking kidding me?" Jody said. "We need to focus."

Twenty minutes later, the cab dropped them a couple of blocks from a nondescript gray cargo van. Marisol had rented it under a false name with cash, splattered mud on the plates, and parked on a side street. The three women opened the back door and climbed in.

Kim unzipped the bag. "Okay, ladies," she said. "Time to get manly."

"Sorry to keep you waiting," VanDyke said. He stepped through the doorway in a blue oxford shirt with an open neck and a pair of navy slacks.

Marisol smiled and shrugged.

"You look gorgeous," he said, looking her up and down. "Let me take that." He reached for her coat and led her into the hall. "I hope you've brought an appetite."

"I've brought more than one," she said.

She looked him over. He kept his body in shape. His face was a little pale and narrow-featured. Involuntarily, she thought of Raul.

VanDyke put a hand on her back, as if to steer her down the hallway, his cool palm against her warm flesh.

The entire apartment was characterized by separation. You could wait in the front hall and only see the Ming vase. The central hallway was nothing but doors. She asked to use the restroom and VanDyke opened one of the doors for her.

"I hope you like Burmese food," he said, after she came back out. He opened a door on the opposite wall that led to a cozy dining nook with a view of the East River. The table was set for two with a pair of stemmed glasses, a bottle of wine, and candles.

"My personal chef does great South and Southeast Asian cuisine," he said.

"Is all the help next door in the kitchen or something?" Marisol asked as she sat down.

He laughed. "I gave everyone the night off. The chef left it warming." He opened the cabinet in the wall beside the table, and spicy-smelling steam rushed out. A large platter held portions of food in bright yellows and reds. Even the rice was multicolored. White, red, and black.

"I hope you're not a vegetarian," he said.

"Not at all. I love meat." She smiled and followed his lead as he reached for the chicken dish. Other than the unusually colored rice, the food looked like a combination of Indian and Thai.

In some ways, Marisol hated this most. Pretending it was a dinner date. Like he wasn't paying and the sex wasn't a sure thing. Part of her wanted them to fuck first and get it over with so she could enjoy the meal.

"Would you like some more wine?" he asked.

"Yes, please." She lifted her glass.

She drank. *Relax, Marisol*, she encouraged herself. *Swirl the wine on your tongue. Take it slow, and give the team time to prepare.*

"I must tell you," he said, as he finished a bite of Khow suey, a spicy meat and noodle dish. "Your business concept is brilliant."

"Thank you," Marisol said. "I've always believed that inclusion of the nonprofit industry can create a value added bonus to services that private-sector investors consume." She drank. "The nonprofit provides the services that protect my workforce, and the tax write-off protects wealth for the consumer. It's win-win."

"About the workforce," he said. "What's the long-term incentive? Not everyone can move into management. What's the retirement plan?"

"Most girls want personal benefactors in permanent arrangements."

"What?" VanDyke asked. "You mean, as in some kind of mistress arrangement?"

"No," Marisol said. "Permanent—as in marriage."

"You consider marriage a personal benefactor arrangement?" he asked.

"Happens all the time." Marisol shrugged. "Let me take you away from all this. In the movies, it's almost cliché."

"A retirement plan that the corporation doesn't pay for," VanDyke said. "You have the mind of a Wharton MBA inside the body of a fifties pin-up."

"They're not supposed to go together?"

"It just seems that women who look like you become actresses or singers, or trophy wives."

"I tried the trophy part," Marisol said. "The guy would have married me, but it was boring."

"That's what I mean," VanDyke said. "Other women would have settled for that, but not you. Why not?"

"For the same reason you wouldn't," Marisol said.

"I couldn't find a woman to keep me in the style to which I'm accustomed."

"Oh, come on, Jeremy. You're good-looking. And the billionaire thing could be a big turn-on for some wealthy older woman."

He laughed.

"What if I could find you a buyer?" Marisol asked. "Would you settle? Would you settle for Pilates every day and shopping and charity luncheons? You wouldn't last an hour. You'd be bored out of your mind. And insulted. You'd feel like your genius was being wasted. Then, what's the difference between you and me except gender? And that I'm better-looking."

"I thought you said I was good-looking," Jeremy said.

"You are," Marisol said. "You're a very sexy guy, Jeremy. I noticed it when I met you. There's this pull toward you. Part charisma. Part power. There you are in the suit, and suddenly I want to be alone with you."

"Then why didn't you want to come tonight?" he asked. "You hesitated at first."

Marisol leaned back and crossed her arms. "If you had asked me out on a date, you know I would have said yes. But you made me a business proposition. I know what the product is worth, and I don't undervalue my assets. If I get to have a luxurious, erotic evening with you, that's just a fringe benefit."

"So we could have had this same evening without the donation to your clinic?"

"Absolutely not," she said. "You're paying for expediency. You're paying to get an asset in one night that otherwise would have taken months to acquire."

"I once waited over a decade to acquire a company," VanDyke said. "Laid the groundwork step by step."

"I checked your portfolio," Marisol said. "Both business and . . . domestic. You like a quick merger, sudden turnover, and to let the asset go before it's clear what the long-term prognosis is. If it crashes and burns, you don't take the blame, but if it soars, it becomes part of the VanDyke mystique. How. Does. He. Do. It?"

"A strategy that works," VanDyke said.

"It works better in business than in your domestic affairs," Marisol said. "And I have certain liabilities that starlets and socialites don't have. Liabilities that you wouldn't want in the tabloids. I know why you sent the staff home."

"You do understand my portfolio," he said.

"You wanted to ask me out at the gala, but I hadn't been vetted yet," she said. "You got some background on me and found out I wasn't a contender for a longer-term, more visible arrangement, but you couldn't resist the write-off. You knew we could come to an agreement."

"I'm not used to women who can decode me," VanDyke said, his brow furrowed.

"I raised the price to protect my own interests," Marisol said, pleased and validated by her effect on him, a Puerto Rican girl from the hood, talking finance and business with a billionaire. "When you took the date off the table, I lost out on a massive secondary gain."

"Which was what?" he asked.

"Disclosure," she said. "If we meet as escort and client, I'll never disclose that fact. On the other hand, if we were to meet on a date, no gag order. So I might let it slip in a strategic moment that I had dinner with you. You know exactly what that's worth for a businesswoman. Any personal connection with you puts my stock through the roof."

"You're charging me for the monetary value of bragging rights?" he asked.

"'Everything has value,'" she said. "'The wise entrepreneur gives nothing away for free without a strategy.'"

"Now I'm the one who thinks I'm dreaming," he said. "I'm sitting here with the hottest woman on the planet, and she's quoting my words back to me about how she used my theories to get me to triple my offer."

"Quintuple," Marisol said.

He reached across the table and took her hand. It brought back the dream in which Raul had taken her hand on the beach. Inside the dream, that had felt so right, so perfect.

VanDyke's hand felt wrong. She dropped her eyes, attempting to look coy, steeling herself against the rising sense of repulsion.

She took a breath and retracted her attention from the contact points of his palm on the back of her hand. She pulled some part of herself deep inside, curled it up safely, and met his eyes.

"It's sort of like a mind fuck," he said, his lips parting into a slow grin.

"More than just mind," she said.

She needed to get things moving to keep the plan on time. She reached forward, grabbed his tie, and tugged it.

VanDyke leaned across the table and kissed her. Softly,

his tongue gently touched hers. He put a finger on her jawline and slid his hand around to the back of her neck.

When the kiss ended, she pushed back her chair and walked around the table to him, wrapped her arms around his neck, and kissed him more insistently, pressing against him, tousling his hair with her gloved fingers.

Chapter 20

How similar men's bodies were under their clothes, under their titles and their salaries. Some tiny part of her was surprised to find that Jeremy VanDyke was no different, billions and all. The only difference was the possibility of the heist, bigger than anything she had ever imagined.

The power of it made her skin flush with heat, her pulse race. More than strangers from uptown bars, where she could call the shots. She was every bit as much in control, but the money was a delicious secret, and the combination was thoroughly intoxicating.

"Let's go to bed," he murmured into her neck.

"Yes," Marisol said. On the way out of the kitchen, she grabbed her clutch purse.

The enormous bedroom, done in decidedly masculine colors—slate blue with chrome furniture—looked out on the river. Nestled in the corner was a king-size bed with gray bedding.

He accelerated. His tongue in her mouth, his hands feeling up her breasts through the dress. She moaned to feign pleasure, and peeled off the elbow-length gloves so she could work. She wrapped one arm around his neck while she unsnapped her purse behind his back. She tossed the gloves onto the table.

He unzipped the upper half of her dress, and she let the purse drop to the floor, palming a couple of accessories in her hand.

She had selected the turquoise dress for the waft of the satin and the drama of the unveiling as much as for the way she looked while wearing it. The dress coming off should look like a wave washing down along her body, sweeping her clothing out to sea.

She stood in front of VanDyke: her body in profile, the upper half twisted toward him, full face, cleavage visible. A little snatch, a little ass, a little hip. Perfect.

She reached and undid the rest of the zipper of the dress. She held the bodice up in the front, revealing a slice of her bra strap, and the skin of her shoulder. Finger by finger, she released her hold on the garment, let the fabric fall in a wave to her feet, the remains of the dress crumpled around her ankles like sea foam. Marisol rose up out of the ocean in her deep violet demi-bra and matching thong panties like a bikini.

He looked in awe at her full breasts and narrow waist, her wide hips and round ass.

Marisol tucked a condom and tiny tube of lubricant into the back of her thong. She dropped her hands to her sides, palms up, soft inner arms forward. Head back; neck exposed.

Slowly, without taking his eyes off her, he unbuttoned his shirt and peeled it off, along with his undershirt. The tan was more pronounced on his face, but he wasn't pale like she'd expected. He unbuckled his slacks and let them drop, revealing long, muscled legs with pale blond hair on the calves. He stepped out of his shoes and socks and walked toward her.

She slipped one hand behind her back and pulled out her accessories. He slid both arms around her waist and ran his hands down over her ass. She wrapped one brown leg around his waist and thrust her hips against his. He had a raging erection. He unhooked her bra and slid both hands under it to cup her breasts.

He backed her up toward the bed and she fell onto it, undoing the French twist and splaying her dark wavy hair below her. He climbed up onto her and groped her breasts, kissed her neck, tangled his fingers in her hair.

With her left hand, she popped open the lubricant. As he pressed his tongue into her mouth, she used her index finger to push aside her thong panties and squirted the lube inside her. Let him think she was this wet for him. She tucked the lube beneath the corner of the bed to retrieve it later. Then she opened the condom packet and tucked it beneath the pillow where she could easily get to it.

With both hands free, she slid them down into his underwear, caressing his erection. He moaned and his tongue went slack in her mouth. She rolled on top of him and pressed her tongue into his mouth.

She reached up and pulled the condom out of the packet, dropping the wrapper onto the floor and slipping the condom into her mouth.

She straddled him and pulled off his underwear, checking out his penis at close range. Nuzzling it, to camouflage her inspection.

She leaned in and put the condom on with her mouth. He moaned as she took him deep into her throat, just to the point before she gagged, then pulled out. With one hand, she kept massaging his erection, shielding the condom from his view. With the other hand, she pulled off her thong, and tossed it so it would fall onto the bed within his reach.

He picked it up and saw the telltale sign of fresh moisture on the crotch.

"Oh, you make me so wet!" she moaned. "I just can't wait!" And with that, she thrust him inside her, riding him hard.

It took him a minute to rally. He wasn't willing to be topped the whole time. He rolled her over and finished up in the missionary position. She hated the feeling of him on top of her, but she tuned out from the sensations in her body. Instead, she focused on reaching under the pillows and checking around the edges of the bed to make sure he didn't have any weapons handy. After a while, she began moaning, faking a massive orgasm and wrapping her thighs around him as if her life depended on it.

After their breathing returned to normal, she wiped the moisture from her forehead. "That was amazing," she said.

He smiled.

A moment later, she reached down between her legs. "We should—"

"Of course," he said, and began to pull out. She held the condom expertly, pulling it first out of herself without leaking, and then off of him, all in less than a second. If he even knew she used one, he didn't say anything.

"I'll be right back," she said. She managed to scoop up the lube and wrapper, and held them with the used condom in her hand as she walked toward a pair of doors.

"Door on the left," he said.

In the bathroom, she tied the condom and flushed it with the other stuff. Cleaned up some of the lube and washed her hands.

She ran her fingers through her hair. She wanted to look tousled, but not disheveled. Now came the more awkward part. If they were lovers, they would cuddle. If he were a cheap client, she would collect her money and leave. But he was something in between. The sexual tension and fantasy that had held them together was now gone. Would he be a talker? Or the I've-got-to-get-back-to-work type of businessman? Or, God forbid, the I-could-really-fall-for-you-under-other-circumstances type of guy?

The team was due any minute. She needed to keep him in the bedroom for when they arrived.

She opened the bathroom door. He was lying back on the bed, covers up to his waist, arms folded behind his head, a portrait of satisfaction. She scanned the bed area carefully, still checking to make sure he didn't have a gun within reach.

"Looks like someone satisfied more than just my curiosity." She smirked and sat on the edge of the bed, naked. She didn't want to take liberties—get back into the bed like a lover—but she wanted to continue to be available, interested. She reached over and ran her hand across his chest.

"You are a delectable woman, Marisol Rivera," he said, smiling up at her.

She leaned in and kissed him.

He reached to pull her toward him when the door flew open and two masked gunmen entered. Marisol screamed and scrambled to cover herself with the comforter.

"What the—" VanDyke said.

"Hands where I can see them!" Jody yelled. "One move, one more noise, and you're dead." The intruders had on shades over ski masks and were dressed in black sweat suits. They had on thick black gloves that made their hands look much bigger.

Marisol and VanDyke raised their hands. The comforter slipped down, revealing Marisol's breasts.

"Nice," Tyesha said, and moved toward her, poking her breast with the gun. Marisol wore a terrified expression on her face.

"No time for that shit," Jody growled, and pulled out a roll of duct tape.

She tossed it to Tyesha, who caught it and proceeded to bind the billionaire's hands and feet. Tyesha sat him and Marisol on the floor at the edge of the bed and bound them together, back to back, while Jody held them at gunpoint. Then the gunmen taped their mouths, and bound them to the leg of the bed.

"Anybody comes in before we get what we came for, you're dead, you hear me?" Jody asked. Neither Marisol nor VanDyke moved. "Nod your head if you hear me."

The two of them nodded, their heads bumping by mistake.

"Grab that purse," Jody ordered.

"He's the one with the money," Tyesha said.

"You never know," Jody said, and Tyesha obeyed.

The gunmen stepped out of the room, leaving them taped and helpless on the floor.

Tyesha and Jody walked into VanDyke's study to find Kim kneeling on a chair in front of the safe. The apartment was true to the blueprints Marisol had gotten from the celebrity bachelor site. The safe wasn't indicated on the plans, but Marisol had accurately guessed its location, because the wall was slightly thicker.

Kim was surrounded by neat stacks of paper and wood paneling. The safe was the height of a regular door, but narrower, with the dial above doorknob height. It was nestled next to the solid oak desk, in an alcove just wide enough for the billionaire to stand in front of it. Kim pulled on the fingerprint gloves and pressed the right index finger to the sensor of the Superlative safe. All three women held their breath.

ERROR, PLEASE TRY AGAIN, the red digital display read. Next she tried the right thumb.

ERROR, PLEASE TRY AGAIN.

"Well?" Jody murmured.

"Two tries and it won't open," Kim said, an edge of panic in her voice. "Maybe I'm doing it wrong. Or are the gloves fucked up?"

"My friend said she confirmed the match with a microscope," Tyesha said.

"Then why isn't it working?" Jody asked.

"Try the right middle finger," Tyesha said.

"Why?" Jody asked.

"I saw this photo in the tabloids of VanDyke giving the paparazzi the finger," Tyesha said. "The safe is set up so that it would be really awkward to use the left hand. So let's assume that Kim did the first two correctly. He wouldn't do the ring or the pinkie finger. I think it would be VanDyke's big 'fuck you' to the world."

"Okay," Jody said. "But if it doesn't work, we get the hell out. We cut the video lines, but there could still be a separate alarm system from the safe."

"Fine," Tyesha said. "Go, Kim."

"Don't rush me!"

Slowly, Kim wiped off the print sensor, then placed her gloved middle finger on the small square of glass.

"Well?" Tyesha asked.

"It takes a minute," Kim said.

They kept their gazes on the small display rectangle, which was now blank.

An internal sound whirred. An alarm? A go-ahead? Finally, after what seemed like forever, the combination dial lit up.

"Well, fuck you, too, Jeremy VanDyke," Tyesha said, and Kim went to work on the safe.

Two hours later, the driver came into VanDyke's bedroom.

"What the hell?" he asked, mouth open at the sight of his boss bound with a woman to the leg of the bed, both naked.

He ran over to VanDyke, who gestured with his head for the driver to ungag him first.

"Mr. VanDyke, I came back an hour ago," the driver said as he carefully pulled the tape off the billionaire's mouth. "I didn't wanna interrupt, but after a while I came to the door, and saw it was open, and the cut wires—"

"Get my cell phone!" VanDyke yelled when he could finally speak. "Bedside table! Now!"

The driver scrambled to comply. Marisol watched him run around her, as if she were a piece of furniture.

"Undo my hands!" VanDyke ordered. Marisol heard the ripping of tape behind her, then the beeping of cell phone buttons.

"This is VanDyke," he shouted into the phone. "Now my feet," he barked at the driver. "Get my feet."

Marisol heard more tape ripping a few feet behind her.

"Send the security detail over immediately. We've had a break-in. Don't alert the police just yet. I want an internal response first."

As VanDyke pulled on his boxers, Marisol made muffled sounds behind the gag.

The driver carefully unbound her mouth.

"Oh, thank God!" she said.

"Is the front door still open?" VanDyke asked the driver. "Did they break the lock?"

"I don't know."

"Go look. If it's not secure, stay there until the team shows up. Call me on my cell if anything happens."

"What about me?" Marisol said. "Can he at least untie me first?"

The driver hesitated, looked from Marisol to VanDyke.

"No time," VanDyke said.

VanDyke undid her wrists and rushed to dress himself.

Marisol undid her own feet and rummaged around in the bedclothes for her underwear. As she pulled the bra out of the tangle of sheets, she heard a pair of security guards storming up the stairs.

VanDyke stepped into the hall, his shirt open. "Don't move anything," he yelled. "Just give the place an initial once-over."

"Got it!" the guy yelled from the hallway, as she crawled beside the bed looking for her left shoe.

"You need to go," VanDyke said to her as he scanned the floor and picked up her dress.

The driver appeared in the doorway.

VanDyke took Marisol by the arm and thrust her toward the driver.

She stood naked between the two men, underclothes in one hand and a single platform stiletto in the other.

"Take her home," VanDyke said.

"What about my—" Marisol began. She was about to say "dress?"

"Money?" He pulled an envelope from his pocket and handed it to her. "Hurry."

Marisol took the envelope. "Can I get my clothes on?"

"No time," VanDyke said. "You can't be here when

the police arrive. Things always leak to the press. For the moment, I'm assuming that you had nothing to do with this. If my team finds any evidence to the contrary, I will prosecute."

"What?" Marisol said. "I wouldn't—"

VanDyke cut her off. "She can get dressed in the limo." He handed her dress, her coat, and her other shoe to the driver. "Get her out of here now." He turned to Marisol.

"Jeremy," Marisol said. "Just lemme put my—"

VanDyke turned and spoke to her as if to a dense and disobedient child. "I said, there's no time for that."

"I'm supposed to walk out of here naked?" she asked, all Lower East Side attitude.

"Spare me the false modesty," VanDyke said. "I've certainly paid enough that a few of my staff can see you. We're done here." He turned his eyes to his phone and began dialing.

Marisol's fist clenched around the crumpled bra and panties.

"What are you waiting for?" VanDyke snapped at the driver.

The driver took Marisol's arm and marched her out the door. Several of the security guards did a double-take.

Marisol stood naked in front of five men in uniform. She didn't meet any of their eyes. She could feel blood rushing to her neck, her face.

"I'm sorry VanDyke is such an asshole," the driver murmured to her in Spanish, and tried to pull the dress up in front of her body.

She snatched the dress and flung it over her shoulder, strutting down the hallway, with one breast out, like an Amazon, pulling him along. The humiliation burned beneath her surface.

Her grandmother used to cook *lechon* like that—she

would slay the pig, then bury it in the ground with hot coals.

At the bottom of the stairs, Marisol put her dress on. When she got back into the limo, the driver was so flustered, he shut the door on her stiletto heel and broke it. He began to apologize, but she raised a hand to silence him.

She sent a text to her team that said: **leaving now**, and leaned back in the seat, jaw tight.

She was still fuming silently when the limo pulled up in front of the same Central Park East apartment building the driver had picked her up from. Neither of them had spoken throughout the ride. She kept her phone face-up in her lap, looking for the all-clear signal from her team.

"Keep going uptown," she told him.

He nodded and pulled away from the curb, letting her direct him to a bar in Washington Heights.

Marisol limped out of the limo and into the bar.

The clock on the wall with the faded Dominican flag read 1:47 a.m.

"ID, miss?" the bouncer asked.

"My purse got stolen," she said.

"Sorry, miss, we need ID."

The place had a low ceiling and was smoky, despite the ordinance against smoking in bars. It was more than half empty, and they still had Christmas lights and a little neon "*¡Feliz Navidad!*" It looked pathetic this late after the holidays.

Marisol couldn't believe they were carding her in this dump. "Do I look underage?"

"Do I look like this is optional?"

"Fuck you!" she spat and left.

She hobbled down the street to the second place. It was her least favorite in Washington Heights. Seedier spot, watered-down drinks, sleazier guys. She saw a couple of girls who were definitely working. They looked her up and down and grimaced.

Marisol went straight to the bathroom, which was dark and smelled like piss. There was more toilet paper on the floor than in the dispenser. She looked at herself in the mirror through the scratched-on graffiti. Her hair was a mess, and her eyeliner had seeped down to make hollows beneath her eyes. She ran her fingers through her hair to shape it, and wiped off the excess eye makeup. The top of the dress was okay, had pressed itself with the heat of her body. Just the skirt was irredeemably wrinkled. She could wear the coat down off her shoulders. Which also worked to cover the broken shoe. She still looked hot.

She sat down on a stool at the bar. The place had begun to clear out. No one came over to buy her a drink. She ordered a glass of rum.

"*Hola, mami.*" She noticed that the guy had on way too many gold chains, as he slid onto the bar stool next to her. "What's your name?"

"Can you fuck?" she asked him in Spanish. "I don't have time for bullshit."

"Yeah, I can fuck." He looked more startled than excited.

"In a condom? Can you fuck with a condom on?"

"I think I can manage," he said.

"Lemme pay for my drink and I'll meet you in the bathroom." She downed the rum and pulled out a ten-dollar bill.

On her way to the bathroom, she heard a phone ring across the bar. Was her phone on?

She fished it out of her pocket, and there was the text, a winking face from Tyesha that had been sent fifteen minutes before—the "all clear" sign.

She laughed out loud with relief and did an about-face, limping out of the bar.

Marisol came in through the clinic's alley door, carrying her broken invincibility shoes in her hand. Her bare feet thudded gently on the wooden steps as she ascended. She pulled up the hem of the rumpled dress as she climbed past the community room, clinic offices, and exam rooms.

In the lobby of her fourth-floor office, everything was quiet. Yet when she opened the office door, she faced off with Jody and Tyesha, guns drawn.

"What the fuck?" Marisol asked, her heart banging in her throat.

"Thank God it's you," Kim gasped, as the two other women lowered their guns.

"You didn't get my text?" Marisol asked, collapsing on the couch.

"An hour ago," Tyesha said, laying the automatic on the table. "VanDyke's place is only fifteen minutes away."

"We came straight here after we left his apartment," Kim said.

"We thought something happened," Jody said.

"I'm fine," Marisol said. "Let's see what we got."

She picked up the two heavy duffels of cash and heaved them onto the desk. Her heart began to race again. "Are the bricks hundreds or twenties?" Marisol asked.

"We just grabbed everything in there," Tyesha said. "And you said not to open it until you got here."

As Marisol unzipped the duffels, Tyesha locked the door behind them, and Kim pulled the shades. All four women peered into the bags.

Benjamin Franklin stared up at them from a hundred different angles. Apparently, the cash was in ten-thousand-dollar bricks. Each compact packet held one hundred, crisp hundred-dollar bills.

"Holy shit," Jody said.

"There's at least four million here," Marisol breathed.

They counted the bricks. Marisol had underestimated by half.

An hour later, they'd emptied a bottle of rum, and Tyesha's impressions of VanDyke had everyone in hysterics.

"I demand to see the manager," Tyesha sputtered. "I did not order a tie-up by two men. I ordered a woman to fuck me and listen to my long, narcissistic monologue afterward."

The women's laughter filled the office. Marisol howled until tears ran down her cheeks. Jody sat on one of the armchairs with Kim on her lap. The two women laughed against each other, unable to sit up straight. Tyesha nearly spit out her last drink of rum. It took over ten minutes for the hysteria to subside.

When they could all breathe again, they felt spent from the buildup and release of tension. But still high from the sight of the money. Eight million. Cash. All theirs.

"You all," Marisol said, heaving herself off the couch, "are the best fucking team any woman could hope for."

After she sent them home, she carried the duffels up to her apartment.

She closed all the blinds, and crept across to the kitchenette island. Moving aside the two tall stools, she pried off the plywood front of the island counter.

When she'd redone the apartment, she had a shallow false back built. Empty until now. She put the panel aside and stacked the bricks of cash into tall columns.

She looked up at the graduation picture of Cristina. "Not bad, huh?"

She replaced the plywood. The exterior of the island looked the same. But now, she would drink her coffee inches away from a fortune.

"The team knows how much we got," she told Cristina's photo. "But you're the only one I'm showing where I put it."

Chapter 21

On Friday, two days after the heist, the team met in the deli across from the clinic. As they ate, they scanned the papers and the Internet for any news of the heist. Not a word.

"I paid off the clinic mortgage today," Marisol said. "After a certain donation check went through."

"We're free and clear?" Tyesha asked.

"The clinic building at least," Marisol said, as Jody's phone rang.

Jody stepped outside.

"What the fuck?!" they heard Jody yell into the phone.

"What's that about?" Tyesha asked.

"If it's who I think it is," Kim said, "that girl is toast."

Through the plate-glass window, Kim, Marisol, and Tyesha could hear Jody screaming into the phone: "Whitman, you've been a VERY bad boy! You're in big trouble, do you hear me? . . . Now you are NOT going to do anything like that. You're going to do EXACTLY as I say. When I hang up this phone, you're going to call the doctor. And tell him what you just told me . . . NO EXCUSES! DO IT NOW!"

Jody returned. "Sorry about that," she said sheepishly.

"I can't believe you," Kim said. "After giving me shit about Mr. Potato Head wanting free time, but you just gave Whitman a free domme session."

"On the phone," Jody said. "Less than a minute."

"Lotta people charge by the minute," Tyesha said. "You're undervaluing your services."

"And setting a serious double standard," Kim said.

"Look," Jody said. "Every six months or so, the guy goes off his meds, and he gets all suicidal and calls me. So I yell at him a little and make him call his doctor. Then he's fine. It's like a public service."

"That rich guy doesn't need your charity," Kim said. "Doesn't he have his own foundation?"

"He calls every six months," Jody said. "I'm not setting up a phone sex operation for two calls a year."

"Not cost-effective," Marisol said.

"Not fair," Kim said. "The next time MPH calls, I don't want to hear shit from you. Not one fucking word."

"That's different—" Jody began.

"Not really—" Marisol broke off as she saw something through the front window. "Gotta go." She dropped fifteen dollars on the table.

As Marisol crossed the street, Eva stepped out of the clinic with an arm around Dulce.

"I told Dr. Feldman not to interrupt you," Dulce said.

"I would never let you go without saying good-bye," Marisol said as she embraced the girl. She had texted something encouraging to Dulce every day since she'd arrived at the clinic. After letting go from the hug, she smoothed Dulce's hair back from her forehead where the cut had nearly healed. *"Tú eres preciosa,"* she said.

"Do you hear me? More valuable than money or diamonds or anything."

Dulce beamed under Marisol's words, and tears ran down her cheeks.

Marisol could feel her own eyes beginning to well up.

"Remember," Eva said to Dulce. "Your world is full of choices now, and we'll always be here for you."

"Is Eva taking you to the safe house?" Marisol asked, blinking back the tears.

Dulce shook her head. "I wanna visit my grandma before I leave town."

"Are you sure?" Marisol asked. The first mistake with a guy like Jerry was to drop your guard. Marisol would never have gotten free of her uncle if she'd underestimated him.

"My *abuela*'s in her nineties," Dulce said. "If I don't visit now, I may never see her again."

Marisol kissed Dulce's cheek. "Good luck, *mi amor*."

Head high, Dulce strode down the busy street toward the subway.

"I worry less about them when they walk in half-dead than when they strut back out," Eva said.

Marisol nodded. "Pretty faces and short memories."

"How'd it go this morning with VanDyke?" Eva asked.

"He didn't come in person," Marisol said. "His head of security came and questioned me about the robbery. Asked what I saw, then insinuated that they might suspect me."

"What'd you say?" Eva asked.

"I acted outraged, and what could he say to that?" Marisol recalled her exact words: "First I get tied up in a robbery. Then that asshole sends me out of his bedroom naked, and now he's acting like I was somehow involved? Tell your boss to go fuck himself. Oh, and—

not like you asked or anything—the police did recover my purse. Thanks for your concern."

Later that day, Marisol sat in her office attempting to create a paper trail for several large sums of cash, when Serena buzzed to say that Raul Barrios was there to see her.

"Show him in," Marisol said.

Raul had on an old-school nylon sweat suit with matching navy blue sneakers and carried an athletic bag. Marisol had the impulse to run her finger along the bag's strap across his chest, from one broad shoulder to the opposite narrow hip. She worried she just might grab him and have him right there on her desk.

"I know you're busy," he said. "I just have a question about your fund-raising."

"I really appreciate your continued interest in the clinic," she said. "Our organization depends on the generosity of our volunteers and donors."

"Are you sure about that?" Raul asked.

"About what?" Marisol asked.

"Maybe the organization depends on the ingenuity of its executive director," Raul said. "I ended up consulting with Central Robbery. Maybe not all your donors are intentional."

"What are you talking about?" Marisol asked, all the heat draining out of her.

"NYPD couldn't find links between all those uptown burglaries," he said. "So I started looking at the partial links."

"Let me guess," Marisol said with a laugh. "Several of the burglary victims were former sex workers who had come in to the clinic."

"You know that's not it," Raul said. "A lot of the victims had the same IT consultant."

"And she was a former sex worker who came to our clinic?" Marisol said.

"No, he was a guy, and the closest link they had," Raul said.

"Just because he was a guy doesn't mean he wasn't a sex worker," Marisol said.

"Not much demand for short, middle-aged balding guys."

"Maybe it's a fetish niche," Marisol said.

"I went to his office," Raul said. "And what did I see on his desk, but a photo of him and his 'girlfriend,' Kim."

"You're here accusing me of robbery because someone you met here is dating the IT guy of some of the people who got robbed?" Marisol asked. "What is that? Like, ten degrees of separation?"

"I'm here because he told me he went to parties at all of the apartments that were robbed," he said. "I'm here because he's an ongoing donor to your clinic at the rate of ten thousand dollars a month."

"Are you saying he robbed those places and is donating the money to our clinic?" she asked.

"Of course not," Raul said. "He made the money in IT and took Kim to all those parties. Kim is way too young and hot to be his girlfriend, especially when she's obviously Jody's girlfriend."

"She's not exclusive with Jody," Marisol said.

"Obviously," Raul said. "Because she's a sex worker. Maybe Jody, too. I think the ten-thousand-dollar donation is paying for Kim's services."

"I don't—" Marisol began.

"Were you at Jeremy VanDyke's house the night he was robbed?" Raul asked.

Marisol's mouth fell open.

"We know VanDyke had a date that night. Was it

you? Don't look at me like I'm crazy. I know he was into you at the gala. And you said you're not dating anyone else."

"Whoa." Marisol put a hand up to stop him. "What's happening here?"

"Okay, I get it. You don't have to say anything," Raul said. "I'm not sure how you did it, but I know it was you. My sister always said you were a genius in math class. I never knew why you didn't go to college."

"Raul, you're crazy." She forced a laugh.

"Central Robbery was totally stumped," he said. "Of course the cops missed it, because they didn't recognize the guy's girlfriend. And wasn't she on your . . . what did you call them? Your 'outreach team'?" He grinned. "More like 'alternative fund-raising committee.'"

"Raul, I have to—"

"Work, I know." He popped up from his chair. "I just came to congratulate you for becoming the stickup kid I always dreamed of being."

He gave her a half smile, and walked out of the room, leaving Marisol stunned.

She called her team for an emergency meeting.

"We need to pull a few more jobs ASAP," Marisol said.

"I thought VanDyke was the final one," Tyesha said.

"We've hit a snag," Marisol said. "An ex-cop is able to link the burglaries to us via Kim's client."

"Does he want a payoff?" Kim asked.

"Who knows what the hell he wants," Marisol said.

"Raul?" Jody asked.

Marisol nodded. "He just—"

"Did you ever hook up with him?" Kim asked.

"Of course not. I just—he didn't set off my cop radar.

He seemed . . . genuine. I mean, I considered dating him until I learned his ex-partner was investigating our burglaries. *Coño!*"

"Don't get all confused straight girl on us now, Marisol," Jody said. "Those broad shoulders are clouding your judgment."

"Jody, please," Marisol said. "Me? You know how I get down: 'Hoes before bros.' "

"Right," Jody said. "Sorry."

"The situation is under control," Marisol said. "I've got a plan. We need to hit two or three uptown Manhattan safes, with our usual MO. Guys who can't be linked to Kim's client in any way. Just to muddy the waters. But we have to do the recon as quickly as we can."

"I've got one," Tyesha said. "Asshole owner of the gentlemen's club I worked at. I used to hook up with his son. He showed me the safe to impress me."

Jody rolled her eyes. "Rich boys and their daddy issues."

"Do you remember enough about the apartment to set up a hit?" Marisol asked.

"Definitely," Tyesha said.

"Count me in for revenge burglaries," Kim said. "We could do the guy's house my mom used to clean."

"Didn't they get her deported?" Tyesha asked.

"When she insisted on minimum wage," Kim said. "Fuckers. I know that apartment like the back of my hand. All the days I spent there while my mom scrubbed the floors."

"You sure they wouldn't suspect her?"

"She's been in Korea for eight years," Kim said. "And we have different last names. The cops would never put it together."

"Great," Marisol said. "We'll look into both of those

leads. Meanwhile, Tyesha and Jody, I'll pay you each the standard escort rate to pick up wealthy guys until you find three good prospects."

"What?" Tyesha asked. "We get to fuck whoever we want and you'll pay us?"

"As long as they have money, and you fuck them in their apartments to scope the place for a safe."

"How come I can't get in on it?" Kim asked.

"Sorry," Marisol said. "Raul already suspects you're casing the apartments. And Tyesha and Jody, I want you disguised. Change your hair color. Dark bars. Lights low at their places. If the cops show photos later, I don't want positive IDs, but I hope it won't come to that. Let's start tonight."

"What are you gonna do about Raul?" Jody asked.

"I'll tell you what," Tyesha said. "Fuck his brains out. Make him think twice about turning you in."

"Not a bad idea," Jody said.

"Worse ways to spend an evening than with a hunk like that," Kim said.

Later that night, while Tyesha and Jody were looking for rich guys to pick up, Marisol pulled Raul's address from the volunteer file. No one answered his doorbell, so Kim and Marisol stood watch on either end of his block. Marisol sat at a bus shelter, and Kim huddled on the steps of a nearby building.

They'd been there a few hours, when Marisol got a two-ring signal on her phone. She quickly stepped out onto the sidewalk, carrying a pair of large shopping bags. She recognized Raul's tall, broad-shouldered form walking toward her down the block.

"Marisol?" Raul said as he got closer. "Is that you?"

"Raul?" She pretended to squint into the gloomy evening to recognize him.

"Let me help you with those bags," he said.

"No." She waved him away. "The clinic is only a few blocks down."

"Exactly," he said. "Which is why it's no trouble to help you."

"Thanks," she said. "You're such a Boy Scout."

"I was going for more of a supermarket Superman," he said.

Marisol laughed. "Everybody loves a hero."

"Or is it just brainwashing?" Raul asked. "I'm one of those guys who grew up with comic books. Big, stoic guys going around rescuing everybody."

"And women with painted-on clothes," Marisol added.

"Yeah," Raul said, laughing. "And can I just say that shit was confusing for a Puerto Rican kid? My dad had this comic book collection that dated back to the late fifties. All the usual ones, Superman, Batman, but also these Robin Hood comics."

"I bet those were worth a lot by the time you were a teenager," Marisol said.

"They helped my folks buy their house. But don't change the subject."

"Which is what?" Marisol asked.

"Two subjects," he said. "Confusing messages boys get, and how I admire you for being like Robin Hood."

"Let's stay with subject number one," Marisol said.

"Well, it was weird," Raul said. "My dad had all these American white guy heroes. Even Captain America. And we weren't really Americans, but he had kept those comics in perfect shape. Which was like a miracle given the moisture in the air in Puerto Rico. He used special bags and mothballs and stuff. He fucking lost it when we tried to read them in the middle of winter in New York, like we were still in PR and the humidity was gonna ruin them."

"I remember your folks being all about Puerto Rico," Marisol said. "Like they were only here for a minute to make some cash and go back."

"They had all this hostility toward America," Raul said. "Those comics were the one American thing my dad really loved—other than sports. They still want me to move to PR to be closer to them."

They stopped in front of the clinic. She opened the front door, and he set the groceries down on a chair in the lobby.

Marisol turned on a lamp, and sat on one of the couches. She motioned for him to join her.

"So, you think you'll move to PR?" she asked.

"My life's been here since I was two," he said. "My job. People."

"Anyone in particular?" she asked, moving toward him.

"Maybe," he said, and leaned in to kiss her.

Marisol had faked thousands of kisses. She knew just how to move her head and hands and body to convey excitement. But with Raul, she just sat still. Utterly still, and felt a flush of heat and desire, invisible, unexpected, and overwhelming.

He finished the kiss, and pulled back to look at her.

"I've been wanting to do that since I first saw you," he said. He reached for her hand and kept his eyes locked with hers.

Marisol cleared her throat. The kiss was nearly an out-of-body experience, and his gaze further unsettled her.

"So . . . uh . . . so, what's next for you, Raul? You got the NYPD begging you to come back. You thinking about it?"

He shook his head. "I plan to stay strictly freelance."

"But they want you to consult, right?" Her words felt disconnected. Like a time delay. Her mouth spoke her uncensored, anxious thoughts, and two seconds later she'd find the words she'd wanted. She meant to say, *clearly, you're a man in demand*. But instead she said, "You've been working with them, right?"

He drew his head back from her. "What is this?"

"What is what?" she asked.

"First you're kissing me, then you're grilling me about the police?"

"I wasn't—"

"No, for real," he said. "I been trying to make a move on you for months. And you been telling me no, no, no. Then I come in here yesterday to congratulate you and suddenly, I'm irresistible?"

Before she could even piece together a response, he had stood up and stalked to the front door.

"Save your bullshit, Marisol," he spat. "I'm not about to be played like that."

He slammed the door behind him.

She stared after him. How had she fucked that up so badly? The kiss had been like a sucker punch. It had her too shaken up to play it right.

Now she would have to depend on her team.

Just before dawn, the four women met up at the office.

"I bagged a corporate lawyer with a Montgomery safe," Jody said.

"I struck out," Tyesha said. "So many guys pretending to be rich to get laid. The guy I fucked mighta had money, but no safe."

"Let's do these hits ASAP," Marisol said. "We've got Tyesha's old boss, the family Kim's mom cleaned for, and this new lawyer."

"I'm on it," Tyesha said. "Just let me cancel my flight to LA."

"That's right," Kim said. "The Oscars are tomorrow."

The three young women looked at Marisol.

"Go catch your plane, Tyesha."

"You sure?" she asked.

"You're not doing the B-and-E," Marisol said. "And you gave the full download on your old boss. Go. Just be reachable for questions."

"I love you!" Tyesha said, and she kissed them all before she ran out of the office.

"Do we start these hits tonight?" Jody asked.

Marisol nodded. "Jody, you stand lookout. Kim, you hit Tyesha's old boss."

"Why not you?" Kim asked. "I only did VanDyke because you were tied up."

"I'll be doing one of the other jobs," Marisol said. "It's Saturday night; at least one of them has gotta be out. I'm hoping we can do the hits at practically the same time. Muck up the waters as much as possible."

"Who'll be lookout for you?" Jody asked.

"Eva," Marisol said. "I learned my lesson."

Two days later, on Monday afternoon, Marisol met up with Jody and Kim in the office. Several piles of small bills made little crosses on the desk.

"Six thousand, four hundred twenty-three," Kim said, confirming the count.

Marisol gathered the bills. "Neither are donors to the clinic, and two hits went down simultaneously on Saturday—"

She broke off when someone knocked at the door.

"Who is it?" Marisol asked, as Jody swept the bills off the edge of the desk into a drawer.

Kim opened the door and Tyesha waltzed in with the *New York Post* and a huge grin.

"Page six, motherfuckers!" she crowed and slammed the paper down on the table.

Kim found the photo right away.

Marisol leaned over her shoulder and read: " 'Rap sensation Thug Woofer on the red carpet with his lovely date, wearing Dilani Mara.' Damn, they didn't even give your name."

"It was amazing!" she said. "I met Shonda Rhimes, and Taraji and Laz Alonzo and Laverne Cox."

"So, where did he take you afterward?" Kim asked. "Did you fuck him?"

"To the Beverly Wilshire," Tyesha said. "That was the craziest part. We didn't fuck. He said good-bye at the hotel and went to catch a plane."

"Marisol!" Serena yelled through the open door.

Marisol locked the desk drawer full of cash as her assistant ran into the office.

"The pimp with the gun is back!"

Chapter 22

In front of the clinic, Jerry smoldered on the sidewalk. The women inside had run to the windows, twenty sets of eyes peering out at the street. His Hummer was parked at a hydrant.

"Where's the head bitch in charge?" he had said. "The executive director bitch. Marisol Rivera."

Eva stepped outside the door and leaned on her cane. "She's busy," Eva said.

Jerry fired into the air. "I'll wait."

Eva flinched, but set her jaw and stood ramrod straight.

Lower Manhattan traffic breezed by, oblivious.

Marisol stepped out and stood next to Eva.

"What do you want?" Marisol asked, arms folded across her chest. She kept a good five feet between herself and Jerry's thick arms and scowling, stubbly face. Jerry had sweat stains underneath the armpits of his designer warm-up jacket. She could see a light sheen on his forehead, even in the cold midday air.

Without his shades, his eyes looked dead and hungry at the same time.

"I wanna make some introductions," Jerry said. He gestured toward his Hummer with the gun barrel.

"You already know Dulce."

Marisol's heart sank as she saw the girl's profile in the backseat. Dulce averted her eyes.

Marisol fantasized swinging the SUV door into Jerry. She, Eva, and Dulce could sprint for the clinic, where they could protect the girl. This time she wouldn't let Dulce go so easily.

It wasn't so much Jerry's gun that made the plan impossible, as Dulce's defeated expression. Marisol knew that despair. She could rip off the Hummer door and beat Jerry to death, and Dulce would still wait for the next backhand.

"And that's my little brother, Jimmy." Jerry indicated the guy riding shotgun.

Jimmy was thinner and clean-shaven. He looked Marisol up and down. "Nothing little about me, sweet thing."

Marisol kept her jaw set, as the two brothers laughed.

"And some more introductions," Jerry said. "Lupe, Jenny, Star, and Spice." The girls waved, a spectrum of young brown women.

"These are my girls, okay?" Jerry said. "They don't need your help. I'm their help. Sometimes they might be a little forgetful about who takes care of them." He turned to the Hummer. "Dulce," he said. "Get the fuck down here, you stupid little bitch."

Marisol couldn't stand that word. Her uncle had fired it at her so many times. It stung even when women used it jokingly. Coming out of Jerry's mouth, it felt lethal.

Dulce stepped out of the vehicle.

"Show them your ass," he barked.

He pulled down the waistband of her hot shorts a few inches, to show a tattoo of a flower with his phone number on it. The flower had been there for a while, but the number tattoo was a fresh wound.

"See?" He snapped the waistband, and slapped her on the ass. She winced and climbed back into the vehicle, eyes still on the concrete.

"She's lucky I didn't tattoo it on her face," Jerry spat. "Or slice it in. But if any of my girls set foot into your building, for a checkup, a visit, a tissue, I will burn that motherfucker to the ground with all you bitches in it. You got that?"

"Is that how you want it, Dulce?" Marisol asked.

Eva's eyes flashed her an *are-you-crazy?* look. But Marisol had to hear it from Dulce's own mouth.

"Jerry didn't mean nothing before," she said in a quiet voice. "It was a misunderstanding." Tears ran down her face.

"Okay," Marisol said. "Jerry, we're a service center. We provide service to women who need it. If they ask, we provide. It's your job to keep your hoes in line. Not mine."

Marisol took Eva's arm, and they walked back into the clinic. She prayed he wouldn't shoot. For assholes like him, her strategy was to show no fear.

Just like her previous confrontation with Jerry, Marisol didn't start to shake until the door closed behind her.

An hour later, Raul showed up.

"What the fuck?" Marisol asked. "Did one of your cop friends tell you about the shooting?"

"What shooting?" he asked, taking off his leather jacket. Underneath, he had on a zip-up work shirt. He looked like he belonged in a factory. Or better yet, a men's cologne ad set in a factory.

"Some idiot shot up into the air," Marisol said. "Nobody hurt, and we didn't call the cops. Raul, what are you doing here?"

"Two more burglaries went down Saturday night," Raul said, sitting down in her client chair.

"Really?" Marisol asked, sarcastically. "I wonder if the victims had thrown parties with some link to one of my donors."

"I was wondering the same thing," Raul said. "So I checked."

"And?" Marisol asked.

"MO matched perfectly, but no link to this place," Raul said. "No link to the IT guy, no Asian girlfriend. Well done."

"Is this our little game now?" she asked. "You come and make innuendos? What's my move?"

"Your previous move was to try to get me thinking with my dick instead of my brain," he said. "But I won't be making that mistake twice."

"Don't act like some innocent victim here," she said. "Your cop connections could get me arrested on your word alone. Telling a woman you've got info that could put her in jail isn't an attempt at seduction, it's an attempt at extortion."

"Extortion for what? I don't want your money."

"Money?" Marisol asked. "If you think you're the first guy who ever tried to use leverage to get laid . . ."

"Are you fucking kidding me? I would never do that," he said. "I told you. I wanted to become a stickup kid."

"But you didn't," Marisol said bitterly. "You became a cop. And your partner was notorious for using his leverage. He used to extort blow jobs from girls working in Times Square—did you know that? Some of them were even underage."

"I heard the rumors," Raul said. "I told him from day one how I felt about that shit. He never did anything like that when we worked together."

"Extra points for you, Boy Scout." Marisol sneered.

"You ever encourage him to turn himself in? Isn't that what you do? Investigate crimes? What's the statute of limitations on statutory rape? Or do you forget it's a crime if the minor is a sex worker?"

"Look, I'm sorry," he said quietly. "When you put it that way, I can see how my last visit to your office would look fucked up—like I was trying to manipulate you, but I swear I wasn't. It doesn't matter at this point, because I couldn't go to the cops with my original theory, even if I wanted to—which I don't. I couldn't rat you out without implicating myself, because the MO changed after I opened my big mouth and told a suspect what I knew."

As he spoke, her outrage ebbed away.

He stood up. "So no need to revive the fake I-like-you act. Whatever threat you thought I posed has been neutralized."

She didn't know what to say.

"I know I'm an ex-cop and everything, but I'm a *barrio* boy at heart." He walked to the door. "If it comes to a choice between my former colleagues and my people, there's no contest." He stepped out of her office and closed the door.

That night, Tyesha stood in front of the clinic waiting for Thug Woofer. She felt a little humdrum for a date with a rap star. Nothing in her own wardrobe could compete with the rented Dilani Mara, so she just wore designer jeans, boots, and a snug-fitting black sweater.

"You look beautiful," he said, opening the passenger door of his SUV.

"Thank you," she said, checking out his jeans that didn't sag to his knees and a similarly casual sweater. "No limo?"

"Did you want one?" he asked. "I can call right now—"

She put a hand on his. "This is nicer," she said. "A real date."

"Our first date was all business," he said, steering the vehicle away from the curb. "Our second date was all publicity. Tonight is just you and me."

He turned at the end of the block, headed uptown. "So, what kind of food you like?"

"A lot of food," she said. "Someplace where a walnut and a stick of celery is not considered a meal."

"I know just the spot," he said.

"How long you lived here?" Tyesha asked.

"Lived here?" Woof asked. "I'm mostly on the road. To be real, this is my first date in the city."

"Your first date?"

"Out the house, I mean," he said. "I can be honest, right?"

"By all means," she said.

"So, do you enjoy your work?" he asked.

"I enjoy studying public health," she said. "Sex work just pays the bills. I could be a waitress, but I'd make much less and have to work a lot harder. I could be a topless waitress, and I'd still make less, and deal with half the shit I do now. As it is, I work one night a week, and I've got an IRA and savings for vacation."

"Damn." Thug Woofer laughed. "I might need to get into your line of work."

"Don't get it twisted," Tyesha said. "This job is fucked up if you're working for the wrong people. I just got lucky. Marisol is the best in the business." Tyesha smiled, thinking about how she was practically retiring.

"How'd you get started?" he asked. "A job posting online or some shit?"

Tyesha laughed. "I was waitressing. My girl Lily was quitting to make better money in this gentlemen's club. I went along." They were stopped at a light. Tyesha looked out at the traffic whizzing past. "One day Lily had a date—you know, a date for money—who had a friend." Tyesha shrugged. "It wasn't that dramatic. The friend was cute, so it was cool to hook up and get paid, too."

"Win-win," Thug Woofer said.

"A year later, I heard Marisol on a panel at Columbia talking about women and public health. She sort of mentored me."

"And became your pimp?"

"Marisol is not a pimp," Tyesha said, a note of outrage in her voice.

"She sets you up with dates for money. She tried to block a real date with you. Isn't that classic pimp behavior?"

"Marisol wanted me to stay out of the business," Tyesha said. "I was an intern at the clinic, and she didn't even tell me she had an escort service. Only when I was going to another escort agency did she ask me to work for her. And she made me promise to quit when I got my degree, and take a straight job at the clinic."

Woof nodded. "You date much outside your work?"

"Not for a while." Tyesha shrugged. "I was dating this guy. At first, we went on some regular dates, but before we really hooked up, he said he was married."

"Mood killer," Woof said.

"I had been thinking we had a future," Tyesha said. "He already had his future with some white woman. And two kids."

"But he said he didn't really love her," Woof said. "Blah blah blah. My old manager used to run that game."

"Yeah, well, I wasn't trying to hear that," Tyesha said. "I was like, only two job descriptions at Tyesha, Inc. Unmarried boyfriend or sugar daddy."

"Is tonight a sugar daddy job interview?" Woof asked. "Am I dressed right? Should I have worn more bling?"

"No." Tyesha laughed. "That was a long time ago. I got a good gig now. No more sugar daddies."

"Whew," he said. "Pressure's off."

"And how about you?" she asked. "Do you like your work?"

Woof sighed. "Sometimes I think you and me, we in the same industry. But enough talk about work."

He pulled up in front of a cozy-looking soul food steak house in the east seventies, and handed the valet his keys.

"I hope you like it," he said as they walked in. "They know how to feed a sister up in here."

The host took them to his usual table near the back of the restaurant.

Tyesha opened the menu and was delighted to see big steaks and Southern cooking.

"This is perfect," Tyesha said.

The waiter took their order. Woof ordered a bottle of wine, and the steak with greens and mashed potatoes. Tyesha got the fried chicken with yams and corn bread.

Tyesha heard someone across the room gasp and ask, "Where?" and figured somebody else had recognized Woof.

"So," Woof said. "What's your family like?"

"Far," Tyesha said with a laugh. "That's how I like it. I had a full scholarship to University of Chicago, but I transferred to Columbia my junior year, with a much less attractive financial package."

"Why?" Woof asked.

"I'm the sister everybody depends on. I was gonna end up failing out of school with all the close-up family drama. 'My girlfriend threw me out, can I stay on your couch?' 'Can I drop off my kids just for the night?' 'Can

I borrow a hundred bucks?' It's easier when you just listen on the phone and wire money, you know?"

Woof laughed. "Yeah."

"I'm the first one in my family to go to college," Tyesha said. "Now I'm in grad school, and I work nights."

"Night," Woof corrected.

Tyesha laughed. "Right. I work night."

"What do you do the rest of your nights?"

"Woof, I'm kinda confused here," Tyesha said. "You're laying on the romance game pretty thick, and I thought we were past that."

The waitress set two steaming plates in front of them.

"Thank you." Tyesha smiled at her. The waitress tried to catch Woof's eye.

"Looks good," he said, without looking up, and the waitress went to help another customer.

Woof cut his steak. His eyes closed as he chewed, then he looked at Tyesha.

"I can't tell who my friends are half the time," he said. "Are they down or just trying to get something? I really can't tell with females. I don't know. You're fine as hell. I knew where I stood from the beginning. I don't mean to sound rude, but in my business most females offer up the pussy and hope to get paid later. You asked in advance. I didn't even get it and you got paid." He cut another bite of steak. "And you checked me on my manners, because it wasn't about the money. Then I took you to the Oscars and you held your own. I never meet chicks on my level who also make me feel at home."

The two of them ate quietly for a while. She had to admit that he cleaned up well.

"So how come you said yes to going out again?" he asked. "You already got your red carpet moment."

She finished eating a mouthful of yams. "Some of the same reasons, I guess. In my experience you can't tell a dude you're a sex worker. But you can't really build something with somebody if you can't be honest about what you do for money."

"I feel that," he said, draining his wine glass. "But I feel the brothers, too. I mean, if we keep talking, at some point, I might trip a little off your job."

"If we keep talking, at some point, I might trip a little off *your* job."

They both laughed.

Later that night, when Woof drove Tyesha to her apartment in Brooklyn, he walked her to her door. Tyesha had rehearsed her "not yet," for when he asked to come in.

"I had a really nice time tonight," he said, lingering for a moment on the steps, then leaned in to give her a good night kiss. She could smell the oil in his hair and feel the heat of his body. He pressed his closed lips softly against hers. The kiss lingered, then he stepped back and said good night.

She watched his long frame swagger down the street. He didn't look back. She savored the feeling of excitement in her body. Turned on and nothing she had to do.

The following day, Marisol and Eva sat in Marisol's office. There was a tentative knock on the door, and they both said, "Come in."

Dulce's hair and makeup were a mess, and her cheek was bruised. Her white dress was smudged with dirt, makeup, and blood.

Marisol took the girl in her arms.

"This time it's for good," Dulce said. "I swear. I don't care what he promises or threatens. I'm leaving the city when I get healed up. I got a cousin in Detroit."

"Dulce, you don't need to promise us anything," Marisol said.

"Our support is unconditional," Eva said. "You get to decide the right next step."

Dulce began to sob into Marisol's shoulder. "I don't know what's wrong with me. I'm one of the lucky ones. I was born here, but all the other girls are illegal. All I have to do is get on a bus, and I can't do it. I'm weak and I deserve what I get from him."

Marisol's stomach burned hearing the words aloud. "*Mentiras*," Marisol said. "Nobody deserves to be hurt like that."

"You're not weak, sweetheart," Eva said. "You just have patterns. As a result of trauma. It's not your fault."

Dulce nodded.

"Men like Jerry use your vulnerability against you," Marisol said. "He knew you needed a family. But we're your family now. And you don't have to earn it."

Eva peeled Dulce's arms from around Marisol. "Let's go to my office and make a plan for you, okay?"

Dulce nodded.

Marisol wiped Dulce's eyes. "I'll check on you later." She kissed her on the forehead and slipped out the door to set up additional security.

After midnight, a firebomb sailed through the front window, right past both security guards. The sound of breaking glass and the explosion woke half the building. A stack of magazines in the front lobby caught fire and the game table started to burn. The fire alarm and the sprinkler system engaged. The shrieking alarm woke up the remaining women in the building, plus half the block. Women went running out into the street.

Marisol called the fire department on her way downstairs. She stood out on the sidewalk in socks, jeans, and a pajama top. Many women wore only T-shirts and underwear. The pavement was near freezing. One of the women stood with a baby and a small toddler, shivering.

Women continued to spill out from the clinic's side exit.

The Hummer idled in the shadows. When Dulce ran out of the building, one of Jerry's thugs grabbed her.

Dulce screamed as the thug pulled her in front of him. He was wiry with ropy, muscled arms.

"This is what happens to bitches who disobey," Jerry yelled from the Hummer. "Watch closely, you stupid cunts."

His thug went to cut Dulce's throat, like a performance, grinning at Dulce's terror. He held her in a vise grip under one arm, and waved the knife in front of her, watching all the women clench in horror each time it drew close to her throat.

Everyone, including Jerry, had their eyes on the knife and Dulce. Marisol crept around behind them. She pulled a gun from the waistband of her jeans. She had a good angle, and a nice dark spot next to a minivan. She aimed and the shot rang loud in the street. Women hit the pavement. Jerry looked around, shocked.

The thug took the bullet in the back and collapsed. Dulce shrieked and jumped away from him. The knife clattered to the ground.

A siren wailed in the distance, and the Hummer screeched away from the curb.

Marisol shoved the gun in the back of her waistband and gathered the screaming Dulce into her arms.

Chapter 23

Eva had just taken Dulce up to Marisol's apartment when the emergency vehicles arrived. The ambulance took the bleeding thug to the hospital. Meanwhile, Serena explained to the fire department that the sprinkler system had doused the blaze in the lobby. Fortunately, the damage was contained on the first floor.

Marisol's body had just begun to shake when she heard a knock on her office door. She clenched her body against the wave of trembling. "Come in," she said.

Raul stepped into the office.

"What the hell?" she asked. "Did your cop friends call you?"

"Clinic security called me," Raul said. "Unlike you, Marisol, they realize when they need help."

"I don't need your help," she said.

"Is it true you're the one who shot that asshole?" Raul asked.

Marisol nodded.

"If you don't want to spend time in jail, then you do need my help."

"You wanna help?" she asked. "I hope you're ready to back me up with the cops, because the gun is only registered in Florida."

"You have a clear case of self-defense," Raul said. "But why have a gun lying around?"

"We've gotten death threats," Marisol said. "From pimps, fundamentalist Christian extremists, and nearby landlords who threatened to torch our building for bringing down property values. I hoped never to use it. But he was gonna slit her throat. Right there in front of everyone, including children."

"I'll vouch for you, but I can't promise," Raul said. "NYC gun laws are strict."

Over the next hour, Marisol told her story to two different officers.

Raul came back into the office. "Guy's in critical but stable condition, so no homicide. They'll drop the gun charges, but they confiscated the weapon," he said.

"What about Jerry?" she asked.

"Did he shoot up in the air the other day?" Raul asked. "The one you said was no big deal?"

"I can't believe he fucking firebombed my clinic," she said.

"I know you're not crazy about NYPD, but I can make a call," Raul said. "The new head of the precinct isn't a dick like the last guy. You need to let them help you."

"How? Jerry got past the security guards with the firebomb. What can the cops do?"

"Cops carry guns."

"Their guns aren't worth shit unless they're pointing at the psycho pimp in front of my building. Cops can't be here twenty-four-seven."

They headed back out to the street, where the smoke was clearing.

A woman firefighter came up to Marisol. "You're the executive director?"

Marisol nodded.

"It was just the waiting room. Good thing your sprinklers activate only in the area they detect smoke. Otherwise you woulda soaked the whole building. Oughta be able to get that front room back in shape within the week."

"Thank you so much," Marisol said.

Raul walked back over to Marisol and pointed to the front door. "Has this door been open the whole time?"

"I guess so," she said. "But the security guards would have—"

"Half the time, the security guards were being questioned by the cops," Raul said. "One of them was getting treated for a minor injury. Plus, the fire department was in and out. I don't know how well the cops had it cordoned off."

"Shit," Marisol said. "I didn't even think to—"

"Jerry could have come back and be waiting somewhere inside."

"Just in the front area," Marisol said. "The upstairs and the back are secure."

"I'm not leaving until we search the whole place," Raul said.

Marisol didn't like it. She still suspected Raul might be trying to set her up, but she liked the idea of Jerry hiding in the office even less.

They searched the building, all the patient rooms in the clinic, the conference room, the medical and psych staff offices. Marisol looked into the large multipurpose room.

Dulce sat on one of the beds, huddled beside a platinum blond African American girl rubbing her back.

"You have people living here?" Raul asked, after Marisol had closed the door. "How did I miss that when I volunteered?"

"It's only at night," Marisol said. "A limited, temporary shelter for a few clients. Women who need protection from pimps and boyfriends. Tonight's drama is why it's such a risk to have clients living in."

Raul nodded. They searched the rest of the lower floors. When they went into the supply room, Marisol remembered them on hands and knees in the dark. The adrenaline from the shooting was subsiding, but her pulse quickened again.

Marisol shook it off, as they confirmed the last few rooms were empty.

"I hate feeling like someone's coming after me," Marisol said. "I shoulda shot Jerry while I had the chance."

"Then you'd be getting booked for murder," Raul said.

"Justifiable homicide," Marisol said. She turned away from the softness of his lips, the open caring on his face. "I need a fucking drink."

She swiped her card at the security door and they walked up to the fourth floor. She went right to the office's liquor cabinet, and poured them two glasses of rum.

For nearly an hour they drank in silence, on opposite ends of the couch. Marisol put away the better part of the bottle. She stared out the window.

She heard every swish of fabric against the leather sofa when Raul moved, every tap of his glass against the coffee table, every swallow of liquid down his throat.

She considered asking him to leave, but she didn't want to be alone. She should have asked Eva to stay, or Serena.

"You ever kill anyone?" Raul asked, out of nowhere.

"Just once," Marisol said. "You?"

"Bunch of times." He shrugged. "Part of being a cop."

She took another swallow of her drink.

"What happened?" he asked.

She knew she shouldn't say anything, but having been raised in part by her Catholic grandmother, the confession felt inevitable. "I came from a super fucked-up family," Marisol said. "I finally figured a way to improve it."

"My sister always suspected something," Raul said. "Wanna talk about it?"

"Nope." Marisol leaned back on the couch with her rum.

"You were always like that," Raul said. "Smart and a badass, but nobody could figure you out."

"That's how I like it." She stood to refill her glass.

"It seems like it might get lonely under that mysterious exterior," he said.

"Guys lust after the mystery girl they can wonder about," Marisol said. "The yet-to-be-sorted girl. Good girl? Bad girl? The not knowing kept everybody interested. If I had slept with half the football team or gone steady with one guy for a year, I wouldn't have been half as fascinating."

"How come you keep lumping me with all the other guys in high school?" Raul asked. "I wasn't some dog. After you graduated, I had a girlfriend all through junior and senior year."

"So what happened?" Marisol asked. "Why aren't you two married now?"

"She went off to Duke," Raul said. "Then medical school. She's a surgeon in Ohio. Married another doctor."

"When do I get to learn all about you?" Marisol asked. "You've been pretty nosy in my alleged love life. My girls think you're hot, even the gay ones. You must have had some luck with the ladies since high school."

"I don't really care if all your girls think I'm hot,"

Raul said. "I don't like girls, I like women. Grown, smart women who happen to—"

"Don't change the subject," Marisol said, smiling. "Tell me about your love life."

"You first," he said. "Have you ever been in love?"

"Nope," Marisol said. "I've always been married to my work." She wasn't ready to tell him about her history of sex work. Or uptown hookups. But he had asked about love, not sex. "I've . . . dated . . . a bunch. But . . . love wasn't really on the table . . . I lived with a guy for a while."

"Okay," Raul said. He accepted her words at face value, and she felt uneasy. She hadn't lied, but she could see he had gotten a distorted picture.

"I dated a woman I met in the police academy for a while," he said. "I was engaged to somebody else when I was a rookie." He looked down at his glass. "A lot of smart women are freaked out by cops. Once I joined the force, I kept meeting these badge bunnies. Women with a thing for cops. It was cute at first, but then it got creepy. Like the guy didn't matter, they were just turned on by the uniform."

"Come on, Raul," Marisol said. "You're good-looking, smart, friendly. I can't believe you have trouble meeting women."

"Not trouble meeting women." Raul shook his head. "Trouble staying interested. At some point, the cop thing got in the way. Either they couldn't handle the lifestyle, or they had a thing about it, always pulling some damsel-in-distress shit to manipulate me."

"'Damsel in distress'?" Marisol said. "Aren't you here tonight on a rescue mission with me?"

"That's different," Raul said. "Your building got firebombed. You shot a man trying to slit a woman's throat.

That's calling for backup, not calling with some bullshit. I can't tell you how many times women have called me after we had a fight or I was mad and I walked out, talking about, 'Oh, Raul, I heard a noise in the apartment and I'm scared.'" He took a swig of the drink. "Be woman enough to say that you're sorry and you want me to come over. I'm not turned on by helplessness."

"I can see how after a day of rescuing people, it would get tired pretty quick to do that at home."

"Bingo," Raul said, downing the last of his drink.

"But you stopped being a cop," Marisol said. "Then what got in the way of your love life?"

"Me." Raul laughed. "I was bitter after the NYPD burned me, just sort of a brooding jerk." He poured himself another shot of rum.

"You?" Marisol laughed. "I can't see it."

She emptied the bottle into her glass. When she set it down, it clacked loudly against the glass coffee tabletop. She stood to get another bottle and the room tilted. The back of the couch was her safety rail as she crossed the carpet to the liquor cabinet.

"Can I get you a refill?" she asked.

"I shouldn't," he said. "I can't be hungover tomorrow."

She crossed back to lean on the end of the sofa. "Don't go home," Marisol said. "Stay." She put a hand on his arm.

Between the shooting and the alcohol and him showing up to help, she was unraveling. All the rules seemed absurd, irrelevant. The space between their bodies seemed wasted. He looked down and took a deep breath. "I can't, Marisol. I—you shot a man tonight." He looked at her. Those improbably long lashes, the brown of his eyes that hid the pupil. "You've been drinking. I don't know if this is what you really want or the rum talking, or you're just reaching out for somebody." He looked down again. "I can't be that guy who fills the gap. I been in love with you since I was thirteen."

She closed her eyes and felt the impact of his declaration. She wanted his body—but more than that, she didn't want him to leave. "We don't have to do anything. Just stay."

"I'm not capable of staying and not doing anything," he said. "If I lie down in a room with you, I'm coming after you."

"Sleep on the couch," Marisol said. "I'll be upstairs. A whole floor away. You'd be safe."

"Don't count on it," he said with a dry chuckle. "But I'll stay."

She opened the cabinet behind the couch and took down some bedding, careful to keep her balance.

"This place is a maze. I'd never be able to find you," he said.

"I feel like such a punk, even asking," she said.

"You saved a life tonight," Raul said. "You deserve some backup."

In the morning, Marisol felt paranoid again. She ran her fingers through her hair and brushed her teeth before coming downstairs.

"*Buenos días*," she said.

"Hey," Raul said. He rubbed his eyes. "What time is it?"

"Nine thirty-five," she said. "I didn't know what time you needed to get up."

"Oh shit," he said. "I had no idea. It's pitch dark in here."

"Heavy drapes," she said.

He stood and stumbled around in a tank top and boxers. She turned on the overhead light, and he blinked as his eyes adjusted, gathering up his clothes and personal items.

She surveyed his muscled legs, his ass holding up the boxers, his shoulders and chest visible inside and out of the thin undershirt.

"I got a meeting at ten," he said. "Thanks for waking me."

Marisol waved it off as she walked him across the outer office lobby.

He stopped at the door to the stairway. "I—" He leaned forward as if to hug her good-bye. "I should go," he said, and headed down the stairs.

She stood staring after him. The door banged shut at the bottom of the stairwell. She wanted to run to catch up with him. Tell him she wasn't drunk anymore, that it wasn't about shooting a man, that he wasn't just some guy. Some scrap of her dream at the beach came back to her, not the image but the feeling. The way it felt so right to be with him.

She shook her head. *Noooo, girl. No.* She didn't have time for daydreams. Back at her desk, she called the insurance company.

Eva walked into her office as she waited on hold.

"I want you to have something," Eva said.

"Don't give me a gun," Marisol said. "I don't think the NYPD will let me off twice."

"I keep my gun at home," Eva said, and handed Marisol a key ring with two buttons.

"A panic gizmo?" Marisol asked. "I already have one."

"Now you have two," Eva said. "You know how it works. Siren button left, silent signal right. You okay?"

"I don't know," Marisol said, as she took the key ring.

Eva studied Marisol through her granny glasses. "I saw Raul leaving. As long as I've known you, you've never had a guy spend the night."

"He just slept on the couch in my office," Marisol said.

"Your idea?"

"His," Marisol said. "He thought I had PTSD, and I wasn't up to making good sexual decisions."

"I like this Raul," Eva said. "I'm thrilled you're dating some sort of cop."

"I don't know if we're dating," Marisol said. "And he's an ex-cop."

"The best kind," Eva said. "Close enough to have connections, but enough distance to be loyal to you first and foremost."

"I hope so," Marisol said, and dropped the panic key ring into her purse.

By that night, Marisol was emotionally drained and mentally exhausted. Still, when she got a call from Raul, she felt an excited pull in her solar plexus.

After they greeted each other, he sighed. "Rough night. I'm just sitting waiting for this woman to call me."

"Maybe I should hang up," she suggested. "You know, keep the line free."

"No, it's okay," he said. "I have call waiting. It's nice to have someone keep me company while I pine away."

"So what is it you like about this chick?" Marisol asked.

"She always surprises me," he said. "She's tough, but she's got this soft side she showed me last night."

"How do you know she won't surprise you with something you're not expecting, something you're not ready for?"

"If I was expecting it, it wouldn't be a surprise," he

said. "So I'm thinking maybe she trusts me a little, and I'm getting my hopes up."

"That's obviously a mistake," she said, laughing.

"I know," he said. "But now that I see she's a really sensitive person, I'm hoping she'll take pity on me and call."

"You need to work on your self-esteem," Marisol said.

Raul laughed. "Can you help?"

"Yeah," Marisol said. "With the advent of cell phone technology, you can wait by the phone and go out with me at the same time."

"Are you asking me on a date?" Raul asked.

"Of course not," Marisol said. "Just helping you pass the time while you wait for Ms. Right to call."

"What time you wanna get together?" he asked.

"I've got a board meeting," Marisol said. "We could have a late dinner at my place around ten?"

"Aren't you worried that she'll call in the meantime?" Raul asked.

"I'll take my chances," Marisol said.

"Okay," he said. "Let me charge my phone."

Later that night, Tyesha and Woof were drinking at an uptown bar that looked out over the river. She had come from the clinic's board meeting and he had been at an industry function.

"Look at us," Tyesha said. "With your artist gear and my suit, we're like some kind of romantic comedy."

"Or a porno." He laughed. "The executive and the bad boy."

Tyesha chuckled and drank. "When I graduate and work at the clinic full-time, this is gonna be my everyday look."

"Will you miss your current job?" he asked.

"Hell, no." She ate a handful of Marcona almonds from a bowl on the bar. "Public health is my real job."

"I thought you said a lot of the clients you'd date anyway."

"More the exception than the rule," Tyesha said. "The very first guy, for sure. The friend of a friend with my girl Lily. But it went downhill fast with the second guy."

"He wasn't cool?"

"More like a nightmare," she said. "Do you really wanna hear this?"

Woof shrugged. "I'm definitely curious."

Tyesha took a sip of her drink. "I would never have messed with that guy in a million years—I just got the offer when my tuition was due."

"Bills gotta get paid."

"I didn't even end up paying the bills," Tyesha said. "I ended up with a broken jaw after he wouldn't pay because he couldn't bust a nut in a condom. No amount of money is worth risking HIV."

"Damn," Woof said. "I'm surprised you didn't just quit."

"I did quit," Tyesha said. "Went back to waitressing in the neighborhood bar with my jaw wired shut. But I learned from Marisol how to set up escort situations that are much safer. Since then it's been pretty cool. But not cool enough to do if I didn't need the money."

Woof traced a finger along her jawline. "I'm glad you're okay," he said.

A group of young frat boy types exploded into laughter.

"Come on, baby," Woof said, putting a fifty down on the table. "Let's get out of here."

They strolled along the river, arm in arm. The night was warmer than usual for March, but they could see their breath. Street lamps reflected off the water, as well as distant moving lights of ferries and party boats.

Woof stopped and put his arms around her. "So," he said. "I was wondering if maybe we could go home together tonight."

Tyesha blinked and stepped back. "Whoa. Can you wait a minute before you make a move?" She shook her head. "I'm still trying to get the taste of broken jaw out of my mouth."

"I can make it better," he said, leaning in to kiss her jaw.

"Seriously," Tyesha said. "Back up please. Give me a minute."

He stepped back. She folded her arms and stared out at the river.

"Woof." She turned to him. "I realize this is our third date."

"Our fourth date, Tyesha."

"Third," she said. "It doesn't count if I got paid."

"You expect me to be up here going on dates with you, and not get none, and sit around and listen about you fucking other dudes for money?"

"You asked—" Tyesha broke off. "You know what? Never mind. This dating thing isn't working."

"Not working?" Woof asked. "I don't even date usually." He began to pace. "I been a gentleman, I brought you flowers and took you out. Isn't it time for me to get my reward?"

"I'm not gonna fuck you as a 'reward,'" she said. "I'm certainly not gonna fuck you if you act like an asshole. Not for cash or a fancy dinner. Obviously you can only think of me as a hoe."

"It's what you do, isn't it?" Woof said.

"Fuck you, Woof," she said. "That's the only fucking you're gonna get from me, tonight or ever."

"Don't you walk away from me!" He caught up to her and grabbed her arm, spinning her around.

"Get the hell off me," Tyesha said. She reached for her panic keychain and pressed both buttons. An alarm split the air.

"What the fuck?" he said.

She twisted free and ran along the river.

Chapter 24

Half an hour later, the front door of the clinic was still boarded up, so Marisol let Raul in through the alley door.

"Hola, guapa," he said. "Guess what I brought you."

"I'm bad at guessing games," she said, as they walked through the back hallway to the stairwell. "Besides, you didn't need to bring anything."

"Flowers seemed cheesy," he said. "So look what I found at the music store."

He pulled out a cassette tape of the Puerto Rican reggaeton singer Ivy Queen.

"En Mi Imperio?" Marisol said. "I haven't heard this in twenty years!"

"I remember how you and Gladys used to blast it in her room," he said. "My parents hated it. They were always trying to get Gladys to go back to listening to Menudo and Yolandita Monge."

Marisol laughed. "I know. Gladys listened to pop before we met, but I couldn't stand that tortured teen-love shit."

"Of course not," Raul said. "A badass girl needs badass theme music. I looked for a digital recording, but I couldn't find one."

"Thank you," Marisol said. "I have a tape player somewhere in my office."

"*Bueno,*" Raul said. "So while you're saving the hood and plotting your world takeover, you can listen to this and think of me."

"Come on up," Marisol said, taking the cassette and closing the hall door behind him. "I hope you like Ethiopian food."

"If I'm eating with you, I'm pretty enthused about it," he said.

They had walked up the same staircase the night before, but this time, the walls seemed to press them together. Every accidental brush of their shoulders sent a buzz through Marisol's system.

"I wanted to let you know how much I appreciate what you did for me after the shooting. I think you were the factor that gave me the benefit of the doubt."

On the fifth floor, she let him into her apartment. She'd never before had a guest other than Cristina or the team or that one visit from Dulce. Raul's presence made her self-conscious, and she was aware of the light film of dust that had settled on everything except the bed, bathroom, and kitchenette. She noticed the unfinished attempt at washing the windows: One was clear and the other still grimy.

"I'm almost never here," she said, setting her laptop and the bag of takeout down on the counter. "I mostly live in my office downstairs."

Raul sat down on the armchair and sank into its ancient springs. "Is this Cristina?" he asked, looking at a snapshot of her in front of her clinic in Cuba.

"All grown up," Marisol said. "I'm hoping to visit her before she moves back in December."

"I been wanting to go there myself now that they've opened up travel," he said. "Maybe next time I visit my folks in PR. It's been five years since they retired."

"Gladys always said it was their dream," Marisol said.

"Yeah, they have a little house in Aibonito," he said. "My ma's got the garden she always wanted. My dad plays dominoes every day."

Marisol crossed to the dining area, where the takeout bag sat on the counter. She arranged the food on a large platter, bright sections of green, yellow, and red.

She set out the *injera* and some salad, plus two glasses of honey wine.

"I hope you don't mind eating with your hands," she said, washing up at the kitchen sink.

"Not at all," he said, taking the soap from her and washing his own hands. "I never had Ethiopian food before, but it smells great."

Marisol beckoned him over to the pair of bar stools at her kitchen counter. His knee bumped against the plywood of the counter's false back.

She tore the large circle of *injera* in half and handed it to him.

"Do I make a burrito or what?" he asked.

She laughed. "I'll show you." She tore a small piece off and used it like a tortilla to scoop up some red lentils.

"Here," she said, and placed the food gently into his mouth.

"That's really good," he said. "Let me try."

He tore off a piece and used it to scoop up a chunk of savory chicken.

"Para tí?" he asked.

Marisol smiled and opened her mouth. Her eyes widened as the spice hit her tongue. "Whoa," she said, fanning her mouth. "I told them to make it medium."

"It's hot?" Raul asked.

"Definitely," Marisol said.

"Show me," he said.

"I don't know if you can handle it," she said, scooping up some more chicken for him. "Let me add some vegetables to cool it down."

"Oh no," he said, grabbing her wrist before she could dip into the vegetables. "Give it to me full strength."

She placed the food in his mouth.

Raul chewed it and blinked, pressing his eyebrows down and trying to keep a straight face.

Marisol watched him. When he finally swallowed, he busted up laughing. "Okay, that was hot. But did I play it off?"

"Not at all," Marisol said.

"I can't hide anything when I'm with you, Marisol," he said. "I should know that by now. But you're so hot I thought maybe it would cancel it out or something."

"Wow," she said. "That was so cheesy."

"It sounded so much better in my head." He laughed.

"Moving on," she said. "I just wanted to thank you for everything. Everything you did yesterday. Last night."

"I was glad to do it," he said. "But I hope I'm not reading this wrong. I hope this is actually a date, and not just a thank-you dinner."

"It's a date," she said.

"Good." He smiled and ate a mouthful of salad and chicken, licking the sauce off his fingers.

"I also appreciated the way you didn't—you waited—" Marisol searched for words. "The way you slept on the couch."

"Curse of the nice guy." He shrugged.

She smiled and drank her wine, hoping he would say more, but he stayed quiet.

"How long you been cursed?" she asked.

"I think it's a Catholic curse," he said. "Goes back to seeing *Santa María* as 'blessed among women' and going to hell if you have sex. It sort of screwed with my head. Didn't seem like you could be good and happy. Being good was supposed to make you happy, and if it didn't, you weren't being good enough."

"We went to church briefly with my grandmother," Marisol said. "Back in PR."

"Did you grow up mostly here or there?"

Marisol shrugged. "I was conceived in Puerto Rico, but my dad was bad news, so my mom moved to the States when she was a few months' pregnant. I was born here. We lived in the Bronx until she met another bad news guy—Cristina's father—and moved back to PR to get away from him."

"Bad news guys," Raul said.

"It was nice to live in PR," Marisol said. "Those were the good years. Until middle school when my *mami* died and *abuelita* died a few years later and we moved back to New York."

"I'm sorry about your mom passing away," he said. "And your grandmother."

Marisol laughed. "Yeah, I'm sorry, too."

He raised his eyebrows.

"I've always laughed at inappropriate times," she said. "You should see me at a funeral." He laughed, too, and it broke the tension.

"Maybe one of these days we could go someplace," he said, almost shyly. "I gotta admit, I have this fantasy of taking you to the beach in Puerto Rico."

Marisol swallowed hard, remembering the dream.

"My parents' place is in the mountains, so the beach is really a day trip," Raul said. "But my folks have this little cabin they rent out. We could stay there."

"With your parents?"

"It's up the hill from them," Raul explained. "They wouldn't bother us. It even has a couch for me to sleep on."

"If we were going to Puerto Rico together, you wouldn't be sleeping on the couch." She moved toward him.

"I was kinda hoping the same thing." He leaned in and kissed her, put a palm on her shoulder, and gave her skin the gentlest of caresses.

"I just need you to know—" he began.

"Raul—"

"Just, just let me finish, okay. I can't just do some one-night shit. Or one-week shit. Not with you. If you don't want to, that's cool, but just let me know, okay? I wouldn't want—"

"Shut up and kiss me, Raul."

She could feel him sink into the kiss, his hands firmer on her skin, pulling her close to him, the warmth of his body, the fierceness of his embrace.

"There's something you should know about this apartment," she said.

"What's that?" he asked.

"No couch." She smiled and led him to the bedroom.

He sat back on the bed as she stood in front of him. She had worn a tank top that snapped up the front, and he kissed her softly as he undid her top, snap by snap. Her skin buzzed everywhere his fingertips touched. After he'd undone the top, he slid it gently off, kissing the tops of her breasts and reaching around to unhook her bra.

She unbuttoned his shirt, and slid her hands beneath

his undershirt, feeling his smooth skin, hard muscles, and a bullet scar just above his hip.

He unhooked the bra and buried his face in her breasts, kissing, licking, nuzzling, taking them each in his mouth.

She gasped, unbuckled his belt, unbuttoned his jeans, and slid her hands down over his hips, his ass, his thighs. He moved toward the edge of the bed, and she straddled him, feeling his erection against her belly.

She was ravenous for him. All his skin against all her skin felt like it wouldn't be enough. She yanked off his shirt and wrapped her arms and legs around him. He hoisted himself onto the bed and lay on top of her. She kissed his neck, his shoulders, his chest. He pushed himself up, straightening his arms, to give her room to maneuver. She kissed his navel, bit the top of his boxers and slid them off, then moved back up, brushing her lips past his erection.

He moaned and threw his head back. She undid her jeans and slid out of them, then pushed off the bed, turning over, on top of him. He lay back, smiling with a tenderness that she had never seen before. Like his heart might break from the joy of it.

She rolled on the condom and slid him into her. She started on top, then they rolled over and he slowed down, kissing her gently, stroking strong and slow. She had never felt like this before. She just couldn't seem to get him deep enough into her. She wanted more of him. More of him, more inside, more connected, more. The air between them seemed like an unbearable obstacle.

She let herself fall. She blinked up at his dark eyes, so open and clear, wrapped her legs around him and held tight.

"*Sí, mamita,*" he said, stroking slowly, looking right in her eyes.

The deliciousness of the sensations between their bodies edged out all thoughts. The only moment she could feel was this one.

"*Te gusta así?*" he asked her.

Yes. Yes. She liked it like that. Oh, just like that. Just like that. "*Sí, papi*," she managed, just as she came, hard and unexpected, calling his name and thrusting against him so intensely, she made him come, too.

When the tremors subsided, he caught his breath and pulled out.

"I couldn't help myself." He smiled at her. "I wanted to keep going. I wanted to give you more." He smoothed the curls from her moist forehead and kissed her, open-mouthed and deep. She kissed back, one arm tangled in the coarse, curly hair on the back of his head, the other hand still holding his ass.

He pulled back from the kiss and rolled them onto their sides. Looked her right in the eyes. "Marisol, *mami*, I want to give you everything."

He kissed her neck, her shoulder, as she started to cry.

"Just let it out," he murmured in her ear. "That's right. You don't have to be tough right now."

"I'm a mess, Raul," she said, wiping her face on the pillow. "I don't know how to trust anyone. I don't know how to let my guard down."

"You seem to be doing an okay job, *mi amor*." He kissed the tops of each of her cheekbones, her eyelids.

"Part of the reason I never dated anyone in high school is that I didn't want anyone to really get to know me. Boys, I mean."

"Hey," Raul said. "I can see you've had some really bad guys in your life early on. That would cause anyone to have a hard time trusting, *verdad*? And I'm not perfect. But I'm serious about you, Marisol. Not just fucking around for fun. I been in love with you since junior high."

"I'm not ready for the L-word," she said with a laugh, wiping her eyes with the back of her hand.

"I'm just saying," Raul said.

"Raul, I'm not an angel," she said, sniffling a little.

"Neither am I," he said. "We're over thirty, Marisol. Neither one of us is a virgin. I can guess that you were probably with VanDyke. My only question is, are you still seeing him?"

"VanDyke?"

"Are you seeing him? Are you seeing anyone else? Is there another man in your life, Marisol?"

She laughed. "No, Raul." She shook her head as she spoke. "I'm not seeing VanDyke, and I have no interest in doing so. I'm not seeing anyone else."

"Good," he said and leaned forward to kiss her.

"Yuck," she said, pulling back and covering her nose. "I've got *mocos*."

"I don't care, *mujer*," he said. "I want you, *mocos* and all."

She reached for a tissue, and blew her nose, then kissed him back.

He pulled out of the kiss. "There's something I need to tell you," he said. "I—that girl Nalissa—the last night I worked at the clinic—"

"You all had sex?" Marisol asked.

"She told you?" he asked.

"No, but I could see she wanted to," Marisol said.

"It was just that one time," he said. "A major lapse in judgment."

She put a finger to his lips. "No apologies," she said. "No explanations. I would never hold anything in your sexual past against you. Let's just start fresh."

"The freshest," he said. "Same here. I'll never hold anything in your sexual past against you. I'm much more interested in your sexual future." He propped himself up on one elbow and ran a finger along the side of her breast, her waist, her hip.

"What did you have in mind?" she asked.

"Well, I'm not quite ready for round two," he said. "The equipment is cooling off for a minute. Maybe I could use some alternative methods."

"Like what?" she asked.

"Just a little old-fashioned kissing," he said, kissing her neck. "And sucking," he said, putting her breasts in his mouth and running his tongue across her nipples until they were hard.

"And more kissing," he said, working his way down across her belly, keeping one hand on her breast, rubbing his fingers back and forth across her nipple.

Marisol moaned.

"And some good old-fashioned licking," he said, sliding his tongue down through her pubic hair. "See this is the place where women are so clearly superior. You all can have an infinite amount of pleasure."

He glided his tongue down between her lips and she gasped. Slid his tongue inside her and rubbed his upper lip across her clitoris, and she arched back on the bed.

"See?" he said, gently guiding her hand down to feel his returning erection. "I like this at least as much as you do."

"Come back inside me, Raul," she said.

"Oh no, *mami*," he said. "Not yet. Not until I make you come again."

He buried his face between her legs until she was screaming with the pleasure of it, then he rolled on another condom and slid back inside her.

"*Ay, Dios*, you're so wet," he breathed into her ear.

Marisol felt spent, liquid, fused to the moist sheets. And yet with him licking her breasts, and sliding a thumb down between her lips, rubbing her clitoris again, he managed to awaken the pleasure in her, and she came, but softer this time. Her body undulating with waves of pleasure. Her hips trembling as if they could barely contain all of him, all of the sensation. And then, grinning down at her, he opened his mouth and gasped, as if startled.

"*¡Ay, Marisol!*" he choked out, and then he shuddered and jerked, falling down onto her chest.

She could feel him slipping. They fumbled together to remove the condom. She barely had the energy to tie it and toss it into the bedside trash, before she collapsed back onto the bed and they slept.

Sunlight streamed in the blinds she had forgotten to close. She blinked at the brightness, and looked for Raul. She found him on her laptop at the kitchen counter.

"What are you doing?"

"Shit!" he said. "Caught red-handed. I'm trying to find a place that delivers breakfast."

Marisol walked over and closed the laptop. "For patient confidentiality reasons, I can't let anyone use my laptop."

He put an arm around her and she tensed.

"What?" he said. "You think I was snooping around?"

"You were using my laptop," she said.

"My phone network was too slow," he said. "And I didn't wanna wake you up to get the wireless password. If I overstepped, I'm sorry."

They were interrupted by a knock at the apartment door.

"Who is it?" Marisol asked.

"Eva."

"It's a bad time," Marisol said.

"I know we haven't talked a lot lately since the—"

"Eva, I'm not alone," Marisol said.

"Oh. Sorry," Eva said. Marisol waited to hear retreating footsteps. "But, um, something happened."

"Is it Tyesha?" Marisol asked as she went to get her clothes.

"Not Tyesha," Eva said. "Somebody vandalized the front of the building."

"Like firebombing it wasn't enough?" Marisol said. She pulled on a pair of jeans, and Raul's T-shirt, then realized it was his and threw it to him as she struggled into her own shirt.

Marisol peeked around the door.

"You really need to come take a look," Eva whispered. "We had better figure out what to do. Do we call the cops? Or should we call your friend Raul?"

"I don't think we'll need to bother with that call," Marisol said.

Hastily scrawled graffiti on the wall beside the door:

Marisol Rivera is a dead bitch.

Marisol swallowed hard.

Two men stood next to the lettering with a bucket of paint.

"I'm gonna have them paint over it right now," Eva said. "But I didn't want to hide it from you."

"Wait," Raul said. "I gotta call this in. They need to get a forensics team out here, or at the very least photograph it first."

"Come on," Marisol said. "You all freak out over every little wall tag in New York City?"

"Marisol," Raul said. "In the past couple of days, this has been the site of an attempted murder, a self-defense shooting, and a firebombing. I think this is a credible threat, and I intend to inform the authorities. Do you have a problem with that?"

Marisol shook her head, afraid to speak, lest her voice betray either her wounded pride or her relief.

"Last night was amazing," Raul said to her after he hung up the phone. "Dinner again tonight?"

"Let's check in later, okay?"

"Whatever you say, *mami*," he said. "Just call me."

Serena walked up to the front of the clinic. "What now?" she asked.

"Just graffiti," Marisol said. "No big deal."

"Okay," Serena said. "I need that narrative for the pregnancy prevention grant ASAP."

"I got a higher priority issue," Marisol said as they swiped in to the security area of the stairwell.

"What's higher priority than twenty-five thousand dollars?"

"I need you to look at my laptop," Marisol said as they climbed the three flights of stairs. "Can you tell if someone was snooping around on it?"

"Like who?"

"Don't worry about who," Marisol said. "Can you check what they did online and what files they looked at?"

"Sure," Serena said and sat down with the laptop.

"Here's what I got in the browser history for today," she said. "A search for 'breakfast delivery lower east side.' A check on a website that lists crime reports in Manhattan and someone checked their Q-mail account. That's today. You want yesterday?"

"No," Marisol said. "What about files they opened?"

"Spreadsheet file," Serena said. "Vega financial complete."

"What?" Marisol squeezed in next to her and peered at the laptop. "That was this morning?"

"It autosaved this morning," Serena said. "It was opened last night."

"Was it viewed this morning?"

"No way to know if it was viewed," Serena said. "The file was open."

"Could someone have sent the file on Q-mail?"

Serena raised her eyebrows. "Hold on, let me try something."

She pulled up a program with mostly text and codes, and clicked through several screens. "Whoever used Q-mail today didn't move a lot of data. It's unlikely that they sent a file. But I can check one other thing."

She opened a word processing document. "Let's see what was on the clipboard."

She hit the paste function.

"*messaging consistent with the goal of making health care available to everyone, regardless of their legal status or engagement in sex work, as well as*" popped up on the screen.

"That's from my board meeting last night," Marisol said.

"Then it doesn't look like anyone cut and pasted from your document into their e-mail," Serena said. "Does that mean we're okay?"

Marisol shrugged. "I just wish I knew what was in that e-mail," she said. "I'll have the grant proposal info for you in an hour. And then I want you to put a security password on this motherfucker."

When she got her laptop back, she did a search for Raul online. Several stories corroborated what he'd said: the police brutality case, the kid dying, the settlement out of court, the other cops fired. Barrios was offered his job back, but the story didn't say whether or not he'd taken it.

Part of her had almost hoped to catch him in a lie. At least then she wouldn't have to keep wondering about him.

Chapter 25

Two evenings after the shooting, Marisol sat at her desk looking at the *New York Daily News* website. "Firebombing and Shooting at Lower East Side Hooker Clinic." She wasn't as upset about the headline or even the article, as she was about the photograph. In it, she was pictured talking to one of the firefighters. She had her mouth open, but she was clearly identifiable. They got the name wrong, María Rivera, and thank God no one had identified her as the shooter, but it wasn't the low profile she had hoped to keep.

Marisol was rereading the article when Raul tapped on her office door and stuck his head in.

"*Hola, guapa*," he said.

"How'd you get past the boarded-up door?" she asked.

"Eva let me in," he said. "Can I take you to dinner tonight?"

She felt almost shy from the night before. Some part of her was trying to use the issue with the computer as a reason to hold back, but the pull was so strong. To want him, to trust him, to say yes.

Marisol smiled and closed her laptop. "Where did you have in mind?"

"Your place," he said, holding up a bag of takeout.

Marisol laughed as she gathered her things and turned off the lamp on her desk. "One of these days, we'll need to go to your place. Unless your girlfriend would mind."

Raul looked stricken. "The place is a wreck," he said as they walked upstairs. "But I'll take you over there right now. I swear I'm single. Except you. And you haven't even agreed to be my woman."

She didn't know what to say as she unlocked the door to her apartment.

He set down the takeout. "I have another present for you." From the front pocket of his jeans he produced a half page of scratch paper.

He handed Marisol a handwritten list of about twenty alpha-numeric sequences, each with thirteen digits—mostly numbers.

"What is it?" Marisol asked. "A secret code?"

"Better," he said. "It's a complete list of all the marked bills stolen from VanDyke."

Her smile disappeared. "Why are you giving this to me?"

He shrugged. "What do you get for the woman who has everything?"

"What the hell?" she said. "Are you trying to set me up?"

"Am I what?" he asked.

"First I catch you sniffing around on my laptop—"

"I wasn't sniffing around," he said. "I was getting breakfast."

"—now you want to plant evidence on me from the VanDyke case?"

"Plant evidence?" His mouth fell open.

"Are you wearing a wire?" she asked, then leaned into his chest and shouted, "ARE YOU WEARING A FUCKING WIRE?"

"Have you lost your goddamn mind?" he asked. "I came here with every intention of feeding you dinner, giving you a present that might save your ass, then fucking your brains out. So unless I have some kind of recording device UP MY ASS, I'm not wearing a wire."

"I don't believe you," she said, and ripped off his shirt. Buttons flew across the floor of her kitchenette, and she ran her hands up and down the front and back of his undershirt.

"Fine," he said. "Search your little heart out."

She unbuckled his belt and let his jeans drop. She sat on the floor at his feet and unlaced his boots, took off his socks, felt around in the shoes.

She grabbed his jacket and turned the pockets upside down. Pulled out his billfold, his ID, his keys. She tossed them on the armchair and ran her hands across all the jacket fabric.

"If you wanna do a cavity search, maybe we could work that in later," he said.

She turned back around and looked at him, naked in the middle of her kitchenette.

She felt stupid, embarrassed, out of control. "I'm sorry, Raul," she said. "I—"

"I think there are a few external spots you missed," he said.

Marisol buried her face in her hands, and felt a flush of embarrassment. "I can't believe I fucking lost it," she said. "You must think I'm a lunatic."

"You definitely missed a spot." He took her hand and slowly guided it between his legs. "Under here," he said, pressing her fingers under his testicles. "You gotta be thorough."

She felt around, massaging underneath. "I don't feel anything that could be a wire," she said.

"What about here?" he asked, guiding her hand up to his erection. "I could be hiding something in here."

"You could hide a lot in there," she said. "Maybe two or three wires."

He laughed. "I got excited watching you search," he said. "So driven."

"Maybe I'm wearing the wire," Marisol said. "You might have to search me."

"A great idea," Raul said, leading her to the bed. "But I'll use the horizontal method."

Marisol laughed. "Oh really?"

"It's very innovative," he said. "You work from the bottom up."

"Interesting," Marisol said, as he took off her shoes.

"This is going to require your full cooperation," he said as he unzipped her jeans and pulled them down. "Step away from the jeans, miss."

She laughed and he pulled her gently onto the bed. "Now, here's the tricky part," he said, and lay back on the bed, pulling her up to straddle him.

He moved his hips to grind his erection against the wet spot in her thong underwear.

"Are we still searching?" she asked.

"I got distracted," he said.

"Very unprofessional," she said.

"Sorry. Back on the case," he said. "We'll work our way up." He began to unbutton her blouse from the bottom up, and slid it down over her shoulders. He unhooked her bra and ran his hands from her waist up to fondle her breasts.

"Just one area left to search," she said, hooking her finger into the waistband of her thong.

"One final safety precaution," he said, pulling out a condom.

"Did you learn this in the police academy?" she asked.

"No, ma'am," he said. "Just basic common sense."

As she rolled off her thong, he rolled on the condom.

"I think you might need to do an internal search on me," she said.

"Great minds think alike," he said. "I was just preparing the equipment."

She slid him into her, riding him, slow at first. She maintained eye contact. Watching his eyes, his face, as his pleasure built. Every intake of his breath, every low moan, every involuntary parting of his lips.

She watched him with a tenderness that took in everything. The five o'clock shadow on his face, the tiny mole beside his left eye, the plum color of his lips, the subtle indentation where his left ear had once been pierced.

She watched him, fascinated. The feeling of him inside her was familiar, but the connection was so different. She touched his cheek to make sure he was real. It was different to enjoy a man's pleasure. To enjoy herself enjoying him.

She didn't want to miss anything. She saw the moment that he slid under, could barely contain himself. Then she rode him harder, at just the angle she liked. Rode him to a climax, first her then him, feeling him quaking deep inside her, with her heart in her throat, her breasts in his hands, her tongue in his mouth. She swallowed his inarticulate gasp of ecstasy as his hips thrust against her, into her, over the edge.

"What happened to dinner?" she asked. "Is there any food in that bag, or were you just trying to plant more evidence on me?"

"As I recall, you started the search party," he said.

"Can I get a temporary insanity plea?"

"I forgive you," he said, kissing her. Then he brought the takeout to bed. He gestured to the pile of his clothes on the floor of the kitchenette and all the scattered buttons. "Actually, I forgive you conditionally," he said, grinning and opening the bag. "You owe me a shirt."

The following morning, Marisol was surprised when a police cruiser pulled up in front of the clinic and two uniformed officers came looking for her.

Her mind flashed to the list of unmarked bills. Was it still on the counter in plain view? She couldn't recall, and she hadn't bothered to clean up this morning. Sex had her way off her game.

"Ms. Rivera," one of the officers said. "We'd like you to come in for questioning."

At the ninth precinct station, she sat in a cold, windowless room. One officer sat across from her, and the other stood by the door. Nothing on the walls, nothing on the desk but a digital recorder.

"You really needed me to come in because of some graffiti?" Marisol asked.

"This is actually in reference to another matter, Ms. Rivera," the officer said.

"Didn't I answer all of the questions about the shooting with the detectives?" she asked, exasperated. "They said they'd just take the gun and drop the charges since the guy is out of critical condition."

"This isn't about Jerry Rios or his associates," the officer explained.

"Well, what then?" Marisol demanded.

The door opened and two plainclothes detectives walked in. Marisol immediately recognized the steely cop whom she'd met with Raul at the gala. Detective Mathias of Central Robbery introduced himself and his partner, Delano. They sat down across from her in the metal chairs.

"Sorry to keep you waiting, Ms. Rivera," Mathias said.

"We have a few questions with regard to Mr. Jeremy VanDyke."

Marisol sat silent, stunned.

"Approximately nine days ago, you witnessed a robbery at his residence. VanDyke's driver ID'd you as the witness from your picture in the *Daily News* that ran yesterday, after the shooting at your clinic."

"I was at VanDyke's," Marisol said. "We had dinner."

"The driver says you were there, but VanDyke denies it," Mathias said. "Why?"

"Who can understand these billionaires?" Marisol said. "I'm used to men bragging about having dinner with me, not hiding it."

"So how come your fingerprints didn't show up on anything?" Mathias asked. "Glasses, silverware, doorknobs?"

"I wore gloves," Marisol said.

"What?" Delano asked.

"Elbow-length gloves," Marisol said. "Part of a Dilani Mara ensemble. I can model it for you."

"Just answer the questions," Mathias said. "How many intruders?"

"I saw two guys," Marisol said. "One tall and thin, one shorter and thicker. They both had guns."

"Thank you, Ms. Rivera," he said, standing up. "Sit tight until we get back. I want to show you something."

Mathias and Delano stepped out, leaving the sergeant at the door. He offered Marisol a cup of coffee. She declined.

After five minutes, a light went on in the adjacent room, and the mirrored wall turned into a window. Through the glass, Marisol could see an identical room. Bare walls. Big metal table. A few chairs.

Mathias and Delano stepped into the adjacent room. Mathias glanced up at Marisol and the sergeant through the two-way mirror.

Jeremy VanDyke entered. He was dressed in a dark suit and wore a grim expression.

"Thank you for coming in, Mr. VanDyke," Mathias said.

"You pulled me from a conference call with Japan," VanDyke said, sitting at the desk. "How can I help you?"

The door to the interview room opened and Raul entered.

"Mind if I sit in?" Raul asked.

Mathias pulled out a chair for Raul and made introductions.

Under any other circumstances, the sight of Raul would fill Marisol with pleasure. But not here. He was too close to the case, and his proximity to VanDyke seemed even more dangerous.

Raul's expression was neutral.

"Mr. VanDyke," Mathias said. "In a previous interview, you said you dined alone the night of the robbery. Would you like to change your answer?"

"No," VanDyke said.

"This morning, your driver identified this woman"—Delano put the paper in front of VanDyke—"Marisol Rivera, as your dinner date that night."

"He must be mistaken," VanDyke said.

"That's what I thought," Mathias said. "We didn't find her fingerprints at the scene."

"What is this about?" VanDyke asked.

"We're working on a theory," Mathias said. "There's only one explanation that fits the evidence as it stands."

"And what's that?" VanDyke asked.

"Your driver is certain he brought her to your residence," Mathias said. "You insist you didn't have dinner with her. Our forensics team found no evidence of her presence at your house. They swept the area where the alarm was cut, and the study where your safe was broken into. We found no hairs, no fingerprints of hers. So our theory is that she was the robber."

Marisol saw Raul's face twitch.

"That's ridiculous," VanDyke said. "The robbers were men."

"You sure?" Mathias asked, flipping through pages. "In your statement, you said the robbers wore masks. They bound and gagged you in your bedroom, then closed the door. Couldn't Ms. Rivera have helped them break in? Once that door was closed, anybody could have entered."

"Technically, yes," VanDyke said. "But I would have—"

"So either your driver is mistaken," Mathias said. "Or Marisol Rivera helped rob you, or you're lying. Which is it?"

VanDyke opened his mouth to answer, when Mathias cut him off.

"It's not really fair to single you out," Mathias said. "We have both of them here—Ms. Rivera and your driver. In nearby interrogation rooms. I'll just get the two of them and we can straighten this out."

VanDyke's jaw clenched. "I'll admit," he said, "I have been less than forthcoming. Ms. Rivera and I did dine together."

"Did she also witness the robbery?"

"Yes."

"You can confirm that your driver picked her up near Central Park?"

"At my request," he said. "People watch me. They watch my car. They follow my staff. I didn't want to be seen picking up a woman from her office location."

"What?" Raul asked. "The neighborhood isn't gentrified enough for you?"

"Not the neighborhood," VanDyke said. "But a clinic that serves prostitutes."

"Are you kidding me?" Raul said. "Marisol Rivera is the executive director, not some girl getting a pregnancy test."

VanDyke looked down at his hands. "Perhaps my focus on protecting my privacy may have underresourced my security. I'll be reordering my priorities." VanDyke looked over at Mathias. "Are we done here, Detective?"

The cop nodded and sent him out to sign a revised statement.

"He tried to clean it up," Raul told Mathias and Delano. "But I know what he meant. Fucking racist. She's too brown for the billionaire to be seen with?"

"I don't think it's a race thing," Delano said.

"I don't need a white cop to tell me what is and isn't a race thing," Raul said.

"Guys," Mathias said. "Forget it. We got what we came for."

Marisol watched them with a growing feeling of dread.

"I know the race thing happens," Delano said. "I'm just saying not in this particular case."

"Hey, you two." Mathias raised his voice. "Let's go."

"What the hell do you think the issue was?" Raul asked. "Because any guy would be lucky to have dinner with a woman like her."

"I'm just saying," Delano said. "I think VanDyke was worried about her rap sheet."

Marisol did the math in her head. No way could she push past the uniformed cop, run out the door, and get to Raul to explain there was something she hadn't told him yet.

"Rap sheet?" Raul asked. "What the hell are you talking about?"

Raul stepped closer to Delano.

"Back the fuck up," Delano said. "Matty, what's he even doing here? He's not a cop anymore."

"Barrios is consulting on this case, and I asked him to come," Mathias said. "We got what we wanted, so let's move on."

"Not until you tell me about Marisol Rivera's rap sheet," Raul said, turning toward Mathias.

Mathias glanced at the two-way mirror, his expression contrite. "Ms. Rivera has two prior arrests," Mathias said quietly. "Now, can we drop it?"

"Arrests for what?" Raul asked.

Not like this. He shouldn't hear it like this. He should hear it from her. Just the two of them. When she could remind him he'd promised not to hold her sexual past against her.

"For prostitution," Delano said.

Marisol's eyes flew to Raul. He said them like they were just ordinary words, five matter-of-fact syllables that hadn't just changed the course of her life. Raul's eyes widened in shock. His jaw clenched.

"See?" Delano said. "It's not a race thing. It's a hooker thing."

Raul stood, fists balled up.

"Why don't you take five, Barrios?" Mathias asked.

"You knew?" Raul asked, looking directly at Mathias.

"Take five. Okay, buddy?" Mathias asked.

Raul slammed the door behind him.

"What's with him?" Delano asked.

Marisol leaped up and bolted for the door. The officer restrained her.

"Miss, I have orders not to let you leave," he said.

She managed to stick her head out the door. "Raul!"

He turned and looked at her, his face puckered in bitter lines of bewilderment. He shook his head and turned away.

Marisol let the sergeant escort her back to her seat.

She didn't hear the door close or Raul's retreating footsteps. She looked past the two-way glass and through the two men in the illuminated room. She recalled standing in another police station surrounded by men in uniforms. She had been wearing a gold halter top, booty shorts, and platform wedge sandals splattered with mud. She had willed herself not to shiver in the freezing air-conditioned room. The only difference between then and now was that today she had on business casual.

Mathias came back in. "Mission accomplished," he said with a stiff smile. "All the stories match."

Marisol felt a rock where her heart should be.

She kept seeing Raul's face, contorted with hurt, his back walking away. She wanted to bolt for the door and catch him to explain. But fuck that. She wasn't gonna chase down some *pendejo*. For what? She imagined some *telenovela* scene: "*Please, forgive me. I was young and didn't know what I was doing . . .*"

She had nothing to apologize for. More like, "*Fuck you. I did what I had to do to protect my family, and fuck you some more if you're gonna hold that against me.*"

Fuck the whole romance bullshit with Raul. Who the hell was he? Not the fantasy about them having a future together—some bullshit dream on the beach—but the reality.

Just a two-time hookup. The little brother of her friend from high school. Some sex she'd mistaken for something more. All that love he talked about? That wasn't love. That was some immature schoolboy crush. Love was putting on your dead mother's dress and fucking a stranger to keep your little sister out of foster care.

Eva was right: The only person she really loved was Cristina. She could catch a plane to Havana tomorrow.

She tried to reach for a feeling, conjure her sister's

face. She felt nothing. She slid her hand up to her locket. It lay on top of her cotton undershirt, but beneath her blouse, cool to the touch.

Mathias said, "I assumed he knew. Didn't you grow up together?"

Marisol began to feel something. A buzzing started in the soles of her feet and moved up her legs. Rage. So strong, she began to tremble with it. She knew she should leave, but she didn't care. Raul? Cristina? It felt like nothing mattered anymore.

"It's not just some coincidence that I run a clinic for sex workers," she said. "I know how hard it is on the street. And New York's Finest are a big part of the problem. What other guys pay for, NYPD takes for free." She looked at Mathias. She could feel the heat under her neck, her face, her scalp. *Rapist.* The word almost spit itself out of her mouth.

"You can go now, Ms. Rivera," he said.

She opened her mouth, but the rage must have unlocked something else, some whisper of caring about seeing Cristina. She walked out with her back straight and her head held high, the same strut she'd performed down the runway of VanDyke's hall.

Marisol held it together on the taxi ride home, all the way into the clinic and down the hallway to Eva's couch. She lay with her face against the microfiber and sobbed.

"What happened, honey?" Eva asked.

"The cops read Raul my rap sheet."

"I'm so sorry," Eva said.

"I'm not," Marisol said, wiping her eyes with the heels of her hands. She grabbed a tissue. "I don't need him. Fucking asshole. *El amor es una mierda.*"

"Marisol, you shouldn't—"

"No, you're the one who shouldn't," she spat. "You

shouldn't have pushed me to date him. To open my heart. If this is what an open heart feels like, I'd rather have open heart surgery."

"I know," Eva said.

"I'm not cut out for this shit," Marisol said. "If I want a man, I can find one uptown any night of the week. I don't care if you judge me for it. Fuck Raul. He doesn't have anything I need."

That night, or really Saturday morning, she got a late phone call that woke her up.

"So, is it true?" Raul's drunken voice came through the phone, his speech slurred.

"Is what true?" Marisol asked. She blinked at her phone, which said 1:52 a.m. "That I was a sex worker?"

"When I asked you about yourself," he said, "you told me you had dated a bunch. Izzat what qualifies as 'a bunch' these days? Fucking guys for money?"

Marisol was wide-awake now, and pissed. "If you wanna know about me so bad, why don't you go look it up on your cop database?"

When he spoke again, his voice was a malicious hiss. "You fucking lied to me. I've been called *hijo de la gran puta* before. But I never thought I'd be *novio de la gran puta.*"

Marisol slammed the phone down.

This time when she cried, it was equal parts rage and sorrow.

Chapter 26

On Monday, two days later, Marisol stood in the rooftop garden above her apartment. In the dusk light, she could scarcely make out the lavender buds on a bush one of the staff had planted. She looked past the garden, past the opposite buildings with their rows of bright windows and zigzag fire escapes. She looked past the church spires and skyscrapers, toward the horizon and the cloud cover over the city.

Her chest ached. She had been distracted from it all afternoon in the bustle of the clinic, but the minute she was alone, the grief fell on her, heavy and sharp.

Her phone rang, and she felt a pang of hope in her solar plexus. That he was calling to apologize. To beg forgiveness. She didn't recognize the caller ID. *Stop it, Marisol*, she admonished herself. *Don't be that girl waiting for the phone to ring. You're done with him. Just ignore it.*

She picked up the phone.

"Ms. Rivera? It's Jeremy VanDyke. I need to arrange a meeting with you, tonight."

"Tonight's bad," Marisol said, trying to recover from the disappointment that it wasn't Raul, and the even stronger disappointment that she cared.

"I apologize for the urgency of the request, but I can meet any time before I leave for Japan at four a.m."

"Jeremy, what's this about?"

"I'd prefer to discuss it face-to-face."

"As far as I'm concerned, our business has concluded," Marisol said.

She walked into the building, closing the roof door behind her.

"I have a lucrative proposition for you," VanDyke said.

"My workday is over," she said. "Call me when you get back from Japan."

"Five minutes," he said. "There have been some—developments."

"You've already had three minutes, and you haven't said anything. I'm hanging up." She walked down the stairwell.

"Wait!" he said. "Security has been compromised from our previous meeting. Five minutes, Ms. Rivera. Please."

"Security?" she asked, stepping into the clinic's administrative office area.

"Please," he said. "I'd rather not discuss it over the phone."

"Fine," she said. "I'll be in my office for the next two hours."

"My limo is out front. I'll be right up."

Marisol rang off. She called Eva and explained the situation.

The intercom buzzed.

"Do you want me to come up?" Eva asked. "I'm only five minutes away."

The bell buzzed again.

"Definitely," Marisol said. "If you could come in through the back and just be in your office in case I need you."

"Done," Eva said. "I've been carrying around the panic button receiver in my purse, so use it if you need it."

Marisol surveyed the mess in her office. Tax season always trashed the place. Manila folders and forms sat on every available surface, along with several grant proposals.

Marisol looked at the video intercom. Even with the grainy image, she could read the anxiety on VanDyke's face. She buzzed him in.

"I appreciate you making time on such short notice," he said.

"Your five-minute clock is ticking," she said.

"I understand that the police brought you in for questioning today about the robbery."

Marisol shrugged and nodded.

"The police also mentioned your prior arrests—" he began.

"I'm familiar with my own police record, Jeremy," Marisol said.

"I fired my driver for identifying you," he said. "His dismissal included a generous severance package with a nondisclosure agreement. No leaks from him." VanDyke pushed up the arms of his sweater. "My concern is about leaks from the department."

"I can't control leaks from the department," Marisol said.

"I'm concerned about what you might say that would corroborate their information," VanDyke said.

"Jeremy," Marisol said, "I told you I might have said something if we had gone out on a real date. We didn't. You hired me as an escort, and I won't be bragging about my reentry into the business, even for two hundred and fifty thousand dollars. It would jeopardize my professional reputation as an executive director, and leave me vulnerable to criminal charges."

"But if the word gets out about your past," VanDyke said, "your professional reputation will already be compromised. And the income potential of selling your story to the tabloids, or better yet, some tell-all memoir, would easily offset any losses of disclosure."

"Are you kidding me?" she asked.

"Ms. Rivera," he said. "You're a businesswoman who covers all the angles. I can't imagine this hasn't crossed your mind. Particularly with your account of the robbery, it would be quite marketable."

"This is why you're here after-hours? This is your urgent business?" Marisol asked. "You're worried I'm gonna say some shit, since the cops know I did sex work ten years ago? How did I ever find you attractive? What I mistook for charisma is really just arrogance and self-centeredness."

"I will ignore the name-calling and clarify," he said. "I want to offer you another donation, in exchange for you signing a nondisclosure agreement." He reached into the inside pocket of his jacket and produced a document.

"I—" He ran a hand through his hair, his face flushing a bit. "I wouldn't be so insistent, but the deal I have going in Tokyo is very big, and with an extremely conservative corporation. The cost of exposure would be quite significant right now."

"Don't waste my time," she told him, leaving the paper untouched on the desk. "At age seventeen, I learned to keep my mouth shut as a sex worker. If I could do it then, I can do it now. I don't want my picture in the *Post* with some lurid 'I fucked a billionaire and all I got was this lousy two hundred fifty grand' story. I'm not gonna write a kiss-and-tell memoir about you."

She looked around at the piles in her office, all the things she had to do. How was she supposed to do it all with a fifty-pound weight on her chest, pining for a guy whom she'd never even really had? Now Jeremy was coming with this bullshit?

"You, Jeremy VanDyke, have played a very minor role in the movie of my life, and your screen time is over," she told him. "I'm gonna keep running my damn clinic, and continue—as I have—not thinking about you, not plotting any scheme that concerns you, and not even mentioning your name."

"Ordinarily I would leave it at that, but this deal is very significant in our Asian market," he said. "It's a question of timing."

"No, it's a question of trust," Marisol said. "You contracted a confidential service with a competent professional. And you need to get on your plane to Japan with your reputation in the hands of a whore. And you need to ask yourself, did the woman who went from street sex worker to running a two-million-dollar agency get there by shooting off her mouth?"

"Everything has a price," he said. "Just name it."

"Jeremy," Marisol said. "Your five minutes are up. Why should I resell you something that came with the package of our previous transaction—my professional integrity?"

"Please," he said. "Just look at the figure I'm offering."

She opened up the paper. "Seventy-five thousand, huh? Okay, I'll sign," she said, pulling a pen from the cup on her desk. "You'll just need to take your clothes off."

"Excuse me?" he asked.

"The cost of exposure." She nodded, uncapping the pen. "You'll just need to exit the building naked in front of my staff."

He closed his eyes. "I really regret—" he began. "I was panicked and I—I should have allowed you to dress. I apologize."

"No need for apologies," Marisol said. "Like you said, you paid for the privilege. Everyone has their price. Is this yours? I sign this paper in exchange for you walking out, stark naked, in front of my all-female staff?"

"But if the press was ever—"

"No one will recognize you without your suit on, Jeremy," Marisol said. "You'll just be a random, naked white man. But I can put a bag over your head if you're worried."

"Ms. Rivera, please—" he began.

"Tick tock, Jeremy," Marisol said. "Your Japanese investors are waiting. You need to decide if it's worth it. This offer expires in thirty seconds." She crossed her arms over her chest and gave him her hardest stare.

Slowly, jaw set, he stood up and loosened his tie. When he opened the first button on his shirt, she put up a hand.

"Stop," she said.

"Thank you," he said.

She scrawled a signature on the agreement and tossed it onto the desk. "This meeting is over."

He stood up, refolded the paper, and put it in his jacket. He pulled out a check and handed it across the desk to her.

"I can also see I made the right choice," he said, turning in the doorway.

"About what?" Marisol asked.

"When I picked you to join me for the evening. I couldn't have foreseen the robbery, but—assuming you can be trusted—I was wise to get not only a thoroughly enjoyable evening, but a level of integrity that I might not have gotten from any of your . . . associates. Again, I apologize for my rudeness that evening."

"Good night, Jeremy," she said. "Good luck on your trip."

She folded the check. A legitimate way to pay their taxes.

"Good luck to you, too," he said. "I understand your clinic has come into a large sum of money."

"Excuse me?" she said, her body suddenly chilled.

"The Operations Excellence grant," he said. "I read it in one of the philanthropy papers. One-point-three million, is it?"

She nodded.

"Congratulations," he said. "Be sure to spend it wisely."

The eight million in cash barely fit on the coffee table in Marisol's office. She had the bricks of bills in three black garbage bags, each doubled against the razor-sharp corners.

The day after she met with VanDyke, her team sat on the couch as she set the third bag on the table. The days were staying light a little later, and they could see the last glow of daylight through the slit in the closed curtains.

"It's a good thing that we waited to divide up the money," Marisol said. "Because some of the bills were marked."

"Holy shit," Jody said.

Marisol held the scrap of paper in her hand that she'd gotten from Raul with all the bill numbers on it. Her only souvenir from their little—whatever it was. Several days had passed since she had seen him in the police station. The sting wasn't as fresh, but the heartache was a constant presence.

"Let's find these marked bills," she told the team.

"I fucking hate loose ends," Tyesha said. "Marked bills? And what about Nalissa?"

"With her dumb ass," Kim said, "she's gonna get herself arrested and then try to make a deal by snitching on us."

Marisol shook her head. "What could she say? She worked with us as an escort, until she stole a bag of cash and started her own operation?"

"Maybe they'd care about the cash," Jody said.

"Too small-time," Marisol said. "Maybe if she knew something about VanDyke, but she doesn't."

"Thank God," Kim said.

"After we weed out the marked bills, let's sit on the cash for a few more months just in case," Marisol said. "You should each have your cut by the end of the summer."

Given the fifty-fifty split with the clinic, then the four-way split, each woman would get just under a million dollars.

"Speaking of loose ends," Marisol said. "Jerry—"

"Loose ends or loose cannons?" Kim asked.

"I motherfucking hate pimps," Tyesha said. "Even when they're someone else's pimp they can still fuck up your life."

"I know," Marisol said. "I was seeing our friend Jerry as a problem. But then I started seeing him as the solution."

"Solution to what?" Kim asked.

"I had a talk with Dulce today," Marisol said. "Jerry has a wall safe."

"I say we rig it to blow up in his face," Jody said.

"I second that motion," Tyesha said.

"Even better," Marisol said. "For the first time in our burglary careers, we'll be leaving a little tip."

"Explosive?" Jody asked.

"Nope," Marisol said. "I like to tip in cash."

Marisol handed out latex gloves, face masks, and hairnets, and they began the arduous task of sorting through the take from the VanDyke heist to find the bill numbers on Raul's list.

They searched for a while without speaking.

"Got one!" Kim said, her voice muffled behind the mask.

Tyesha snatched the hundred-dollar bill from Kim and pulled down her mask. She sang the hook from a popular rap song: "*I gotta give my pimp all my money*."

The women all laughed.

"When do we do the hit?" Kim asked.

"Tomorrow night," Marisol said. "I got info from Dulce."

Marisol's upper body felt sweaty and awkward in the male bodysuit. It was Wednesday, the night after they'd found all the marked bills. She stood in front of Jerry's safe, stuffing the pimp's cash and guns into her knapsack.

She felt around in the back of the safe, and her fingers came across something flattened against the rear wall. She aimed the flashlight, and found a manila envelope taped to the back of the safe.

It held six passports of various colors, each from different countries. Five girls, including Dulce, aged eighteen to twenty-one. On the bottom was Jerry's passport. He was forty-four. She stuffed them all into her pack.

From her pocket, she pulled out a plastic bag with a mix of marked and unmarked hundred-dollar bills. She wedged the stack of cash into the back corner of the safe. She jammed them behind the envelope and pushed a corner under the tape to make it look as if the bills had gotten caught. She closed the safe door, and walked back to the front of the apartment.

In the unlit living room, Jody's face was illuminated by a streetlight, and the glow of the New York sky that never went dark.

Jody pointed to an SUV double-parked in front of the building. "We may have company."

Two men got out of the vehicle and walked toward the building.

"Shit!" Marisol said. "I think that's Jerry's brother. We better go out the fire escape."

"Give me the pack," Jody said. "You're awkward enough in that damn suit."

They ran to the back of the apartment and tried the window.

"It's painted shut," Marisol said.

"That fucker is practically holding these girls hostage," Jody said.

"We gotta go out the front," Marisol said. She reached into the pack, removed two guns, and checked them for ammo. Both were loaded. "If they catch us, we can hold them at gunpoint and run, or shoot if we have to."

"My pleasure," Jody said.

"Only if we have to," Marisol said.

Back in the living room, the only two places to hide were behind an armchair, or underneath a large coffee table with a tinted gray glass top.

Jody dove behind the chair, and Marisol tried to squeeze in next to her, but she was too bulky in the suit.

Marisol knelt beside the coffee table and waved a hand under it. She couldn't see her hand very well, but it was far from invisible. She squirmed under the table.

"Jody," Marisol whispered. "Will they be able to see me?"

Jody peeked out from behind the chair. "No, it's dark enough."

"What if they turn the lights on?" Marisol asked.

"Just shoot those fuckers right through the table," Jody said.

Marisol drew in a ragged breath. When she heard keys in the lock, she broke out in a cold sweat under the thick bodysuit, her hands and feet twitching with nerves.

She could hear a man's voice just outside the door. "This bitch Nalissa? Trying to act like some kind of pimp moving in on our territory? She's not a fucking pimp, she's a hoe and Jerry's gonna fuck that bitch and slit her throat."

The door opened and the light flipped on. Two men walked into the apartment. The voice belonged to Jerry's brother, Jimmy, the pretty boy. The other man was tall, pale, and looked high on something. Both were dressed in hip-hop gear that looked too young for them.

"Gonna put that bitch in her place," Jimmy continued. "You want a drink?"

"Sure," the drugged-out guy said, trailing after him into the kitchen. They walked right past Marisol.

They heard the fridge open and the clink of glasses and ice. Jody slipped out from her hiding place and headed for the door.

As quietly as she could, Marisol wriggled her body out from under the table in the heavy suit.

Jody turned the apartment doorknob.

"Wait a minute," Jerry's brother said from the kitchen. "Did the alarm go off when we came in?"

"I don't know, Lil J," the other guy said. "I don't remember no alarm."

He headed into the living room. The two women flew out the door.

"What the fuck?" Jerry's brother yelled, just as the door was closing.

Marisol ran for the stairs, but Jody stayed behind.

When Jimmy flew out the door behind them, she Maced him and cracked him in the head with the gun. He moaned. She shoved him back in the apartment, and slammed the door behind him.

Half an hour later, they met up with Tyesha and Kim back at the clinic. Marisol was locking up all of Jerry's stuff, except two of the guns. She stuck one down the back of her waistband.

"We have to find Nalissa before Jerry does," she said.

"Fuck that," Tyesha said. "I know you tryna save everybody, but—"

"Marisol is the original captain save-a-hoe," Kim said.

"Nalissa knows too much," Marisol said, and handed the other gun to Jody.

"You said she was no threat if she went to the cops," Jody said.

"The cops?" Marisol said. "I'm worried about Jerry. Everybody knows he's got it in for me. Including Nalissa. She would definitely snitch to him trying to save her ass. Maybe even make some shit up."

"Good point," Kim said. "But where is she?"

By 3 a.m., they had found Nalissa's Bronx apartment, only half a mile from Jerry's place. Kim and Jody stood on the front stoop making out. Marisol knelt hidden behind them, and worked to open the door.

She wore a bulky black jacket with loose black jeans and sneakers. Her hair was up under a cap. Both she and Jody wore black latex gloves, in case the place was already a crime scene.

"Kim," Marisol whispered as the lockpick slipped once again. "I might need you to take over."

"Okay," Kim said. "But no kissing my girlfriend."

"Marisol is kinda hot, though," Jody said. She was

also dressed to look boyish in thick sweats and work boots.

Marisol ignored them and the lock finally clicked.

The two women stopped kissing. Marisol and Jody stepped inside, as Kim went down to the car to sit lookout with Tyesha.

On the fourth floor, they could hear thudding bass from behind Nalissa's door. Marisol managed the apartment lock, and opened the door a crack. She saw a cheaply furnished and dim living room. A couple was having sex on a foldout couch. The woman was on all fours, and both had their backs to the door. The woman moaned with exaggerated excitement, and the man's neck was flushed with concentration.

Marisol and Jody crept inside, the music covering the sound of the closing door.

Down the hallway, they found three bedrooms. The first two also had sounds of thumping and moaning, but the third was quiet.

Marisol and Jody kicked in the door, guns drawn.

Nalissa sat in an armchair in jeans and a T-shirt, smoking a cigarette. When the two women burst in, the cigarette fell onto the carpet.

"Marisol," Nalissa said, wide-eyed with hands up. "Don't shoot. I'm sorry. I'm so sorry."

Marisol stepped forward and punched Nalissa in the face. The young woman fell onto the bed.

The smell of singeing plastic filled the room, and Marisol ground out the cigarette with her boot, leaving a char mark on the carpet.

"Please, Marisol," Nalissa whined. "I was always planning to pay you back. I got five thousand here right now." Very slowly, with her other hand raised, she removed a small blue backpack from beneath the mattress. "A down payment. Another five by next week, I swear. Don't kill the goose that lays the golden egg. I just wanted to be like you. Be the boss." She held the backpack out to Marisol.

"It's not about being the goddamn boss," Marisol said, slapping the backpack out of Nalissa's hand. "It's about doing what you fucking have to do for your folks. How you gonna have some girl getting fucked in your living room while people walk in and out? That's not being a madam. That's being a little girl playing dress-up. You thought you stole some play money? You stole the rent money. The whole fucking clinic almost got shut down behind your ass."

"I didn't—"

"Of course you didn't," Marisol said. "Didn't know. Didn't care. But I cleaned up that mess, just like I'm here to clean up another mess. You pissed off the wrong people."

"I promise, I'll make it up to you," Nalissa said.

"Not me," Marisol said. "Jerry the pimp, the fucking psychopath who firebombed the clinic? You're operating on his turf."

"No," Nalissa said. "His brother, Jimmy, told me—"

"Then Jimmy played you," Marisol said.

Jody's phone beeped and she checked it. "Jerry and his boys are on their way up," she said. "He plans to fucking kill you."

Marisol stuck her gun back down her waistband. "Let's go out the fire escape," she said, opening the window. She pushed Nalissa out, then climbed out with Jody.

Jody lowered the ladder. From inside the apartment, they could hear the music stop. Then the thundering of Jerry's voice.

Marisol and Jody had begun to descend down the fire escape, but Nalissa climbed back into the bedroom.

"What the—" Marisol began, and started to climb back up.

Through the small window, Marisol could see into the bedroom. Nalissa was grabbing the backpack.

Nalissa had one leg back out the window when Jerry burst in, cursing. With his hefty frame and booming voice, he seemed to take up all the space in the small room. Nalissa rushed to the escape, backpack in one hand.

While Jody had climbed down two flights, Marisol had been crouching in the relative darkness of the fire escape ladder. As Nalissa's leg hit the fire escape landing, Marisol began climbing down fast.

From below, she could see most of Nalissa's body squeeze out the window, and then a man's arm pulling on the backpack. Nalissa yanked hard and the man's hand let go. Nalissa fell back against the iron of the fire escape, banging her head. She sagged in what seemed like a daze, one hand loosely clutching the backpack, the other crumpled beneath her.

Jody was on the ground now. Marisol continued to climb down, as quickly as she dared. Meanwhile, above her, she saw a thick leg climb out of the window. Then a second leg, then Jerry heaved his ass and trunk out the window.

Marisol froze. She could see Nalissa rally and scramble for the ladder. Jerry was big—unwieldy on the small fire escape—but he was fast. He crossed the landing in a single step, the metal groaning with the movement of his weight. His hand clenched over Nalissa's arm. He ripped the backpack away from her, tearing the bag from the straps and tossing it back in through the window.

"You ain't no pimp, bitch," he said, his voice echoing into the alley. "Only one pimp around here."

He grabbed her by both of her shoulders and wrenched her from the ladder, holding her for a moment in the air. Nalissa was frozen, her face a mask of terror, her hands clenched on the thin pair of blue backpack straps, now ragged at the ends.

And then, as if she were an oversized doll, he tossed her off the fire escape.

Marisol ducked her head, both to avoid being seen, and to avoid seeing. So she heard, rather than saw, Nalissa fall the three floors and land on the concrete with a sickening *thud*.

Pulling her hood up to shade her face, she glanced up at Jerry. He was barely illuminated by the weak glow through the window, as he peered down through the gloom. Marisol was over two stories below him. It was dark. She had on men's clothes. She knew he could barely see her, let alone recognize her. Yet she felt her insides liquefy under his gaze. A man who flicked a woman off a fourth story like ash from a cigarette.

He lumbered back to the window, first his trunk, then both his legs, climbing back out of view.

Marisol hustled down the final length of the ladder and jumped to the ground. Jody grabbed her hand.

"I called nine-one-one on the burner phone," Jody said, pulling her toward the other end of the alley. "I texted them to meet us."

Jody took off running, but Marisol turned back.

"Marisol," Jody hissed. "He's gonna come looking for us."

Marisol ignored her and ran back to Nalissa. A pool of red was spreading behind the girl's head, making her usually bright carrot-colored hair look washed out. She reached into Nalissa's pocket for the girl's phone.

As she ran down the alley, she could feel the phone's warmth through the latex gloves. In contrast to the cold night, it felt almost hot, as if it could burn her.

Chapter 27

Two days later, Marisol sat at her desk, wearing the same clinic T-shirt and cotton leggings she'd slept in. She hadn't put in contacts, and she stared at a spreadsheet through slightly grimy glasses. Even after twelve hours of sleep, she felt tired. She was halfway dozing off, when Eva came in.

"Serena's hilarious," Eva said. "Since that foundation check came in, she's walking around here like the female Ed McMahon. Or a white Oprah. Ladies, look under your seats—Pap smears and HIV tests for everyone."

Marisol forced a weak smile.

Eva laughed. "Seriously, though. We did it," she said. "Really you did it. You should be so proud."

"I don't really feel anything," Marisol said, leaning back in her chair. In the two weeks since she had last seen Raul, the ache had dulled, replaced by a heavy weight in her torso. "I know I should be grateful. But I'm just going through the motions."

"It's burnout, honey," Eva said. "You should go visit your sister in Cuba."

"I can't go right now." Marisol ran a hand through her hair. When had she last combed it? "I'm a mess."

Eva crossed her arms. "Cristina doesn't care what shape you're in."

Marisol shrugged. "After everything with Jerry and Nalissa, I just ran out of gas."

"Nalissa's still in a coma?" Eva asked.

Marisol nodded. "But her phone was full of escort clients she'd stolen. Now they keep calling. I just handed Kim and Jody the escort operation. They can turn down those disloyal motherfuckers."

"Look, honey," Eva said. "For the last year, you've been living from crisis to crisis."

"Really my whole life."

"Exactly," Eva said. "You're used to being so pumped full of adrenaline. The crash was inevitable."

"What do I do now?" Marisol asked.

"Nothing. Just let the waves of feeling wash over you," Eva said, putting an arm around Marisol. "It'll shift in time."

Marisol recalled the waves in her dream of Raul. Previously, the memory of him had stung. But now, like everything else, it just made her feel tired.

"Eva?" Marisol asked. "Can you prescribe something for me?"

"I already did," the older woman said. "Go see Cristina. You don't need meds. You need rest, new scenery, and love."

Marisol closed her eyes. The thought of buying airline tickets seemed like more than she could manage.

Marisol's phone buzzed. The receptionist said Dulce was there to see her.

"I gotta get outta New York," Dulce said as she clacked into the office on stiletto ankle boots, and sat down on the couch. "I ran into Jerry's brother, Jimmy, today. He kept following me, squinting like he wasn't sure if it was me or not."

She had dyed her hair back to a dark brown. "He saw me come out of my sister's building. Jerry could find me now. He'll look there and then at my ma's apartment."

Marisol sat down next to her on the couch.

"I won't let him find you," Marisol said. "I promise he'll never touch you again."

Dulce burst into tears. "I've been so scared. Scared he would find me, and scared you wouldn't help because of all the shit I've caused. The fire and then you had to shoot that guy."

"You didn't cause that shit," Marisol said. "Jerry caused it. That's what we do here. Protect girls and make sure they have choices."

"So is it true?" Dulce sat up and wiped her eyes. "Is it true that you broke in a couple of weeks ago and got everyone's passports back?"

"No." Marisol hugged her tight, looking over her shoulder as she lied. "Someone delivered them here anonymously."

"Star went back to Jamaica, and Spice went back to the Philippines. I don't have any real family outside the city, except my cousin in Detroit." She jiggled her foot and looked around the office. "Things didn't work out with that backstabber. Her boyfriend tried to fuck me. When I told her, she threw me out instead of him. Good luck with *ese cabron, pendeja*."

"What about your brother in the Dominican Republic?"

"He got locked up," she said. "And my mom's family down there are all dead or moved to the States."

"What about family on your dad's side?"

"My dad is long gone," she said. "All I got is a grandmother I've never met, somewhere in Cuba."

"Why don't you try to find her?" Marisol asked. "It's legal to travel there now."

"What if she won't take me in?" Dulce asked. "If I'm gonna be a homeless hoe, I'd rather be in the U.S."

"If I went to Cuba, would you come with me?"

"Are you fucking kidding?" Dulce laughed. "If I'm going with you, I'm already packed."

Chapter 28

Two days later, Marisol got hassled at every security checkpoint at JFK because she had left the panic key ring in the inner pocket of her purse.

Finally, the five women touched down in Havana at José Martí International Airport.

Dulce had clung to Marisol through the whole trip. Without the girl's hard New York face, Marisol could tell she was practically still a teenager. She'd never been on a plane before.

Cristina had sent word and a photo to Dulce's grandmother. As the women walked through security, they hit a wall of brown faces. Whole families had come to meet their people. Adults and elders waving. Children jumping up and down. Babies dozing in parents' arms.

They trooped past the reunions. Dulce gripped Marisol's hand, scanning the crowd.

Tyesha gave Marisol the *what-should-we-do?* look. Marisol was ready to ask the authorities when a middle-aged man stepped forward, wearing a *guayabera* shirt. He led an elderly woman who shuffled slowly with a walker made of bamboo.

"Dolores?" the old woman asked.

The girl lit up. "*Abuelita?*"

"*Sí, mi amor.*" The grandmother stepped forward and embraced her.

Dulce sobbed and clung to her.

The grandmother laughed and wiped Dulce's eyes with a handkerchief. "We didn't recognize you without the blond hair," she said in Spanish.

"You look better like this," the man said.

"I don't know how to thank you," the grandmother said to Marisol with tears in her eyes. "I didn't think I was ever going to see her."

"*De nada*," Marisol said.

They made their way out through the airport, where they were properly introduced to the man who turned out to be Dulce's uncle. They also met three aunts, five cousins, and Dulce's half sister.

Marisol accepted their thank-yous and promised to come over for dinner before she left. She and her crew all hugged Dulce good-bye, as she sobbed.

Dulce squeezed Marisol hard. "If it wasn't for you," she stammered through her tears, "I know I'd be dead. I owe you my life, Marisol."

"No, *nena*," Marisol said. "I didn't give you anything more than you deserved."

Marisol felt her own eyes misting up. She knew Eva was right—she couldn't save everyone. But this victory was particularly sweet. Just like in her own fantasy from decades ago: The long-lost relative had appeared, and Dulce would be safe. Marisol embraced both women, absorbing their tears of gratitude.

In the 2 a.m. light, they could barely see the city from the taxi. Marisol rolled down her window and drank in the thick, humid air. A heady cocktail of sea salt, tropical plants, and red dirt. Eva had been right. This was exactly what she needed.

* * *

The Hotel Palacio was a large, historic building with Spanish-style architecture, tall, curving archways, columns, and balconies. The suite was lovely, with thick carpets, high ceilings, antique décor, and modern amenities.

"I like this country already," Tyesha said, collapsing onto the queen-size bed.

Kim and Jody had one room and Tyesha had the other. Marisol slept on the foldout couch in the living room. In the morning, she would see Cristina.

Jody and Kim wheeled their suitcases into one of the bedrooms.

"Good night, ladies," Jody said.

"Just keep it down," Tyesha said as Kim closed the door with a grin.

Tyesha turned to Marisol. "Pair of goddamn howler monkeys. If it gets too loud, you can always come crash with me."

"I bet I'll be knocked out before the party even starts," Marisol said.

"I didn't realize how much I needed to get away," Tyesha said. "I been studying my ass off, but underneath it all, I've been kicking myself for not taking your advice about Woof."

"Really?" Marisol said. "I never got details."

"I was blinded by the bling," Tyesha said. "But he was a dick."

"Powerful men are really appealing," Marisol said. She hadn't told the team about her interactions with VanDyke, or that she had hooked up with Raul.

"We never even had sex, but do you know how hard it is to get your mind off the number-one rapper in America?" Tyesha said. "I swear, if I hear one more '*hey, girl, hey, pick up it's me*' ringtone, I'll smash someone's fucking phone. I wish I was more like you, Marisol. All about work, and not tripping off men. You must think I'm a mess."

"On the contrary," Marisol said. "I didn't think you could handle yourself, but you did. You got out after a couple of dates, before you even had sex. That's admirable."

"Seriously," Tyesha said. "If I'd been open like that and actually fucked him? I'd be walking around with my heart dragging on the ground."

"Yup," Marisol said. "That's for sure."

In the morning, Marisol was crashed on the sofa bed when she heard a knock at the door of the hotel room. She rolled over and rubbed her eyes. Her watch said 9:45, and Cristina wasn't due until eleven. She had forgotten to put up the Do Not Disturb sign.

"*Momentito*," she said, wrapping a sheet around her bare legs. She would tell the housekeeper to come back later.

She peeked her head out the door and shrieked, then covered her mouth with both hands. Cristina threw her arms around her. Marisol hugged her back, and they started crying. The sheet fell to the floor, and they hung on to each other and sobbed.

Marisol half-released Cristina and invited her in. They lay on the sofa bed, shoulders pressed close.

"Your shoulder is so fucking bony, *flaqita*," Marisol said.

"*Cállate*," Cristina said. "Juan keeps trying to feed me, but I'm always rushing and tired."

"I need to get you some damn food," Marisol said. Cristina's sandy curls were pulled back from her face with three black bobby pins. Marisol smoothed a lock back from her sister's forehead. "When did you start wearing glasses?" Marisol asked.

"When did your ass get so big?" Cristina asked. "You better watch out for these Cuban men. They're gonna be all over you."

"Whatever," Marisol said. She had always been curvy, and she had filled out a bit more in her thirties. Cristina was slender and practically flat-chested, with lighter coloring. They had both inherited the underlying bone structure of their mother's face—large, close-set Taino eyes, high cheekbones, and full lips.

Cristina had on a pair of loose shorts, a tank top, no bra, and flip-flops. "I see you dressed up for me," Marisol said.

"Let's get outta here," Cristina said. "Juan should be downstairs by now."

Marisol stepped into jeans, and grabbed her shoes and purse. Cristina zipped up the open suitcase and wheeled the bags out of the room.

Marisol followed her into the hallway. "Is that a gray hair?" she asked, tugging at one of Cristina's short curls.

Cristina laughed. "One for every year of medical school."

"My baby sister with gray hair," Marisol said as they went down on the elevator.

"You dye yours like *abuelita* or pull them like *mami*?" Cristina asked.

"I pull them," Marisol said, as the elevator opened. "But I'm getting too many now. I have to start dyeing or I'll be bald."

They walked through the lobby. The restaurant was full of tourists having breakfast.

"Or you could just let them be gray and natural," Cristina said.

"Please. I live in New York, not Havana."

"Just saying," Cristina said. "Maybe *mami* would have eventually let hers grow in gray."

"Ha!" Marisol said. "She would have taken to the bottle just like *abuelita.*"

"No way to know," Cristina said, as they stepped outside.

Cristina's boyfriend, Juan, waved from across the street. He was tall with caramel skin, a short Afro, and dark eyes behind wire-rimmed glasses.

"Welcome to Cuba!" he said in Spanish, kissing her cheek. "Sorry we couldn't pick you up at the airport, but we worked overnight at the hospital."

He took her suitcases and loaded them into the trunk of his boxy Eastern European eighties-make car.

"Our house is no Hotel Palacio, *pero mi casa es tu casa.*"

"Thanks so much for having me," Marisol said. "I know you all are busy—"

"Busy is an understatement," Cristina said. She and Juan proceeded to share several recent hospital anecdotes. Juan talked about the time the tube on the ventilator broke and they used a krazy straw that a tourist had brought. Cristina said she always wore extra bobby pins because she never knew when she'd need a short piece of metal to hold some piece of furniture or equipment together.

"I'd been picturing you starring in *Grey's Anatomy,*" Marisol said. "But it sounds more like *MacGyver.*"

Cristina laughed and explained the joke to Juan.

Cristina and Juan's place was a two-bedroom pink cement house they shared with Juan's sister and her two kids. The rest of the family had gone to live for a while with Juan's ailing grandmother in Santiago, so Marisol got their room. She set down her suitcases among the crib, child's bed, cloth diapers, and toys so old they might have belonged to Juan or his sister.

While Juan slept, Cristina and Marisol sat on opposite ends of the creaking wicker sofa, with their feet tangled up in the middle.

"*Mami*, don't let me keep you up," Marisol said. "If you need to sleep, go ahead. I'll still be here when you wake up."

"Sleep?" Cristina asked. "I'm so excited you're finally here, I couldn't sleep."

"I brought you a present," Marisol said. She pulled out a copy of *From Red Light to Red Carpet,* signed by Delia Borbón.

Cristina squealed and hugged Marisol. "Oh my God!! You're the best."

"*Cállate*," Marisol said. "You'll wake up your boyfriend."

"Please," Cristina said. "*Ese tipo* could sleep through Armageddon."

Sure enough, they didn't hear a sound from the bedroom until around three, when Juan emerged, eyes puffy and half-closed.

The kitchen and living room were separated by a low partition. He didn't speak until after he'd made them all a pot of coffee.

As they sat sipping from chipped, mismatched mugs, their neighbor knocked on the door. Vladimir was strapping and pecan-colored, with hazel eyes, golden dreadlocks, and an easy laugh. He offered Marisol the customary kiss hello, but lingered, holding her hand, looking her up and down.

"*Un placer*," he said, and invited them all over to his house later that night for a party. A little welcome to the neighborhood.

"We'll be there," Juan said.

* * *

"Did I misunderstand?" Marisol asked after the door had closed behind Vladimir. "Is he throwing me a party?"

"Trust me," Juan said. "It's better this way. Otherwise, they'd all have to come over individually to check you out."

"You're kidding," Marisol said.

"Word has already traveled across the neighborhood," Cristina explained. "I'm La Puertorriqueña. You're Sister of La Puertorriqueña."

"What?" Marisol asked. "I don't get my own identity?"

"Not unless you stay awhile." Cristina laughed. "I'm hoping to graduate to 'Juan's girlfriend' after a couple of years. If I stay for a decade, I might get to be 'Cristina.'"

"Havana is a city of gossip," Juan explained. "Be careful of Vladimir. He wants to host the party to—you know, mark the territory."

"Let everyone know he met you first," Cristina said.

"I gotta get to the hospital," Juan said, and kissed Cristina good-bye.

Cristina refilled their coffee cups.

"'Mark the territory'?" Marisol asked.

Cristina laughed and switched to English. "I told you, these guys'll be all over you."

"Why?" Marisol asked. "I look just like all the Cuban women here."

"Yeah, but you're not a Cuban woman. You're an American woman."

"I'm a Puerto Rican woman," Marisol said.

"With a purse full of American dollars."

"They wanna rob me?" Marisol asked.

Cristina burst out laughing. "Hardly."

"Then what?"

Cristina poured some sugar into her coffee. "A lot of these guys, Vladimir in particular, are *jineteros*."

"Gigolos?" Marisol asked.

"Not exactly," Cristina said. "I don't think there's an English equivalent. They see a woman like you, and you're . . . you're coming from the States, and you have money, and you're Latina, and beautiful, and any one of them would gladly be your boyfriend for the time that you're here. And if you wanted to marry them and bring them to the States, all the better."

"Did you get the same treatment when you came?" Marisol asked.

"I was an incoming medical student, not a woman on vacation." Cristina drank her coffee. "Most Latino students come from countries poorer than Cuba."

"They see me as a sex work client?" Marisol asked.

"It's different here," Cristina said. "After the revolution, the government outlawed prostitution. I came back when Cuba broke ties with the Soviet Union, but women have a lot more control."

"Which is good," Marisol said. "But what does that have to do with your neighbor?"

"*Jineteros* like Vladimir—male or female—are more like gold diggers than sex workers. Maybe no money changes hands. Maybe you come back twice a year, and Vladimir is your boyfriend when you visit. Maybe you bring clothes or stuff for his family, even furniture. Vladimir is attracted to you. He assumes you're good people because you're Juan's girlfriend's sister. He's excited because he can get to know you better than his Swedish or German girlfriends who don't speak good Spanish."

"Would he marry them, too?" Marisol asked.

"Probably not." Cristina shrugged. "They live too far. Too hard to visit his family."

"I just can't wrap my mind around that," Marisol said. "In my experience, it's only a fantasy that sex workers would have done it for free under different circumstances. As a client that would be a total turnoff. I'd always be worried that they didn't really like me, that they were just doing it for the money."

"Maybe socialist sex work is different," Cristina said. "Maybe the money is just a bonus."

"Picture that," Marisol said, noticing her coffee had grown lukewarm. "Some young stud wanting to marry me for my money."

"He's a complete hunk, right?" Cristina said, fanning herself. "The first day I met him, he was wearing his jeans so low I could practically see his pubic hair. Those lower abdominal muscles are insane." Cristina carried the coffee cups to the sink. "And I hear he knows how to handle his business."

"As in financial business?" Marisol asked.

"As in handle his business." Cristina thrust her hips forward a few times.

"How do you know all that?" Marisol asked.

"Like Juan said, Havana is a city of gossip."

Later they took a taxi back to the hotel and lay down for an evening nap in the air-conditioned suite. Kim and Jody had turned in for the night. Tyesha studied in the living room while Marisol and Cristina slept in her bed.

"Just like at *abuelita*'s house under the mosquito net," Marisol said.

"Except without the heat and mosquitoes." Cristina laughed. "God, I've missed the luxury of AC."

"I'm surprised you don't get that here as a doctor," Marisol said.

Cristina shook her head. "I'm still a student. And being a doctor in Cuba is nothing like being a doctor in the States. That's why I wanted to study here. It's all about public health."

"Are you still gonna come back?" Marisol asked. "And work at the clinic?"

"I have to," Cristina said. "It's a condition of my education."

"But you would anyway," Marisol asked. "Even if you didn't have to?"

"Of course," Cristina said. "That's our plan."

That Thursday night, Cristina kept vetoing Marisol's dress options for the party. "You know people don't have a lot of money here."

Marisol looked at the fuschia halter dress. "I got this for twelve ninety-nine on Twenty-seventh Street."

"It's not just about cash," Cristina said. "*La gente* don't have access to a lot of cheap consumer goods, either."

She rummaged through Marisol's suitcase. "How about this?" Cristina held up an emerald-green spaghetti strap top. "With the jeans you're wearing."

"I guess . . ." Marisol said, but when they got to the party, she fit right in.

Everyone greeted each other with a hug or kiss. Even more so than in Puerto Rico, there didn't seem to be a concept of personal space. Vladimir welcomed her to the party, hugged her, stood with his arm draped over her, heedless of the moisture on her skin and under his arm. Cristina's other neighbors did the same. Men and women, standing close enough to smell her breath, touching her shoulder for emphasis as they talked.

Vladimir attended to her every need. More rum? Was she hungry? She must let him take her to the beach, to the *discoteca* during her stay. His brother was in a folkloric dance ensemble. Could he take her to their next performance?

He put his arm around her waist. He did it casually,

like Juan, across the room, had an arm around the shoulders of one of his buddies. Marisol could feel a heat between them that crackled independently of the thick, humid evening. His firm thigh pressed the side of her ass with a pressure that was just shy of insistent. He finessed it, so that she could easily move away if she didn't like it. She stayed.

Vladimir was a paradox of hard and soft. His frame was tightly muscled, but his body was relaxed. Confident but not tightly wound. Unlike the Latino men in the United States. It wasn't so much the confidence that he could get her—would get her—in bed. More the confidence that everything would work out for him one way or another. That his life would be filled with beautiful women and good times. Such confidence was quite appealing. Particularly when packaged in such broad shoulders and such a firm ass. The cotton T-shirt clung to the ridges of muscle in his chest and abdomen. The shirt itself, an American relic from the eighties, was bright green with giant letters that said RELAX across the front. The shirt might be older than Vladimir himself.

He stayed close, but didn't monopolize her time. Friends and neighbors were eager to meet her, inquire about her life in *Nueva York*. Many were doctors, so she had to explain several times why she needed to run a community clinic in one of the most industrialized cities in the world.

Around 2 a.m., neighbors went down the block to their houses with sleeping children in their arms, little open mouths lightly snoring in the night air. Medical students hopped onto bicycles and rode off into quiet streets.

"So has our boy swept you off your feet yet?" Cristina asked, back at the house.

Juan had crashed out in the bedroom a few hours before. The two sisters lay on the couch, talking.

"He's very attractive," Marisol said, stifling a yawn.

Cristina laughed. "What are you trying to say? 'He's so sexy it's boring'?"

"I don't know," Marisol said. "I was sort of dating someone for a minute."

"You were dating?" Cristina asked.

"Do you remember Raul?" Marisol picked at a stray thread in the sofa. "His sister was my friend Gladys from high school."

"The skinny one?"

"Not anymore."

"What happened?" Cristina asked.

"I guess I fell in love." Marisol shrugged. "Since we go so far back, he sort of slipped past my defenses. I never felt that way about anyone before."

"You broke it off?" Cristina asked.

Marisol gave a bitter bark of a laugh. "He did," Marisol said. "Damn hypocrite. So down for a woman who runs a clinic for sex workers, but when he learned I used to be one myself?"

"What the fuck?" Cristina said.

"I don't know," Marisol said, her eyes filling. "Maybe it was me. Maybe all the crazy shit when we were kids has made me—"

"Scared of men?" Cristina asked. "You and me both. Juan had to work so hard to get me to trust him."

"It's more than that," Marisol said, blinking tears back. "I feel kind of shut off, split into pieces. Like I could love somebody or fuck them but not both."

Cristina raised an eyebrow.

"And even the loving part is kinda not happening. I mean, the only person I really love, as in, think-about-them-when-they're-not-even-there love, is you."

"Because coming up, we only had each other," Cristina said.

"Nobody else feels permanent," Marisol said. "It's fine when they're there, but if they left, I'd just shrug it off."

"I love you, too, Maiso," Cristina said, using her baby nickname for her sister. "But you gotta open up to other people. You can't spend your whole life just loving me."

"What do you suggest? Vladimir?"

"Definitely," Cristina said. "A heartbroken woman could always use a little stiff dick to get her mind off it."

Marisol's mouth fell open. "You did not just say that."

"Your baby sister isn't a baby anymore," Cristina said. "It wasn't just Juan's sensitive demeanor that won me over, *tú sabes*?"

"Whatever," Marisol said, and kissed her sister good night.

Chapter 29

Havana's Spanish colonial architecture, botanical outdoor plazas, towering Catholic churches, and brightly colored stucco apartment buildings reminded Marisol of Puerto Rico. The unexpected visual factor was the presence of Soviet buildings throughout—hulking, gray, industrial blocks. Nineteen fifties–era American Fords and Chevrolets dotted the landscape like dinosaur remains, but they still ran.

A couple of weeks after the party, Marisol told Cristina not to wait up for her.

She and Vladimir walked along the *malecón*—the seawall in Havana. It was humid, twilight, with a few dark clouds threatening rain, but the *Habaneros* were out in droves. Couples, families, clusters of young people, strolling up and down the sidewalk next to the sea. Cars driving by with windows wide open.

Marisol wore flip-flops with a low-cut pink top and a peasant skirt. Vladimir was gorgeous in a Brazil soccer jersey and jeans.

"You're very beautiful, Marisol," he said in Spanish, as a wave crashed against the railing in front of them.

Marisol shrugged. "I just look like the average *trigueña* here in Cuba."

"Much more beautiful than average," Vladimir said. "And you're very interesting—different. I've never been able to travel outside of Cuba, so I'm always curious about foreigners. You'd rather stay in a crowded house than at a big hotel. It makes me want to know about you, about your life in the United States. I wonder why aren't you married."

Marisol laughed. "I got close to getting married once," she said. When she had told the sugar daddy she was leaving, he had suggested marriage. Like a business negotiation. She'd proved her worth, and he was willing to improve the compensation package.

"You didn't love him?"

"How old are you, Vladimir?" she asked.

"Twenty-four," he said.

"I was around your age," she said. "He was okay, but he couldn't offer anything but money."

"Not a bad thing to have," Vladimir said.

"But I could never be independent," Marisol said. "It would always be his money. And I'd be the one earning it by sitting around all day, waiting for him to come home and then waiting on him. That's no life."

"But it would be better after you had children," Vladimir said.

"He didn't want kids," Marisol said.

Vladimir shook his head. "A wealthy man who doesn't want children?"

"Guys like him have no concept of family," she said.

Vladimir frowned and tilted his head to the side. "I can see that," he said. "I've dated foreign women who took me to nice hotels and restaurants, and for spa massages, but I wouldn't want to live in their countries with them full-time. I'd miss my family."

"Exactly," Marisol said.

"No amount of money is worth being apart from the people you love," Vladimir said.

"Or the work that you love," Marisol said. "I've had plenty of jobs I didn't love just to pay the bills. But now I'm passionate about what I do. Aren't you socialists supposed to believe in the working class?"

Vladimir laughed. "I'm not much of a socialist. I'd move to the States if I could."

"What about your family?" Marisol asked.

"I'd get settled and send for them," he said. "My heart will always be in Cuba, *pero no es fácil*, even with the blockade lifted. If I want to start a family with someone, where will we live? All together in one bedroom in my parents' house, like my sister? Maybe my time in fancy hotels has spoiled me, but I want more."

"And you think it's in the States?"

"It's definitely not here," Vladimir said. "My life is fine for now, while I'm young. But in the future, I want options."

"Cristina thinks you want a woman to take you to the States."

Vladimir laughed. "Guilty as charged. But it's not you. If you didn't want the older man who could keep you, then you don't want to be the older woman who can keep me."

"So what do you want with me?" Marisol asked.

Vladimir laughed. "I'm hoping you'll take me to a nice hotel and let me make love to you. And let me show you Cuba. And make love to you some more. I want to enjoy you, Marisol."

His arm had been slung over her shoulders, but now he walked his fingers gently, stealthily, down toward her breast, not groping, not tickling, just brushing.

"Would you still want to make love to me if I didn't

have any U.S. dollars? If I was Cuban? A woman who lived in your neighborhood?"

"If you were Cuban, I would have already made love to you."

Marisol checked them into the Hotel Palacio. The moment they stepped into the room, Vladimir pulled her into his arms and kissed her. He was incredibly tuned in to her. Like in dancing salsa, the pressure of the man's hand against the woman that maintains the connection and checks in: *Are you ready for me to turn you?*

His kisses were like questions. *Do you like this?* He didn't crowd her; he held her close, but not crushing. Just when she worried that maybe it really was a gigolo act, she got close enough that she could feel his erection. From the hardness between his legs, she could tell that whatever the context, the circumstances, his desire was real. She surrendered to it.

She kissed him back, pressed her tongue into his mouth, answering: *Yes, I like it.* She pressed her body against him, her navel against his erection, her breasts against his chest. He caressed the back of her neck, delicately licked along her earlobe, slid a hand down the side of her thigh.

He didn't rush. He moved with the confidence of a man who was used to getting and giving pleasure, without worry that anyone would have to do without. Vladimir slid a hand down the back of her skirt and caressed her ass, pressing her hips into him.

Suddenly, Marisol had a flash of her Washington Heights hotel. Vladimir was the taste of home she'd been chasing all those nights. But without the random, razor edge of danger. And without the mutual suspicion of immigrants armored for a game of take-or-be-had. She could relax with him. Let him lead.

She slid her hands up under his shirt, her fingers stumbling for a second over a scar on his side. His hands were under her shirt, sliding beneath the wires and fabric of her bra, cupping her breasts, gently stroking her nipples, and she felt a surging ache. She walked backward, pulling him toward the bed, kicking off her flip-flops.

Vladimir looked into her face and grinned. Lifted her up and sat her on the bed, sliding his hands up her thighs. He hooked one of his index fingers in the front of her panties, and Marisol lifted up her hips so he could slide them down over her ass. When he had pulled them off, he hiked up her skirt and began to kiss her thighs. Marisol tangled her hands in his hair, ran her fingers along the strong bones in his jaw, caressed his shoulders.

He kissed her outer lips, tangling his tongue in her hair, nuzzling along the opening. She moaned and he placed a string of tiny kisses along the line where her lips met. He had an authentic enthusiasm and curiosity about her body.

Marisol threw her head back and gripped his shoulders.

Vladimir pushed the skirt out of the way, reached up, and unhooked her bra. As he ran his tongue up and down, just inside her lips, teasing, he slid his hands around to the front of her body and caressed both her breasts, stroking his thumbs back and forth across the tips of her nipples.

Marisol groaned with anticipation, feeling her own eagerness, feeling his enjoyment of her pleasure, feeling, even without seeing or touching him, that he was just as turned on.

And then, without warning, he plunged his tongue

right to the tender spot of her clitoris, and she gasped and collapsed back on the bed.

"Sí, cariño," he encouraged in a low murmur that vibrated between her legs.

He teased her. Used his tongue slowly and skillfully. His fingers on her breasts, tongue on her clit. He moved one hand down and gripped her ass, pulling her in closer to him, sliding his tongue inside her. He felt her tense up and slowly pulled his mouth away.

"Don't stop," she murmured.

He pulled back and she could hear him unbuckling his jeans and stepping out of them. He produced a condom, and rolled it on himself.

As she looked down across the tangle of her blouse, unhooked bra, hiked-up skirt, and open thighs, she beheld a huge erection.

"Te gusta?" he asked.

Marisol blinked in surprise, as he leaned down and teased her with just the head. She felt the pleasurable pressure of his size, the welcome intensity of his hardness.

But then he pulled back, licked her, kissed her some more.

"Ay, Dios," Marisol moaned.

And then, with both arms, he lifted her up and moved her farther back on the bed, so he could get purchase, leverage.

"Are you ready?" he asked her in Spanish.

"Sí," she breathed, through open mouth, open thighs, open pores, open.

He entered her slowly, with care. As he pressed into her, Marisol was aware only of the sensation of him, the sweet pressure, the gentle hardness. And then, slowly at first, he began to move. He held himself up over her on strongly muscled arms, rocking his hips. She ran her hands down the muscles in his back, grabbed his ass, caressed his chest. He lowered himself down onto the bed, onto one shoulder, and caressed her breast with the other hand.

Marisol sank into the bed with the pleasure of it, the surrender of it. Her body melting to liquid.

He pushed a little harder, tilted the angle. She cried out with the pleasure.

Now that he had found the right stroke he was merciless. Slowly gliding himself down along the fault line of her pleasure. She felt her body tense as it headed toward climax. His rhythm became insistent. And then, with a final acceleration, she screamed and grabbed him around his chest, coming hard and sweet.

And just as she would have lay back, spent, he heated up. Vladimir opened his mouth as if to speak, and with a gasp that was half groan, thrust his way to his own climax.

"You are a delicious woman," he murmured to her a few moments later, as he gripped the top of the condom and pulled out.

Marisol lay back and sighed. She felt an uncomplicated satisfaction in the present moment that she'd never felt before.

Cristina was right, a stiff dick was good medicine. But not the kind that heals, just the kind that temporarily relieves the symptoms.

A week later, Marisol was reading on the couch when Cristina came in.

"Honey, I'm home," Cristina said, and they kissed hello.

Marisol set down her book. "I was walking on the *malecón* this morning," she began. "I met this nineteen-year-old *jinetera*. Are there still travel restrictions? Would the Cuban government let me take her back to New York? Her family situation is fucked up and I think—"

"Marisol, what are you doing?" Cristina asked.

"I'm trying to help this girl," Marisol said.

"In the middle of your vacation, you manage to find someone in crisis?"

"She asked for help," Marisol said.

"Of course she did," Cristina said. "And if you were a man, she'd ask if you wanted a date. She's trying to hustle you. The girl just wants a few bucks, not an intervention."

"Cristina," Marisol said. "You didn't see the look on her face. She really needs help."

"You think everybody needs your help," Cristina said. "You've got eight million dollars stashed in your apartment to save half the young women in Manhattan. Isn't that enough? Or are you always gonna look for someone to rescue?"

"That's funny," Marisol said. "I thought you were studying to be a medical doctor, not a shrink."

"Oh please," Cristina said. "I know you better than anybody. And you've been in the rescuing business a long-ass time."

"After all the shit that's gone down, you're gonna throw that in my face?" Marisol said. "Like you would even be here if it wasn't for my rescuing?"

"I don't mean it like that," Cristina said. "We both know I owe you my life."

"That's right," Marisol said. "You were little and I had to protect you."

Cristina walked over and put her arms around Marisol. "That was twenty years ago," she said gently. "We were both little and we both deserved to be protected."

"It's not about what I deserved," Marisol said, pulling away. "It's about what I had to do so we would both make it out alive."

"I know that!" Cristina said. "But you're fucking stuck there. Stuck in that stinking-ass crowded apartment, trying to get us out alive. You go walking on the *malecón*, and you don't see the ocean and the waves and the sea spray. You see teenage sex workers who need your help."

"She does need my help!" Marisol yelled.

"This is a Caribbean country with socialized medicine," Cristina said. "She's not gonna freeze to death or be denied health care. She's not gonna get beat up by a pimp . . . She's older than you were when you started fucking for money. What's so goddamn special about you that you could handle the same thing two years younger under ten times harsher conditions, but she couldn't possibly survive without you?"

"You just don't get it," Marisol said.

"Oh, I definitely get it," Cristina said. "You had to rescue me, because it was the only way you could survive what happened—what *Tío*—"

"Don't say his name!" Marisol yelled.

"You don't want to hear his name?" Cristina said. "Then tell me what the hell happened to him. One day he was there. The next he was gone. We never even had a funeral."

"We didn't have money for a funeral, so I just left him in the morgue," Marisol said. "He got mugged in the hallway. You know that."

"Stop lying," Cristina said. "I'm not eleven anymore, but you're still fucking trying to protect me. I knew you weren't telling the truth even back then. I don't know if you killed him, I just know you were different that night."

"How would you know how I was that night?" Marisol asked. "You were asleep."

"Are you kidding me?" Cristina asked. "I was never asleep. Do you think anyone could sleep through what he did to you? I heard everything."

"What?" Marisol asked. It was as if the humid air grew suddenly still.

"The only dignity I could give you was to pretend that I didn't hear what happened." Cristina's voice was barely above a whisper. "I knew your only consolation was thinking that you had protected me. How could I take that away from you?"

"You knew?" Marisol asked. "You knew the whole time?"

"Of course I knew," Cristina said. "I knew you did it for me. The only gift I could give you in return was to let you be the hero. To let you believe you had sheltered me from all of it. It was obvious you stayed to protect me." Tears ran down her face as she spoke, but her voice didn't shake. "When you got older, you could have run away. I know it crushed you that you couldn't protect yourself. At least I could let you believe that you had protected me."

"I did protect you." Marisol shot up off the couch. "He never touched you."

"I know I was the lucky one!" Cristina said. "But you can't honestly believe that it was a party to hear him every night. To live in constant fear that I would be next. I had nightmares of my own. Nightmares that he'd come home and you wouldn't be there. I know why you didn't date, or go out past five. You had to be home every night when I was."

"I can't believe you knew," Marisol said, her voice choking up. "But of course you did. The room was tiny. Nobody sleeps that soundly."

"It was how I protected you," Cristina said. "I played the role of the saved one, so you could be the savior.

Like in church. Christ died for us. Was crucified and suffered for us. But it wasn't noble. It was fucked up. Nobody should have to go through what you did. What we both did. That night he died something was different. I knew but I couldn't say. How could I explain that I had been awake as always?"

"What was different?"

"Every night you'd wait in bed," Cristina said. "Your bed closer to the door, like a sentry. He would have to get past you to get to me. But that night—"

Marisol cut her off. "I wasn't in the bedroom."

"At first I was terrified," Cristina said. "Were you leaving me exposed? I heard the apartment door open and close. I just lay in bed and prayed that everything would be okay."

Marisol shook her head. "He started looking at you. So skinny, but you were sprouting breasts. I know you tried to hide them."

"They weren't hard to hide," Cristina said.

"But somehow he knew you were developing," Marisol said. "I could tell it flipped a switch in his sick head."

"I was panicked," Cristina said.

"I knew I'd rather die than let it happen to you," Marisol said. "But then I thought, what good would that do? If I died, then there would be nobody to protect you. That fucker needed to die, not me."

"But how did you manage it?" Cristina asked. "He was such a big guy."

"I would lie there," Marisol said, "when he was in our bedroom, planning it. I didn't know how to get a gun. I wasn't strong enough to throw him out the window, even when he was drunk. But I could get a kitchen knife."

"A young Latina buying some kitchen shit," Cristina said. "Unremarkable in our hood."

"I was seventeen, but I could have been ten," Marisol

said. "That day I bought four things at the supermarket: a kitchen knife, a flashlight, a knife sharpener, and an onion."

"You bought an onion?" Cristina asked.

"Getting only hardware might look suspicious," Marisol said. "Why kill him if I ended up in juvie and you went to foster care? I had to do it and get away with it."

"You stabbed him down on the fourth floor?" Cristina said.

"No," Marisol said. "I waited for him at the top of the landing, and when I stabbed him, he fell down the stairs."

"You must have waited for hours," Cristina said.

"My hands sweat so much in the gloves," Marisol recalled. "I held the knife in one hand, and the flashlight in the other one. Every time the downstairs door opened, my heart raced. I couldn't watch from the window because the light on the stoop was burned out. Finally, he came up the stairs. Do you remember how creaky the steps were on the last flight up to our apartment?"

"I hated everything about that place," Cristina said.

"And I smelled him," Marisol said. "His particular brand of rum. His particular stink of sweat. The sound of his keys jingling. And as he neared the top of the stairs, I just—I switched on the flashlight and flew at him with the knife."

Marisol recalled how the surprise of the sudden light in his face was surpassed only by the shock of the blade in his chest. His eyes and mouth widened in slow motion as he gasped and fell back, tumbling down the stairs. As she snapped off the light, she caught the glint of his keys on the landing, and scooped them up in the dark.

"Was he dead?" Cristina asked. "Were you sure?"

Marisol shook her head. Before the sound had even

stopped, she had stepped back into the apartment. In the quiet that followed the thudding of a falling man, she locked the door with her own keys. She waited for some commotion of neighbors. Some siren or flashing light.

She had sat by the door, terrified that a bleeding and wounded thing would drag its drunken self up the stairs and claw at the door. "I held his keys in my fist to remind me that he couldn't just walk in. I was ready to stab that motherfucker as many times as it took."

"You never actually told me he was dead," Cristina said. "You just told me he wasn't ever coming back."

"That's what mattered," Marisol said.

"I still have nightmares sometimes," Cristina said, her face puckering.

"Me too," Marisol said.

"Thank you," Cristina whispered through her tears.

Marisol could only nod, as she cried, too.

Chapter 30

Marisol had been in Cuba for nearly two months. Her skin glowed copper, and she'd put on a little weight in her belly from all the slow meals.

Tyesha had gone back after a week, Kim and Jody after two weeks, but Marisol had extended her ticket twice. She also filed for an extension with the IRS, and would have until October to make a paper trail for all the cash "donations." Meanwhile, she took the positive weekly e-mails from Eva and Serena at face value. The clinic was finally stable.

She had gone to the beach and stood alone in the surf, enjoying the sound and feel of the water, the sinking of her feet into the sand. Gazing out to the horizon, she let the warm currents sway her body gently back and forth. The ocean's authentic majesty washed away the memory of her dream with Raul and the bitterness of his final drunken words to her.

The reality of love was Cristina. Marisol spent as much time as possible with her sister. Sometimes, when Cristina came in to crash from her residency, Marisol would lie on the bed next to her, reading a mystery novel in Spanish. Marisol could see that the extra hours

Cristina stayed awake to visit were wearing on her. She became increasingly fatigued. This was a rare morning, when Juan was working but Cristina had a whole day off.

"Too bad Vladimir's not around to keep you busy while I've been at the hospital," Cristina teased.

"Vladimir's been away with one of his paying girlfriends," Marisol said. "He got back last night, I think."

"Any chance you'll stay in Cuba for a while?"

Marisol sighed. "Maybe another week. It's already May, and I can't miss Tyesha's graduation. Besides, you and Juan are coming in December."

"About that . . ." Cristina began.

"You're not having second thoughts, are you?" Marisol asked.

"I'm pregnant," Cristina blurted out.

"What?" Marisol's jaw dropped. "But what about the birth control pills I've been sending?"

"There's that point-oh-one chance."

"Such fucking bad timing," Marisol said.

"Why are you freaking out?" Cristina asked. "This isn't a tragedy."

"What about becoming a doctor?"

"I can be a doctor here," Cristina said. "And have a family with Juan."

"Cristina, don't be naïve," Marisol said. "It's not that simple."

"It's not that simple in the U.S.," Cristina said. "Day care is free here. Doctors practice locally. I know lots of women doctors with kids. They're happy."

"What about me?" Marisol asked.

Cristina shrugged. "What's keeping you in New York?"

"I'm not ready to just pack up and—"

"Why choose?" Cristina asked. "You have plenty of money now. Live there. Visit a lot."

"You're having the baby?" Marisol said. "Is Juan pressuring you?"

"I haven't even told him," Cristina said. "But I'm not having an abortion just because the pregnancy wasn't planned. Maybe a couple of years ago, but not now."

"I don't want us to be apart anymore," Marisol said.

"So don't be," Cristina said. "I love you, Marisol, but not only you. I love Juan, and I'll love this baby."

"You're building a family without me."

"I'm just building a family in Cuba," Cristina said. "You can be as big a part of it as you want. We had a good plan, but this baby changes everything. Why can't you be happy for me?"

"It was supposed to be you and me in the center of this family," Marisol said. "Not you with some man and me as a fucking visiting aunt. What happened to *'tú y yo siempre'*?"

She grabbed her shoes and left the house.

Marisol showed up unannounced at Vladimir's. She was ravenous for him.

After the second round of sex, he looked into her face for a while.

"What's wrong?" he asked in Spanish. "Is it because Cristina's pregnant?"

"She told you?" Marisol asked.

"Juan did." Vladimir shrugged. "She hasn't said anything but he can tell."

"I'm her sister. How come I couldn't tell?"

Vladimir shook his head. "You still see her as a child."

"No I don't," Marisol said.

"She was a child when she first came to Cuba, but she's a woman now," Vladimir said. "You need to let her have her adult life."

"I thought you understood wanting to be near family," Marisol said. "Why shouldn't I expect her to come back to New York?"

"Because I'm hoping this means you'll stay in Cuba."

Marisol laughed. "I don't think—"

"Or at least you'll come visit," he said, leaning in to kiss her.

"I'm thinking about it," she said as they sank back on the bed.

The moment Marisol walked in the door the next morning, Cristina leaped up off the couch.

"Marisol, I can't do this without your blessing. I told Juan I wasn't sure about keeping it."

"You have my blessing," Marisol said, smoothing back Cristina's hair. "I'll be the *tía* who comes from New York all the time."

"You better mean that," Cristina said, tears falling. "No more lame excuses, like thousands of women in New York depending on you to rob corrupt CEOs or billionaires."

"Fine," Marisol said, crying, as well. "But you gotta keep up your end, too. No more bullshit embargoes."

Chapter 31

From the plane's window, Marisol watched the blue-green water turn to a lacy streak of foam at the beach along the Rockaways.

After landing at JFK, she took a town car back to the city. Marisol felt relaxed, unencumbered. The driving force of her life had always been about survival. Surviving her mother and grandmother's deaths, surviving her uncle. Doing sex work to survive, and then fighting for the clinic's survival.

Marisol crossed into Manhattan after more than eight weeks in Cuba, several shades darker and better rested than she'd been in decades. Dusk fell as they sat in Monday post–rush hour traffic, and Marisol leaned back against the seat, unfazed. Her phone sat at the bottom of her purse with zero percent battery. An accident on the bridge had traffic backed up, but she didn't care. There was nowhere Marisol had to be until Tyesha's graduation the next day.

A sentimental, old school salsa song came on the radio, and she found herself filled with thoughts of Raul, even with the taste of Vladimir's good-bye kiss still on her lips.

Once the car crossed into the Lower East Side, her

senses heightened. When they pulled up to the curb of the clinic, everything looked okay. It was just after 9 p.m. The street was relatively quiet. No new graffiti. Nothing on fire. She planned to stop by the office to pick up her mail.

In the pile was an article Serena had clipped with the headline, "Mexican Women's Organization Gets Huge Anonymous Donation." It was dated seven weeks before. She read it as she climbed the stairs, her mouth splitting into a grin.

> . . . the grassroots organization in Mexico of former sex trafficking victims helping current victims, has reported receiving their first U.S. donation—$250,000 in cash from an anonymous source. The organization's founder and director says the funds will be used to. . . .

Marisol knew something was wrong the moment she walked into the outer office of the fourth floor. She smelled a slight odor of cigarettes. Pulling her keys out of the door, she turned around and headed back into the hallway.

She'd almost reached the stairs when Jerry yelled after her.

"I've got your little bitch assistant."

Marisol froze at the sound of his voice, that sneering, swaggering arrogance.

"If you're not here in thirty seconds, I'll blow her ugly head off," his voice echoed down the quiet hall.

Marisol walked back toward the inner office—her office—not feeling the carpet under her feet. Her numb fingers fished the panic key ring out of the pocket inside her purse.

Jerry had a gun to Serena's head. Desk papers had been thrown around, file cabinets emptied onto the floor. Plants dumped out, their dirt sifted through. Cabinet doors stood open with papers spilling out. Several cigarette butts were strewn across an award plaque that lay atop the chaos on her desk. There were burn marks in the surface of both the desk and the plaque.

"Welcome home," Jerry said.

Serena seemed tinier than ever.

"Did he hurt you?" Marisol asked. "Touch you?"

"Please, bitch." Jerry sneered. "I got more pussy than I know what to do with. I don't need this dog here."

Marisol's heart banged against her ribs. With her hand still buried in her purse, she tried to remember Eva's words that day in her office.

"You know how it works," Eva had said. "Left button siren, right button signal."

Marisol gripped the key ring and pressed the signal button.

"I heard some bitch gave all my girls their passports."

Marisol slowly slid her hand from her purse.

"Dulce called me just before she left town," Jerry said. "Said she was going to Cuba and wanted to say good-bye. See? I told you they were my girls!" He thumped himself on the chest.

Marisol stayed quiet.

"I ask who's taking her, and she wouldn't fucking tell me!" he yelled, and then his voice lightened. "But I figured it out. She left the same day you left."

He slammed his free hand against the arm of the couch.

"I put it together," he growled. "You got some motherfuckers to break in my place and steal my shit and gave my bitches their passports so they could go back to their countries, where they'll learn that their pussy is worth a lot less." Spit had gathered in the corners of his mouth. "You think you did them a favor? I was the one doing them a favor!"

He backhanded the vase on the end table, and Marisol watched it crash onto the carpet, spilling blue irises and water. Serena must have brought her fresh flowers.

"I just had to have one of my new girls call here pretending to be some reporter," Jerry said. "*When will Miss I-Shit-Gold Marisol Rivera be coming back?*" he mimicked a female voice. "Your girl on the phone just gave it up like a slut in the back of a car."

He slammed the fist of his free hand down on the desk. The cigarette butts jumped.

"I came here to GET MY SHIT BACK," Jerry said. "All of it. The cash and the guns."

"I told you, Jerry, we're a service center," Marisol spoke with a calm she didn't feel. "Girls ask for something and we give it to them. Dulce wanted to join my trip to Cuba, so I said yes." Marisol leaned back and crossed her arms. "Besides, I didn't take your shit. But I know who did."

"Who?" he asked, advancing on her.

"You won't believe me," she said.

He jammed the gun into her temple. "You better fucking tell me."

Marisol didn't even look at him. "Your brother set you up, Jerry."

"What?" Jerry asked, startled. The gun went slack in his hand. "He would never—"

"I knew you wouldn't believe it," Marisol said. "Especially after he played the victim role so well. '*I tried to stop them from robbing you,*'" she mimicked in a singsong voice. "'*They hit me in the face.*'" She laughed. "That was all part of the heist. Your brother knew just how to play you. You want your guns and money? Ask Jimmy."

A sharp furrowing of his brow let her know she had him unsettled.

"Who knew when you would be out of the house? Who knew you had a four-way hookup with all your girls in Manhattan that night? He had plenty of time to figure out how to crack the safe. You wanna know how I know all this shit? His ass kept coming by here just to brag about how smart he is. How he had a plan to take you down."

Jerry's face was tight, his eyes locked on Marisol. She went on, "Seems guys always need an audience to talk shit for. Jimmy's no different. He couldn't brag to any of your folks, because they would give him away, but he could come brag to me because I was supposed to be the bitch you wanted dead. I couldn't show my face and tell you even if I wanted to. He gave me the passports just to fuck with you. He said it couldn't be him to give the girls their freedom. He said after Dulce left, he got the idea. Make you lose everything."

He still had the gun next to her head. She was close enough to smell his cologne.

"Jimmy came by a couple of days after you introduced him and the girls to us. Said he was gonna show you who the big brother was in your family. I said I didn't want any part of it, but later when he handed me a bunch of passports, I gave them to the girls he sent my way. So now you know. Your brother set you up."

Jerry's eyes were blazing, and his mouth twitched.

Marisol tried to keep her eyes on Jerry as she spoke, staying calm.

"And here you are, with a gun, in a room with two unarmed women. Are you the kind of guy who's gonna take it out on us just because we're here? Or are you the kind of guy who's gonna go find the guy who fucked you and handle yours? Seems to me that pimps always take the easy fight. What the hell can we do? You'll have to beat us both to death or shoot us all or rape us or whatever, because your shit's not here, Big J! Your brother has it. You need to ask Lil J!"

"Shut up!" Jerry said. "JUST SHUT THE FUCK UP!" He raised his hand and smacked Marisol hard across the jaw.

She opened the eye on the side of her face that wasn't burning, and looked at him. He dialed his cell phone, while still holding the gun on them.

Both women waited, barely breathing as they heard the faint, tinny ringing of the phone. Voice mail came on, a man speaking with music in the background.

"Jimmy!" he yelled into the phone. "Where the fuck are you? Call me now!"

He dialed a second number. "*Chuco?*" he demanded. "It's Jerry. Where's my motherfucking brother? . . . He's not with you? . . . Well, find his ass and tell him to fucking call me right now!"

Jerry hung up and stared at the phone. "I don't know who's fucking lying to me," he said. "But my brother's gonna call back in a minute, and I'm gonna get some answers."

As they sat tense, all eyes on the cell phone, the quiet was shattered by a knock. The three of them snapped their attention from the phone to the door.

"Marisol, are you back, honey?" Eva's voice. Calm and ordinary. "I saw the light."

Marisol and Serena sat motionless on the couch.

"Marisol?" Eva knocked again, as Jerry crossed the room to whisper in Marisol's ear.

"Tell her you're fine," he hissed.

"I'm fine, Eva," Marisol said in a cheerful voice. "Just getting some work done."

"I haven't seen you in weeks, lovey," Eva said. "At least come give me a hug."

"Get rid of her," Jerry said.

"Whatever you say," Marisol whispered. "But she'll be suspicious if I don't go hug her."

"Stay where I can see you," he said. "Plus I keep this little bitch as insurance."

"Just for a second," Marisol said to Eva. "I wanna finish this up and get to bed."

Marisol opened the door, and stepped one foot out into the hall. She maneuvered herself to embrace Eva, and felt cold steel as Eva pressed a .44 automatic into her hands. Marisol stuck it down the back waistband of her jeans.

"So good to see you," Marisol said. "We'll catch up tomorrow, okay? Good night."

Marisol stepped back into the room, and resumed her previous position on the couch. She sat with her palms up in her lap. The press of the gun against her spine beckoned to her as they listened to Eva's footsteps retreating down the hallway.

"My brother's gonna call back," Jerry said. "Then it's either his ass or yours."

Marisol looked straight at Jerry. "Then I got nothing to worry about."

They waited. Serena sat motionless. Jerry held his phone but didn't take his eyes or his gun off of them.

A car went by blasting a *cumbia*, out on the street below. Marisol slid her hand down her thigh onto the couch. As the music faded, they heard the sharp burst of a woman laughing. Marisol moved her hand, millimeter by millimeter, back toward the gun.

Jerry dialed again. All three of them heard the faint ringing, then an outgoing message. "*Chuco!*" he thundered. "Why you ain't picking up the phone now, bitch?"

He hung up and looked toward the street. "Those fucks better not have left." Jerry stormed to the window. When he leaned over to look out, Marisol slid her hand back. She had just dislodged the .44 from her waistband when Jerry spun on her with his gun.

"I said don't fucking move!"

"Sorry," Marisol said, putting her hands back up.

Marisol felt a cold object press against her hip. She realized that Serena, who was sitting with her feet tucked under her, was using her toes to nudge the gun forward.

Her assistant stared straight ahead, but Marisol felt the achingly slow but insistent crawl of the gun along her thigh.

". . . the fuck is he?" Jerry muttered.

Finally, the gun butt pressed against her knee. When Jerry looked at the window, Marisol glanced down. A sliver of the metal barrel was visible between the two women. Marisol scooted over to cover it.

"I said don't fucking move!" Jerry roared.

A moment later, an aggressive techno ringtone startled all of them. When Jerry focused on the phone, Marisol snatched up the gun and fired off a single shot.

The blast echoed in the office, as Jerry's gun clattered onto the floor under the desk. A red stain blossomed on his shirt, and his right arm hung limp.

The recoil burned Marisol's side from her shoulder to her fingertips, as the tinny techno ringtone continued to fill the room.

On Jerry's face, shock gave way to fury, as he stood up and lumbered toward Marisol.

She and Serena scrambled up over the back of the couch.

Jerry loped across the rug, the stain spreading across his pale gray shirt.

Marisol raised the gun and shot him again with a weak and shaking hand. The bullet hit his right shoulder. He jerked back, but kept coming, eyes hungry.

The phone stopped ringing. Serena yanked the door open and ran out.

Marisol leapt back and lifted the gun, grasping it with both hands to keep it steady. She pointed it at his head.

Jerry let out a laugh that deteriorated into a cough. "Punk-ass little bitch," he drawled, his eyes locked on Marisol. "What are you waiting for?"

"I'm savoring the moment," she said.

"Bullshit," he croaked. "You're stalling. You don't have the balls, stupid cocksucking bitch."

At first she thought maybe he remembered how they'd first met. But she searched his face for signs of more intimate recognition and found nothing.

"I remember the first man I ever killed." She clenched her hands to keep the gun from shaking. "My only regret is that I'll never be sure he knew it was me."

"Marisol! Marisol!" Eva called from the hallway. "Are you okay, Marisol?"

"Perfect." Marisol laughed. "My name is the last word you'll ever hear. Tattoo that on your ass, motherfucker."

With an animal yelp of rage, he heaved forward and reached for her with his one good hand.

Marisol squeezed off a third shot, and the bullet hit near the center of his chest. As it punctured his lung, the big man deflated. He sagged forward onto the couch, face-first. His hat toppled off, falling at Marisol's feet.

"Eva!" Marisol yelled. "He's down." She gritted through the recoil pain and held the .44 on Jerry.

Eva opened the door as she held her arm around Serena in the doorway. Serena was shaking and sobbing. "It's okay now, honey," Eva said. "It's okay."

Marisol pulled the two women into the office and locked the door behind them.

"He's down, but is he dead?" Marisol asked.

Eva left Serena to feel for a pulse and nodded.

"The guys he came with?" Marisol asked. "They still out there?"

Eva nodded. "When I saw the Hummer, I came in the back."

"You think they heard the blast?" Marisol asked.

"Maybe," Eva said. "But they'll probably assume it's him shooting you. We need to call the cops before they figure it out."

Marisol nodded. "But we can't have cops here until we secure the place."

"You handle security," Eva said. "I'll take care of Serena."

While Eva took Serena out the back way, Marisol started sliding bookshelves.

She covered the doors in the hallway that connected to the modeling agency. The specialty bookshelves slid on casters, completely covering the doors, and then slid flush with the wall, so there wasn't even a gap for the knob. She heard Jerry's phone ringing through the hallway.

When Marisol came back, she surveyed the wreck of her office.

The cell on Marisol's desk began to ring again. Marisol couldn't stand it, and turned the phone to silent.

She sat down to call the cops on her landline. On the desktop were messages that had come in during her trip. Serena always piled them neatly, but Jerry's tirade had disarranged them. The top one said, "Raul Barrios called

AGAIN." Half the messages in the stack were from Raul. "Called to apologize . . . called twice today . . . please call when you get back."

Instead of calling the ninth precinct, Marisol called the number on the message.

It rang three times before he picked up.

"Marisol," Raul's voice came on the line. "*Mami*, I am so—"

"I shot Jerry," she said.

"The pimp?" Raul asked.

"Three times. He's on the floor of my office."

She could see the toe of one of Jerry's dress shoes in her peripheral vision. Shiny.

"Are the cops there?"

"Not yet."

"I'll be right over."

Marisol gave him the three door codes that would get him from the front door into her office. Marisol sat unmoving. Not until the disconnect sound began to buzz in her ear did she hang up.

She felt her stomach heave, and she leaned over to vomit into her wastebasket.

She wiped her mouth and sat frozen at the desk, gun in hand, watching the dead man's shiny left shoe for any sign of movement. She couldn't shake the irrational fear that, unless she stayed vigilant, Jerry would rise from the dead like a zombie, an unkillable mass of vengeful rage.

Jerry was still dead when Raul arrived fifteen minutes later.

"Marisol," he said, crossing the office with his arms outstretched.

"Don't," she said.

Raul stepped back to survey the body.

Jerry lay in a wide bloodstain on the carpet, weapon peeking out from beneath the desk.

"He had a gun," Raul said. "He broke in and threatened you. It was a clear case of self-defense."

"I had to shoot him three times," Marisol said from the desk. "He kept coming at us."

"Us?" Raul asked. "Who else was involved?"

"Serena, but we have to keep her out of this. She's transgender and undocumented."

"She still here?"

"Eva took her home."

"Eva?"

"She slipped me the gun," Marisol said.

"Anything else?" Raul asked.

"I'm glad he's dead."

Raul nodded. "Don't lead with that."

Chapter 32

"So let's go over this again," the cop said. He was fortyish, short, and had a crew cut.

"I had just come back from visiting my sister in Cuba," Marisol said, taking a sip of water. "I stopped by my office to find Jerry had broken in and threatened to kill me. I shot him three times."

"With an illegal, unregistered weapon," the cop said.

"It's registered in Pennsylvania to Eva Feldman."

"Does this look like Pennsylvania?"

More cops came trooping up the stairs, including two homicide detectives. Marisol felt nearly claustrophobic with all the police in her office.

"What do we got?" one of the homicide guys asked.

"Hispanic male, mid forties, three shots through the chest," his partner said.

As he spoke, Raul arrived with Robbery Detective John Mathias.

"We've got some info on this case," Mathias said, flashing his badge. "We're out of the Central Robbery Squad."

Raul stood in the background.

"Let's have it," one of the detectives said.

"Miss Rivera here was a witness in one of our cases," Mathias said.

Raul jumped in. "Around the same time, she was publicly threatened by this guy, Jerry Rios, local pimp." He explained the situation.

"Pimp connected to your robbery case?" one detective asked.

"Not that we know of," Mathias said.

"I say let the forensics team do their job," Raul concluded. "But let's assume that everything's gonna check out with ballistics. You could just confiscate the gun and call it a night."

"What do you think?" one detective asked the other.

"I think I'm ready to go to bed," the other replied. "But I don't want ballistics to find out that he was actually shot with some other gun that's linked to seven different homicides and the women involved have skipped town."

Raul made eye contact with Marisol. "I can vouch for them."

"Our sergeant isn't gonna like a man with three bullets in him, an illegal weapon, and no one in custody," one detective said.

"That's Sergeant Brooks in homicide, right?" Raul asked.

They nodded.

"Brooks and Detective Mathias here go way back to the academy," Raul said. "Like Detective Mathias said in the car on the way over, he'd stake his badge and his career on this woman's innocence."

"Detective," Mathias said, "this situation is not worth missing any more sleep."

"Good enough for me," one detective said. "If anything goes wrong, we released her on your word."

"Done," his partner agreed. "You're free to go, Ms. Rivera."

Marisol felt a slight loosening in her solar plexus as the two homicide cops headed down the stairs.

"You hear that?" Raul said to Marisol after the detectives had gone. "You're free to go."

"Only because you put my reputation on the line," Mathias hissed at Raul. "And because they think you're a cop."

"Should I be flattered or insulted?" Raul asked.

Mathias put a warning finger in Raul's face. "It's not a joke," he said. "If this comes back to bite me in any way, it's your ass, Barrios."

"Nothing's gonna come back to bite you, Matty, because she's telling the truth," he said, all the humor gone from his voice. "I don't have a badge or a career, but I would stake my life on that."

"How noble," Mathias muttered as he walked out.

Raul pulled Marisol aside, out of range of the coroner's staff.

Marisol slumped down on the couch. She watched like a sentry as they put Jerry on a stretcher, and the forensics staffers bagged and tagged his gun, phone, and hat.

"Marisol." Raul sat next to her on the couch. "Can we talk? I—"

"You should leave," she said.

"Okay, but first I just wanna apologize—"

She tensed back up. "Not while there's still a single cop in this building."

Marisol rested her head on the back of the couch. Her hair fell back, revealing the bruise on the side of her face.

"Are you all right?" Raul asked. "What happened?"

"One hit," she said. "It's nothing."

"Hold on," he said, and fetched an ice pack from the

mini-fridge in her office. He raised a hand to put it on her face.

She pulled away. "I'll do it."

He clenched and unclenched his jaw. "You guys just about done?" he asked the forensics team.

"We'll seal the place in a few minutes."

Marisol held the ice on her face, eyes closed against the cold.

When the front door clicked behind the last of the forensics team, Marisol slumped down onto the couch and let out the breath she'd been holding. She looked across the downstairs lobby at Raul, who was standing with his hands in his pockets.

"Okay," she said. "Say whatever you need to say."

"Marisol, I'm so sorry," he said. "I was drunk when I called you, but that's no excuse. I was totally outta line. I get why you don't want to talk to me. I'm just glad you called me. Glad I was able to help and you're free."

But Marisol didn't feel free. She felt like a seventeen-year-old girl standing at the top of the stairs with a dead man's keys in her hand.

She had been so alone then, some part of her had been braced for the next nightmare ever since. But this time it was different. She had called Raul and he'd come. He'd backed her up with the cops, even putting Mathias in the line of fire. No man had ever done anything like that for her before.

So what? This didn't change anything. She tried to cling to the memory of his drunken voice slurring hate through the phone. She tried to do it the way she always did it. Bite back the feeling. Keep moving. Nothing to see here, folks. She wanted to tell Raul to leave. She wanted to go up to her apartment and sleep.

She tried to stand but her legs wouldn't hold her. When

she opened her mouth, she couldn't form any words. Her jaw trembled. Then her shoulders. Then her whole body. She tightened her core, trying to hold the trembling at bay, but the tremor increased.

"Marisol," Raul said and reached for her.

She tried to pull away, but she was all fault lines. She collapsed against him, shaking and weeping.

He held her, stroked her hair, wiped the tears with the hem of his blue cotton T-shirt.

When Marisol was no longer overcome, when she was herself and could have a coherent thought, she wanted to throw him out and retreat back up the stairs. But it felt so good. He felt so good. The firmness of his chest, the strength of his embrace, his hands in her hair, and the softness of the cotton against her face.

Marisol didn't know how long she cried. It felt like forever. But at some point she stopped being a seventeen-year-old girl and became a woman. Became aware of the heat where her body pressed against his.

Slowly, she sat up, swung around to straddle him. She moved her mouth toward his.

For a moment, he leaned in to kiss her, but then he pulled back.

"Wait," he said. "What are we about to do?"

Marisol blinked. "I don't know what we're about to do." She shook her head. "Maybe I planned to fuck you and ask for some money." She began to untangle herself from him.

"Marisol," he said, holding her wrist. "I told you. I'm so sorry. I was drunk and angry and—"

"*En vino hay verdad,*" Marisol said. "Maybe that's what you really think."

"It's not like that," Raul said. "I was calling myself *novio de la gran puta*, because I still wanna be with you. But you hung up—fair enough. I thought we were just having a fight. I took a few days to cool off. But when I called back, you were gone. Cell number disconnected."

Marisol pulled her arm away and reached for some tissues on a side table. She wiped her eyes. He still wanted to be with her? He had always wanted to be with her?

"A fight?" Marisol said. "A fight is when you're mad but you call the next day. You left me hanging."

"I fucked up," he said. "I needed time to get my head together. I was just a little flipped out. It took me a while to make a clear decision."

"A decision?" Marisol said. "Every fucking minute you didn't call me was a decision."

"Yeah, but you don't understand how it is for guys," he said. "It's hard to think about your girl fucking anybody else. We wanna invent time machines to go back twenty years and kill motherfuckers before they even touched our girl, you know? But to think that any asshole with a hundred bucks could have—it's just—shit, Marisol. And I didn't even hear it from you."

"I would have told you eventually," she said. "I just wanted to get to know you a little better before I sprang my fucking sex work history on you. You said you wouldn't hold my sexual past against me. Like I didn't hold it against you that you fucked Nalissa."

"As I recall from that same conversation," Raul said. "It's not like you just didn't mention your past. You intentionally lied to me. 'I dated a bunch'?"

"I didn't lie," Marisol said. "I minimized it because I knew you couldn't fucking handle it. Who the fuck are you, really? The *barrio* boy who understands that we do what we have to? Or the Boy Scout who wants to marry a virgin?"

"Wait a minute," Raul said. "There's a lot of territory between virgin and sex worker."

"That's still the Boy Scout talking. Was it him or *barrio* boy who fucking called me *la gran puta*? You and your little fucking feelings trying to decide if you could fucking handle the fact that I was a sex worker ages ago," she said. "It's not like it was my first choice of a job."

"Okay, already," Raul said, his voice rising. "You. Are. Right. I should have called you up the next day to apologize. I fucked up. Are you gonna give me a second chance?"

"At what?"

"A second chance to be with you, Marisol," he said.

She shook her head. "Look, you apologized. I accept your apology. Can we just leave it at that?"

"Hell, no," he said. "Marisol, my only regret in life is becoming a cop. But now that I found you again, if I didn't do everything in my power to be your man, I'd have an even bigger regret."

"Well, that's all fine and good, but I can't be with someone who puts me on some Robin Hood pedestal," she said. "And then knocks me off when he finds out I'm not Maid Marian."

"Fair enough," he said. "But, baby, I'm ready for the real. I just want to know what I'm signing up for."

"I don't know what you'd be signing up for," she said. "I don't understand this 'be with me' or 'be your man' shit. I've fucked plenty of guys. Sometimes for money. Or because I had no choice. Or sometimes because I needed a good fuck. You want a guarantee? You want a road map? I can't give you shit."

"What can you give me?"

"I don't know, Raul," she said, tears filling her eyes. "All I know how to do with men is to fuck them."

"Those nights we were together?" he asked. "That was just fucking to you?"

"I don't know what that was," she said. "I never had anything like that before . . . or since."

"It's called making love, Marisol," he said. "It's what two people do when they care about each other."

"What are you gonna do, Raul? If we have some kind of relationship, and we run across some guy who I fucked for money?" she asked. "Or some guy I picked up in a bar?"

"I don't know what I would do," he said.

"Or your cop buddies start to talk smack about you dating an ex-whore who fucked VanDyke?" She poked him in the chest. "What are you gonna do when they start asking you how you compare to billionaire dick? Huh?"

"I don't know," he said, banging his fist against the wall. "I don't fucking know."

"Then don't come to me with this fairy-tale shit until you have an answer," she said. "Because I was falling for you until I saw your face when your friend read my rap sheet. And I'm not gonna let myself fall again unless I know you can handle it."

"Marisol, I've been in love with you since junior high school," he said.

"Then show me you're not still in junior high," she said. "All the guys want to fuck the school slut, but then they find out they like her, and they can't face the peer pressure at school the next day."

"Is that what happened to you?" Raul asked. "Is that why you're so goddamn scared?"

"No," she said. "I got all my high school fucking from my family, thank you very much."

He sat stunned for a moment.

"I'm sorry," he said.

She rolled her eyes. "Let's drop it," she said.

"Your uncle," he said. "I met him once. He was such a creep."

"Yeah?" she said. "You remember I said I had only killed somebody one time? Well, it was him."

"Shit."

"You happy?" she asked. "Wanna call one of your pals to arrest me?"

"No, Marisol," he said. "But I wanna talk about it."

"There's nothing to say," she said.

"But it explains so much," he said.

"Don't psychoanalyze me," she said. "I have my own damn shrink."

"What does your shrink say?" Raul tilted his head to the side and looked right in her face. "About me. What does your shrink say you should do about me?"

"What are you talking about?" she asked.

"I've talked to a shrink before," he said. "I had to after I shot a guy, and I kept seeing her because my fiancée and I broke up. The shrink said it's good to open up your heart after you've been hurt. Your shrink say anything like that?"

"I think you need to leave," Marisol said.

A smile spread across his face. "I think your shrink says I'm good for you," Raul said. "And you keep saying things to piss me off so I'll leave, but it's not gonna happen, Marisol. I love you. I fuckin' love you."

"Shut up," she said.

"No." He shook his head. "This is real. I love you, and there's nothing you can do about it. I'm good for you. And neither of us knows what's gonna happen. That's how it works." He reached across the couch and took her hand. "You know I'm right."

"Fuck you, Raul," she said, looking away, but she didn't pull her hand out of his.

"Oh no, *mujer*. No more fucking," he said. "We're making love."

He leaned in and kissed her, sliding his arms around her waist, pressing their bodies close.

Her body responded. She kissed back, running her hands down his back, across his chest.

They both moved more slowly than they had before, eyes locked on each other.

She let herself really take him in—the smile lines by his eyes, the trio of gray hairs in his stubble, the hint of hazel in his brown eyes. This beautiful face belonged to a man who loved her. Who knew all about her past. Who was sorry he'd left her hanging. Who wouldn't let anything stand between them—not even her own fears.

As she took it all in—that she could be loved, would be loved—she opened up to him from somewhere deep inside. She swooned with the fullness of her desire for him. She wanted to have every possible inch of skin pressed against him, inhaling him through every pore.

Her apartment, her bed, was four whole floors away—too far. She couldn't wait. She pulled him onto the couch in the lobby.

She kissed him as if she would devour him, and began to take off her clothes.

"Marisol, wait," Raul said as she slid out of her jeans. "I don't have a—"

"Shhh." She pressed her finger to his lips. "This is a clinic that serves sex workers. We keep condoms just about everywhere."

As he removed his shirt, he didn't take his eyes off her. He watched her as she walked in bra and underwear over to the front desk, and pulled out a condom from a safer sex display.

By the time she got back across the lobby, he had

stripped naked. She handed him the condom, and took off her underwear and bra. He rolled the condom onto his erection, as she lay back on the couch. He slid inside her, so tender she could barely stand it.

"I love you, Marisol," he said, kissing her gently and stroking in and out of her with a sweetness and precision that made her shudder.

"I know you love me, too, even if you're not ready to say it," he said, grinning down at her, moving his hips up and back, until she could barely breathe. "You don't have to say anything until you're ready. Just take your time."

I love you, Raul, she thought as she tumbled over the edge of the orgasm, moaning unintelligibly, the words clear in her mind.

After they had migrated up to the apartment, they lay on the bed, kissing in the half-darkened bedroom.

He touched the bruise on her cheek, and she winced.

"You know," he said. "You get into so much trouble, I'm just gonna have to be your boyfriend. For your own protection."

"Oh really?" she said.

"Yeah," he said. "Then we'll have to spread it all over the neighborhood that we're going steady so nobody will mess with you."

"'Going steady'?" Marisol laughed. "I hope you're kidding."

"Only about what we call it," he said. "You ready to let me be your man?"

"Okay," Marisol said.

She felt shy. It seemed strange. And corny. And wonderful. They lay on their sides, facing each other on the bed. She took a finger and traced the outline of his face.

He took her finger and kissed it. "So now that you're my girlfriend and everything, I'm definitely gonna get some shit from guys on the force."

"Especially if you spread it all around the neighborhood," Marisol said.

"I don't care what shit they say," he said. "You're totally worth it. I just need to ask, is there anything else I should know?"

"Well, you know I was a sex worker," she said. "And why I killed my uncle. After that, anything else seems kinda anticlimactic."

"And yet, we may be heading for another climax," he said, sliding close to her and running his hands down her back, over her ass.

"You're kidding me," she said, laughing. "Again? What is that, like the fourth time?"

"I'm taking the fifth," he said, and rolled on top, landing with an openmouthed kiss.

Chapter 33

The next day, Marisol and her crew were celebrating in the conference room. Her office was still sealed as a crime scene by order of the NYPD.

They were all dressed up from the graduation, and Marisol wore concealer over the bruise on her face.

"To Columbia's Mailman School graduating its first former escort and grand larceny conspirator with a master's in public health!" Marisol said.

"Cheers!" Tyesha, Kim, Jody, and Eva said and drank their champagne.

"To Marisol," Tyesha said. "For helping a bunch of young hoes retire before the age of thirty!"

"L'chaim," Eva said as they all drank again.

"To Jeremy VanDyke, for being such a committed philanthropist!" Jody said.

"Fuck, yeah!" Kim said.

"To Tyesha, the new associate director at the clinic!" Eva toasted.

"Salud!" Marisol said.

"Okay, Kim," Tyesha said. "What's your toast?"

"To all the hoes everywhere."

"I'll drink to that," Marisol said as they all laughed and drained their glasses.

* * *

After everyone had left, Marisol picked the champagne flutes off the table and walked upstairs to her apartment. She kicked off her brown suede stiletto pumps, and was surprised to see Raul sitting at the counter of her kitchenette reading the paper.

"How was graduation?" he asked, standing up and pulling her into a kiss.

"Good," she said.

It had been great to see Tyesha walk across the stage. However, when Marisol had agreed to go, she had expected it to be on campus at Columbia, not further uptown at The Armory, a track and field center in Washington Heights. On the way back, the taxi drove past one of the bars she used to frequent. It was unsettling to see her old hunting ground during the day.

"I wasn't sure you'd still be here," she said.

"It's cool, though, right?" Raul asked.

"More than cool," she said, kissing him again.

He pulled back from the kiss and held her by her waist. "So, I got two pieces of news while you were gone."

"Good news?" she asked.

"I think so," he said. "First is cop news. Looks like they've linked the pimp to the VanDyke job and maybe even that string of robberies uptown."

"Really," she said. "You wouldn't have thought that Jerry would be smart enough to pull those off."

"You can't argue with evidence," Raul said. "They found bills from the VanDyke robbery in his safe, and the Ivy Alpha ring of one of the uptown victims. But they didn't find the big money. So they're looking for an accomplice."

"Seems like your boys at Central Robbery got it wrapped up pretty tight." Marisol smiled. "What's the other news?"

"My folks are in town," he said. "So my aunt is having a family get-together thing in the Bronx."

"A thing?" Marisol asked. "You want me to meet your family?"

"Meet my family?" Raul said. "You know them already."

"From high school," Marisol said. "How do I explain what I've been doing since?"

"Just say what you do now," Raul said. "Nobody's gonna scrutinize the gaps in your résumé."

"I don't know," Marisol said.

"Come on," Raul said. "This is what girlfriends and boyfriends do. They go to each other's annoying family things and they make the best of them."

Marisol laughed out loud. "You make it sound so tempting."

"Come on," he said. "My sister will be so happy to see you."

Marisol nodded slowly. "I need to show you something first."

She walked around closing all the window shades.

"Oh," Raul said, raising his eyebrows. "I might like this."

"Maybe not," Marisol said.

"Does it involve nudity?" he asked.

"In a way," she said.

"I'm flexible," Raul said. "I'll work around a bra. I can keep the jeans on, baby. What do you need?"

"A crowbar," Marisol said, rummaging through her closet.

"Whoa," Raul said. "I'm not that flexible."

"It's not about sex," Marisol said.

"Then what's it about?" he asked.

Marisol pushed the two tall bar stools aside and slid

the flat end of the crowbar behind the plywood in the kitchenette island.

"Can I help?" Raul asked, as she pushed and the wood of the board squeaked against the nails.

"Nope," Marisol said, leaning down in her burnt orange silk dress, her cleavage nearly spilling out of the surplice front. "I got it." She pushed the board free. It swung open like a drawbridge, and she caught it squarely in her other hand.

Raul's gasp was just audible as the plywood swung out of the way of the naked stacks of bills.

"Holy shit," he whispered.

Marisol laid the crowbar down on top of the plywood. "If you're really trying to be my man, and you wanna take me to visit your family, I want you to know exactly who you're fucking with."

Carefully, Raul walked around the plywood. He squatted down to get a closer look.

"From VanDyke?" Raul asked.

"Mostly," she said.

Raul hovered there, staring at the money. "How much did you take him for?"

"Eight mil," Marisol said. "Give or take."

"Did you fuck him?" Raul asked without taking his eyes from the cash.

"Yep." Marisol stood her ground. "Are you having second thoughts?"

"Did you enjoy it?" he asked.

Marisol laughed. "No," she said. "I pretended to. Like I pretended to be terrified when my team came and held us up at gunpoint."

"Who were the guys?" Raul asked.

"No guys," Marisol said. "Women in bodysuits."

Raul set aside the crowbar and stood up. He lifted the

board and rested it against the counter, leaving a slightly open gap. He started to unbutton his shirt.

"Come here, you genius," he said. "VanDyke? Eight mil? Your team dressed as men? I told you smart women turn me on. *Coño*, we might not make it to visit my family today."

"What?" Marisol asked. "Now that you know every single one of my secrets? You're definitely taking me to visit your family."

"Okay," he said. "But don't tell them what we're about to do."

He slipped the strap of the dress off her shoulder.

"You never got to be a stickup kid," Marisol said, peeling off his shirt. "You'll just have to settle for being an accomplice after the fact."

"I accept," he said.

"*Bueno*," she said, leading him over to the bed. "Why don't you come here and let me jump you into the gang?"

Raul laughed as he unbuckled his jeans.

They made love again in the bedroom alcove. The edges of the bills danced in and out of sight as the two of them laughed and rolled and tangled on the bed.

A READING GROUP GUIDE

UPTOWN THIEF

Aya de León

ABOUT THIS GUIDE

The suggested questions are included to enhance your group's reading of Aya de León's *Uptown Thief*.

DISCUSSION QUESTIONS

1. The entire adventure begins when Marisol and her team are furious to learn that a corrupt corporate CEO has won a humanitarian award when he's also a sex trafficker. Can you identify any instances in your life or in the current news where corrupt individuals or groups are being rewarded or singled out for praise, when they actually deserve legal or ethical consequences?

2. Marisol operates both in and outside of the law. What are some of the laws that she breaks? How does she justify her illegal behavior? Do you agree that her actions are justified?

3. Advocates for safe and healthy working conditions for sex workers often use the slogan "sex work is work." As with any job, different individuals have different relationships to the work: Some love it, some hate it, and for some, it's just a job. What are some of the different relationships that the sex worker characters have with their work?

4. The sale of sex operates on a spectrum from those who do so voluntarily to those who are trafficked or coerced. Advocates for decriminalization of commercial sex between consenting adults are careful to separate sex trafficking from sex work. Can you identify the following in the book: In which instances do we see women choosing sex work from a variety of options? In which instances do we see women choosing sex work from a very limited set of options (sometimes known as "survival sex work")? In which instances do we see women threatened, pressured, forced, or coerced to sell sex?

5. Throughout the book, there are many different types of sex that Marisol and others have. What are some of the different types of sex that you see? What are each of the people hoping to get out of those sexual encounters? How do those goals or intentions change for Marisol throughout the book?

6. Marisol has trust issues. Whom does she trust at the beginning of the book? How is that different by the end of the book? Who takes advantage of her trust during the book? During her life before the book? Who in the book has to earn her trust? What is it about Marisol and Raul's previous connection that allows them to get past some of their defense mechanisms?

7. Women are conditioned to compete for male attention and favor. Who are some women in the book who attempt to succeed at other women's expense? Do their plans work out?

8. Marisol hates cops. Is her attitude justified?

9. Marisol's life is a complicated mix of risk and protection. What are some ways she engages in risky behavior, and what are some ways she engages in protective behavior?

10. Marisol is bold and courageous and brings out those traits in people around her. If you had someone like Marisol in your life, what might be some areas in which you would accept her encouragement to be bold? Where do you wish you had more courage?

1
The Sky is Crying

Rashad Eason reached across the desk and handed the woman a fifteen-hundred-dollar cashier's check. She had pasty, pimpled white skin, a buzz haircut, and a thick mustache. She was very unattractive. To Rashad, she resembled a proud lesbian but that didn't matter. He had extensively researched Lily Tangaro online. He admired her track record and needed a competent person to do the job.

"You think you can get me everything I want?" he asked.

Lily examined the check, then reclined in her leather swivel chair. "You're serious about this, aren't you?" she said.

"More serious than a triple bypass."

"But it hasn't been that long since you physically separated from your wife."

"I know that. But if I don't do something fast, I may change my mind."

"I see." She paused. "We always recommend that the plaintiff think about the decision for six months."

"I can't wait that long. Thinking about this for six months would kill me."

She nodded and secured the retainer payment inside a

classified file folder. "Sign these documents and we will get started on your case right away."

Rashad eagerly reviewed several papers that Lily gave to him. He took a blue pen and scribbled his name and the date. Then he stood and shook her hand.

"Thank you, Ms. Tangaro."

"Call me, Lily."

"Will do, Lily. And my son, Myles, really thanks you."

"Seriously? He's only six—"

"He's seven. Myles knows what's up. He's seen a lot, unfortunately. And this is why I gotta do this. It may be the only way I get to spend quality time with him. Plus, I don't want my son around his crazy mama any longer than he needs to be."

"Totally understandable. We'll be in touch."

"No doubt, Lily. I appreciate this."

Rashad drove away from his new attorney's office feeling more hopeful than he had in weeks.

It was a rainy Friday in Houston; the day after Thanksgiving. Rashad was lucky that Lily had agreed to meet him briefly in her office to sign his paperwork.

Light drops of water drizzled from the sky. Rainy days made Rashad feel depressed. But he had to shake it off and keep it moving. It was time to go see Myles. And spending time with his son was one of the few things he could be happy about these days.

When Rashad arrived at the designated pick-up spot, which was in front of Mama Flora's house, he let the car idle next to the curb. Technically, she could be considered his grandmother-in-law. Mama Flora was his wife's maternal grandmother, and the woman that raised Kiara. She was sensible and didn't stand for drama. Rashad and Kiara both agreed that exchanging Myles for visits at Flora's place would be the best option.

Rashad impatiently drummed his hands on the steering wheel. He listened to raindrops splatter on the ground. Minutes later, Kiara drove up and parked directly behind him. He observed her through the rearview mirror.

"Damn, I can barely see her but the woman still looks good," he admitted to himself. He hadn't laid eyes on Kiara in weeks. And after all they had been through, she still tugged at his heart.

He saw her mouth moving and assumed she was talking to their son. After a while, both Kiara and Myles emerged from the car. Wearing white gym shoes, the little boy ran behind the car then raced ahead of her. He fled into the street instead of staying on the sidewalk. Soon he tugged at his father's locked door handle and yelled.

"Hurry up, Daddy. I'm famished."

Rashad laughed and popped the locks. He got out of the car and scooped Myles off his feet and hugged him tight.

"Really Myles? You're famished? Where'd you learn that word?"

"The Food Network."

Rashad chuckled as he set him back down.

"Oh, so I don't get a 'hey, Daddy, how you doing? I miss you. I love you, man'?"

"Hey, Daddy, I missed you. Can we go to Steak and Shake for dinner?"

"Myles," Kiara interrupted as she hurriedly approached them wearing a short, purple long-sleeve dress and four-inch wedge heel sandals. "I told you about running in the street. Are you crazy? Do you wanna get hit by a car? It's raining and that makes it harder for drivers to slow down in this weather."

Kiara eased up next to Myles. She thumped him on his forehead.

"Ouch, Mommy."

"Don't do that," Rashad scolded. "My little man misses me, that's all. It's been a minute."

"Whatever Rashad," she spat at him. "None of that matters. He knows better than to do something reckless like running in the street. He doesn't listen."

"I do listen, Mommy." Myles mostly ignored his mother as he happily gave his father a few daps. The little boy always seemed calm and sure of himself when he was in Rashad's presence.

"You're a chip off the old block, son," his father said. He knew the danger of Myles not looking where he was going but Rashad didn't notice any cars coming down the street. He could tell how much his boy deeply missed him and that made him feel good.

"Damn, I've been dying to hang out with my little man. Has he gotten taller? What the hell you been feeding him?"

"That's a stupid question and you know how I feel about those."

"I was just joking, Kiara. Lighten up."

"Ain't got time for jokes."

Suddenly the air grew tense. Rashad felt himself getting agitated.

"Look, this is the holiday season. People are supposed to be merry. But you act like you on something. You been drinking? Can't you ever be happy and just chill?"

"Lord Jesus. More stupid ass questions. Don't start."

Kiara gave Rashad a sober look as she handed him Myles's backpack.

"Lucky for you, Mama Flora is away from her house right now. At the last second, she had something to take care of and she had to leave. So we both have to be mature enough to handle this without her."

"That's cool. I got no problem with that."

"Anyway, all his things are in there: two pair of pants, some shirts, underwear, pajamas, favorite electric toothbrush, all that."

"Hmm, seeing this makes me realize I gotta stock up on some stuff for him to keep at . . ."

He wanted to say he had to buy clothes for Myles to keep at his other place, a home he started sharing with his pregnant lover, Nicole Greene. Weeks ago, when his wife forced him to leave the house because she got sick of Rashad's lies, Nicole instantly suggested that he come stay with her. On that short of a notice, he had nowhere else to go. So he took her up on her offer. And now he was adjusting to his 'new normal.'

Rashad mentally switched gears as he gazed at Myles.

"Damn shame we couldn't eat turkey and dressing together, and watch the Lions and Cowboys game. That's what I did with my dad every Thanksgiving when he was still alive. I was *always* with my daddy on that holiday. Sitting up in that cold ass living room. Eating good food and talking smack. I wish we could have done that, Myles."

Rashad stared at his son but he was talking to Kiara.

"Um," she responded. "We had the whole day already planned so he wouldn't have had a chance to come by anyway. We went to the parade downtown. We ate a wonderful dinner. And then we drove down to see the Festival of Lights at Moody Gardens. Myles ended up having a *real* good time with us, didn't you?"

"Uh huh," he said.

"Cool," was Rashad's clipped response. "I'm glad for you."

He acted like he was unbothered. But Rashad hated that Kiara stopped him from spending time with his child two holidays in a row. *She* got to pick his costume and take Myles trick or treating. And *she* got to eat turkey with him too. What gave her the right? Just because she made him leave the house, does that mean she could enforce all her own rules as well?

Rashad fought to hide his anger as he leered at Kiara on the sly. She was holding one of those huge pink and black golf umbrellas in her hand. Even on a dreary looking afternoon, somehow this woman managed to appear elegant and beautiful. Her eyes were full of spunk and passion. It seemed she didn't have a care in the world.

And he hated it.

But at the same time, Rashad was strangely tempted to grab his wife in his arms, slap her one good time, kiss her, and tell her that they were both acting silly. He wished they could get their emotions in check, work things out, save the marriage. He really didn't want to file on her, but she was acting unreasonable. He wished she could get some sense into her stubborn head. Maybe she'd listen and let him come back home where he felt he belonged. But that scenario was a hopeless fairy tale. He knew Kiara was still pissed and he didn't want to risk getting swung at in public.

"All righty then," Rashad spoke up, anxious to leave. "Since I have less time than I originally thought, we need to make that move right now. I will have little man back here on Sunday night around eight."

"Eight?"

"Okay, then. Seven."

"Sunday *afternoon*, Rashad. I need him here by two so I can make sure he has time to take his bath, complete his homework, and eat dinner. Plus, if we decide to go check out that new Madagascar movie he's begged us to see, we will probably want him around noon."

We.

Rashad knew his wife was referring to her new man when she said "We."

"Back by *noon*? That means I won't even get to spend, hell, even a full twenty-four hours with him—"

"Sorry, but that's just how it is."

"You're not sorry, Kiara. You're selfish. I haven't seen my son in God knows how long. I have a right to be with the boy just like you do. And I will bring Myles back when I'm done with him."

"Wait one second here. I find it so strange that all of a sudden you are so desperate to spend time with him. You should have thought about how important he was back when you were sacrificing time with your son to go lie up and bump your nuts on that whore."

"W-what did you say?"

"You heard exactly what I said. If you hadn't done what you did, we wouldn't be out here on these streets doing this; exchanging a child like he's a drug or a piece of currency. Do you know how mad this makes me? I did everything and I mean *ev-e-ry*-thing I could to make you happy, but no, no, no. Nothing I did was good enough. You had to go get yourself a damned side piece. Her pussy must taste like Skittles."

"Kiara, you best better shut your mouth."

"So it's true? Her coochie taste like Gucci?"

"I'm warning you."

She was ready to attack him with more angry words, but she grew alarmed when she noticed a frozen smile gripping her son's face. He resembled a mannequin; he looked like he was scared something bad would happen if he moved an inch.

Kiara realized she'd gone too far. But she usually did when it came to Rashad. She hated that his whorish ways had destroyed their perfect family life. She hated that not only had he knocked up that heifer Nicole Greene, but he'd also been hiding a two-year-old daughter that he had with another woman who worked for her: Alexis McNeil, her own administrative assistant. Her hubby hiding baby mamas and side chicks that worked in her office was too much. Rashad made her look like a fool. The more Kiara thought about it, the crazier she felt in the head.

She reached and grabbed Myles's hand as if to snatch him back toward her car.

"What are you doing?" Rashad asked.

"Let me be clear. I don't know if we're ready for this informal custody sharing thing. I know it's the decent thing to do, but hell, I'm not feeling 'decent' right now. I think we need to take baby steps. So if you can't bring him back by noon, then he's going home with me right now. I'll let you have him in two weeks. For a full weekend. Promise."

"See, this is bullshit. I was supposed to get him last weekend, remember? You broke that so-called promise. Why you always got to be in control?"

They were still standing in the street next to Rashad's idling sedan.

"Why you always try to run shit like I'm your child? Or your employee. Huh? I'm a grown ass man." He stepped closer to her. "Who the hell put you in charge of me?"

Kiara snatched Myles's bony little arm and pulled so violently that he screamed, "Ouch! That hurts."

"Your crazy ass better let go of my son." Rashad grabbed Myles's other arm.

"Shut up! I don't like how you're talking to me."

"I don't like the fact that you fucked another nigga; now you pregnant. I guess we should go on the Maury show to find out who the real father is."

"What the hell? That's it. Forget this. Come on, Myles." She yanked him again.

"Mama, I want to stay with my daddy. I want my daddy." Myles inched closer to Rashad.

"I don't care what you want. He doesn't deserve you. We're leaving. Come on."

Raindrops poured from above as if the sky was crying. Kiara tried to hold her umbrella in one hand and drag away Myles with the other.

But the boy wrestled with her, pulling back from her, and tried to free himself.

"My arm. It hurts. It *hurts*. I don't like this. Let me gooo."

Kiara wouldn't release Myles, but Rashad did.

He'd been taught that real men don't cry. But right then, he was filled with uncontrollable rage and a lingering frustration that made his throat swell with pain. It wasn't fair that since Kiara banned him from their house he hadn't played with his son, hadn't looked him in his eyes, or helped him with his homework. He missed fixing Myles's breakfast and shooting hoops with him in their backyard. Little things meant a lot. And Rashad resented the legal system which granted numerous women so much power when it came to a man, his money, and his children.

He stared at his wife, almost in disbelief that feelings of pure hatred were boiling up in him and making him flush with so much anger that he started sweating.

"Mommy, I want to be with my daddy. Let me go."

"Stop all that yelling, Myles. I want you to come back home with me."

Several cars slowly drove past them, which infuriated Rashad. "Look at this shit. You got people staring at you like you're crazy."

"The hell with them. I'm not crazy. I'm just doing what I have to do to protect my son."

"He's my son, too, Kiara. I don't know why you seem to have forgotten that." If his wife wasn't pregnant there was no telling what Rashad would have done to her. He didn't want to fight, but her unpredictable reactions drove him to respond in ways that he hated.

"All I know is, it's damn near Christmas," he continued in a choked voice. "I wanted to take Myles shopping this weekend. I-I-I have all *kinds* of plans for him, don't you understand that?"

"I don't give a damn about your stupid plans," she retorted. "You better learn how to speak to me like you have some sense. You can't just say anything in front of a child."

Rashad felt like his wife was a hypocrite. She clearly saw his sins but was blind to her own. But he counted to ten and calmly told her, "Kiara, I apologize if it seems like I was disrespecting you. But can we let go of this argument? Please. And let me give Myles the chance he deserves to hang out with his father . . . his *real* father."

"Oh hell no. I know you're not trying to throw shade at Eddison who's been nothing but remarkable to us. Plus, that boy's not stupid. He knows who his daddy is."

"Mommy, you're hurting me. Please let me gooo."

Kiara then realized she had Myles in a death grip. She felt his fragile bones between her fingers. She heard the hurt in his voice. She released him.

"Oh God. I'm sorry baby. I-I . . . please forgive me."

With tears in his eyes, he nodded and leaned on his father's stomach.

"Kiara," Rashad said in a gentle tone. "So you're going to let him be with me till Sunday night?"

She hesitated and reached in her purse. "Fine. I'll let him go with you since we went through all this trouble in the first place. We can negotiate a fair time for his drop off. But I want you to know that I bought him his own cell phone today. Whenever he's away from me, he must keep it on him at all times. And we taught him how to use it. In case of an emergency."

"You really don't trust me, do you?"

"No, I do not. But that's beside the point. I just want Myles to be okay. I just want him to be happy." Kiara's voice caught in her throat as she wiped tears from her eyes.

She kissed Myles's little cheeks and allowed a brave smile to brighten her face. "Bye baby. I love you."

"Love you, too, Mommy. Come on, Daddy. My stomach is growling. Can't you hear it?"

"That's a damned shame. We'll go eat right now, son."

Kiara swiftly turned around to leave. The street was slippery and wet. In her rush to get away, her feet got tangled together. The wedge heels were narrow and clumsy. Her right ankle twisted and gave in underneath her. Her umbrella plunked to the ground. She slipped on a pothole, and fell forward, but landed on her thigh. Her hand scraped the rugged, scraggly surface as she braced herself from injury.

"Ugh, ouch. Dammit."

She lay on her side feeling totally embarrassed and wincing. Rashad wanted to ask if she was all right, but he simply stared at her.

Rain water sprayed her hair and cheeks. Her hair became a matted mess.

"I can't believe this. Rashad! Can you help me up or are you just gonna stand there?"

He gaped at Kiara and wondered if she just got what she deserved.

She'd made life so difficult for him recently. Rashad knew she was now seeing that man from her job, Eddison Osborne, and Nicole told him that they'd had an affair.

Rashad could clearly see Kiara's tiny baby bump. He wondered if the baby was his, even though she'd told him that it was.

"Rashad, did you hear me? I need your help."

"Why should I?"

"Huh? I can't believe you said that!"

He had the eyes of a reptile; cold, curious, and calculating.

"I don't know whose baby you got inside of you."

"Rashad, oh my God. How can you go there?"

"Because *you* went there—with that other nigga!"

"Now is not the time. Help me up, please."

He stared down at her belly. And so did Myles.

Kiara felt completely humiliated. She never wanted their son to see her like this.

"Rashad, show your son how to treat a woman. *Show* your *son* how to *treat* a *woman*!"

Rashad looked skeptical and unmoving.

"Myles baby, please."

Myles raced to his mother and immediately grabbed her outstretched hand. His tongue stuck out of his mouth as he struggled to help Kiara. Rashad suddenly rushed to the other side of her and held out his hand too.

Wincing in pain, she got on her knees, and leaned on Rashad as he hoisted her to her feet.

"Thank you, baby." She ignored Rashad. "You are my precious son. You must always remember to be a gentleman, and help your mother. And always be good to a lady. Promise me."

"I promise, Mommy."

"Ha!" Rashad muttered.

"All right, okay. I can do this," she said to herself. "I can make it to the car."

"Bye-bye, Mommy. Don't forget to pick me up on Sunday."

"I can never forget anything that has to do with you."

She watched Myles excitedly race around to the other side of Rashad's sedan. He went and opened the passenger door for his son. Kiara waited until Myles was safely inside the car. She rubbed her hip and hobbled over to Rashad.

"You didn't act concerned about our unborn baby for one second."

"I don't know whose baby that is." He paused. "How many times did you fuck that dude?"

"How many times did you fuck both your baby mamas?"

"Oh, so you hooked up with him just to get revenge? Was his dick bigger than mine? I don't care how big it was, no man could ever love you like me!"

"Oh my God! Just be quiet with all that. I can't believe I used to love your pathetic ass. And you best believe that part of my life is gone. I'm moving on. And you're acting like a dick and trying to shame me in front of Myles is unforgivable. You'll never get this pussy again."

She turned away again, this time moving more slowly than the first time. Then she quietly limped away. Hair soaking wet, but head held high.

After Kiara slid into the vehicle, she slammed her door, revved the engine, and waved her middle finger at Rashad as she drove past him.

Eason v. Eason had officially started.